# The
# Secret Unknown

*DILLON WATSON*

BELLA
BOOKS

2016

Copyright © 2016 by Dillon Watson

Bella Books, Inc.
P.O. Box 10543
Tallahassee, FL 32302

Printed in the United States of America on acid-free paper.

First Bella Books Edition 2016

Editor: Medora MacDougall
Cover Designer: Sandy Knowles

ISBN: 978-1-59493-512-1

## Other Bella Books by Dillon Watson

*Keile's Chance*
*Back to Blue*
*Full Circle*

## Acknowledgments

I want to thank the Golden Crown Literary Society (GCLS) for providing me the opportunity to interact with readers and fellow authors during their annual convention. It's food for my soul.

I also want to thank the people responsible for putting on NANOWRIMO (the National Novel Writing Month program) every November. Three of my four novels got their start there.

Finally, I want to thank Medora for helping me to write righter.

## About the Author

Dillon Watson resides in the southeastern United States. During the day, she slaves away as a Regional Planner. At night, she sits down with her trusty iPad and conjures up romance. She has won Goldies (Golden Crown Literary Society) for Best Debut Author and Best Contemporary Romance. She has also been short-listed for a Goldie in the Best Paranormal/Horror category and a Lammy for Best Lesbian Romance. Her novels include: *Keile's Chance*, *Back To Blue* and *Full Circle*.

# PROLOGUE

"Please don't hurt me. I'll go away, never come back. I promise." Tears trailed across Lucy Mae Brown's round face and pooled on the car seat as she pleaded for her life and the life of her unborn twins. She was laid out on the backseat of an unknown car as big as a boat with her hands and feet bound behind her. The two masked men in the front seat had dragged her from her bed, and her nightgown was providing little protection against the roughness of the pock-marked vinyl seat.

"Shut up or I'll shut you up," the big man in the passenger seat said.

The coldness in his tone made her believe he'd like to do more than shut her up. It had been the other one, the shorter of the two, who'd stopped him from back slapping her after she bit him trying to escape. Lucy had seen a glint in his eyes as he watched her kick her legs in struggle, watched as her nightgown exposed her panties. So when he grabbed at her legs, spread them, rape had been on her mind and, she thought, his as well.

A hard bite to his hand had transformed that glint into anger to her relief.

But the bite, combined with her struggles, hadn't been enough to get away from the men. They'd learned their lesson because they tied her feet first, then her hands and carried her to the old Caddy. She hadn't wasted her breath or energy on screaming. Her grandpa Jimmy was the only one not at the Christmas Eve revival, and he was as deaf as a rock. Plus she'd been so sure she could talk them into letting her go. Everyone always said she could talk her way out of anything. Anything but this, she thought and choked back a sob. She couldn't cry, didn't dare draw *his* attention again.

By her estimation they'd been on the road for a good hour and she wasn't sure how much longer she'd be alive. They most likely had orders from the queen bitch to kill her babies, maybe leave her in some wooded area to die from the abortion. Soon they'd be far enough from Savannah, from her home and the people who would care what happened to her, to her twins.

The worst part was that her predicament was mostly her own fault. Her arrogance had led her to believe that after their talk that Eugenia Tanner had understood she wanted to have nothing to do with her or her son. That she wanted her babies to have nothing to do with them. Her uncle Gene had told her more than once that her arrogance, her not knowing her place, would be her downfall. She could take some comfort he wasn't here to say "I told you so," to lecture her once again on the sins of sex outside marriage and her audacity to be keeping the results.

It didn't matter now that she'd ignored what she'd been taught of how the world operated to be with the boy who made her heart sing. A boy she'd wrongly believed had the same commitment to their relationship as she. And maybe he hadn't loved her enough to go against his mother and society's dictates, but surely he would feel *some* loss at her death. He didn't know about the babies, so he wouldn't have to carry that loss as well.

As sleep beckoned, her short-lived relationship with Jackson Tanner played through her mind—the wild beating of her heart when he looked at her and saw what was on the inside, the joy when he confessed his feelings, the hours squirreled away talking about goals, about a shared future. It had been a heady time that no one could take away from her.

Lucy came awake to pressure building in her abdomen. She felt more than heard a pop followed by a flood of wetness between her thighs. Her babies were trying to be born and she was tied up in the back of some car with men she didn't know, men who wouldn't care if she and the babies got through the experience alive and well.

She started to call out, then changed her mind. It was better for her to keep quiet for as long as possible. If she were about to give birth, maybe the shorter one would hesitate to kill her, hesitate to kill babies who were close to being born.

So Lucy bit down on her lip when the first shot of pain rippled through her stomach. She panted softly through the second, the third, the fourth contraction, but she hadn't counted on the strength of the contractions or the pain that kept coming until it felt like her lower half was a ball of fire. Pain that got more and more intense until she couldn't keep silent anymore. A low groan escaped before she could bite it back.

"You be quiet."

"My babies. My babies are coming."

The mean one turned on the overhead light, took one look at her and said, "Shit! Thought she wasn't due for a couple of weeks."

"She's not," the driver said. "Minnie said she could even be late as it's her first one. What're we going to do?"

"Nothing. These things can take hours, right?"

"I guess so. We could stop at a gas station, give Minnie a call. She's the one knows all that birth shit, not me."

"They take a long time on TV and that's good enough for me. Another hour and we'll be there. Let him deal with her. He's gonna get most of the money."

"I don't like it. We should at least untie her so she can do it better."

"What? Escape?"

"No, fool. Bear the pain. Having babies hurt."

"So you know that, but you don't know it can take hours. Pull over then. If she gets away it's on you to deal with him and that knife he likes to use."

Lucy could have told them escape was the last thought on her mind, but she was saving her strength to stay conscious through pain that seemed to paint the very air around her.

She felt the car stop, heard the back door open, and there he was, scowling at her.

"Don't try anything," he warned.

She thought it was hysteria that made her want to laugh at the statement. The way she felt, she couldn't have taken down a day-old kitten, let alone a grown man with bulging muscles. But she did find a measure of mental relief when her feet and hands were free. She also felt physical relief at being able to curl up in the fetal position when the next contraction struck.

It seemed to Lucy that hours had passed by the time they slowed down and turned off the road. She wanted to sit up, try to get her bearings, but the motivation was lacking. She could only brace herself as the car dipped and shook on what had to be an unpaved road. When she wanted to scream from the constant jostling, they came to a stop.

Worn out, she didn't make a fuss when the mean one told her to get her ass out of the car and into the house. On some level she realized they weren't going to kill her yet, that there might be some hope for her babies. Surely they could fetch some money, even though she was not worth a cent to them alive.

She took one step toward a ramshackle building that was barely bigger than a shed and the ground shimmered and rolled. Only grabbing the car door kept her upright, kept her from losing the contents of her stomach.

Letting lose on a string of curses, the mean one picked her up. "I sure as hell hope he's ready for this."

What followed for Lucy was more body-wracking pain until she was told when to push, told when to stop. She heard a baby's cry, heard a woman say it was girl and felt some of the dread leave her. When they let her hold the little body, stroke and kiss skin that was impossibly soft, she cried. Love burst fast and furious as she counted fingers so amazingly small, so amazingly perfect.

"My sweet, sweet April."

She felt bereft when they took her baby away, but then the pain cycle began again. With what little strength she had left, Lucy pushed, stopped, and pushed so more.

"There's too much blood with this one," Lucy heard one of the women mutter. "Something's not right."

"Should I get the doc?"

"And do what? Have the girl tell him everything? Let someone know you're here? No one can know you were here. No one can know about any of this, Letha. I thought you understood. Tell me you know what could happen if you ever tell."

"But she could die. We can't let her die, Minnie."

"Sometimes you can only do so much. Now give the girl some more ice and let me deal with this mess. Remember now, nobody can ever know about this."

*I'll know*, Lucy thought, floating in a sea of pain. *I'll know and I'll tell everyone about my babies and about Jackson Beauregard Tanner being their father.*

But Lucy was dead moments after her second daughter was pulled from her body with forceps. She wasn't around to give this baby girl a welcoming hug, wasn't around to hear the exclamation of shock, didn't see Letha cross herself at the sight of the white baby that had come from between Lucy's dark brown thighs or hear her say reverently, "It's a miracle."

# CHAPTER ONE

Shock fought anger as Eugenia Tanner watched the recording for the third time. She might be old, but she certainly wasn't feeble enough to miss the unmistakable resemblance between the thirty-four-year-old woman in the video and the young pregnant girl she thought had been taken care of thirty-four years ago.

What a fool she'd been to trust that boy to take care of anything when he could barely take care of himself. But he'd begged for the chance to help the family, to pay her back for giving him a place to stay after his parents washed their hands of him. And because she believed he had potential, could be of further use to her, she'd given him that chance to prove himself. Lucky for him, he was long dead from the drugs he never could shake, sparing him the necessity of answering to her, of feeling her wrath.

It was anger, not age that made her tremble as she placed a call. With few words she told her personal soldier, as she thought of him, what had to be done. There could be no mistakes this time. She also had to make sure the buffoons the boy had hired to get rid of the girl were found, interrogated to see if there had been others involved in the operation and then silenced.

In an attempt to regain her usual calm, she crossed to the window overlooking the well-kept yard and let the sun play on her pampered skin. The yard didn't have the stately appearance of the one at the Tanner estate where she'd lived the majority of her adult life, but that was okay. Her son was finally about to play the role she'd raised him for, and he and especially his eminently suitable wife didn't need her underfoot while they ramped up the campaign to make Jackson Georgia's newest US senator.

A smile softened her face as she thought of her beloved son. Sure, he was the cause of the current problem, but he'd only been a teen when it happened. As his mother it had been her job to see he didn't suffer from that mistake the rest of his life. She'd believed she'd done her job. Until now. Until she'd seen the photo of that woman. Pressing her fingers against her temple, she could feel the blood throbbing in her veins.

Lord knows she'd almost been as arrogant as that foolish black chit who'd had the nerve to come sniffing around her Jackson. She'd thought nothing of the little flirtation, thought it wasn't so bad that he sow his wild oats with one of the little well-mannered house servants while he was home from college for spring break.

How wrong she'd been in many ways. She hadn't expected the girl to intrigue him, to make him think he was in love to the point where he began to get crazy notions of marriage and forever to a no-name black girl, of all things. It wasn't done. It just was not done. Not on her watch. It was a good thing the housekeeper was on her toes. After hearing of their plans, she came directly to her. In turn, she went to the girl, and with a few words sent her on her way, clipping that relationship before it had a chance to really bloom. Jackson had been hurt, but she'd made sure he got over it. The little red Ferrari had been the first of many gifts to soothe the pain of separation.

She frowned as she heard the approaching footsteps of her current housekeeper. She wanted to be alone, to gather her thoughts, plot out a backup scenario should there be another mix-up or worse, outright failure. The thought wasn't to be borne. The Nevada woman and all the people involved in her birth had to be dealt with before someone else noticed the unmistakable resemblance and began to wonder how a very pregnant Lucy Brown had managed to escape a fire and give birth without anyone noticing.

She could be grateful Jackson was too busy preparing to run for office to be bothered by the story of another school shooting. If he did catch a glimpse of Adeena Minor, she'd make sure he dismissed the resemblance between her and his former girlfriend as purely coincidental. There were plenty of people who could attest that Lucy Mae Brown had died while she was pregnant.

"What can I do for you, Miss Eugenia?"

She turned at the sound of her housekeeper's too cheerful voice and recalled she'd been the one doing the summoning. "Ah yes, Martha. I believe I'll call and invite Jackson and his family to dinner tomorrow. Make sure the dining room is set just so. And see that Delilah has the ingredients on hand to fix his favorites. This is a very important time for him."

\* \* \*

Thomasina Angelica Salamander tried for sophistication as she sipped the, to her, deadly dry white wine. She was hoping it would make her date see her in a different light if she was sipping a glass of wine rather than guzzling the rum and Coke— sans rum—that she usually ordered. And since she was close to being the female version of the guys on that TV show about physics geeks, she knew she needed all the help she could get to keep Trin's interest for a little longer. She did have an advantage those guys didn't and that was money. So far it had worked to attract the cute blondes she lusted for, but it hadn't worked to keep them for very long.

Her best friend, Cyn, kept telling her to switch types, to try for not as pretty, not as blond. Well, she'd tried that once and had the trampled heart to prove it. While the cute ones might ding her feelings, it was the smart, geeky ones who had the power to cut her deep. Dinged feelings she could shake off in a few days, usually assisted by the purchase of a new toy. Sal was still working to fully recover from the slicing open of her heart that happened two years ago. So she tended to let Cyn's advice drift free in space while she settled for the cute, the blond, the superficial.

A movement caught the corner of her eye, and she straightened her thin shoulders and fixed a smile—only to discover it was the snooty waiter, come to check on her yet again. Before he could ask if she was ready for another drink, her cell alarm pinged to let her know Trin had officially stood her up for the second time in a row.

"Check please," she announced, taking a little pleasure in the fact that he wouldn't be living off the hefty tip she would've had to pay if Trin had showed. The busty waitress and Broadway-star-wannabe had a habit of ordering the most exotic item on the menu. She'd take a few bites, declare it unsatisfactory and only then would she order something with ingredients she could pronounce. For reasons that obviously had nothing to do with logic, Sal had found that rather endearing.

*That should have been a sign*, she told herself. A sign Trin only tolerated her for a taste of the big-ticket items on the menu. Apparently that and great sex weren't enough anymore, and that Sal couldn't understand.

"Your check, madam. Please come again."

She really wanted to knock that knowing smirk off his face. Instead, she threw down a twenty and said in her best British accent, "Not bloody likely, sir. The service leaves much to be desired." With her own snooty lift of her chin, she walked out, all dressed up in an outfit Trin claimed made her look hot and with no place to go.

Outside, New York City was bustling with people who, unlike her, looked like they were going to have a good evening.

A lot of them probably had a good chance to get laid, again unlike her. For all Trin's faults, she did enjoy having sex after spending Sal's money. No doubt some other woman was going to be the beneficiary of her enthusiastic calisthenics tonight.

Sal liked to think that Trin—and all the others of her ilk who had come before her—eventually came to miss what she brought to the bedroom. Being skinny and at best plain, at worst not pretty, she prided herself on being an attentive lover. *And inventive*, she added as she fought her way through the hoards of tourists who kept Times Square bustling at all hours.

Normally she would have taken the time to stop and gawk at the lights and the colorful electronic billboards, because she absolutely loved the look, the vibe of the area. Her love for the flashing lights, the neon signs, must have come from her mother. According to her father's mother, who'd raised her, it hadn't come from her father.

Sal hadn't walked a full block before the magic of Times Square broke through her disappointment. She stopped, unmindful of those behind her, and breathed in the energy of the crowd, of the lights, of the best place on earth. Pouting about being stood up again was no reason for her to miss out on enjoyment. In fact, she was due a treat for getting her heart dinged, she reasoned. She turned around and headed to another of her favorite places, this one a toy store of the three-story variety.

Inside, she took the escalators up to the building block section on the top floor. As usual, she took the time to enjoy the large Lego replicas of buildings and monuments that New York City was known for, most of which could be found in the smaller-scale city that was taking over her home office. Before too long she was going to be forced to call her carpenter about adding more shelves so she could have full use of her desk again. Not that she would let that stop her from adding onto the city in the meantime.

While trying to decide which Lego set would follow her home, she stumbled onto a section with building sets of miniature monuments of not just New York, but the world.

Sal would be the first to admit her eyes glazed over with joy at the number of sets to choose from. And okay, she might have drooled at the thought of the hours of fun laid out before her.

After much backing and forthing and going round and round, she picked the White House building set in honor of the first African-American president. She added the Eiffel Tower and the Empire State Building sets because she deserved them for the damage done to her heart. With her selections paid for, Sal hurried to the escalator. She wouldn't be having sex, but that didn't mean she wouldn't be having fun. The blaring of her grandmother's ringtone had Sal reaching for her phone.

"What are you doing answering your phone on a Friday night?"

"Because it rang?" she guessed. "No, wait. Because I knew it was you."

Betty Salamander's snort came through loud and clear. "You forget I'm not one of those bimbos you find so irresistible. You get stood up again, kiddo? That must be yes because I can hear kids in the background. And if there's a kid around you, it has to be in a toy store. When are you going to learn that you're more than that illegally gotten money of yours and leave those gold diggers alone? You need to settle down with a nice girl. I'm not getting any younger and you need someone who'll watch over you."

*This is new*, Sal thought. *Something must be wrong.* "Not getting any younger? Nobody is, Nan," she joked as she walked down the escalator. "Everything okay in Beantown?"

A loud sigh was eventually followed by, "Yeah."

The sigh and silence were unnerving. Her grandmother was not one to complain or be at loss for a word. "Tell me quick. I can take it."

"There was another school shooting—"

"At your old school? Anyone you know get hurt?" Damn, why did she have to choose today to go off the grid? "I can be there in a couple of hours tops."

"Nevada. It was Nevada. One of the teachers died saving the lives of the kids in her class. She taught English. Had been at the school for a long time."

"Oh, Nan. I don't know what to say anymore. I know high school's no picnic, but this? It shouldn't be the answer."

"Middle school. He was only in seventh grade and he sees this as his only way out. It breaks your heart. For his parents and everyone else whose life will be changed forever."

Sal remembered her school days. Being skinny, awkward and nerdy on top of having brown skin, glasses, red hair and freckles, she'd gotten plenty of looks of derision, words that could and did hurt. She supposed she was lucky she was a girl and therefore hadn't suffered much physical abuse in addition to the verbal. "How many? How many were lost this time?"

"At first they thought it was only two. And how terrible is that? What have we come to if two dead can bring relief? Not a good place, I tell you. There were more. Six in all, including the boy."

"I know it sounds selfish, but I'm glad you got out without that ever happening to you. I'm glad I don't have to worry about that for you anymore, Nan."

"Days like today make me glad too. She had a daughter your age. The teacher from Nevada. That poor child barely had time to take a breath before those jackals were in her face, asking how she felt. Couldn't help think it could've been you. Could have been my hard-headed granddaughter having to face something like that. Lord, if it didn't hit me hard, baby girl." Her grandmother had lived north of the Mason-Dixon Line for longer than Sal had been alive, but she hadn't lost her southern roots.

"Don't do this to yourself, Nan. It wasn't you and it wasn't me. I'll catch a plane, come up and keep you company for a few days. You'll see I'm okay."

"You will not be wasting your money that way. Or your time, since you must be really busy not to call your Nan like you've done for every other school tragedy. It's not such a hard hit now that I've talked to you. Tell me you're okay. Tell me that this little girl you've been seeing didn't break your heart."

"I'm okay and I have the new toys to prove it. Tonight was a slight setback, that's all. I'll get it right with the next one. I promise. Now tell me what exciting things you did today."

After she ended the call, Sal thought about her promise to "get it right." She wondered if it had sounded as hollow to her grandmother's ears as it had sounded to hers. She couldn't count on her fingers the number of times she'd tried and failed to get the love thing right. Maybe it was time to stop trying. Time to stop giving the promise and, more importantly, time to stop thinking there was the possibility of her finding "the one." That person didn't seem to exist and wouldn't, no matter how many times she dusted off her dinged heart and put out the "open for business" sign.

Six months. She'd give herself six months of leave from the pretty, the sexy, the blond. No more chasing them down, being at their beck and call or drooling at their feet. She was better than that, damn it, and now she would prove it to herself and those who knew her best. She would use this time to figure out what she really wanted and, more importantly, figure out if she was letting the one who got away dictate her life.

"New start," she said as she went through the gate at the subway station, then rushed down the stairs to catch the coming train.

Once she was headed north to her apartment on the Upper West Side, Sal browsed the reports of the Nevada school shooting on her cell phone. She couldn't help but look at the photos of the sweet-looking shooter, his devastated parents, the shell-shocked students, and wonder what drove these shootings. Like she'd told her grandmother, school could be a special hell all of its own, and yet there had to be more than the bullying that set these kids off.

She'd crossed paths with plenty of kids who'd been angry, who'd felt helpless. To her knowledge, none of them had gone on rampages. Now when she looked back on the two years she'd felt most angry and hopeless, could see them as a blip on her life timeline, she wondered if perhaps it was worse to feel helpless and unloved when you had a safe place to stay, plenty of food and parents in the picture. Maybe there were levels of hopelessness, levels of feeling unloved and unwanted. Or maybe there were simply nasty human beings who sought out and found reasons to take a life.

Seeing photos of the families who'd lost children pushed thoughts of the shooter's psyche out of her mind. These poor people were probably too numb to analyze what the boy had been thinking when he sighted his gun on their kids like they were prey. It was all so senseless, so tragic and too common.

Sal was surprised when the photo of the daughter her grandmother had mentioned caused her a fleeting pain. She had lost her parents to senseless violence, so she could empathize with this Adeena Minor, could imagine the what-if scenarios running through her brain on a continuous loop. Unlike this poor woman, Sal hadn't had to deal with a microphone stuck in her face, a camera seeking to record her grief. Her heart went out to the other woman, who probably only wanted a quiet place to grieve.

She looked closer and thought she saw a deeper kind of grief in the daughter's eyes, then laughed at herself for being fanciful. Adeena Minor probably wouldn't be considered beautiful, but there was something about the big brown eyes and the almost arrogant tilt of her head that made her worthy of a second and third look.

When her stop was announced, Sal pocketed her phone and jockeyed into position near the closest door. As she waited for the train to come to a stop, she realized thoughts of the shooting, of Adeena Minor, had taken her mind off Trin and being stood up. She wished the other woman well, knowing that getting over the hard pain of losing her mother would be a very long process. At least the short attention span of the press would assure they'd quickly move on to the next big story.

Sal's phone gave three quick beeps as she took the escalator up and out of the 72$^{nd}$ Street Station. A glance at the information displayed brought a muttered curse. This seemed to be her day for heavy conversations with family. Cynthia Kennedy wasn't related to her by blood, but Sal had considered her a sister since they roomed together freshman year at MIT, and for Sal family was everything. So she would do the hard, call her sister of choice and give her and her parents a heads-up about what tomorrow's news would bring.

Before she made it the four blocks home, Cyn's ringtone blared out. "Listen, I'm five minutes from home. Call you back when I get there."

"Wait! It's not that important. I can wait. In fact, forget I called. Forgot you have a date tonight."

"Had. Stand-up number two if you're counting."

"Not me who should be counting. Anyway. You probably don't want to talk right now. Call me tomorrow. I only want to bitch."

"Four minutes now," Sal said and disconnected the call. Cyn's bossiness was alive and well. She gave Damon, the dapper-looking doorman, a fist bump, wished him an uneventful evening. Normally she would take the time to ask about his boys, his thoughts on the latest happenings in the city, but that had to wait.

Sal caught the elevator to the top. A little bit of luck in a lucrative, though illegal, card game had fattened her bank account. She'd used that money and honed computer skills to build a successful business. Information was the name of her game these days, and it paid very well.

Once inside her apartment, she ignored her rumbling stomach and took the curving staircase to the second floor where her office was located. She dropped her package on the desk with thoughts of getting to it later, then placed the call.

"Technically that was five minutes," Cyn announced.

"Yeah, yeah. Here now, so bitch away. I'm all yours."

"It's Nate. He's not getting any better." Cyn sighed. "He barely talks, never smiles and nothing I do works. I feel helpless. And you know how much I hate feeling that way."

Nate was Cyn's four-year-old nephew. His mother, Cyn's only sibling, had died five months ago. Nate lived with his dad in Boston but was currently visiting Cyn and her parents in Georgia. "You're going to accuse me of repeating myself, but—"

"I know, I know. To be expected. Heather's death hit us all hard. Why should Nate be any different? I just…" Another long sigh. "I just wish he would reach out to me or to Mom or Dad. It's kind of hard to justify pursuing the custody deal if he doesn't want to be with us."

"Give it time. Sure, he's been there before, but this is different. The first time without either of his parents." Sal wasn't telling Cyn anything she hadn't said a million times before. Her hope was for repetition to lead to acceptance.

"Stephen has never been here."

Sal went with the segue she was offered. "Uh, yeah…well, speaking of Stephen, I have, uh, good news and bad news."

"What?"

She'd clearly caught Cyn off guard. "Simple really. Bad or good first?"

"Bad. Bad should always go first."

"He was cheating on Heather. The good news is that his girlfriend's tell-all interview will be airing tomorrow morning. The whole world will know the kind of man he is." Sal had expected the silence, and she was sorry to be the one to add to Cyn's already heavy burden. "As soon as we're done, I'll try to get my hands on a copy. Let you know what's what."

"Great. Just great." There was nothing humorous about Cyn's laugh. "That bastard. That low-down, slimy bastard. All this crap about how Nate was his last remaining link to Heather, the love of his life. He had tears in his fucking eyes when my mother said how maybe it was best Nate come live with us until he could adjust. Tears. Wonder how long he's had that thing on the side."

"I'll check, get back to you. Maybe then we can talk about how *you're* dealing with all that's been thrust on you."

"I'm fine. Call me ASAP. This is more important."

"At least try not to worry too much," Sal felt compelled to say before ending the call, knowing it wouldn't make a difference. The past six months had given Cyn plenty of reasons to continue to worry. Along with her sister's death and her father's heart attack, had been the move from Dallas to Seneca, Georgia, to take over her father's job as CEO of Kennedy Industries. While Cyn had been prepping for the job most of her life, Sal knew the suddenness of having to take on additional responsibilities on top of worrying about her family had been very stressful.

Cracking her knuckles, Sal sat down in front of her desktop computer. It didn't take her long to hack through the system at the television network and find the interview. She downloaded a copy, then decided to view it before she forwarded it to Cyn.

The interview was everything wanted in a "mistress tells all exposé"—and more. She could only shake her head as she sent Cyn an encrypted message, including instructions to watch the video before sharing it with her parents. Cyn's father, who was recovering from a heart attack, should be prepped first.

After watching the interview again, disbelief crowded out all her other emotions. Disbelief that Stephen had fallen in with a skanky, no-class, gold-digging stripper when he had Heather. Disbelief that he would look at any other woman when he had beautiful, smart, loving Heather as his wife.

"Come on, what normal person would do that?" she demanded of her computer monitor. "You're exactly right. No sane person would be taken in by that silicon-breasted, low IQ, second-rate bimbo."

While she'd never liked the guy, never thought he was good enough for Heather, she had believed he was somewhat intelligent. It burned her butt she'd been wrong. Burned her butt he hadn't been the caring, loving husband Heather deserved and that she hadn't seen that in him when Heather was alive. Sal could only hope Heather hadn't seen it either.

When her office phone rang, she took a moment to throttle down. Cyn was sure to be angry enough for the both of them. She was right.

"That bastard!" Cyn raged. "Can you believe it? And her? Looking like something the cat wouldn't drag in and trying to pretend she was sorry for cheating on my sister. That's bullshit! The only thing she's sorry about is that Stephen has no plans to marry her. It's almost enough to make me glad Heather isn't here, that she can't see this. It would've broken her heart."

Hearing the catch in Cyn's voice, Sal could easily imagine the tears beading in Cyn's eyes. "On the good side, after that performance, getting custody of Nate should be easy. If they spent a tenth of the time together that she claimed, I don't see how he could've been spending any time with Nate. And that means that someone had to be with Nate."

"That's right. He claimed the nanny only worked during the day. That he made a point of being home every night. Claimed family was important to him. That fucking liar. How could he do that to her?" Cyn was sobbing now. Softly, so that it hit Sal in the heart.

"I don't know." Sal swiped at her own tears and thought about Heather, whom she'd thought of as her little sister though they were the same age. "It's…Oh god, I really do not know." She stayed silent, fighting for control and waiting for Cyn to find hers. "He couldn't have been bringing her home, right? I know stripper girl said he only took her to the best restaurants, the best clubs, but come on. The way she claims they were going at it, he'd have run out of money. Unless…" She made a mental note to do an in-depth financial search on both Stephen and the bimbo. He worked in finance after all. There were ways for him to get his hands on money, and luckily she knew the majority of them.

"Unless what? What do you know that you're not sharing?"

"He works with other people's money, right? What if he found a creative way to get money so that Heather wouldn't know?"

"No. No. Wouldn't that be the smelly rose on top of the shit pile?" Cyn blew out a breath. "Problem is, I can see him doing it. His type is arrogant enough to believe he won't be found out, that he's entitled to it. How much do I tell Mom and Dad? They don't need this on top of the other."

"Nothing but the interview for now. Let me work my magic. If I find something, then *we* can break it to them gently."

"I can't ask you to come down here, Sal. You've been a rock these last months. You have your own work to worry about. You shouldn't have to worry about us as well."

"That's what family's supposed to do. You're my sister and if I can't help out my sister when she needs it, I'm no good. And you know I loved Heather too."

"You certainly saw her more than I did these last few years."

"Geography, Cyn. New York's much closer to Boston than Dallas. Then with being up there to help Nan downsize to her new place, it only made sense that I saw her more than you did. Maybe if I'd been paying better attention, I would've seen what Stephen was up to. Though I don't think I saw him more than twice in all the times I was up there. Heather made excuses, said he had a new account that was eating up his time. But I swear to you, Cyn, she didn't seem worried or upset. If she had…well, I would have done something, said something. You know me."

"If you don't beat yourself up over this, I won't either. It's done. I love my sister, but let's face it, she had a bit of a blind spot when it came to Stephen. She wouldn't have wanted to hear anything negative about him from either of us. What you can do now is help us get as much damaging information as possible. Nate deserves better than that cheater."

"If Stephen left the tiniest crumb, I'll find it. Use it to hang him with. Heather deserved better too."

"You always did have a little crush on my baby sis. No one would have been good enough for her in your mind."

"Hey, you never liked him either."

"Because I didn't like what he wanted for her. I always thought she'd end up at some think tank solving the world's problems. She used to talk about that before he showed up and bowled her over."

"She had the brains for it. She also was smart enough to find other ways to stretch her brain once she married him. And she did love being a mom. Wanted to have another one, but he convinced her to wait."

"I didn't know that."

"Come on, Cyn. I didn't tell you that to make you feel sad. I told you so you'd realize she was happy with her decision to get married and procreate. Maybe more happy with Nate than the marriage, but she was happy."

"You're right. Every time she talked about Nate you could hear how much she loved him, how happy she was to have him. Happier than she would've been with any job."

"Hold on to that thought. It'll help you get through the coming storm this interview will bring. The media will be all over your ass again."

"You always know how to comfort a girl, Sal."

# CHAPTER TWO

With a smile she didn't feel, Adeena Lynne Minor shut the door on the last of the well-wishers. Alone. She was finally alone. No more having to be on display. No more having to show emotions she couldn't feel no matter how hard she tried. Yes, she was proud of what her mother had done. But that pride couldn't erase the distance of the past twenty or so years. That pride couldn't make her love her mother more now that she had died a heroine.

Too restless to settle, she wandered around the room her mother had set aside as strictly for company. *And not just any company*, she thought with a nagging bitterness. Her friends had never been good enough for this room. *She* hadn't been good enough for this room in her mother's eyes. Just one of the many points of friction that had kept her and her mother from being close.

Adeena shook her head. There was no use for her to gnaw on that bone now. Her mother was gone, and there'd never be the opportunity for them to have the kind of relationship

Adeena thought a mother and daughter should have. Maybe if her dad hadn't died when she was fifteen things would have been different. He'd been the center, the one who kept the family on the right road. Without him, she and her mother hadn't known how to interact, how to be a family anymore.

With one last look around a room that could have easily come from a magazine on sterile living, she went to take care of the things she could control. Though her death had been unexpected, Joy Minor had saved her daughter the trouble of figuring out what should happen next. Every detail had been seen to, as was in keeping with Joy Minor's way. Adeena was grateful, but deep inside she wondered if it hadn't been done because her mother didn't trust her non-doctor, non-straight daughter to do anything right.

"Oh, get over yourself," she told herself sternly. "Everything is *not* about you."

The sooner she did the necessary, the sooner she could leave this house where the mostly good memories of the first fourteen years were overshadowed by the not-so-good memories of the last twenty.

In her mother's office, Adeena opened the folder where everything that needed doing was detailed, not in her mother's neat script as she'd expected, but typed. She was pleased to see the many check marks next to the items already completed. Her mother's friends had overridden her half-hearted objections and boxed up most of the house, then moved the boxes to storage for the yearly fete that raised funds for a number of charitable organizations. Once the house sold, they would come back for the furniture Adeena didn't want. Adeena was now left with going through the few boxes from the attic, going through the contents of her mother's home office and scattering her mother's ashes.

She'd given herself a day and a half to finish up, and then she'd go back to Las Vegas, knowing she'd sort of fulfilled the promise she made to her dad to take care of her mother. Diablo, her one-year-old miniature pinscher, would be happy to have her back. This despite the fact he was undoubtedly being spoiled rotten not by her best friend and coworker, Ian Zucker, but his elderly neighbor, Mrs. Gardner.

Adeena spent the next few hours going through the old, four-drawer file cabinet that had been a Mother's Day present from her and her father—Joy Minor only stood for getting practical gifts. Most of the files were from classes her mother had taught over the years, and she relegated them to the recycle bin. According to her mother's instructions, anything that needed keeping would be on her computer, in her locker in the teachers' lounge of the middle school where she taught or in the briefcase currently locked down in her mother's classroom. When classes started back, the person who took over her mother's language arts classes for the remainder of the school year would be able to find everything they needed. No disorder for her mother.

A sob caught her by surprise and she wiped at the tears impatiently. She was done with the crying. Crying wouldn't help her complete the tasks so she could leave this house, this town and the walking wounded, as she thought of a lot of the town's people. The shooting at the only middle school in Dayton, Nevada, had affected a lot of people.

*Another school shooting*, she'd thought, overhearing colleagues discussing it as she made her way to yet another meeting. Had felt superior hearing the mix of horror and excitement in their voices, then disgust when they put the blame on the lack of armed teachers. She'd been tempted to ask about the sanctity of assault rifles but had known it would only rile them up and she didn't have time to enjoy their sputtered response.

It was later, after the meeting that her boss had dragged out as long as possible, that she returned to her desk, that she listened to the message from one of her mother's good friends, a fellow teacher. Adeena had replayed the message two times, and even then, it hadn't seemed real, hadn't sunk in that this time it wasn't about someone else's family. She'd immediately called her mother's cell and gotten no answer. When she called the school and got the same response, she began to believe.

Then Ian had rushed into her cube with news of the shooting. News that it had happened at the middle school where he knew her mother worked. News that one teacher and the shooter had died. He'd asked if she shouldn't call her mother, make sure she was all right.

Looking back now, Adeena thought her tears might have clued him in that she already knew about the shooting, that her mother wasn't okay. Whatever it was, despite the fact she knew he dreaded crying women, he'd taken her in his arms, patted her on her back while she cried buckets of tears because she and her mother would never be able to get to a place where they could accept each other for who they were.

The sound of a car horn brought her back to the present. She closed her eyes and bit down on her lips until some sense of control returned. It wouldn't do any good to wonder what set the boy off or to wish someone had known how to convince that kid he had other options. There were enough people in the town, in the nation, doing the pontificating for her. If she had to listen to one more person quote what they'd heard the supposed experts say, she was going to start screaming and not stop until maybe next year.

Her cell phone buzzed, breaking through the building anger. She saw Ian's name and smiled. "Yes, I'm okay. No, you didn't need to come with me."

"Who are you to decide? Maybe me and Diablo wanted to see the city of your birth. Ever think of that?"

"No. But if you do, nothing's stopping you from making the eight-hour drive up here to nowhere."

"Who cares about Dayton? If I'm driving that far, I'm going to Lake Tahoe."

"You're such an asshole."

"We all have our strengths, babe. But really, how are you holding up? I know it can't be easy being there, accepting the condolences graciously."

"That part's over, done. Although there were a few times I thought I was going to explode if one more person told me how proud I must be. Like the dutiful daughter I don't play on TV, I smiled and nodded while terrible thoughts ran through my head. But I couldn't bring myself to thank them for their words.

And okay, I did boohoo during the service. It was so sad. I mean, these people are so sad and…I don't know…downtrodden? Don't get me wrong, I understand the illusion of safety's been ripped away. It's just, I don't know them, didn't know the kids, didn't really know my own mother, so it's hard to be in the middle and yet not be in the middle." The tears wanted to start up again, so she pressed her fingers against her eyes. "We have to talk about something else now or I'll turn into a blubbering idiot."

"Diablo misses you. This despite the excellent care I've been lavishing on him. Not that he doesn't deserve it. I can't believe you never told me what a chick magnet he is. I'll need to borrow him more if he continues to produce."

She could only laugh. Ian was Ian. "Fitting as it's from one dog to another. Make sure you close the bedroom door before you get your freak on. My baby doesn't need to see all that carrying on."

"Goes without saying. That would be cruel, seeing as you've already taken his manhood."

"Fool. Anything happening at work I should know?"

"Contrary to your and most of your coworkers' opinion, we can function without you for a few days. Though Bobby-boy's been asking about you, wondering when you're going to get your ass back here. My words, not his. But you know how he likes to throw his weight around. Pretend he's so important."

"I'll be back in town day after tomorrow. I may make it to work the day after that. I have to see how I'll feel after spreading the, uh, the ashes."

"Don't hurry back on his account. I've got everything under control. You worry about you and take the time you need."

"Thanks."

"That's what friends are for. Hey, you want me to sing that song?"

"No!" She ended the call laughing, as she was sure Ian meant her to do. He was the best, best friend she'd ever had. He'd wanted to attend the funeral though he'd never met her mother. She'd put him off, thinking she needed to handle everything by herself. Now she was willing to admit she'd been wrong. Having him, and his understanding of her relationship with her mother, around would've made everything easier. One day she might even tell him and then step back as his ego swelled.

Adeena's mood was measureably lighter as she finished emptying the file cabinet and added another check mark to her list. She moved to the desk, another office fixture that had been around as long as she could remember. Of course everything in the center drawer was neatly arranged.

"Everything has a place, Adeena," she said, parroting the admonishment she'd gotten too many times to count. She figured her leaning toward messy—with drawers, her office, everything really—was a form of rebellion. "And isn't that pathetic?"

She frowned as her fingers closed over a tiny envelope. Unlike everything else she'd come across, there was no notation of purpose or instructions on what to do with it. Peering into the unmarked envelope revealed a small key. She wondered about it briefly, but quickly dismissed the notion of her mother wasting money by having a second safety deposit box. She'd already emptied the one at her mother's bank in Carson City and found some important documents, a few pieces of unfamiliar jewelry, but no mention of another box or anything else that needed a key.

A thorough search of the desk had her coming up empty. It was totally out of character for the super-organized Joy Minor to leave things to chance. Maybe she'd go to the tiny bank up the street, see if it fit their boxes. She hated to think it could belong to a box in Reno, given the number of bank branches she'd have to visit to find a match.

A closer study of the key revealed no distinguishing marks she could use for an over-the-phone identification. It could be for anything. "Interesting." Intrigued that her mother may have had a secret, she sat back and twined the key through her fingers. It would be a hoot if the box held sex toys or a porn stash, she decided. The very proper Joy Minor would not want to be caught dead with those things.

But surely her mother would have entrusted the key to a friend if that was the case. Even dead, her mother wouldn't have wanted her daughter to have knowledge of such things.

Thoroughly amused, she turned her attention to the boxes from the attic and rediscovered her childhood. Every scrap of paper from her school years took up one box. She opened the second and with a cry of delight pulled out a stuffed purple miniature unicorn. Adeena couldn't remember how old she was when the unicorn had come to live with her, but at five Pegasus had been a constant companion. She could remember wanting to cry when she found out he couldn't go to school with her. She didn't because her mother told her she was a big girl and big girls didn't cry. Then one day Pegasus was gone. She and her dad searched everywhere to no avail. Adeena had cried herself to sleep and never allowed herself to get attached to another toy.

"Oh, Mother." Hugging the unicorn close, she gave in to tears. She would have to find a way to live with the possibility her mother had only been capable of loving the child she'd wanted Adeena to be.

Adeena woke early the following day. Sitting up, she stretched and looked around the room she'd grown up in. The twin bunk beds had morphed into one queen with a matching dresser and vanity. Nothing was the same as it had been in her youth, and yet it felt like her old room. She could go downstairs, dig through what she considered "her" box and find the rolled-up posters of Einstein, of the human skeleton. Her mother had picked them out, determined her bright little girl was going to grow up to be a doctor.

For a long time, Adeena had also believed she'd grow up to be a doctor. She'd gone to the University of Nevada at Reno at the tender age of fifteen, proud to proclaim her major as pre-med. And along with the classes in science and math, which she excelled at, she'd taken a class in social geography because it was reported to be an easy elective and it fit her schedule. Over the course of the semester, she'd gotten interested in how geography shaped the human experience and that was, as they say, "all it took."

She couldn't say informing her mother she'd switched her major in her junior year had been the beginning of the end of their relationship. No, the end had started before that. It was more like the end of the end. Her mother had continued to support her financially, had allowed her to stay in the house when the dorms were closed, but they lost even the uneasy interaction that had previously defined their relationship.

With a sigh, Adeena slid back the covers. She was wasting time jolting down memory lane. Time she didn't have if she wanted to be done with this place for good.

First thing on the agenda was spreading her mother's ashes in a spot near Virginia City and saying a final goodbye. Although her father's ashes had been spread there, she'd been surprised by her mother's request for the same thing. She guessed in the end, the very practical Joy Minor had put that side away and given in to the romantic side that had seemed to only show itself when her husband had been alive to nurture it.

Downstairs Adeena grabbed her bag. As she did, she spied the envelope with the pesky key. Somehow she had managed to forget about it and her fruitless attempts the day before to uncover its mystery. Neither the calls to her mother's inner circle of friends or the trip to the local bank branch had provided her with answers. As she fingered the old envelope, it occurred to her that it might be fitting to let whatever secret the key held die with her mother and that Joy Minor might finally applaud a decision her daughter made.

Despite the early morning nip in the air, Adeena opened up the sunroof before starting the trip west, then north. As her Subaru ate up the miles between Dayton and Virginia City, her heart grew heavier. She was officially an orphan, a fact having to take care of all the arrangements had successfully let her forget. *Not that you weren't on your own before*, she reminded herself and blinked away the sting behind her eyes. And yet this was different. She'd no longer be able to claim to have a mother, to have family. Exhaling, she turned on the radio and let Top 40 tunes keep her company.

Virginia City was now more a tourist attraction than a city that had sprung up almost overnight with the discovery of the first major silver deposit in the country in 1859. But her dad had loved to come here, eat in the restaurants and tell himself he was back in the past. Adeena liked to come because it was usually just her and her dad and the chance to get away, to do something fun.

Near the spot where she and her mother had freed her father's ashes, she did the same for her mother. "I hope you find happiness again," she said as the wind picked up the ashes and blew them away. "Good-bye." Her eyes dry, Adeena sat for an hour in the weekday quiet, sad because she probably would never be back. Her job was done and she was ready to leave Dayton, Las Vegas, even the state of Nevada behind.

She wasn't sure where she wanted to go, but she did know she was ready for something completely different. The DC area was a possibility. Two visits there for conferences had given her a chance to spend time in the National Museum, the Smithsonian and other national treasures, and she thought she could be happy there with much to explore on the weekends. She'd gone so far as to put out feelers with a couple of companies, but she had yet to hear back. Something would come up, she was sure of that. Until it did, she had a good job and a great friend in Vegas. And when her mother's house sold, she would have money to make the move, to help pay the bills until she found a job. Not a bad situation to find herself in.

Adeena stretched her arms to the sky and said her good-byes. With something like freedom lifting her spirit, she made her way back to the car. The first task of the day was done, leaving her plenty of time to get back, go through the house and decide what she wanted to keep. It wouldn't be much. Her mother's tastes were different from hers, and given that she hoped to relocate soon, she didn't want the extra baggage.

Deciding there would be loud, off-key singing on the way back, she turned on the radio. After checking for coming traffic, she pulled onto the narrow two-lane road that would take her back to the highway. When she was learning to drive, the summer after her sophomore year in college, her mother had insisted she master this stretch of road before she could get her license. She'd hated the road, so twisty and curvy and so high up there was nothing to catch you but air. Eventually, with lots of practice and advice, she'd gotten over that fear and learned to enjoy accelerating into the curves, going as fast as her mother would let her. When alone, she would go as fast as her nerves allowed. The older she got, the more her nerves could withstand.

From habit, she checked the rearview mirror and her heart leapt into her throat. Some idiot was coming up behind her much too fast for anyone's safety. Luckily no one was coming from the opposite direction for now. She couldn't guarantee that would be the case once they made it around the next bend in the road.

Adeena increased her speed, but the white SUV continued to gain on her. There was a place to pull off and put on snow tires a little way up, and maybe she could make it there before the SUV caught up with her, before anyone got hurt. Then the idiot could have it his idiotic, suicidal way. Gripping the wheel, she increased her speed again and prayed.

When the SUV clipped her on the rear driver's side, panic clouded her mind. She jerked the steering wheel and went into a spin.

"Steer into the skid!" she shouted to no one in particular and managed to bring the car to a stop, facing the wrong direction. Shaky, shocked and somewhat mad, she looked for the other vehicle and saw it still barreling toward her, head-on. She threw the car in reverse, spun around with a spray of gravel from the minuscule shoulder and floored it. Finding a pull-off wasn't going to do her any good, she realized, and she took curve after curve at dangerous speeds, managing somehow to stay ahead of the SUV.

After what seemed like forever, she spotted the marker signaling the Mulberry Farm was up ahead. If she could make it there, where there would be witnesses, surely the idiot would back off. She could then call the police and get the other driver off the road before they killed someone. She didn't slow, then at the last second, made the sharp right onto the dirt road. Her sedan fishtailed, and she quickly corrected without much loss of speed. When she didn't see the other vehicle pull up behind her, she pumped the brakes, slowed down and eventually came to a stop.

Resting her forehead against the steering wheel, she tried to get her breath, tried to control the trembling. An adrenaline junkie she was not, she thought as she gulped in air, felt the pounding of her heart. She couldn't say if praying had helped, but surely it hadn't hurt.

She was alive. Alive enough to be shivering so hard she had to clench her teeth to keep them from knocking.

A knock on her window brought a scream and had her looking for the white SUV. They'd followed her, not satisfied with near death, was her first thought. When she finally looked at the grizzled man, the horse standing placidly behind him, she exhaled and rolled down the window.

"You hurt?"

She shook her head and gathered her thoughts. "Some crazy idiot decided to play chicken. I thought…" She took a deep breath, let it out slowly. "I didn't want to play."

"What kind of car?"

"Big and white. They chased me from almost Virginia City."

"Don't have to worry about them now," he said serenely. "Saw them go off the road myself. Looked like they tried to turn around too quick and lost control."

She didn't know what to think. Going off the road up here was serious, could even mean death. The person driving the car had been an idiot for sure, but they didn't deserve death. Before she could figure out what this all meant, she heard the sirens. A patrol car must have been close by. Too bad it hadn't been closer.

\* \* \*

Vicki Adams had known there could be some difficult questions raised the second she saw the news report about the school shooting. It had been more than three decades, and still the name Joy Minor was etched on her brain. Add to that the Dayton location and a daughter who couldn't look more like her mother, and there'd been no doubt the house of cards she'd cobbled together in desperation could come tumbling down. On some level she had known this day could come. Had known of the possibility around thirty years ago when Jeremy Winston's link to the Tanners was revealed through his death.

She took a sip of her nightly glass of wine and began to plan for any fallout. There was enough time to formulate a careful response if the secrets of the past were revealed. Her uncle Kenneth, as she called him, would have to be apprised of this new development. He had the most to lose if he was linked to two illegal adoptions and assisting in identity fraud. Well, he had been making noises about retiring. Still, disbarment, if it came to that, would be a crushing blow to a man who valued his integrity. Which meant she should wait to mention this until he returned from his annual vacation, giving him time to relax and unwind. He deserved that for all the good work he did.

Vicki exhaled. She'd have some things to answer for as well. She was ready. What she'd done thirty-four years ago had saved two innocent lives. At the time she hadn't known the whole story, hadn't realized the Tanner connection, but that wouldn't matter. What she had known was that her college pal Walter needed help. She'd known that a relation of his wife had come to them with an unbelievable story of kidnapping, miracles and having spirited away two newborn babies—one black, one white—whose lives were in mortal danger. Walter said he and his wife were willing to take one of the babies. He'd been hoping Vicki's lawyer uncle could find a good home for the other baby, could quietly arrange the adoptions.

Because she knew Walter, knew the kind of man he was, she'd agreed to discuss it with her uncle. When she'd discussed it with him, when he'd reluctantly agreed to consider helping for the babies' sake, Vicki hadn't known about the fire, hadn't known the identity of the dead mother or about the search a vicious drug dealer was conducting for two babies he'd planned to sell. When Walter had come back to her hours later, had told her everything he'd managed to uncover about a murder for hire, Vicki had acted decisively. She was going to have to do the same now…

The slap to her face jarred Vicki back to the present where every part of her body hurt. She groaned as even taking a breath brought pain.

"Good. You're back. I have more questions and I want the truth this time."

As she looked into cold, pale blue eyes and saw her own impending slow, painful death, she allowed herself to feel some pity for herself for not realizing how desperately the Tanners had wanted Lucy's baby dead—along with everyone who could tell anyone about her.

# CHAPTER THREE

"I have to go…No, really…We're at the gate and the door's gonna open any second…Okay…Okay…It's not my first time… Yes, ma'am…Nan, I solemnly swear to be on alert for men in sheets. Call you tonight." Sal pocketed her phone, pulled her duffel bag from under the seat in front of her and eased into the aisle.

To hear her grandmother talk, one would think the KKK would be at the gate to welcome her to Atlanta, Georgia, because there was an African-American man in the White House and because they somehow knew about her proclivity for dating white women. She couldn't really blame her grandmother, she thought, and smiled her thanks to the first class flight attendant. The South of now was different from the one her grandmother left in the fifties. These days Sal imagined the large African-American population in Atlanta made for a more subtle Klan. She wasn't naïve enough to think there couldn't be issues, but as a female of color, she believed she was less likely to be in mortal danger than her grandmother imagined.

As promised, Cyn was waiting for her in the baggage claim area. After an extended hug, she pulled back to study Cyn's face. Maybe there were more fine lines around her baby blues, but Sal decided her friend looked damn good considering the weight she'd been under for the past five months.

"Do I pass inspection?" Cyn fluffed at her shoulder-length blond hair and offered a dazzling smile.

"Well, you're not the dried-up crone I was expecting," she replied and took a quick step back and out of reach of Cyn's long arms. "You look great. I take it everyone survived the interview mess?"

"Better than survived. Stephen has agreed in writing it's better for me to be Nate's guardian. For now."

"So you took my advice and threatened him with an all-out war?"

"Nope. That would be Mom who was all over that. Once she had a chance to stew about some of the comments Stephen's whore said about Heather, she turned into a fire-breathing dragon. Called our lawyer and demanded he put the pressure on or she'd find someone who would. She didn't say it that nicely."

"Way to go, Mom!" As Sal pumped her fist in solidarity, the beacon over the luggage carousel lit up and Sal's flight number flashed across the screen. "Stephen more than deserves to have his ass kicked."

Amusement faded from Cyn's expression. "You know something."

She nodded, feeling terrible she had to add to the trouble Cyn was already carrying, but it was the reason she'd flown down. "Took me longer than planned to uncover his hidden accounts, then backtrack to the source. Both he and the firm he works for have very good security. I'm better."

"When will this get out?"

"Right now they're assessing the damage." Sal scanned the moving belt, looking for her distinctive bag. "Stephen was smart enough to take the money from an associate's client instead of his own. With a little help from an anonymous source, the good guys were able to figure out the true culprit."

Cyn snorted. "Anonymous source, my ass. Would they have figured it out by themselves?"

"Probably. Would've taken longer though. Like I said, he's pretty damn clever at hiding his tracks. And frankly, I get the impression the bigwigs didn't want to believe someone with his resources would stoop to this. Oh good. There's my bag." Sal slipped through the crowd and pulled her hard-sided suitcase off the carousel.

"Only you would have a suitcase covered with cartoon X-Men, Salamander." Cyn shook her head. "One of these days you'll be forced to grow up."

"Not in this lifetime, baby. I have enough money to make sure of that." She pushed at glasses that were dark and square. More than just correcting her vision, they were her personal touchstone. "And speaking of money, I have more bad news." Sal reached for Cyn's hand. "I wanted to tell you in person because I know this is going to hurt like hell."

"Tell me on the way out. I sent Nick a text to pick us up out front. Mother insisted that I needed to be driven."

Despite Cyn's nonchalant reply, Sal caught the tensing of her shoulders. "Okay. Hard and fast. He was siphoning money from Heather's account. He put it back after the accident. I'm guessing 'cause he knew there'd be an audit."

"That bastard." There was more sadness than heat in her voice as Cyn closed her eyes momentarily and took a deep breath. "He probably planned to do that all along. Probably had it in his head when he signed the damn prenup. God, I could kill him for that alone! She trusted him, was always quick to defend him. And he does something like this?" She pressed her fingers against her eyes, then let her hands drop. "There's no word harsh enough."

"Word? Death's too good for that rat bastard. Now me, I like the thought of him being disgraced, languishing in prison for years only to get out and discover his hidden accounts are empty." Sal's grin was fierce. "That would be worse than death for guys like him who put form before substance."

Cyn wiped at her eyes as a ghost of a smile touched her lips. "Remind me to stay on your good side."

From the back of the Cadillac the forty-five-minute drive from the airport to Seneca seemed to take no time at all. Sal spent most of that time talking about the plans for her annual Vegas trip in hopes of taking Cyn's mind off Stephen's betrayal.

"I would be impressed if it didn't sound exactly like what you've done for the past few years. How many times can you fly over the Grand Canyon? And why go all the way to Vegas to gamble when Atlantic City is practically next door?"

"If I have to explain, Grasshopper, then you don't get it. Atlantic City's okay on a limited basis, but the big boys and girls go to Vegas. How can I win their money if I'm not there? And the Grand Canyon? It never ceases to take my breath away. Once is never enough."

"I've managed it."

"You always did lack imagination." Sal craned her neck, waiting for the first glimpse of the Kennedy mansion. She could still remember the awe she'd felt the first time she'd seen it. The house, set far back from the tall stone wall that surrounded the estate, was ringed by a grove of mature trees. You had to drive a ways to see it in all its glory.

It was out of place to Sal's way of thinking, looking like it should be in England. Instead of the antebellum style popular in the South, the house was a stone behemoth with turrets. It stood three stories high and was wide enough to cover a city block. She'd been told some Kennedy ancestor fancied himself to be a king. "Gets me every time," she admitted as the limo came to a smooth stop in front of the house.

"It's home," Cyn said with a good deal of pride. She got out, then walked around and waited for Sal to do the same. "I forgot to tell you about the puppies."

"Puppies? As in more than one?"

"Mom had this great idea that Nate needed a puppy. When we went to pick it up, there were these two cuties sleeping all tangled up together. I didn't have the heart to separate them.

They're more work than I figured, but you should see the way Nate's face lights up. He's a different boy, laughing and playing. Totally worth it. I can't tell you how good that makes me feel."

"Don't have to. I can see it on your face."

The front door opened before they reached it. Sal thought having a butler was a little much, so she liked to think of Henry as a doorman. Those she was used to. "Hey, Henry. How's it hanging?"

He gave her a stiff nod. "Glad to have you back, ma'am."

Sal laughed. "How many times do I have to tell you I ain't no ma'am."

"Ignore her, Henry," Cyn called over her shoulder and pulled Sal further into the large foyer. "I don't hear the puppies, so everyone must be out back. I forgot to ask. Are you hungry? I know whatever they serve on the plane doesn't go far."

"I grabbed a calzone from Big Al's on the way to the airport." She patted her flat stomach. "Me and the person sitting next to me are full."

Barking followed by laughter spilled from a room down the hall. "And they're back," Cyn said.

"I hope Nate will be glad to see me. Last time I tried to visit, the nanny wouldn't let me in without Stephan being there."

"You took him to the toy store and bought him that monstrous dragon. He'll be happy to see you." Cyn steered them into the sunroom where Nate was rolling around on the floor with the puppies. "Nate, look who I brought with me."

Sal caught the quick look of fear on Nate's face, the stiffening of his body and wondered at the cause. "Hey kiddo, how you doing?"

He looked at her, then checked behind her before he gave her a tiny smile. "You gots me the dragon and you played with me at my other house."

"That's right. How 'bout a hug?"

When he pushed from the floor and ran into her open arms, Sal's heart did a slow turn. She hadn't realized she missed him as much as she missed Heather.

"You've gotten bigger on me." She ran her fingers through his sandy blond curls and thought about how much like Heather he looked with the big, blue-green eyes and the smattering of freckles across his nose. "And heavier." She pretended to stagger at his weight and set him down to greet Cyn's parents. "Mary Francis, you're looking gorgeous as ever. Cyn should be grateful you deigned to share your looks." As Cyn had with her, Mary Francis had taken to Sal from their first meeting, easing her concerns that the wealthy Kennedys would disapprove of their daughter befriending someone not of their stature.

Mary Francis Kennedy wrapped Sal in a hug. "And you're as charming as ever."

Sal shook George Kennedy's hand. He was too thin and not as robust as he'd been before the heart attack, but he'd lost the gray pallor of a few months before and that was a plus. "Good to see you again." She looked down as one of the puppies attacked her shoe. "Looks like you have your work cut out for you."

His blue eyes twinkled. "Who me? I'm a sick old man."

"Only when it comes to cleaning up accidents." Mary Francis ran a hand down his back. "Sit. Sal, can I get you some food or drink?"

"Rum and Coke without—"

"The rum," Mary Francis finished. "I know what the rest of this group wants." She swept out of the room, leaving behind a subtle floral scent.

"While she's seeing to that, I'm going to put a little sleepy body to bed." Cyn pointed to where Nate, tangled with the puppies, was fighting to keep his eyes open.

"Not tired," he said and rubbed his eyes. "No bed."

Cyn scooped him up. "But you need your rest. Big day for you tomorrow, sweetie."

"Do I hafta?"

"It'll be fun having lots of kids to play with. It's only for a few hours, and then you can come home and tell us all the fun you had at school."

"And maybe I'll have a little present when you get back." Sal was rewarded with a smile.

"Will you come with Aunt Cyn to take me?"

"And pick you up," she promised.

He rested his head against Cyn. "Like Mommy used to?"

Cyn rubbed his back. "Like that."

After a round of hugs and kisses, prolonged by the return of Mary Francis, Cyn, followed by the puppies, bore Nate off to bed.

"Thank you," Mary Francis said once Cyn's footsteps faded away. She held up her hand when Sal opened her mouth. "Your name might not have been mentioned, but I know you're the one who sent Cyn that horrible video. Because of you we were able to anticipate the press and have a statement ready for the vultures."

"So take the thanks," George said gruffly. "For that and for being a good friend to Cyn. It hasn't been easy for her. What with Heather, then me and this damn heart. But she stepped up, our Cyn did."

"Like she always has." Mary Francis put her hand on top of George's. "We worry about her and all the new responsibility. But we worry less because of you." She smiled at Sal. "I'm so glad you came so I—no, we—could have a chance to tell you in person. Oh, I know you young people and your texts and tweets, but face to face is nice."

Sal rubbed the cool glass against her heated cheeks. "Cyn, well, man, she's been like my sister from the start. I couldn't do any less for her or you. Family's the thing." She'd learned that lesson early from her parents. No matter what game they might be running, it never came before doing right by the family. Even back then, she'd been taught family was more than the people related by blood, by race or by creed. She'd been taught families were made by love and intention.

"Just know we appreciate you and your sentiments," Mary Francis said. "Now how is your grandmother? I do hope we can get together and go shopping again."

"She'd love that." Sal suppressed a shudder. That type of shopping was not her forte.

# CHAPTER FOUR

The next morning, after a light workout and a hearty breakfast, Sal fulfilled her promise to accompany Nate and Cyn to preschool. Nick left first in the empty Caddy to draw away any curious media personnel. Fifteen minutes later, they pulled out in Cyn's sedan with the tinted windows.

The private school was a twenty-minute drive away. It housed preschool up to the twelfth grade in two buildings that had been added on to over the years. To Sal, Weston looked more like a college setting than any school she'd attended.

Unlike the majority of parents, Cyn pulled into the parking lot instead of using the designated drop-off lane.

"How does it feel to have Nate going to your alma mater?" Sal asked as Cyn backed into a parking space. "Like a parent?"

"More like strange. And older." She lowered her voice. "But I'd like to think someone up above is getting a big kick that her son's following in her footsteps. I just wish…"

"I know." Sal patted her thigh before turning to look at Nate. "You ready to take over this place, kiddo?" When his expression said otherwise, she added, "I bet there are some kids waiting to be your friend."

"Will it be like my other school?"

"Sort of the same and sort of different," Cyn said. "I bet you'll have fun."

Nate insisted on wearing his backpack once he was out of his car seat. He also insisted on holding both of their hands.

"To Oz?" Sal asked.

"To Oz," Cyn agreed.

They walked to the school, swinging Nate into giggles. Once inside they had to sign in and show ID.

"That's new from my time," Cyn said as they walked past a guard. "But necessary, I guess."

"No guessing about it. Nan called me the other day, upset after that incident in Nevada."

"I heard about that one. I should have called her."

"Nan knows you have a lot to deal with. She kind of freaked because one of the dead teachers had a daughter my age. And when I didn't get in touch like I usually do, it got her worried. She worries about me too much."

"Shouldn't she? Considering what you do?"

"No. I'm always careful about who I deal with. You should know that by now." Sal opened the door to a colorfully decorated front office. "This is nice. Hey, Nate, look up." She pointed to the fairies dancing on the ceiling. "I should get some for my office."

"I like 'em," Nate said.

"Good morning," the cheerful, grandmotherly-looking woman standing behind the counter called out. "Welcome back, Nate. We're so happy you could join us. I'm Miss Susan, remember? I'll let Miss Annabelle know you're reporting for duty."

"I went to school with her," Cyn murmured while the call was being made. "Annabelle, that is. Nicest popular girl I've ever known."

Annabelle was tall, blond and beautiful. Sal felt a tug on her libido.

"Cyn. Good to see you again." Annabelle smiled down at Nate. "Welcome back to Weston, Nate. I'll take you to your room and maybe next time you can walk by yourself since you're a big boy."

Nate's response was to reach for Cyn's hand.

Cyn got on her knees and pulled him close. "It's okay, sweetie. Sal and I will be here to pick you before you know it."

"Promise?" he whispered with a glance at Annabelle.

"Promise. Now you go have some fun."

"Cyn, if you have a minute, I'd like to talk after I deliver this young man."

"Sure." Cyn frowned as Annabelle and Nate disappeared down a hall. "What do you suppose that was about?"

"School stuff. So you went to school with her?" Sal blew out a breath. "Be still my heart."

"Straight and married with two point five kids."

"Crushed." Sal put a hand to her heart. "Or would be if I hadn't given up blondes for my own version of Lent."

They moved to the side as more parents arrived to drop off kids. Sal was impressed that Miss Sally greeted parents and kids by name. "Busy place."

"Lucky for us, they made a space for Nate because of his situation and the fact my parents have donated plenty of money over the years."

"Money always helps."

Annabelle beckoned them from the open door. Sal could barely hear the sound of kids as they passed four rooms on the way to the end of the hall. Annabelle's office was spacious. Sal figured the clear walls gave the appearance of transparency.

Once they were seated, Cyn made introductions. "Sal can hear anything you have to say."

"It's not much. There was a man, a private investigator. He got in somehow late yesterday and was asking questions about Heather. Sally referred him to me, and of course, I immediately sent for security, who escorted him to Headmaster Doyle's office."

"Do you remember his name?" Cyn asked.

She picked up a card and handed it to Cyn. "I would have called you, but I knew you'd be here this morning and I wanted to tell you in person."

"What did he look like?" Sal asked as she peered at the card over Cyn's shoulder. "I mean, how was he dressed? Suit and tie, neat, wrinkled, clean-shaven? That type of thing."

"He was well dressed. I thought at first he was looking to place a grandchild."

"So he was older?" Sal prodded.

"Late fifties, early sixties and in good shape. He was very polite, but we have strict rules about disseminating information on students or parents."

"What did he ask?" Cyn finally looked up from the card.

"If I remembered her. Sally heard later he'd asked someone if Heather knew she was adopted."

"That doesn't make any sense. Of course she knew she was adopted." Cyn stuck the card in her pocket. "Headmaster's office still in the same place?"

"Yes. And he usually sticks close to it around this time. If not, his admin can summon him."

"Thanks for bringing this to my attention, Annabelle. I assume you heard about the interview with—"

"Yes. Don't worry. We'll keep an extra eye out for anyone snooping around looking for a story."

"I'm impressed," Sal said as they made their way to the headmaster's office. "They not only know about the situation, they already have a solution in place."

"They've always been aware of the need for privacy and have attracted a good number of prominent families over the years because of it. That certainly played a role in why we wanted Nate to come here. Here we are." Cyn knocked on the open door.

With a smile, Headmaster Doyle came around his desk, his arm outstretched. "Cynthia Kennedy. One of my brightest and most challenging students."

"Challenging I can agree with." Cyn shook his hand and made quick introductions. "My mother was sorry we missed you when we came to enroll Nate."

"Meetings. Always meetings. What can I help you with today?"

"I have a few questions about the investigator who was asking questions about Heather. With what's been in the news lately, you can understand my concern."

He nodded and gestured toward the chairs in front of his desk. "I'm afraid there's not much to tell. I quickly sent Mr. Burlett on his way after making it very clear there would be no information forthcoming from my office or anyone under contract with our institution. I must say he took the dismissal very well and left without the need to get security involved. Perhaps I should have informed you and your family, but I can assure you he received no information from anyone at Weston."

"Understood. However, I'd like to ask that I be informed if anyone else comes asking for information on Heather. The press has been very aggressive of late and we want to make sure we stay ahead of them."

"I understand. His full name was Roman Burlett. I do not have any more information to give you as I refused to take his card. I imagine you can look him up on the Internet."

"The name is enough, Mr. Doyle. Can I say how much I'm impressed by the changes you've made since my time here?"

They left Doyle's office ten minutes later with a promise to come back for a tour.

"He should have called you," Sal said as she worked on her phone. "Though I think he realizes that now. He seems to be legit."

"Of course he is. He wouldn't be associated with Weston if he wasn't."

"Not Doyle. Roman Burlett. From the looks of his former clients' list, he does the job. Impressive even."

"Could it be Stephen? Trying to, I don't know, find dirt on Heather to make himself look better?"

"Nada. I dug deep, deep, deep into his financials. Even if he paid cash, the withdrawal would have shown up."

"Maybe I should call this Burlett guy. Ask him what he wants and who he's working for."

Hearing the agitation in Cyn's voice, Sal put a hand on Cyn's shoulder. "Not the way to go. This guy's been in business for years. Couldn't stay there if he made a practice of blabbing. If he'd wanted it known who he was working for he would've led with that."

"Then what do we do?" Cyn ran her fingers through her hair. "I honestly don't know how much more of this bullshit my parents can take."

*Or you*, Sal thought. "They can take more than you think. As for what to do, that's easy. We go back to your place and let me do what I do."

\* \* \*

"Not acceptable." Eugenia Tanner tightened her grip on the phone. "It's been a week. I thought I'd impressed upon you the urgency of the situation...I don't have time for your excuses. My instructions were certainly clear enough...Then I suggest you get yourself to Nevada and deal with the matter personally. I've counted on you in the past, Conlin, and I would like to continue to do so in the future." She disconnected the call in the middle of his pathetic excuses. There was too much riding on this to accept failure and he had to be made to understand that.

"Problems?"

Eugenia cursed herself for having forgotten she wasn't alone. She forced a smile for her favorite grandson. "Nothing that can't be solved, Beau." Holding out her hand, she said, "You never did tell me what brings you here." The sulky expression marred his handsome face, she thought. He was like his father in looks only, much to her disappointment. His constant talk of wealth distribution, global warming and human rights had become quite tiresome. But he was young and spoiled by the lifestyle he railed against. She was sure age and experience would season his views and turn him into a man who could follow his father into politics.

"Why, you ask? Maria! She drives me crazy! She practically lives at the house now, so it'll only become major torture once Dad announces his candidacy. If I have to take one more family portrait or listen to her tell me what I can and can't do, I'm gonna hurl." Groaning, he flopped down in a chair and swung his long legs over the side.

She deplored his deportment and could well understand the frustration Jackson's campaign manager, Maria Cousins, must be feeling. "Maria is doing her job, Beau. As any good manager would do. Don't you want to help your father get elected?"

"Why would I? His platform is totally lame. The Republican Party is like a dinosaur. They're hurtling toward extinction because they don't see that the country—hell, the whole world—is changing. Dad would be much better off running as a moderate Democrat or an Independent."

"Please do not let the press hear you saying that, dear." Eugenia clasped her hands tightly. The situation was worse than she thought. "Rumors of the death of the Republican Party are being fed to you by the liberal media. You mustn't believe everything you hear or read."

"But it's true." He swung around to face her, his expression earnest. "If Dad really wanted to make a difference, he'd support some of the issues my generation cares about. It's time to get out of the pockets of big business and help the people who are struggling. What does it matter if guys marry guys? He should be more concerned about the effects we're having on the climate, on the animal species that are going extinct daily. But no, all he does is listen to that talking head of a manager, who wouldn't know a fresh idea if it came in that junk she sprays on her hair. He should be forging his own path."

"Regardless of what you think you know to be true, I would ask for your father's sake that you tone down your opinions in public. It would be better yet if you kept them to yourself."

"Whatever." He stood with the jerky movement of one who hadn't fully grown into his body. Beau was almost eighteen, almost eligible to vote for those Democrats he loved so much.

"Is that any way to speak to your grandmother?" He seemed to Eugenia to get taller every day. At six-three, he topped his father by an inch. She continually had to remind herself rebellion was normal at his age. But maybe she should talk to Jackson, have him talk to the boy.

"Sorry, Grandmother. Too bad I can't be like Phillip, right? Do everything I'm told. Believe everything I'm told. I should go." He dropped a kiss on her cheek and took off in his long, loping stride.

His increased verbalization of liberal rubbish was something else to worry about, Eugenia decided. She needed to find a suitable place to send him once school was out. In the fall, he'd be going off to college and be too busy worrying about getting into the right fraternity to cause any trouble. But it was this summer, when Jackson would be working hard to get the big money donors as well as the full support of the party kingmakers, that Beau needed to be muffled.

Eugenia mentally worked through her long list of contacts. She required someone who could get him into a project that was away from an urban area, maybe even away from the US. Working with the downtrodden he was so eager to discuss should teach him a few things about real life. He could come back having gained a better insight on how the world worked and with a better appreciation of the financial standing he took for granted. A win for everyone if they leaked his charitable deed to the press.

She reached for the phone. The first place to start was with her daughter-in-law, Hope. Convincing Beau's mother shouldn't be a problem. Jackson's beautiful, accomplished wife seemed to want that senate seat as much as he did, if not more.

"So you're just leaving it as that? A mystery?" Ian raised his bottle of beer, then set it back down without taking a sip. "What if it's a safe deposit box filled with money, gold coins, jewelry? Maybe your mother was a bank robber before she toed the straight and the narrow."

Adeena rolled her eyes. "Get real. My mother a former criminal? No. Joy Minor was never on the wrong side of the law."

"Well, what about the lawyer? What did he have to say?"

"He's as baffled as I am. I'm telling you, the key is likely leftover from when she and Dad were younger. Think about it. I didn't find anything related to their lives before I was born. I bet they dumped that stuff in a trunk when they moved, got rid of it later and forgot about dumping the key."

"No. *You* need to do the thinking. You only put valuable stuff in containers that lock. And if she did decide to throw it away, she would have tossed the key along with it. How do I know that, you ask? Easy. She would've had to have the key right there to open the trunk to see the junk. She wanted you to find the key. Probably meant to tell you about it. Maybe she's dropped hints over the years."

She propped her head up with her hand and silently admitted he had a point. Her mother would not have gotten rid of the trunk without checking the contents and that meant the key would have been in the lock when she made the decision to dump the box. And even if she had emptied it, Joy Minor would not have thrown away a container unless it was falling apart.

"Well?" He prodded her with his elbow.

"You may have a small point." She demonstrated how small with her fingers. "But number one, that still doesn't tell me how to figure out where this lock may be. It could be attached to something she left in Georgia for all I know."

He frowned. "I forgot they moved here before you were born. What about her relatives?"

"Doesn't have any. Neither did Dad. But back to point number two. I've lived for thirty-four years without knowing the contents of said thing. You agree on that point, right?" She didn't continue until he nodded. "So I can live another thirty-four years without knowing. Boo-yah. End of story." Adeena raised her empty bottle and nodded at the bartender for a refill.

She hadn't been to Maxim since she got back from the funeral, and she was glad she'd let Ian talk her into coming today. She'd missed the casual atmosphere, the camaraderie with the other regulars. "So, how're things with the latest Ms. Supermodel?"

"They're not. She wanted more and you know me." Ian shrugged. "What I don't get is why a beautiful woman like her, one whom you'd expect to keep a couple of men at a time on the line, would try to limit herself to one."

"No. That's what *you'd* expect. You, Ian Zucker, the king of the Playaz. Maybe she wants to be someone's baby." She laughed at his sneer of disgust.

"No, no, no. We are not going there, Rick Springfield."

"I thought it was clever. So maybe she's decided a stud like you looks good on her arm." She waved off his glare. There was no doubt Ian was gorgeous. High cheekbones, thick black hair and burnished skin that showcased his Native American heritage. Add the long lashes surrounding his hazel eyes, a body he kept fit and trim like a religion, and you got eye candy for days. Even with her sitting next to him, women came up to give him sultry glances. Some discreetly left their digits when they thought she wasn't looking. Once a woman, who'd obviously had too much to drink, told him he could do better and she was that better. Adeena had wanted to punch her for principle's sake.

"Hey, shouldn't that be opposite? She's supposed to be thinking about how good she looks hanging on *my* arm. And I have to admit we looked good together. But then I look good with everyone."

"You, sir, are a pig." She smiled her thanks when the bartender placed a cold one in front of her. "Gorgeous as sin, but a pig nonetheless. Makes me glad I'm not straight or I'd probably be falling at your feet like all the rest."

He flashed a grin. "Probably? I'd have you in knots and you know this."

"Please. I'm not your type. Too smart, not thin and lacking in the chest department. You wouldn't give me and my brown hair a second glance."

"But you got that cute face." He pinched her cheek and laughed when she slapped at his hand. "A little makeup and who knows what could happen."

"Makeup? Really? I'm a natural beauty. Makeup and I don't need to know each other. Not ever."

"Never say never." His expression went from teasing to serious in a heartbeat. He reached for her hand and cradled it between his. "I know we never dated, but now's a good time for you to pretend. Why did I tell her about this place?"

"Are you crazy?" She tried to get her hand back and failed.

"So this is my replacement. That was quick."

Adeena's first impression was of masses of blond hair, big blue eyes and the prerequisite impressive cleavage displayed by a tight-fitting tank top. "Uh, I...think I need the ladies' room." She yanked her hand and again Ian didn't let go. "Guess I don't. I'm Adeena, by the way," she added with a simpering smile. "Have we met? I don't think so. You I would have remembered."

"I'm his ex." Supermodel's smile was decidedly frosty. "I hope you're not looking for permanent because I can assure you, you *won't* get it from this one."

She tried to look indignant. "No! Say it ain't so. I mean, he's like already talking about rings." She managed to keep a straight face when Ian choked on his beer. "This is awful. Don't tell me he used the same ploy to get you in the...you know?"

"No. I fell for his dog. An adorable miniature pinscher. Not that guys haven't tried to pull one on me before." She flipped her hair over her shoulder. "Look at me."

"I am," Adeena said, wondering what would happen if she announced she was a lesbian. "You're so gorgeous. Do you model?"

Supermodel preened. "You're sweet, but no. I'm a stylist. If you ever feel the need for a makeover Ian knows where to find me."

"That's so sweet of you. I really appreciate you coming over and giving me the four-one-one. I might have bought his act." She yanked on her hand, and this time Ian let go. "Take care of yourself, girlfriend. Remember, you can do better than him."

Supermodel flipped her hair again. "So true."

"Rings?" Ian asked, once Supermodel was out of hearing range. "You had to go with that?"

Adeena laughed. "You said pretend. I was in character and the words flowed. You know, one scorned woman to another. She needs a new name. While she is gorgeous, and I hate to say that word again, she's much too short to be a supermodel. Just saying," she added as he tried to cut her with a glare.

"And I'm just saying you got her all riled up. Rings." He huffed, obviously disgusted. "She'll be drunk-texting me next. Asking why I never talked rings with her. See if I let you be my pretend girlfriend anymore."

"Now you've crushed my feelings." She wiped at dry eyes. "Maybe I should go join her, dish about what a heartless ass you are. Bet I could get her riled up enough to do some of that drunk-texting right now."

"Shut up. What kind of friend are you anyway? Don't you know that kind of shit will give a man like me nightmares?"

Adeena rested her head against the bar and howled with laughter. "Priceless," she said, wiping away tears once the laughter was under control. "Your expression was priceless. If you do have nightmares, will you tell me about them?"

"That's not right." He pointed a finger at her. "Not right at all."

"But it was funny." She downed the rest of her beer. "Now that I've had my fill of entertainment, I must go home, take my baby for a walk. Hey, maybe I could use Diablo to snag me a lesbian supermodel."

"Not even in your dreams."

"For that, my boy, tab's on you. And now to make my exit." She couldn't flip her hair over her shoulder because it was too short, so she gave him the neck movement, shook a finger in his face. "If you're lucky, she'll think I'm dumping you and be willing to give you sympathy sex." She held her head high as she stalked out of the bar.

The heat enveloped her the minute she stepped foot outside. Las Vegas in May was hot, but bearable. The temperature wouldn't rise to triple digits until later and by then, she might be somewhere else. Of course it would be hot in DC too, and she'd have to add the humidity on top of that. But it wouldn't be here and that's all she was looking for right now.

It was a short walk back to the office to pick up her car, then make the thirty-minute drive to the massive apartment complex she'd called home for five years. It seemed to her as she got older, the other residents got younger. Another reason she was ready to move.

Diablo welcomed her home with his usual abandon. She would dare anyone not to get a lift from his show of unwavering love and affection.

It had been a lucky day for both of them when the need for new work clothes had forced her to venture to the mall. One look at the dog, peering out of the crate with something like hope in his eyes, and she'd been hooked. Out came the wallet, not for clothes, but for adoption fees and all the accessories the little rescue dog shouldn't have to live without. Since the poor baby was nameless, she'd chosen Diablo because obviously the devil made her do it. She hadn't regretted that decision, not one second.

"Okay, you attention hound, go get your leash while I change and we'll go for a walk." She thought he only understood "leash" and "walk" when he gave a happy bark, then raced off to do her bidding. Once she'd traded work clothes for shorts and a tank, he was sitting patiently by the front door. The obedience classes had paid off.

"Ready to go, baby?" Diablo danced on his back legs and barked his agreement.

Adeena's neighborhood was a maze of apartment complexes. Each one tried to outdo the others with move-in specials, so it seemed to her that there was always someone moving in or moving out. She'd stopped trying to keep up with her neighbors.

Diablo's pull on the leash grew more insistent as they got closer to the park. This time of day, on a Tuesday night, the park would be full of people walking their dogs, jogging or taking their kids to the playground.

"Chill, Diablo." Adeena refused to be dragged over to where a Great Dane named Molly was catching a rest. The fact that Diablo's love for Molly was unreciprocated hadn't yet put a damper on his adoration. It helped that Molly seemed to view him as an acceptable annoyance and not a chew toy.

"Wish men were that loyal."

Adeena hoped her internal cringe didn't show on her face. She'd forgotten to keep an eye out for Lola and now she had to pay the price. "How's it going? Haven't seen you for a couple of days." Days when she'd been more alert.

"Some days are better than others." Lola Kemper sighed loudly. "Jerry's a thing of the past. Cheating bastard."

"Sorry to hear that." She couldn't remember if she'd met Jerry. Lola was fifty-five if she was a day. She admitted to being fortyish and had a love for men who were twentyish. Lola kept up her appearance, Adeena had to give her that. But it seemed money couldn't keep her twenty-something boy toys from eventually seeking out twenty-something women, leaving Lola heartbroken for a couple of weeks until the next soon-to-be ex captured her devotion.

"He's the last one. I mean it this time, Adeena." Lola put a hand to her chest. "My heart can't take the rejection one more time without dying. I'm going to take a page from your book and go it alone. Let Princess be my only companion."

Adeena looked down at the stylishly dressed Pomeranian and she would have sworn Princess rolled her eyes. She, like Adeena, had heard this refrain too many times before. "Don't give up hope. The right guy's out there somewhere."

"Easy for you to say. I don't see you out there looking. Maybe there's more going on with that hunk I saw you with that one time than you're letting on."

*Here it comes*, she thought. Lola had caught a glimpse of Ian one time, two years ago, and she never failed to bring him into their conversation. "He and I are strictly friends with *no* benefits. And even if he weren't a friend, take it from me, he's not the kind to settle with one woman. You know he's in his thirties, right? A little old for you."

"For him I'd make an exception. I'm glad you don't think of him that way." Lola put a hand on Adeena's arm. "You should know I saw him with this gorgeous blonde while you were seeing about your dear departed mother. And Diablo was with them."

Adeena's lips twitched, but she didn't grin. Lola made it sound as if trysting with Diablo was the worst sin of all. It made her think Jerry had committed that particular offense. "To prove my point, she's already history as gorgeous as she is. That's Ian for you. Strictly the 'love-'em-and-leave-'em' type."

"So...he's available?"

Yup, she could always count on Lola. "He is not. Not in the sense you mean. Besides, you don't want to repeat past mistakes. Give yourself a few weeks and you'll have forgotten all about Jerry and be ready to get back out there."

"Did I tell you he was sleeping with a stripper? In my house, no less." Tears beaded in Lola's eyes.

Adeena patted her on the shoulder, but she couldn't find a drop of sympathy. She'd known Lola for four years and it was always the same thing. Maybe Lola was doomed to repeat her mistakes until she righted a wrongdoing committed in one of the past lives she liked to talk about. "Have you thought about having your psychic look into past lives for answers? That might be what you need to move forward. Now I should go, get Diablo's walk in."

"What a great idea. I'll call her tomorrow. But one day you're going to tell me the secret of living without men."

"One day," she agreed and gave Diablo a pull. "Silly woman," she muttered under her breath and began the walk home that included circling the park at least one time. She wasn't sure what Lola would say if she knew the supposed secret. Not that she kept her sexual orientation, and didn't she hate that expression, a secret. It was just that Lola wasn't really a friend, and to be honest, Adeena would hate to be the one who gave her the idea to start chasing twentyish women.

Her stomach rumbled and she dismissed Lola from her mind, preferring to think about what she had in the fridge. She should eat the leftovers. She really should. It was certainly more sensible than ordering a calzone from Rosa's. Not as good, she conceded and sighed, but more adult-like to eat what was in her fridge before it spoiled.

And yet, a calzone with pepperoni, onion, peppers and mushrooms seemed to be calling her name. She didn't have to strain to hear it either. She could take the pasta primavera for lunch tomorrow, she rationalized, and enjoy the calzone tonight. And if she added spinach it would almost be healthy. A win-win for her body and her mind.

The squeal of tires drew her attention to the street. A beat-up white van was going in the opposite direction much faster than the posted speed limit. Dangerously fast, factoring in the number of kids out and about in the area.

"Hey," somebody yelled. "Slow that piece of crap down."

The driver either didn't seem to hear or care. "Another idiot driver," she told Diablo, thinking of the man who'd almost caused her to wreck in Virginia City. That driver had certainly paid the highest price—his life—for a stupid game. Her price hadn't been nearly as steep, but since they were never able to identify the guy and therefore his insurance company, she'd paid for the damage to her car out of pocket rather than risking a higher insurance premium. Lucky for her, the guy a coworker had recommended charged her only a little more than what her deductible would have been. And luckier still, she'd made it through the ordeal with her life intact.

"And isn't that what I should be focusing on?" She might be living in the same state she'd been born in, but she was living. She had a good job, a great dog and her best friend Ian for entertainment. The dating pool might be a little too shallow and her boss could show her more respect, but all in all, she wasn't doing so badly. Spending another summer in Vegas wasn't the end of the world. Eventually she'd get to DC or further east than she was now. Until then, she'd practice some of that thing called patience her mother had always talked about and enjoy a calzone for dinner.

She pushed the walk button and as she waited for the light to change, her phone buzzed. She laughed when she saw Ian's name. "Miss me already, lover?"

"I might if you hadn't so totally jinxed me."

"Me? What did I do?"

"You just did, okay."

"I'm not giving you carte blanche to demean my character." She laughed silently when he let loose a long, loud sigh in response. "Drunk calling, texting? What? You gotta give me something."

"You can't laugh."

"Fine. But hurry it up. There's a calzone screaming my name."

"Okay. So after you left, I got to thinking about what you said. You know, about my preference for a certain type of woman."

"Curvy, stacked, blond." She punched the walk button again. "But we know this. How can it be a problem now? And how can I be the cause of it?"

"Because you left me. The woman who grabbed your seat was tall, athletic looking, size A cup."

"I know who you're talking about. She's cute."

"Okay, yeah, but that's not the point. We started talking like you do. She even joked about Di running off my date. Of course that meant I was forced to explain the true situation and she laughed. Not a prissy one, but a full one. I kind of liked it, so I bought her a beer and we talked some more."

"The horror."

"No sarcasm needed. So long story short, she's in the bathroom and I'm standing here freaking out while I wait for her to come out so I can take her to dinner even though I'm the one who did the asking."

"Finally!"

"I just met her, what's this 'finally' about?"

"The walk light. It finally came on. And it's already counting down." She quickened her pace. "I must be missing something. When did taking an attractive woman out to dinner constitute a jinx?"

"Did you *not* hear the part about her *not* being my type? Oh God, here she comes," he whispered. "She did something with her eyes, her lips. I might be in love."

"Watch out!"

The strident cry brought Adeena to a stop. It didn't take long to notice the beat-up van bearing down upon her. She froze like an animal caught in headlights until Diablo's strident bark snapped her out of it. She dropped his leash, told him to run and tried to jump the remaining distance to the sidewalk. The side of the van caught her hip, sending her face first toward concrete. She managed to twist, landing on her hip and elbow with a jarring thud and skimming the concrete with the side of her face. She heard the screech of metal on metal followed by the squeal of tires on pavement and hoped the van was driving away and not toward her.

"Don't try to get up." A woman knelt down beside her. "You could make your injuries worse. I've already called 911."

As aches and pains ramped up to screaming level, moving was the last thought on her mind. "Diablo! My dog? Is he hurt? Has anyone seen my dog?"

"Right here," another woman said and moved into Adeena's line of vision with Diablo in her arms. "Don't worry, he's okay."

"Thank you." She closed her eyes as the shaking began. *Two times this month*, she thought. Two accidents so close together when she'd gone her first three decades without any. Hopefully the two accidents and the death of her mother equaled her three things. She didn't know if she could survive another event, especially since they were getting worse.

She managed to smile when Diablo curled up beside her and rested his head on her arm. "I'm okay," she said, despite the deep ache coming from the hip she was lying on. Lifting an arm, she ran her hand over his body to find him trembling as well. The thought that he could have been hurt as well made her feel sick, then mad. How dare someone almost run over her baby!

"Can you feel your legs?"

Adeena looked at the woman crouched beside her and realized she lived in her complex. She didn't know in which apartment, but she did know the other woman drove a fiery red BMW convertible that had caused many pangs of envy. "Oh, yeah. No nerve damage here. I can probably sit up. Maybe even make it home."

"You should wait for the police," said the redhead with the nose ring who'd found Diablo. "The driver took off, but I got the license number. He must have been very drunk."

"I agree. You should wait and file a report. It was almost as if that guy was aiming right for you. I'm Lisa Perdue, by the way. We seem to leave for work at the same time."

"Adeena Minor. Nice to officially meet you, no matter the circumstances."

"My car! What the hell happened to my car?"

"My first guess would be someone hit it," Lisa said under her breath.

The man, who was as tall as he was wide, pulled at thinning hair. "I was only gone five minutes. How could this happen?" He seemed to notice them and his eyes narrowed as he pointed at Adeena. "You hit my car?" It was more accusation than question.

The redhead put her hands on her narrow hips as Diablo growled. "The same person who hit your car hit her. The police are on their way, so chill."

He had the grace to look ashamed. "Sorry. I'd better call my insurance and the wife. Looks like dinner's going to be late."

At least he had food, Adeena thought. Despite the pain, visions of calzones danced in her head. She deserved it now. Had earned it. When she got home, first thing would be to call Rosa's. Second would be a nice, long soak in the tub while she waited the usual hour for delivery. It always took an hour despite the fact Rosa's was a seven-minute drive from her apartment.

But before she could make that call, she needed to get up. Bracing herself, she sat up gingerly. Oh yeah, there was no problem with numbness. Not when she could feel every bump and scrape in triplicate.

Adeena wondered if the calzone could be delivered to her current resting place. They would have to. There was no way she was going to be able to get up and no way was she going to the hospital. Bad things happen to you in hospitals. Her father had withered away in one, so she knew that for a fact.

The sound of a siren drew her attention to the street. An ambulance pulled up, followed by a cop car.

"I don't need an ambulance," she protested and turned her attention to the cop. He was Hispanic and very official-looking in his pristine uniform. When he looked at her, she thought she read compassion and figured this interview would go much better than the one near Virginia City. Hopefully this cop wouldn't assume she was in any way responsible for almost getting run over.

"Standard procedure," Lisa said. "They can't make you get in."

"Good."

# CHAPTER FIVE

Adeena surfaced around noon the next day and cried for her mama. Well, she would have cried for her mama if her mother had been the type to coddle. She'd managed to stay out of the hospital thanks to Ian, who'd rushed to her side and then stayed the night to monitor her condition.

Cursing up a storm, she rolled over onto her back and panted. Obviously the hounds of hell had slipped into her bed last night and had their way with her. She could stay where she was, she thought on a sob, and die in her bed and preserve what little dignity she had left. The fullness of her bladder suggested otherwise. There would be no dignity if she died in her own piss. Sure, she knew from TV, the body regularly flushed itself after death, but she was sure as hell that some overzealous tech would figure out she'd peed *before* she died and then where would she be?

Whimpering, she sat up and eased off the bed. If she could've gotten her hands on that drunk driver at that very moment, things would've turned ugly. Her hips sang a tune of pain in a duet with the elbow she'd fallen on. Why hadn't she listened to Ian, she wondered? He'd told her to get up, walk around a little, loosen the muscles. But no, she hadn't wanted to hear that. She said a quick prayer of gratitude that he was not here to see her hobbling around like the hunchback of Notre Dame.

In the bathroom, she peed for what seemed like days, then downed some painkillers that would most likely only make the pain laugh. Thinking longingly of another long soak, she nixed the idea, afraid she wouldn't be able to get out of the tub. For her, having to be rescued while naked was right up there with dying in her own pee.

After doing a half-assed job of brushing her teeth and washing her face, she went back to bed. She'd made the effort and could now die with a modicum of dignity. Her doorbell rang the minute she was down and she made the executive decision to ignore it. Whoever was there could damn well come back after she was dead. There was no way she was getting back up again until her bladder forced her to.

She heard the telltale click of nails against hardwood and braced as Diablo jumped up on the bed. He seemed to sense she was injured and settled for licking her hand.

"Diablo and I brought lunch." Ian entered her bedroom moments later waving a large brown bag. He'd obviously gone home, showered and changed yesterday's work clothes for jeans and a T-shirt. "You do not want to look at the news for the next week or so. Stay away from the Internet as well."

She made herself sit up, jostling Diablo, who then jumped down to sniff at the bag by Ian's feet. "Tell me fast."

"Someone caught the bump and the fall." He winced, his eyes full of sympathy. "It looked like you flew a little. I don't know how you didn't break any bones."

"Any news on the driver?"

"They found the owner of the van. Turns out he lent it to a friend of a friend—well, after further questioning, it turns out he lent it to an acquaintance of a friend of a friend."

"And nobody knows who that is, right?"

"No. See his name is Shaggy or Woody, and maybe he's white or Hispanic. Apparently they were sitting around drinking and other things, so when this Shaggy or Woody offered to go get more supplies, they were all for it. Not surprising, he never came back with the supplies or their money or the van. You hungry?" He placed a bone in front of Diablo. Diablo picked up the bone and ran off. "Not that I'm going to feed you a bone."

"Not really." She leaned back. "This has been a bad month for me. Really bad. But I should quit whining, be grateful my three things are behind me now."

Ian paused in the act of removing a container from the bag. "Three? What three?"

"The bad things that come in threes. Number one, my mother getting shot." She held up a finger. "Number two, that asshole in Virginia City who almost ran me off the road." Another finger went up. "And num—"

"Wait! What number two asshole? There was no mention of said asshole, of getting run off the road."

"Almost," she corrected with a grimace. She'd meant to keep that one to herself. "I'm sure I meant to tell you. Let me think. That's right. You were at the conference in San Fran when I got back to work and then I kind of forgot about it. Compared to today it was nothing."

"I'll be the judge of that." He gave her a stern look. "Give."

"I was leaving Virginia City after releasing my mother's ashes when some guy decided he wanted to play road games. Managed to clip my back bumper before I was able to outwit him. He was joyriding in a stolen car and felt frisky, I guess. We'll never know because he didn't make the next curve."

"Didn't make as in…"

She nodded. "Crashed and burned."

"And now this. *You* need to stay off the streets for a while. We'll say six months."

"Didn't I just tell you I've done my three? They say things come in threes, not fours."

"And who are these '*they*' to be so narrow-minded?" he demanded. "Sometimes things come in only one."

"Listen to you. When have you ever stuck to one of anything?" She watched him unwrap a sandwich and her stomach rumbled. "What else is in that bag?"

"Thought you weren't hungry."

"I wasn't until you started flaunting food in my face."

"A little of everything. Wasn't sure what you'd feel like eating." He pulled out another container. "Got some of that chicken salad you like so much."

She held out her hand. "That works."

"Here. Fork, crackers, napkins. Of course it's going to be hard to sleep with all those crumbs later."

"I'll find a way. What did Bobby-boy have to say about both of us being out?"

"Nada," he answered around a mouth full of sandwich. "He saw the replay and probably kissed the ground that you won't be out permanently."

"As if. Me being out permanently would be his wish come true."

"Not really. He may hate your smart mouth, your way of always being right, but he knows he needs you. And so does Lara. She's already talking about needing you, and only you, for the needs assessment."

"Give me a break. That's not on the schedule for, what, four months?"

"Didn't stop her from trying to have a meeting today. She canceled because you couldn't be there. Dan and Stevebo send their gratitude."

"Guess I owe that drunk something. And speaking of owing, I owe you big for last night. Sorry about messing up dinner with un-Supermodel."

"I accept your apology, unnecessary as it is. I got the feeling my stock went up when I explained to Andi why I was begging off. We rescheduled for tonight."

"Wow. I was sure you'd ditch her after you had some time to think it over. I have vague memories of someone telling me she was so not your type."

"But then you were hit with a van, now weren't you? Your memory is bound to be faulty."

"Smirking bastard. You'll probably end up married, have five girls."

"Wait, wait, wait," he said, patting the air. "You can't be putting stuff out there like that. It might stick. All I'm saying is I'm willing to see where this goes. Maybe meeting her while I was contemplating things was like some kind of omen thing. Who knows what might happen if I don't see this through."

"You getting all mushy on me, Zucker?"

"Kiss my ass, Minor."

\* \* \*

"I can certainly take care of that for you." Sal perused the stories trending on Yahoo while she halfway listened to her client ramble. Technically she was on vacation, but given the offer of generous payment for an easy job, she was willing to be flexible. "I'm writing it down now…Two weeks works, no problem." Though all the important decisions had been taken care of, she'd figured out over time that Joe wasn't comfortable ending the call until he regurgitated their conversation. "That's exactly right, Joe. And yes, you'll have everything in hand in two weeks."

As she gleefully ended the call, a story about "van versus woman" caught her eye. She scanned the text about a drunk driver clipping a woman as she was crossing the street in Vegas, then watched the video clip of the said woman meeting the sidewalk. Sal gave her an eight for the landing, then upped it to nine when she factored in the limited skull-sidewalk contact. Still, it had to have hurt like hell, she decided, and added another half point. There was a postscript which mentioned the woman's recently deceased mother had been one of the victims in the Dayton, Nevada, middle school shooting.

"It's her!"

"Her who?" Cyn put down the report she'd been reading. "And aren't you supposed to be on vacation until after Vegas?"

She shrugged. "You know me and money. I like to—"

"Steal it," Cyn interjected.

"Really, Cyn, you know that type of behavior belongs to my youthful past. Now I like to earn it. Not as much fun, and yet still lucrative. Joe has more money than sense, so it's only fair I relieve him of a few cents."

"Ha not. Go back to the 'her' you were talking about."

"It's the woman I told you about. The one whose mother was killed in the Nevada school shooting. Well, some drunk caught the poor woman, the live one, as she was crossing the street. And of course someone else caught the resultant sidewalk splat." Sal turned her laptop to face Cyn and played the video clip.

"Ouch. This isn't her month. Probably not her year. They catch the driver?"

"No, and the owner isn't sure who he lent the van to. You know, someone needs to start a beer delivery service. Think of the drunks that would get off the road."

"I doubt it's legal or someone would already be out there. Liability issues would make the insurance sky high."

"Spoken like a true businesswoman."

"Forget that and get back to 'it's her.' What gives? You've met her before and didn't think to tell me?"

"What? No." Sal shook her head for emphasis. "Why would you even think that?"

"You're the one with the excitement in your voice, that expression on your face. I have to ask myself why."

"Then ask yourself."

"Anybody else in here notice how our friend Sal's avoiding the question?" Cyn looked around her home office as if seeking agreement. "It's unanimous. You *are* avoiding the question."

"And you need help. But just so we're clear, I do not personally know this woman. I know of her because of my grandmother. Is that clear enough for everyone?" Now it was Sal's turn to query the room. "It's unanimous. I *did* answer the question."

"If I need help, you need help." Cyn propped her feet on her desk and grinned. "I've missed being crazy with you."

"Back at you."

"Then why don't you forget your sojourn to Vegas and stay here. You're pretty damn handy as a kid and puppy minder."

"No can do. Vegas is in the cards."

"And the showgirls, no doubt."

Sal rubbed her hands. "We all do what we have to do. Speaking of which, vacation or not I'll continue to search for the deets on our mysterious Mr. Burlett. It's a shame he's so security conscious. Takes longer when they know what they're doing." She pushed up her glasses. "The question is why he's looking. Can you think of anyone other than Stephen who would be looking at Heather? Maybe I can go about it that way."

"No. You knew Heather. There's nothing about her life that would call for an investigation. She never had a job, got married while in grad school and settled down into domestic bliss. Could it be something with Stephen and work?"

"Checked and no. What about the adoption? Could there have been anything…unusual about that?"

"You can say illegal. But with *my* parents? No way. Everything would have been strictly by the legal book. And why would anyone wait until she's dead to try and claim foul play?"

"Money. Could be looking to get their hands on Nate and his money. But that doesn't feel right either." She took a sip of Cyn's diet soda and grimaced. "Speaking of foul."

"Not all of us can suck down sugar and keep our stick figure."

"A compliment." Sal smiled sweetly. "Could be someone gathering info so they can make you think they were Heather's birth parents. A would-be father spinning a sob story about having found out about her too late, how now he wants to get to know her son. It's not a bad con, and they could be thinking either of getting control of his trust fund or of taking money to go away."

"Anyone trying to get their grubby hands on Nate's money will be in for a rude awakening. We've taken extra precautions because of this business with Stephen."

"That has never stopped anyone from trying. Remember I grew up with a tribe whose lifestyle was about trying. That should be 'is,' not 'was,'" she corrected. "They're still out there."

"That's the first time you mentioned them in a long time. You in contact with anyone from back then? Slip them money?"

"Some," she admitted and looked away from Cyn's knowing smile. "Old habits die hard. You have, you share. Not the ones looking for a handout though. I help the ones looking for a way out of the lifestyle or a little down on their luck. Despite what my parents taught me, there are some I will never help. My line may not be 'gay and narrow,' but even it doesn't curve some ways." Sal thought about one person in particular, a man she'd known when he was a boy. He grew up and twisted the tenets they were supposed to operate under. He'd sought her out, thinking she'd be interested in getting in on his action. Though his smile had still been dazzling as he bragged about his big house and fancy cars, it wasn't enough to blind her to his dead heart.

"Hey, where did you go?"

She forced a smile. "Nowhere important." Her former family member was not worthy of her thoughts. Her phone signaled a new message. "Toast! Stephen is toast. We need to prepare your parents for another storm of crap."

# CHAPTER SIX

Feeling as she imagined a warrior returned from battle felt, Adeena walked Diablo to the area with the complex's mailboxes. Two and a half days had passed since the accident and she was finally starting to feel human. Any sudden moves, though, and the hip she'd fallen on was not shy about letting her know its displeasure.

She unlocked the box and had to wrestle the mail to get it out of it. As she sorted through the credit card offers and the numerous packets from charities begging for additional money, she found an envelope from her mother's attorney. She'd been expecting it and still it hit hard. This was really the end of the end. Biting her bottom lip, she went back to sorting.

"This is different." The bright yellow envelope had her name and address written in shaky letters, no return address and a Savannah, Georgia, postmark. Her mother had mentioned being from Tifton, Georgia, wherever that was, and as she ripped open the envelope, she found herself hoping she had relatives after all. A couple of photos floated to the ground, but

Adeena's interest was caught by the shaky, looping handwritten words. She didn't notice when Diablo sniffed at the photos and quickly lost interest. She didn't notice anything but the shocking words that couldn't be true. Someone was trying to play her for a fool, she decided after reading the letter for the second time. Someone who must not know that she knew who her parents were, knew where she'd been born. It was after all on the birth certificate she had in her possession. The same document that certified she'd been born on December twenty-ninth and not on the twenty-fifth, as the letter claimed. And she damn well knew she didn't have a dead twin sister named Heather Lynne Garson-Kennedy.

Adeena lowered the letter and finally noticed the photos at her feet. She picked them up gingerly. The one on top was of two babies, one black, one white, lying next to each other on a bed with a light-colored blanket. On the back "December 25" was written, followed by "5:10 a.m." and "6:20 a.m.," matching the times in the fake letter.

"No way." She shook her head violently. That wasn't her in the photo, wasn't her light-skinned twin. She had not been born in some backwoods Georgia town. Nor had her eighteen-year-old mother died shortly after her sister's birth. But most of all, she was *not* in danger because she should never have been born.

It just was not so, she reasoned. Some crackpot had seen the video, connected it to her mother's death and decided to play with her head. This had to be a sick joke played by a sick individual with too much time on their hands.

"People can be so cruel," she told Diablo. "But I'm not that gulli—" The second photo stilled her words and blew doubt from her mind. She could have been looking at a photo of herself—if she'd ever looked this young, this happy, this alive. The other woman's skin was darker than hers, the hair styled differently, but everything else was similar. Eerily similar when combined with her dissimilarity to either of her parents. It couldn't be true, she told herself as acceptance fought with doubt. And yet...

With her heart beating furiously, she turned the photo over. The name, her birth mother's name, read "Lucy Mae Brown." Lucy had been seventeen when the photo was taken. Seventeen and with no knowledge she only had one more year left to live, Adeena thought. It was too much to take in on top of everything else and tears blurred her vision.

If any of this was true, and the resemblance had her believing it was, she'd lost two mothers in only a matter of weeks. Two mothers who hadn't really been mothers to her. One because she never got the opportunity and the other because…well, she couldn't really know why she and her mother had never bonded, never been close. But maybe the reason was in her hand. It was certainly possible the mother she'd grown up with had not been able to accept another woman's child as her own. If that were the case, then it was time for her to let go of the lingering notion she was responsible for the deficits in her mother. Time she accepted that neither she or her mother had been in a situation of their making.

Adeena blew out a sharp breath. The failure in the mother-daughter relationship was not the issue here. The contents of the letter and her two brushes with death were what needed her immediate attention. The "they" who'd taught her to believe in the power of three were wrong. Her three bad things had not gotten her off the "bad things happen" wagon. If the letter was to be believed, and it seemed she did believe it, there was no safety in numbers for her.

"This should not be allowed to happen in my universe," she yelled at the sky. "I'm the one in control." When Diablo barked as if in agreement and licked her ankle, she felt a little bit better. But despite her assumption of control, somewhere up in the vastness of space someone was screwing with her. She'd managed to go thirty-four years without knowing any of this—being adopted, the death of her birth mother, the death of Heather, and, damn, she could easily have gone another thirty or forty more in blissful ignorance.

"Alternate universe." That had to be what she'd stepped into. Her life was simple, even a little boring, but she was okay with that. This new existence where one chance event could unravel the fabric of her life—the simple, the boring—was not for her. Damn it, she wanted her old life back. Wanted James and Joy Minor to be her only parents. But most of all, she wanted her life to be off the chopping block for reasons she wasn't sure she could prove.

Life really wasn't fair, she thought as she looked at Lucy Mae Brown's photo again. She would check, do some digging, but the likeness was too remarkable for her to dismiss the very real possibility that everything her parents had told her about the past was a lie. Adeena fought tears as she rubbed the ache in her chest she couldn't touch. An ache for the mother she didn't have because someone had decided they didn't want that to happen, that they didn't want her or the sister to be born. And she had the bruises to prove that thirty-four years later they continued to want her not to exist.

Self-pity morphed into anger in a flash. "The nerve! The fucking nerve." She didn't deserve this disdain for her existence, this arrogance that had led someone to believe their wants took precedence over another's life. She might not have known Lucy Mae Brown, but she wouldn't believe there was anything that Lucy could've done to deserve what happened to her.

Adeena's exhale did nothing to slow down the anger, the rage. Yes, the threads of her life had been pulled loose, revealing secrets and lies, and surely that meant she owed it to Lucy's stolen life to stand up to the ones who were trying to kill her. Not only stand up, but expose the secrets they so desperately wanted to stay hidden. So far the bastards had tried to make her death look like an accident. Surely that meant an investigation into her murder could lead back to Lucy Mae Brown and the events surrounding her death. And maybe even further back to the man who hadn't been happy with Lucy's pregnancy.

"Come on, Diablo, we have more threads to unravel. And we have to find out when and where my sister died." Eventually, she decided, she would go to where she was buried, pay her respects and perhaps find some closure.

Eugenia clenched her teeth as she watched the video yet again. She was surrounded by idiots, she decided. The girl had survived a second attempt—a well-publicized second attempt at that. Should the girl turn up dead now, it would bring too much attention. Eugenia could almost see the bold headlines about the death of the girl whose mother died in a school shooting, who'd then survived a drunk driver. And the photos!

So far it seemed no one had made the connection between this Adeena Minor and Lucy Brown. She'd make sure Maria kept Jackson too busy with meetings and fundraisers to stay abreast with human interest stories. And that's what Adeena Minor was. What she would stay.

"Miss Eugenia, there's a Mr. Burlett to see you."

"Show him to the sitting area. No need for refreshments."

"Yes, ma'am." Martha hurried out.

Eugenia pushed back from her desk and slowly made her way to the sitting room. She hadn't yet decided how much to trust Mr. Burlett. He'd come highly recommended with a reputation for getting the job done. She needed that, but more importantly, she needed someone who understood the value of loyalty and all it entailed.

She was pleased when he stood as she entered the room. "Mr. Burlett, lovely to see you again." His handshake was firm, his gaze direct. All points in his favor to her way of thinking. "Please sit." Again he showed good manners by waiting for her to get settled before he sat. "You have information for me?"

He removed glasses from his suit pocket, then slid them on before he opened the notebook in his lap. "Heather Lynne Garson-Kennedy was killed in a vehicle accident on December thirtieth of last year. Her son, Nathan Garson, survived the wreck with minimal injury. Per your request, I've gone back and gathered as much information on her life as I could."

"Was she aware she was adopted?"

"Yes, ma'am. I tracked down an old friend of hers. Heather had talked about trying to get in touch with her birth parents. She later changed her mind. Here are all of my findings in detail."

Eugenia accepted the folder but made no attempt to open it. He'd already provided her with the most important information. "It's always a pleasure to find someone who lives up to his reputation. I value excellent work, Mr. Burlett, believe in rewarding it. I have a name of a person that I need a detailed biography on. I would hope that you're up for another assignment."

"Of course, Mrs. Tanner. I'm happy to be of assistance. When do you require the information?"

"As this one is trickier, I'm willing to wait say, two weeks for the information. The name is James Minor Jr. You'll find he's deceased. I am particularly interested in what he was doing thirty-four years ago. That includes where he was living, any family members, friends, acquaintances, employers, the works. The best place to start is a neighborhood that was nicknamed 'lowrents' by the people who lived there, I believe. I have been told it was the place to go for illegal drugs. The neighborhood has changed drastically since then, but I'm sure a resourceful man such as yourself could find something to go on. It's imperative I have enough information to track his movements in December of 1981. And of course, discretion is again the key."

"Part of the service, ma'am."

Eugenia rang the bell, summoning Martha. "Please see Mr. Burlett out." She only opened the folder once she was alone. He'd attached an updated photo of Heather to the typed report. Not that she needed it. Conlin had provided her with one, along with one of the Minor woman and the details of the night Lucy had been kidnapped that he'd managed to get out of the man hired to dispose of Lucy before she gave birth. Eugenia had no doubt the details were truthful. She'd heard Conlin and his bag of tricks were quite motivational.

Eugenia rarely allowed herself to feel regret. She gave herself permission as she studied the head shot of Heather. Heather's skin might have darkened with age, but not enough for anyone to question her racial background. Certainly not enough for anyone to think her mother had been black. If only she'd had this information back then. She could have had the girl placed with relatives, where the slight resemblance to the Tanner side of the family would have been expected. She could have had the girl grow up a Tanner and been proud to have her in the family.

And the girl's little boy. She remembered how her heart had stuttered at the first glance of the mischievous-looking toddler. While she was sure others would look at the boy and see the resemblance to his mother, she'd looked at him and seen the only man she had ever loved. She saw her husband's younger brother, Phillip Marcus Tanner.

Of the few things in her life she would change, meeting Phillip after her marriage to Franklin was number one. He'd had the look of Franklin, only bolder, brighter, livelier. It was no wonder her head had been turned by his charming smile and roguish manner.

Their first meeting had been at a party arranged to celebrate his homecoming from a six-month stay in Asia. Phillip had swept her into his arms for a dance and she'd been intrigued. When he cornered her on the balcony later, she'd been lost under the onslaught of his kisses, his talented hands.

To this day, Eugenia couldn't believe his boldness or her acquiescence to his demands. Over the following months he was gone a lot as his business dealings took him all over the world. But when he came back it only took one look for her to fall into his arms, into his bed, with a wild abandon she to this day didn't understand. He liked to say that he enjoyed loosening the stiffness of her spine. God knows she'd enjoyed it herself.

Then one day he was gone, killed as flamboyantly as he'd lived, while running with the bulls in Spain. Not by the bulls, but by an out-of-control driver. When she got the news, her heart shattered into a million pieces. Franklin had been touched when she mourned his brother as much as he did, never knowing she was mourning the loss of her lover. Finding the stiff upper lip of her British ancestors, Eugenia managed to get past her grief, to play the dutiful wife role. But inside something changed when she was forced to say good-bye to love.

Eugenia gave herself a mental shaking. She was sitting here acting like a sentimental old fool. That had to stop. Phillip, the girl, the boy, they no longer mattered. She had more important problems to deal with that did not include sitting around mooning over the past.

Thanks to Conlin's incompetence, it would now be difficult to make the death of the girl in Nevada appear accidental. She had to come up with another way to neutralize the girl. But first, for her own well-being, she needed to find the connection between the thug her young relative had hired to deal with Lucy and the parents who had adopted Lucy's babies. Then she had to decide if she would use Conlin to eliminate the potential sources of leaks. She'd already ruled out the possibility of the Kennedy family knowingly being involved in anything sordid. The reputation of adoption lawyer Kenneth Nicholson had been solid, his dealings seemingly aboveboard—with the exception of Lucy's babies. The Kennedys had obviously been duped by the attorney. They might have had second thoughts if they'd paid close attention to the name of Heather's supposed birth mother, a name taken from a work of fiction.

Unfortunately, Nicholson had died too soon and without giving Conlin any useful information. Fortunately, Conlin had been able to get his hand on Nicholson's cell phone and track his last calls. One had been to his goddaughter, Vicki Adams. After breaking into her home, Conlin discovered and erased a message warning Adams that she was in danger, which could mean she was on the run, but he was certain he would find Adams and tie up all the strings into a tidy bow.

Eugenia wasn't as certain given what had happened so far. It was so much harder these days to get these pesky problems dealt with in a speedy manner. To even the odds, she'd thought it prudent to bring in another player, someone who would, she hoped, be able to figure out what role the Minors had played in this whole disaster. Even if they hadn't been involved in the kidnapping, they had to have a connection to Nicholson or to Adams. Most likely Adams, given Nicholson's stellar reputation. If that was so, tracking Minor's action thirty-four years ago could lead her to others who knew that Lucy hadn't died in the fire and had, in fact, given birth.

There was a slight danger in sending Burlett to Lucy's old neighborhood, but she was willing to take the risk. If he did manage to fill in blanks she didn't want filled, she'd find a way to spin it to her advantage. She simply had to.

"What a mess." If only she hadn't trusted a boy to do a man's job. Jeremy had come to her when his parents gave up on him. She'd been a fool not to realize the extent of his addiction. His first mistake had been hiring his dealer, who'd seized the chance to make even more money by selling Lucy's baby instead of killing it. How pleased he must have been when Lucy produced a baby he could pass off as white.

Then she'd been a bigger fool for accepting Jeremy's claim the job had gone off without a hitch, for believing what she'd read in the paper about the house fire without sending someone to investigate. But placing the blame was neither here nor there, and it got her no closer to discovering all of the players. It especially got her no closer to figuring the sources of potential trouble.

She rubbed tired eyes and considered taking a brief rest. This situation was fraught with danger and made sleeping through the night almost impossible. Which was unacceptable.

She needed to remember that everything she did now, everything she had done in the past, was worth it. Nothing could hurt Jackson. Nothing could ruin his chance to be Senator Tanner, then Governor Tanner and perhaps more. She would *not* allow it.

\* \* \*

Adeena blew her tender nose for what seemed like the thousandth time, then tossed the tissue onto the used tissue pile. "Five months!" She'd missed knowing her twin by *five* miserable months. And it was her own fault she'd taken this particular punch directly to the heart. When she went into research mode to look up Heather Lynne Garson-Kennedy she'd been under the impression that her twin had died years ago. Only to find out she'd missed her chance to meet Heather by just five months.

This, on top of learning about everyone in Lucy's immediate family dying in a house fire, had been the knockout blow for her tear ducts, her heart.

Contemplating the mound of snot rags by her side, she decided for her nose's sake to focus on the little bit of good. She had a nephew, had family. Heather's son Nathan had survived the accident physically unscathed. He was currently staying with his maternal relatives in Georgia because his father was reported to be a cheating bastard. She was definitely going to consider it a good thing Heather had apparently been spared that knowledge, unlike the rest of the world.

Adeena looked into Nathan's solemn face, thought about what he'd gone through these past months and contemplated if blood was thicker than water. He was her nephew despite their disparate appearances. Through him she might be able to connect in some small way with Heather. Surely the Kennedys would understand that need and let her get to know him. She would work that into her schedule of things to pursue after she unraveled the mystery surrounding his mother's birth—and hers.

Adeena shut down her laptop and made her way to the bathroom. As she'd expected, her eyes were red and swollen. *Not surprising considering all the information processed today*, she thought as she sluiced cold water over her face.

The letter had mentioned that her birth mother was dead. What hadn't been mentioned was that Lucy's official cause of death was due to a fire. A fire that had destroyed the house and all those gathered to celebrate Christmas around the time Lucy was giving birth elsewhere to her second daughter. By the time the fire had been put out there was nothing left but ashes. When the landlord admitted the heater hadn't been working, official cause was listed as a faulty space heater. Case closed.

Someone had gone to a lot of trouble to cover up the birth of Lucy Brown's babies. Adeena couldn't conceive of her parents being involved in anything sordid, let alone the murder of an entire family. Her dad had always told her how much he'd wanted a daughter, so maybe he'd been taken in by a crooked lawyer. She supposed it was possible a Kennedy could have gotten a black girl pregnant, given the light-skinned baby to a relative and put the darker-skinned baby up for adoption. Possible but not very probable. Given what she'd learned about the family who'd adopted Heather, it didn't seem likely they would've used a deadly fire to solve a problem.

If this was TV world, Adeena would ask the Savannah police to reopen the case on the fire. They in turn would search through thirty-four-year-old evidence, find witnesses who remembered the events as if they were yesterday, put all the clues together and figure out who the killer was. Unfortunately in the real world, any official record of the fire had probably been destroyed in some basement flooding, lost in a move or had nothing in it to shed light on what happened.

Exhausted, saddened and any number of other things, she turned away from her reflection and trudged to bed. As she slid between the sheets, she added depressed to the list of things she was feeling. The past would most likely stay the past. *Some of the past*, she amended. The warning in the letter and the two failed attempts said the past wasn't dead.

"It's still being played out," she told Diablo, who was getting settled beside her. Someone still had something to lose. Which made no sense to her. Try as she might, Adeena couldn't come up with a scenario where her death would be to anyone's benefit. She wasn't rich, wasn't famous, wasn't anything. Technically, she now owned a house, had some insurance money and a nice lump sum her parents had stashed away. In total it wasn't enough to kill for. There had to be something she didn't know. Something huge.

And damn, if she wouldn't find it out, she vowed. As she plumped her pillow, she decided her next step should be to take a leave of absence from work and make the trek to Georgia. Once there she would see what or who she could find in the Savannah neighborhood where Lucy had lived. With luck she might find an old acquaintance of Lucy's, might find the identity of the man who helped create her.

What she would do after that she couldn't say. After all, she'd never been the target of a cold-hearted killer before. She'd never had to solve a mystery to keep herself alive. If only her parents had told her she was adopted or anything about their life before she was born. Maybe then she'd have a better place to start unraveling her life and theirs.

"I'm an idiot!"

Adeena threw back the covers and wondered where she'd parked her brain for the past couple of weeks. Of course she knew what the mystery key was for—the shiny box that was hidden in the space beneath the floorboards of her father's shop. Her father had shown it to her, told her where he kept the key. He'd impressed upon her how important it was to tell no one about the box, how she was only to take it out if he or her mother told her to. Her mother had probably moved the key after his death with the expectation her daughter would remember the box when she saw the key.

Her problem now was how to get to Dayton and quickly. She didn't want to drive after recent experiences and she couldn't involve Ian. If someone was out to get her, she didn't want him caught in the crosshairs. A plane ticket would cost a fortune at this late date and be too easy to trace.

"The cheap bus." She could take one of the inexpensive buses to Reno, maybe even Carson, then rent a car for the rest of the trip. If someone was looking for her, they wouldn't be looking on a bus. If she remembered correctly, the bus picked up on the strip. She could dress up like she was going to a casino, walk through a few, then hop on the bus at the last minute.

A quick Internet search and she found a doggy daycare that was open twenty-four seven. Then she bought a ticket for the bus leaving for Reno in three hours and, after weighing the pros and cons, reserved a car to be picked up near a downtown Reno hotel.

A nervous laugh escaped when it sunk in what she was doing. She was actually going to risk death by sneaking off to Dayton on the chance that information about her adoption or her parents' background was still in the shed. Could she do something so spontaneous, so daring?

"Hell yes!" No more sitting around for her, no more waiting to be a victim. There had to be something in that box she could use. Something that would give her an edge. She didn't really have a choice but to chance it.

Once she got back from Dayton, she'd request a couple of weeks off. She could tell Bobby-boy she needed to deal with crucial family matters stemming from her mother's premature death. Even Robert Tolliver bowed to tragedy once in a while. If not, she'd quit and find out how far her money could take her while she searched for another job.

"You're good at what you do," she told herself. Someone would hire her—eventually.

Placing a hand against the flutters in her stomach, she took a deep breath and then got dressed for what could be the show of her life.

# CHAPTER SEVEN

Adeena's nerves were beyond strained by the time she pulled into the driveway of her mother's house the next morning. Everything had gone as planned, and now she was thinking it had gone too well. Halfway to Dayton doubt had reared its ugly head; now she fully expected the bad guys to be waiting for her inside the house.

Marshaling up a backbone, she let go of the steering wheel, grabbed her bag and slowly made her way up the short sidewalk to the front door.

"It's empty," she told herself and unlocked the front door. Stale air greeted her and not much else. To be sure, she walked through every room, checking under beds and in closets. The house was as empty as it felt.

*Doesn't matter because you're not here to look for home*, she reminded herself. Nor did she want to go back to memoryland. She'd come for one purpose and the sooner she accomplished that, the sooner she could take the next step.

The combination lock on the shed hadn't been changed in years. It was a little rusty, but it was nothing a good tug didn't take care of. She pushed open the door and stood for a moment. It was mostly empty now, had been since shortly after her father's death, and was missing the smell of sawdust. As far as she knew, her mother had not stepped foot in the place once the tools had been sold. Adeena used to sneak in from time to time, sit on the hardwood floor and remember doing homework while watching her father create something wonderful from wood. To her young eyes he'd been good at it and seemed happiest when using his tools.

"I miss you, miss our time together, Dad."

When the tears wanted to fall, she had to once again remind herself of her purpose. Her footsteps echoed off the floor as she passed the wall where tools once hung in neat precision, passed the spaces once filled with the table saw, the circular saw and the miter saw. Her father had instilled a healthy respect for their metal teeth and then taught her how to use each of the machines. It had been another of their secrets.

The hidey-hole was in the corner farthest away from the door. The heavy rusted toolbox was no longer standing guard above it, and she wondered if her mother had emptied the contents of the hidden box when she emptied the rest of the place. "But she'd kept the key." No need to keep it if the box was empty or gone.

Dropping to her knees, she felt around for the slight indentation that was easy to miss. A quick yank and the wood pulled back to reveal what used to be a shiny box. Now it was covered with dust as if it hadn't been accessed in a long time.

It took some doing to maneuver the flat box out of the space. When it was done, Adeena sat back on her heels and wiped her sweaty forehead. She didn't want to think what the warm temperature had done to her armpits. She didn't have time for a shower. Not that she wanted to change back into the little black dress she'd exchanged for shorts and a T-shirt in a McDonald's bathroom. Maybe she should have thought ahead and packed an additional change of clothes.

Realizing she was stalling, she opened the box. The sound of her name had her quickly stuffing the contents into her overnight bag and scrambling to her feet. She should have known Mrs. Branson, their closest neighbor, would consider it her duty to stop by and see what was going on. Almost running, she made it out of the shed before Mrs. Branson could come in.

"I thought I saw you go into the house," Mrs. Branson said as she peered over Adeena's shoulder. "Didn't recognize the car."

"Rental. I flew up this time."

"Something wrong with the shed? I've been keeping an eye on the place and I haven't seen anyone over here except the realtor when she put up the sign."

"Nothing like that. I, uh, forgot to look through it before." She squeezed her eyes shut as if fighting off tears. "I'd never forgive myself if I overlooked anything. Dad loved this space so much."

Mrs. Branson patted her arm. "That he did. I remember when he made those beautiful bookcases in the living room for your mother. He was so good with his hands. Good enough to open a shop. No doubt he could've sold a ton of stuff."

Adeena nodded and pressed a hand to her mouth as if she was too choked up to speak.

"You poor girl. Call me if there's anything you need." Mrs. Branson gave her another pat. "Anything."

She waited until Mrs. Branson left through the side gate to return to the shed. After replacing the empty box, she took the time to go through the drawers and cabinets in case she was being timed. It wouldn't do for her to come out too quickly.

To her surprise not all the cabinets were empty. Her mother had gotten rid of the tools but had held onto her father's smaller projects. It made her sad to think her mother felt she had to keep these hidden away, rather than proudly display them in the house. Just one more thing to let Adeena know she would never have the chance to understand Joy Minor, to know what made her tick.

Delight pushed away sadness when she found the wooden family he'd made for her when she was eight. Mother, father, sister, brother and dog. They had to live in the shed so they could be around the other wood was the story her father told. They both knew it was so her mother wouldn't know her daughter was playing with toys instead of learning.

She had no trouble producing tears as she thought about all the ways her father had shown her love. No matter what his role might have been in her birth, she knew he'd thought of her as his child, that he'd wanted her.

The family went into her bag. Instead of searching the rest of the cabinets, she sat down and reminisced about the good times she'd had when it had been the two of them. She'd learned plenty of new things, like how to use a screwdriver, how to tune up a car and how to work with wood. Unfortunately, those skills did not translate well on an application to get into medical school—as her mother had been quick to point out. The skills had however translated well in life.

"Good-bye again, Dad. I love you." She grabbed her bag, looked around one last time and headed for the door. No matter what she found out about Lucy's story, she felt certain her father couldn't have been involved in anything bad. When the story came out, and she was determined it would, James Minor Jr. would be proven to be innocent.

\* \* \*

"Are you sure?" Lilly shook back her long, curly blond tresses, tilted her head and sent out a sultry smile.

"Can't, Lent," Sal muttered. She was having a very hard time saying no to Lilly, her luscious body and hours of enjoyable sex.

Lilly pursed her full, red lips and made kissing noises. "Next time, lover."

Sal watched the sway of Lilly's behind until it was out of sight and sighed. Doing the right thing was hard, she thought, and sighed again. When it came to Lilly, with whom she'd tussled on many other occasions, it was damn hard.

Tomorrow would be easier on her brain and her libido. She'd done her obligatory nights of gambling, so it was time to switch into tourist mode. After grabbing some much-needed sleep, she planned to tour the other hotels, the shops, take bad photos and people watch. Later in the evening, she had a helicopter tour of the city planned where she could get her fill of flashing lights and neon signs. The helicopter ride to the Grand Canyon was scheduled for Sunday morning, then one more night at the tables before she flew back home Monday afternoon. All in all, the perfect vacation for her.

Upstairs in her luxury suite at the Bellagio, she kicked off her shoes, grabbed a soda and plopped her butt on the sofa. A good night at the poker table always left her too revved to fall asleep immediately. If she hadn't been fasting, enjoying the talents of Lilly would have been a great way to burn off energy.

Instead of brooding over what she'd turned down, she tuned in to CNN. There were other ways to get her jollies. To her delight, the clip of Stephen's arrest played on the big screen TV. As it had every time before, the sight of him resisting arrest gave her a nice zing. The simpleminded reports always spliced in bits of the interview with the mistress as if to suggest Stephen had embezzled to keep up with her expensive tastes. Eventually all would come out and they would realize the embezzling preceded the mistress, and then Sal hoped there would be another round of clips, complete with the arrest and the mug shot.

"Couldn't happen to a nicer guy." She saluted the TV with her soda. After checking the time, she decided it was a good time to call Cyn, so she'd have someone to gloat with. Before she could dial, her cell phone dinged, letting her know the search running on one of her two laptops was complete.

"This is my lucky night." She hadn't expected to hack through the lawyer's security so soon. Apparently he wasn't as security conscious as the PI. "Let's see what you have."

An hour later her eyes began to droop after searching record after record. Nicholson certainly had a prolific adoption practice. Setting her laptop aside, she went to the bathroom and splashed cold water over her face until she believed she could last another hour.

More asleep than awake, she returned to the search. When the letters began to blur again she was no closer to finding anything of use. Rubbing her eyes, she bargained with herself for fifteen more minutes. If she focused for a mere fifteen minutes, she got to close her eyes and shut down her brain.

The next document had nothing of use, just another baby girl who was getting a forever home. This one was black and happened to have been born on the same day as Heather, Sal noted. She read the names of the parents and a bell went off in her head. She'd read the same names before. Backtracking, she found another baby born to Laura Wingfield and Harold Mitchell on the same day. There was one big difference—race. Baby Lisa Mitchell and her parents, Laura and Harold, were black, while Baby Dawn Wingfield and her parents, Laura and Harold, were white.

Sal slumped back and stroked her chin. None of this made sense to her. Nicholson had handled many adoption cases over the years, so she had to wonder why he'd chosen to use the same names for the parents of these two babies. They couldn't be twins, not with one being white and one being black. Something was going on, but obviously she was too damn tired to figure it out. She would need a few hours of sleep before she could puzzle out the histories of these two babies and their possible relationship to Heather.

\* \* \*

"What? Are you crazy?"

Adeena had been sure having this discussion with Ian in public would stop him from yelling at her. She'd been wrong, and now everyone in the little coffee shop probably thought she was crazy. "I think they heard you in California."

"Don't get cute with me. What you did was stupid. If you thought someone was out to get you, then you gave them the opportunity to do that *and* without anyone being the wiser."

"Exaggerate much?" she snapped back. She'd done what needed to be done. End of story. "And by the by, you sound like my mother. I knew what I was doing, knew the risk and made the *informed* decision it was worth it. Come on, Ian, it was daylight by the time I got to the house, for crying out loud."

"Like it was the two times you almost got run over. You should've called," he added, a sulky expression on his face. "I could've driven you there since you didn't want to take your car. Watched your back while you were skulking in the shed."

"Again, it was daylight, so no skulking involved. I wasn't there more than five, ten minutes before Mrs. Branson came over. Now there's someone who was watching my back. You can be sure if anyone had killed me, she would have been able to give the cops a detailed description of the bad guys, including the tag number of their vehicle."

"How comforting," he said deadpan. "But here's the thing. You'd still be dead."

"But the thing is, I'm not." She leaned forward. "And here's another thing. The stuff in the box? Totally worth the risk." She tapped on the table to emphasize her point.

He lost his sulky look. "You found the killer's name?"

"Not that good. I did find my original birth certificate. I compared it with my...I won't say my real one, but you know what I mean. The info's almost the same. Different parent names, but their age, birthplace, occupation were the same, along with the judge's name, the date issued and the date signed. Big difference is that one's issued in Georgia and the other in Nevada."

"How is that possible?"

"Can you say fake?"

"You can't tell me you believe your parents were in on it."

She shook her head. "Absolutely not. I thought a lot while I was there, on the trip back. There is no way my father would have had anything to do with what happened to Lucy, her family. But somehow he must have found out after and taken steps to cover himself, my mother and me. He was a good man and he loved me. There's nothing anyone can say to make me believe differently. Nothing."

Ian held up his hands. "Don't have to convince me. Anything else in there? That doesn't seem like it's enough to find our would-be killer."

"Three other birth certificates. Father, mother, twin sister. My father's and my mother's had different names before."

"Time out," he said, making the motion with his hands. "Twins? This is beginning to sound like one of those soap operas my mother used to watch religiously. So you're telling me your parents weren't your parents *and* were not who they said they were? And," he continued before she could reply, "your birth mother had two babies *while* she supposedly died in a house fire?"

"It gets crazier."

"How?"

"One of these came with the letter and the other was in the box." Adeena placed two photos in front of Ian. She took a sip of her rapidly cooling coffee and waited for his reaction. "Uh, you might want to close your mouth."

Ian looked at her in consternation. "What the hell is this?"

"According to the birth certificates it's Lisa Mitchell and Dawn Wingfield. Both born early Christmas Day. I'm the older, darker one."

"No way. I'm willing to admit you look amazingly similar to Lucy Brown and therefore could be her daughter, but this other one? She has blond hair. And I bet blue eyes. Are you hearing me? Someone's trying to play you. They saw the video of the fall and decided to mess with your mind."

"Her eyes are technically bluish-green and her hair darkened to more of a honey-blond as she got older." She flipped through the photos on her phone, then handed it to him. "My twin. Heather Lynne Garson-Kennedy. She was born on the same day, same year as me, only she was adopted by a different family. A white family. Unfortunately…" She exhaled and blinked rapidly. "Uh, she died in a car wreck in January, leaving behind a cheating husband and a four-year-old son. Before you freak out there is documentation of other black and white twins. You know I checked."

He took another look at the photos. "I know black babies are born in all different colors, but they don't grow up to look like the woman you showed me. Skin's not dark enough."

"Bull."

"Then give me an example."

"Jennifer Beals."

"From *The L-Word*? Seriously? She was hot. They all were hot." He smiled. "What was your point again?"

"Would you believe she's part black?"

"No," he said with obvious reluctance.

"Then why can't Heather be half black and my twin?"

"Does Jennifer have a black twin? Never mind. Your point. But…" He raised a finger, then shook it as if he'd just discovered a new wrinkle. "What does it mean? Having a sister's not going to help. Unless you think the people who adopted her have something to do with this."

"No. I think it has to be our birth father, if there's such a word. Being white, he might have had a lot to lose if it came out we—well, me—was his. Could've even been married with kids of his own. You know, the upstanding family man with the dirty little secret."

"What about the father named on your first birth certificate? Could that be him?"

"As fake as the mother. Harold Mitchell. Which wouldn't seem bad until you combine it with Laura Wingfield. Both are main characters in Tennessee Williams' plays. Which is why I want to start the search with the lawyer. He still has a practice in Savannah, where Lucy's from, where maybe the adoption took place, and where according to his real birth certificate, my father was born."

Ian frowned. "And where most likely the person who wants you dead lives."

"I'll have the advantage because he doesn't know that I know. Adeena Minor has no reason to go to Savannah. I have to do something other than sit on my ass and wait like a good girl for them to try until they succeed. I'll wear a disguise while I'm there, find a place to stay outside of town," she added when he continued to look skeptical. "Believe me I want to live. No rash moves for me."

"And going there isn't rash?"

"It'll be well thought out. Planned even, if you will, by a Senior Planner." She hoped to lighten his mood by playing on her job title.

He snickered. "Even better if I go with. I could play the part of your boy toy. Watch your back."

"As much as I appreciate the offer, there is no way Bobby-boy's going to let both of us be out of the office for the amount of time I'm going to need. It'll be a miracle if he lets me go, and that's with me throwing myself at his feet and crying family tragedy."

"What if he says no?"

"I'll quit. If I die he'll have to replace me anyway."

"Oh, stop," Ian said with a glare. "No death talk, and he doesn't want to lose you. You make him look good."

"Meaning he needs me more than I need him. And speaking of need…" She smiled widely. "I'm going to need someone I can trust to watch over my baby boy. Someone whom he already feels comfortable with and loves."

He sighed loudly. "Okay, okay. Drop the fake smile already. But you have to promise you're going to use that big brain of yours to keep yourself safe. I'll be totally pissed if you let those fuckers succeed in killing you. And you have to buy one of those cheap phones where you add the minutes so you can call me the second you think you're in over your head. The cheaper it is, the harder it is to track you. At least that's the way it works on TV. And use cash as much as possible."

"Good, good. Those are great ideas." Some of the tension in her shoulders lessened. She wasn't in this alone. "I'll stop by the ATM on the way home, then again tomorrow."

"I can loan—"

"No. I'll have enough to start. But thanks."

"When will you leave?"

"Fairly soon. Tomorrow night at the latest. Which means I'll have to call Bobby-boy at home. What fun."

"Don't forget to mention your heroic dead mother. Oh, and you should take a bus or drive to Phoenix or Albuquerque and fly from there. You know, this could be kind of exciting. Clandestine getaways, disguises."

"Except for the danger part, you're right."

"No need for sarcasm," Ian said, slapping her arm. "Now, what are you going to do about Heather's family? They're probably not in danger because, hey, she didn't look like Lucy, but they should be told something."

"After. I don't want them brought into this until after I'm no longer in danger. That way they can't get caught in the middle. And they're really rich, so if you think about it, they're much more likely to believe me after the cover-up's exposed."

"I see your point, but I think they need to know *before* exposure of said cover-up. What if you sent them an email letting them know your suspicions? Kind of a heads-up that a shit bomb comes their way. Hopefully the fact that you have the same birthdate and the same adoption lawyer might give them pause. They'll feel even better once they check you out, find you're legit."

"Then what?"

"Then maybe they realize they were duped and start digging. Being the rich kind, they can hire someone to do the digging for them, giving you answers sooner rather than later. Win-win."

"Look at you. Full of the good stuff today." She raised her fist, waited for him to tap it. "And it won't matter if they dismiss me, dismiss the story. I'll still be there doing my own digging. It was smart of me to bring you into this operation, Special Agent Zucker."

"Smarter still if you took me with you, Special Agent Minor." He held up a hand when she opened her mouth. "I accept that it's not possible right at this time. Now for my last bit of morning wisdom. If you take Diablo for a walk today, cross in the middle of a large crowd."

"No worries." She pushed back her chair and grabbed her mostly full cup. "We're giving the park a miss for now. No more emergency calls to ruin another date."

"Good. I have another sort of date tonight."

"How do you have a 'sort-of' date?"

"She has plans to hang with friends at a bar, listen to this band she likes. I said I might stop by, depending."

"You? Two nights in a week?" She smiled. "You are so going to marry her, dude. I'd better be your pick for best man." As she'd expected, her attempt at humor earned her a one-finger salute.

# CHAPTER EIGHT

Sal jerked awake at an unfamiliar sound. She had to shake away the dregs of dreams where she'd been chasing crooked adoption lawyers carrying two babies, one white and one black, before she could identify the noise. "Phone, phone." She let out a pent-up breath, fumbled for her glasses, then felt around for the hotel phone. "Hello?"

"I didn't expect you to answer."

"I didn't expect you to call me at this number. This is my best friend, Cynthia Kennedy, right? The one who's known my cell for years?"

"And who knows you usually don't spend Friday night in your room. Don't tell me the great Salamander struck out."

"Lent." She sighed. "I don't know why I picked this particular time to stop being a slut. You should have talked me out of it."

"As if. It'll build character or some such crap."

"Was there a reason you called with the intention of not talking to me?"

"I told Mom and Dad about the investigator and now Mom's decided we need one of our own. Like you, she believes it has something to do with Heather's birth parents and she's scared we could lose Nate. I assume you've seen about Stephen."

"Oh, yeah. To my delight it's on all the time."

"Well, she, Mom, thinks that could somehow be used against us."

"What? As if somehow you're responsible Heather picked a criminal douche bag for a husband?"

"Now is not the time to expect reason. Anyway, she thinks if we could talk to the birth parents, work out an arrangement, then we could avoid going to court and traumatizing Nate further."

Sal thought about the duplicate names in the lawyer's records, how Heather could easily be one of the girls, and decided to keep quiet for now. Two babies out of hundreds didn't necessarily scream scam. "Getting your own investigator can't hurt. Especially if the interested party is more interested in the Kennedy money than a family reunion. Hey, I, uh, don't suppose your parents got any kind of correspondence from Heather's birth parents? Sometimes they write a letter or note to the kid, explaining or declaring their love. Anything with a first name or initials even."

"There is. From Heather's birth mother. I'd forgotten about it. Mom first read it to her, us, really, when she was four or five. I think that's when the adoption talk started."

"So she always knew?"

"That she was adopted? Definitely. It was never a secret or something we couldn't talk about. In fact, Heather used to tease me about our parents liking her better because she was the chosen one. Of course I had to retaliate by holding one of her dolls hostage until she took it back." Cyn sighed. "I'd almost forgotten about that too. How I miss her."

"I miss her too. But I confess I'm glad she's not here for any of this. Uh, hey, any chance you can get your hands on that letter? Sooner rather than later."

"We got it back…after, along with her other personal stuff Stephen wanted us to keep for Nate. Why? You think we can find them from that?"

"Maybe. I sort of hacked into Nicholson's—"

"You didn't!"

"Well, yeah. You had to have expected that, Cyn. It's what I do."

"You're right. What was I thinking?"

"So I thought if you had a name, I could see if it matches any of the hundreds of files I looked through last night."

"Lucky for you, and me, I have her folder right here. Thought I would need it for our PI. Let's see. 'I love you…Blah, blah, blah. Laura.' It's signed by Laura…"

Cyn continued to talk, but Sal stopped listening. Laura could be the Laura Wingfield who had shown up on two birth certificates in Nicholson's files. Couldn't be a coincidence the name showed up on a letter to Heather. And it would undoubtedly be a miracle if a Laura Wingfield actually existed. It was far more likely they'd pulled the name out of the air or the obituaries.

But there had been two babies. She wondered if they'd dangled Heather in front of two sets of parents, only to sell her to the highest bidder. Or perhaps this Laura character had managed to get her hands on two babies.

"Are you listening to me?" Cyn demanded.

"Uh, what? Yeah. Of course I am."

"Don't lie. What time did you go to bed?"

"I'm not sure. Sometime. This morning maybe?"

"Call me when your brain wakes up. Oh, and can you check out a name for me? Dani Knight. I got her name from an acquaintance. She's supposed to be a top-notch investigator."

"Will do." Sal mentally added it to her growing list of things to do. "Oh, the adoption lawyer. You know how your parents found him?"

"No. Is it important? I can ask."

"Just curious." Sal said an absent good-bye, her focus on the lawyer's files. She'd have to go through them all again, searching for any other mention of Laura Wingfield or Harold Mitchell she'd overlooked. Then she needed to figure out what she had before going to Cyn and her parents with her suspicions. But first she'd start compiling data on Dani Knight, make sure the woman could do the job.

Hours later, her back as flexible as a board, Sal finished searching every file. She could now say with certainty there were only two birth certificates with the names she'd been looking for. She could also say Heather's adoption file was a no-show. Rubbing her eyes, she considered the implications. Her gut told her the lawyer was dirty and that it would take forever to verify if any of the other adoptions were illegal.

She set her laptop aside and stretched her back. The bigger question might be if she cared whether the other adoptions were illegal. "Care" was the wrong word, wrong question. The question was if she had the right to stir up other people's lives as a byproduct of delving into Heather's adoption.

"No." Not without personally verifying each and every adoption. That was her bottom line, and it made her next step, a visit to the lawyer's office, that much easier. Heather's file had to be locked up somewhere the lawyer considered safe. Most likely in a hidden safe in his office or, since he lived alone, his home. Either way, she'd find it and use it to get the lawyer to talk.

On a whim she searched online for Laura Wingfield and Harold Mitchell and found them in plays by Tennessee Williams. Obviously someone was a fan, but wasn't creative enough to come up with names on their own. Didn't matter. The lawyer existed, and he was the key to figuring out the nature of the scam about to unfold.

She smiled. Scamming the scammer was one of her favorite games. She hadn't planned to return to Georgia so soon, but the game afoot was much more entertaining than any Las Vegas had to offer. Good thing she'd had the sense to pack the necessary documents and equipment for sleuthing.

* * *

Scowling, Beau Tanner pulled at his necktie and thought, *Another Saturday night wasted.* He hated these gatherings where the family had to fawn over his father's potential big money donors. Hell, he hated the donors with their potbelly stomachs, their skinny young wives and their worship of the almighty dollar. Much to his disgust, more than one of those skinny wives had let him know they were available.

"Stop scowling."

He looked down his nose at Maria Cousin, his father's campaign manager and lover. They thought they were so slick, but he knew what went on behind closed doors. Beau wasn't sure who he hated more, Maria with her need for power, his father with his weakness for women or his mother for putting up with the long line of other women. And he couldn't forget his dear old grandmother, who'd sell her own mother to see her beloved Jackson Beauregard Tanner succeed in politics. There were many days when he wished he'd been born into a different family. More so lately after being under the almost constant scrutiny of Maria. Yeah, he definitely hated her more. "Stop fucking my father and maybe I'll stop scowling."

"You're going to want to watch your mouth." Maria kept her smile, but her eyes were hard as nails. "You think I'm a bitch now. Do anything to jeopardize your father's campaign and you'll find out how much of a bitch I can be."

"Like you could *be* any worse." He brushed past her and crossed the room to where one of his classmates had just entered. Sinead Tisdale looked about as glad to be here as he was. Sinead, despite her Irish name, was African-American. Her father had come from money and made even more with his national restaurant chain and luxury car dealerships. She was smart as hell and the star of the basketball team. "Didn't expect to see you here."

"That makes two of us. Mom pulled out the poor health card, so Dad drafted me at the last minute."

"What are you getting out of it?"

She smiled and her face became one of beauty. "He was so desperate I could have gotten a new car, but I went for the new PlayStation *and* ten games of my choosing."

"Thought he hated you gaming."

"Exactly. He wants me here in a fucking dress and playing nicey-nice, he's gotta pay. When he got all blustery, tried to renege, I reminded him he's the one who taught *me* how to play the game. Shut him up." She looked around the room. "Anything good to eat here? Didn't have time for dinner."

"Only the best. I could get you the good stuff to drink if you want."

"I leave that to my mother. And I already know I'll be the one driving us home after Daddy Dearest knocks back a few with his upstanding colleagues."

As Beau escorted Sinead to the overflowing buffet, he couldn't help notice his dad and Maria seemed to be having a heated conversation. *Good*, he thought. Let them worry about what he knew, what he might say. *Assholes*.

Sinead grabbed a plate and piled it high. "Good eats. I'll be back for dessert."

"Maria wouldn't let it be anything less, don't you know."

"How is the queen bitch?"

He tried to look sad. "Not doing so well. I might have mentioned that if she wanted me to stop scowling, she needed to stop fucking my dad."

Her eyes lit up as she let loose a shot of laughter. "You didn't."

"Did. I'm sick of that bitch thinking she runs everything in this damn family when she's not a fucking member. Getting so bad, I'm not sure I'll make it to graduation without going crazy."

Sinead picked up some silverware and motioned to a couple of empty seats away from the fray. "You can't let her get to you, Beau. That's what she wants. Then she'll eat you up and spit you out without breaking a sweat. It's what lifesuckers like her thrive on."

Beau knew she'd gone through some of the same issues he was facing during her father's failed attempt to join the state

House of Representatives. Her father might not have been fucking his campaign manager, but he'd sampled his share of the young, female volunteers and getting caught with one of them had ended his run. "She can try to eat me up all she wants. I hope she finds that I'm poison to her system."

Sinead swallowed a mouthful. "Just try to keep it chill. We have less than a month till graduation, and then you'll be out of here for the summer deal your grandmother hooked you up with. Come home for a week and then on to Yale. Time'll go faster than you think. And when she's really driving you crazy, come hang at the house. Play games on my new console."

"You don't know Maria. She's had it in for me from day one. Nothing I do is good enough, unlike my perfect little brother." His lips twisted in a sneer.

"Here's what I think," she said, pointing at him with her fork. "One day Phillip is going to wake up and they're gonna have a werewolf on their hands. You just have to look at him to see he's itching to shed his human skin."

"Won't be soon enough for me. All that ass kissing has to make you sick eventually."

"My father's been doing it to the Republican Party for years. Hasn't affected him yet." She shrugged. "Of course it doesn't do him any good since he choked on that election."

"From what I heard, it wasn't the election he was choking on."

"Dude!" She gave him a shoulder bump. "Careful, you'll scar me for life."

He shot her a quick grin. "As if. More like the other way around," he said, thinking of some of the locker-room escapades she'd shared with him. "How did you know?"

"Know what?"

"That you were…you know?"

"Queer? It's okay to say the word, Beau. I knew because girls were it for me. In the Disney movies I was the one who dashed in to save the beautiful princess, not some totally lame prince. No offense. If the attraction is there, it's there. Not a thing you can do about it. Why, you see someone you like that way?"

His heartbeat sped up at the very thought of saying it out loud. "You could say that. Listen, you can't tell anyone."

"As if. You're more like a brother to me than my own brother." She looked him in the eye, her expression solemn. "What's said between us stays between us. Especially something as crucial as this. You know what. Forget about my dad and his gifts, let's go someplace we can really talk."

He put a hand on her arm to keep her from standing. "No, it's okay. I'm being stupid. I know I can trust you with anything." Beau blew out a breath. "Jarvis." As he expected, her eyes got bigger than the moon. "Yeah, that Jarvis," he said, referring to the star athlete who always had two girls on each arm and more trailing behind waiting for a word of encouragement. "You know I've been tutoring him for calculus, right? Well, uh…" He gave a shaky laugh. "He kissed me yesterday. Just came right out and planted a wet one right on my lips."

"OMG! OMG!" Sinead clapped a hand over her mouth momentarily, then whispered, "What did you do?"

"Grabbed him and kissed him back. I tell you, Sinead, it's like everything became so clear. Like I solved an equation after weeks of trying."

"Okay, okay, okay. Gotta adjust." Sinead closed her eyes briefly. "Wow. And you're just telling me this now why? This is big stuff. The kind of big stuff you tell your best friend in the whole wide world right away."

He rubbed his hands against his heated cheeks. "Put it down to shock. I hardly slept last night thinking about it, wanting to do it again."

"Completely blown away. That's what I am. Jarvis, huh? You the man." She punched him in the arm. "Never would've guessed that in a trillion years. So what happens now?"

"I don't know. We didn't say anything after. He went his way, I went mine. Sometimes I wonder if I made it up."

"Made it up because you wanted it to happen?"

"Maybe." He ran his fingers through his hair. "I don't know. I guess. I went over to see Michelle this morning and broke it off. She said some nasty things, cried, then tried to convince me to change my mind. Even if nothing happens with Jarvis, I can't…with her, you know? Not anymore."

"I totally get that."

"But my parents won't. Maria won't."

"Despite the role Maria has given herself, she is not the boss of you. As for your parents, big deal. I haven't told my dad. Won't tell him until he asks. That's not to say he doesn't suspect, but high school's almost over, I'm doing well in school and haven't been in trouble. Unlike my useless and straight brother."

"Got that basketball scholarship to UConn. Can't leave that out."

"That was pretty sweet. I'll be up there freezing my ass off in the cold, but it'll be a long way away from his evil sphere of influence. I plan on doing what I want to do. You should do the same." She looked down at her plate. "Incoming. Other dragon lady this time."

"Beau, I'm surprised at you, hiding back here in the corner. You know how much your father needs for you to mingle at these affairs. Help with the cause."

He stood and dropped a kiss on his grandmother's cheek. He considered it lucky he'd managed to stay off her radar for as long as he had. "You remember Sinead, don't you, Grandmother?"

"Of course." The smile she gave Sinead was thin at best. "I hope you'll excuse him."

Sinead's smile was closer to a grimace. "Of course. You want to hit the books tomorrow, Beau?"

"That'd be great. Afternoon?" He waited for her nod and then followed his grandmother.

"I know you've been friends with her a long time, but surely you must see how it looks for the two of you to spend too much time alone," Eugenia said once they were out of hearing distance. "People will talk."

"People will talk about anything," Beau replied, thinking of what she'd say if she knew about Jarvis, the kiss. She'd change her tune then, he bet. Sinead would become perfectly acceptable in a heartbeat. "What's the big deal? So I was talking to a friend.

Look around you, Grandmother. You'll see I'm not the only guilty one."

She raised her right eyebrow. "I doubt there is a friendship among this group. What they are doing is networking. It wouldn't hurt you to try it sometime."

"I'm here." He sighed heavily over his grandmother and her faulty eyesight. Instead of riding his butt, she should be worried about her son and Maria. They were so obvious he wouldn't be surprised if a clever opponent used it as ammunition. But no, she had to bring up the fact he spent a few minutes alone with his best friend. A friend he knew would stand with him no matter what. He guessed it was lucky Maria hadn't yet seen their association as a problem, which he knew had a lot to do with the money Sinead's dad could contribute to the campaign.

His grandmother pulled him to a stop in front of a couple. Beau knew for a fact the man had jettisoned his family in favor of his current trophy wife. To his mind that was a worse offense than him talking to a friend.

"This is Jackson's eldest boy, Beau. He'll be going off to Yale in the fall."

Listening to his grandmother rattle on about him, about the family, Beau figured he was going to spend the evening stuck in a form of hell.

# CHAPTER NINE

"You do realize there's a three-hour difference between Seneca and Las Vegas, right?" With a yawn, Sal settled back against the pillows.

"I didn't think. Sorry. Thanks for the okay on Knight."

"Cyn, I love you, but please, please, please tell me you didn't just call me at five thirty on a Sunday morning to thank me." She heard the sigh loud and clear. "What? No! Your dad? I can be—"

"No. No. Not that. He's fine. We're all fine. Sort of. This is going to sound crazy, but I received an email from a woman claiming to be Heather's twin. I dismissed it at first, figuring someone was trying to pull a fast one. But then I got to thinking, read it again."

"The guy. You think she's the one who hired him to get the backstory on Heather?"

"Don't know what to think. She claims to have only recently found out she was adopted. She sent me a copy of her original birth certificate and what she claims is an original copy of Heather's. The information on both is almost identical."

"Hang on a minute." Sal vaulted out of the bed and grabbed a laptop. "What's the name of the parents?"

"Laura Wingfield and Harold—"

"Mitchell," Sal finished. "And the names of the babies are Lisa Mitchell and Dawn Wingfield."

"How do you know?"

"Twins. That explains it. I found two files for Wingfield and Mitchell. No other duplicates in the hundreds of files I went through. I thought the lawyer had pulled a bait and switch, then sold Heather to the highest bidder. But it's twins. He split twins. No. That can't be right. One of the families was Caucasian and the other was—"

"African-American. The woman who supposedly was previously known as Lisa Mitchell is African-American. So not twins. She could be mixed, but she is definitely not white."

"But isn't that interesting? Why would he use the same names for the parents of two unrelated babies? He didn't do it for any others."

"At this point, Sal, I don't know a damn thing about anything and you know I don't like not knowing."

"Why wouldn't you? It's like opening a portal to an alternative universe. You'd hate it. Me? I find it interesting. Good thing you have me for a best friend. I'll check her out, see what schemes she's been running and who she's been running them with. Could lead me right to the Burlett connection. Maybe Nicholson as well."

"Actually she lives in Las Vegas. I thought…well, I thought you could go see her, talk to her, find out what she's after. I already looked her up and according to what I've found, she seems okay."

"Anything can be faked."

"That's why I want you to see her in person. And Sal, here's the really weird thing. She's 'her.' The woman I accused you of knowing. From the hit-and-run video."

"Yeah? Even more interesting." Sal's brain chugged in many different directions, all thought of sleep forgotten. This might turn out to be the best vacation ever. "I was planning to fly your way this afternoon, show you the files, then track down Nicholson, the lawyer. Seems I'll be making a different house call. Forward the email. I'll do a deeper search before I look her up. Confront her if I find anything hinky."

"Be careful. I have an afternoon meeting with Knight. I waved enough money to get her to see me today. If the meeting goes well, she'll hopefully be willing to start right away. Sounds like I should put her on Nicholson."

"Definitely. He knows something." She opened the email from Cyn and did a quick skim. "Yeah, I'll be doing a deeper check on the former Lisa Mitchell who is now Adeena Minor. See if she paid Burlett or if she's tied to Nicholson some kind of way. I'll check her parents as well." Sal read the email again, thought about the video. "Hey, on the off chance this isn't total bullshit, you should consider beefing up security."

"Already went there. Too much unusual shit flying around not to. You should take your own advice. Watch your back, Thomasina Salamander."

"I always do, Mom." Skinny didn't mean Sal was helpless. She knew how to take care of herself, had learned out of necessity years ago.

Despite a restless night, Adeena was up early Sunday morning. She'd spent a good portion of yesterday getting ready for her trip. Her evening had been spent doing research for which she had little to show. At Diablo's insistence, she'd taken him for a couple of walks around the complex. On one of those walks, she'd talked herself into reaching out to Cynthia Kennedy and sharing her story. She hadn't been surprised at the lack of response to her email by the time she finally went to bed. Her story read like fiction and bad fiction at that. Ms. Kennedy had probably been quick to click the trash icon.

Taking Ian's advice, she'd bought a bus ticket with an early afternoon departure. Instead of Albuquerque, she'd chosen

Dallas as her final destination. Her plan was to get off the bus when it stopped in Albuquerque, go to the airport, then buy a ticket on the next available flight to Atlanta. She'd rent a car in Atlanta, spend the night at a hotel and do the six-hour drive to Savannah tomorrow morning. If she couldn't get a flight to Atlanta, she'd try Jacksonville.

Once in Savannah, she was going to the lawyer's office and demand some answers. He had to know something about the people who'd sold her and Heather. Finding one of them should get her closer to finding the person who wanted her dead. Assuming she wasn't killed by the lawyer or the person who sold her first.

But as she threw back the covers, she mulled over what she would do once she found that person who wanted her dead. She wasn't some badass ninja who could take on a killer, knock him out, tie him up, then buff her nails while she waited for the cops to arrive and haul him off. No, she needed to go about this business a different way. Exposing him should be her first step. Then the cops could take it from there.

As she brushed her teeth, she thought about her dad and if letting the police sort things out would be in his best interest. She had his real name, knew he'd been born and had probably grown up in Savannah. Maybe tracking down his whereabouts around the time of her birth was something she should also be doing. He'd loved her and that made it more likely he knew the lawyer or someone associated with the lawyer. Something else to add to her list.

As she got dressed later, she tried to figure out what else she might need to figure out. One thing was the move to Dayton. The town certainly wasn't a bustling metropolis for culture and as one of the few black families there, they had always stood out. It seemed to her they could have more easily gotten lost in a big city like Oakland or LA. Those were also on the opposite side of the country, but much farther away from Savannah than Dayton and with a substantially larger black population for cover.

A sharp bark interrupted her thought. "I'm almost done." Obviously Diablo had remembered her promise of a long walk this morning. Their last until she returned. While it wouldn't include the park, it would get her out of the apartment long enough for her to stop feeling the walls were going to contract on her. After all, she couldn't spend the rest of her life trapped indoors.

*No.* She refused to spend the rest of her life trapped indoors by some madman. And if someone was waiting for them to cross the street, they'd have a long wait, she thought and smiled.

At seven on a Sunday morning the sidewalks and streets were practically empty. Adeena enjoyed this time of day when she could imagine she was one of a few instead of one of many. It felt good to be out of her apartment, so she was content to go slow, stopping and starting to let Diablo sniff and spray at his leisure.

Because it was quiet, the loud rumbling sound of a car traveling at high speeds put her on alert. A glance let her know it was headed in her direction. This time she didn't freeze, this time she snatched up Diablo and ran before her brain had time to send out a warning of danger. Fear fueled her as she raced across the grassy front of yet another apartment complex and ducked under the gate. She felt something whiz past her head before the back window of the car in front of her exploded. Screaming, she tried to keep low without slowing down, hoping someone would hear her, hoping someone would call the police.

As she made the first left turn, she heard the car barrel through the gate, followed by a shout of outrage. *Good,* she thought, struggling for breath, someone had seen her assailant. Someone would call for help.

She came to another intersection and this time she made a right and ran up the stairs. At the first door she came to, she banged for all she was worth. When there was no response, she moved on to the second, then the third. Finally when she could hear footsteps running up the stairs, she got a reply at the fifth door.

"Can I help you?" The tiny woman who opened the door had a surprisingly robust voice.

"Call 911! Somebody's trying to kill me." As she bent over gasping for breath, Adeena tried to think of her next move. Knowing she couldn't stand it if she put someone else in harm's way, Adeena thrust Diablo forward. "Please, watch my dog. And find a good place to hide."

Taking a breath, she realized she was spent, realized she couldn't outrun a bullet. But maybe she could keep the would-be killer talking long enough for help to arrive. It probably wasn't the dumbest move she'd ever made, but she thought it was in the top three as she turned to the person who was trying to kill her.

"You got me." She raised her hands in surrender and mentally cataloged his features. He was probably six feet tall, big and beefy with a crooked nose and thin lips. She added bushy eyebrows and no visible scars or tattoos to her list. "Please don't hurt anybody else."

"Mighty noble of you." The man had a pronounced Southern accent to go with the big gun. "You come quietly and I won't have to shoot anybody else who tries to stick their nose in our business."

She nodded, trying to keep her expression blank. "I'm Adeena Lynne Minor. I hope that's who you're looking for. The Lynne has an e on the end," she went on to say loudly, hoping to mask any noise that the topless, barefoot man creeping up on her bad guy might make.

"I know exactly who you are, bitch. Now quit stalling."

She took a step, then stopped, bent at the waist and rested her hands on her thighs. "Sorry. Need to catch my breath. Not used to running for my life."

"Let's see if I can do something to speed you up."

His smile warned her what that something ⌐ she dropped down a second before he raise⌐ position on the ground, she saw her r⌐ assailant's ear.

"You might want to lower that gun t⌐ and get on your knees, or I'll have no ch⌐ brains out."

The way he said it, so nice and easy, had shivers running down her back. If she'd been on the other end of that gun, she would've done anything asked. She saw with relief that her would-be killer was quick to comply.

In a smooth move, her rescuer pulled cuffs from the back of his jeans and secured the other guy's hands behind his back. "Are you okay, ma'am?"

Nerves forced a shaky laugh that verged on a sob. "Thanks to you." She drew up her legs, dropped her head on her knees and rocked back and forth as it sank in someone wanted her dead.

For the third time in two weeks, Adeena found herself giving a statement to the police. Only this time they had a suspect and a witness who was a cop. Not knowing who she could trust, Adeena pleaded ignorance as to a motive. She kept to that story even when she was taken to the station for a more thorough round of questioning.

When it was finally over and she had assurances the matter was going to be pursued, she called Ian. She was too unsettled to register much surprise when he brought the new woman with him. And when he pulled her into a strong hug, she finally felt safe enough to let go, to release pent-up tears.

"Sorry," she said once the storm slowed to a trickle.

He rested his forehead against hers. "Hey, it's me. No sorry for this."

"Okay. Okay. I'm going to, uh, wash my face." It was then that Adeena remembered his new woman, who as luck would have it, was sitting quietly nearby petting Diablo. She wiped her eyes. "Oh, uh, sorry about this. I swear I didn't know you were, well…" She bit down on her lip to stop the babbling. "Just uh, sorry."

Ian's new woman smiled. "It's okay, really. I've got my thanks right here in my lap."

"I'll…I'll be right back." She scurried to the bathroom, and water on her face and tried to regain some modicum She realized almost immediately that calm, or any semblance thereof, was not in the cards for her heart, her body, her mind. Someone had shot at her, would have kidnapped and killed her if not for a quick-acting, off-duty cop. "Kind of hard to be cool and composed after that," she told her reflection and put a hand to her rapidly beating heart. So maybe it was even okay not to find that Zen place for hours, maybe days, weeks even.

When her legs felt numb, she slid to the floor and put her head between her legs. Her life was in danger and she didn't have a clue who the enemy was. To make matters worse, they were no longer content to make her death seem like an accident, and that stank of desperation. Her only hope was that desperate people sometimes made mistakes.

"And mistakes keep me alive." That should be her focus, not the fear eating at her insides and forcing her to sit on a public bathroom floor.

"Eww." Adeena pushed up, looked at her hands and remembered the other time she'd found herself on a bathroom floor. She could still see the look of horror on her mother's face when she discovered her almost eight-year-old daughter curled up on the floor as she waited for her stomach to stop hurting. Back then she'd been sick from the pressure of having to ace yet another high-stakes test.

As she scrubbed her hands now, she decided the advice her mother had given her then—to straighten up and do what had to be done—still applied. Sitting on a public bathroom floor was not going to make her less of a target or help her learn the identity of the person who wanted her dead. She wasn't going to go straight, but she could get her ass in gear and catch that bus.

She returned to find Ian's girlfriend by herself.

"He took Diablo for a walk," the other woman explained. "I'm Andrea. Andi Dwyer."

Adeena took the offered hand, liked the friendly concern on Andi's face. "I guess you figured out I'm Adeena Minor. Sorry we had to meet this way, but still glad to meet you," she added. She thought how she'd said something similar not too many days ago. She didn't want to have to say it again anytime soon.

"You too. Ian talks about you a lot."

"Without curse words?"

"Mostly. But I knew I was going to like you as soon as I heard about that stunt you pulled at the bar. Served him right."

"And I knew I was going to like you when I heard you weren't one of his…usual types." Adeena frowned, realizing how that might sound to someone who didn't know her. "I mean that in the best kind of way."

Andi smiled. "He's told me your opinion of his usual type. I agree."

"Now I like you even more. We should find Ian. I'm more than ready to leave this place behind." Outside, she filled up her lungs with fresh air and wondered how people could stand spending their days breathing in police station air.

When Diablo ran to her, she scooped him up and cradled him close. "Hey, baby. Mama's okay. We're okay." His response was to lick her face.

Ian slung an arm around her shoulder and gave her a hard squeeze. "So I'm thinking maybe now you'll want to relocate to my place."

"Hiding at your place wouldn't have done any good." She rested her head on his shoulder. He was such a good friend. "He waited for me to come out, Ian. He's obviously studied me. Probably knows where I work, who my friends are. He could've followed us from work to your place and hurt you too." She cleared the lump in her throat. Nobody should get hurt because of her.

"Then I think you should leave right away. To Seneca." Ian held up a finger when Adeena opened her mouth. "They think you're here, and it'll take at least a little while for someone to pick up where the other guy left off. I could drive you to Phoenix or Albuquerque and you could catch a flight from there. It would confuse them long enough for you to get there, talk with Cynthia Kennedy and begin to figure out what this is about."

"I work for Delta," Andi said. "I can swing a buddy pass. You'd be subject to getting bumped, but you'd get there eventually and for a lot cheaper."

"I do need to go soon. Thanks for the offer, Andi, but I got it covered." She shared her plans to get off the bus early and fly to Atlanta. She'd tell Ian about going from there directly to Savannah after she came back.

"As good as anything," Ian said. "Let's swing by your place, get what you and Diablo need. That should give us plenty of time to get you to the bus station."

When they returned to Adeena's apartment complex, they found a nerdy-looking guy knocking on her door. "Shit! How could they have gotten somebody else out here so soon?"

"They couldn't," Ian said. "Andi, drive around the corner and let me out. I'll pretend like I'm a neighbor, wondering who's knocking on your door when everyone knows you're in Dayton to see about your mother's house."

"We'll go together," Andi countered. "Two against one. I know some moves."

Adeena believed it. Tall and nicely muscled, Andi looked like she had athlete stamped on her DNA. "I think Diablo and I should stay within seeing distance in case you have to get out in a hurry. The other guy wasn't afraid to use his gun. No offense to your moves, Andi."

"None taken." Andi backed into a parking space. "I'll leave the keys in the ignition."

Adeena held Diablo close as she watched the scene unfold. It quickly turned anti-climactic when the nerdy-looking black guy removed his phone and pointed to the screen. Moments later, a wave from Ian had her grabbing the keys and scrambling out of the vehicle. She thought she did a great job of hiding her surprise when up close, the he turned out to be a she.

The mistake was easy to make. At first glance the red hair cut close to the scalp, the dark, square glasses, the short-sleeved shirt with the manly cut, the baggy pants and the pocket protector filled with gadgets said male of the black geek variety.

"She seems to be legit," Ian said. "Cynthia Kennedy sent her your email, and since Ms. Salamander was visiting our lovely city, asked her to look you up."

*And that really meant she's here to check me out*, Adeena thought. She couldn't complain. She would have done the same thing if the situation was reversed. "And you just *happened* to be in town?"

Ms. Salamander frowned. "Just as I *happen* to be here this time every year. R and R. It's not yet a crime."

"Rest and relaxation in Vegas? Really?"

"Really." Sal shrugged. "We relax in our own way. I happen to find winning large sums of other people's money relaxing. But is that important?"

"Could be. Your timing's a little too good. We're returning from the police station. Pesky little thing like being shot at." She didn't offer her hand, instead she watched for a reaction and she wasn't disappointed. Salamander's gaze sharpened and she lost the laid-back demeanor. "So you showing up now is more than a little suspicious."

"You serious about the shooting thing?"

"Very serious. I won't say dead serious because, hey, I'm not. Some guy tried to shoot me while I was walking my dog this morning. Which means now you can inform Ms. Kennedy that I meant what I said in the email about being in danger."

"Okay, yeah. I will. I'm Thomasina Salamander, but everybody calls me Sal. Do you have any idea who's behind this? You weren't exactly specific in your email."

"Do you?" she countered.

Sal pushed her glasses up her shiny nose. "How could I?"

"Then why are you here?"

"You send my friend a strange-sounding email and you have to ask why I'm here? Talk about more than a little suspicious. You're lucky she sent me. Most people would have ignored it."

"But she didn't, did she?" Adeena felt compelled to point out. "So, yeah, I do have to ask why you're here. Maybe it's because your friend has questions of her own. Questions about her sister's adoption that she can't answer."

"Point. Some private eye type's been snooping around. Asking questions about her sister."

"My sister too," she asserted. "My *twin* sister."

"We don't know that for a fact, now do we? I knew Heather very well and you look nothing, and I mean nothing, like her. No offense."

The "no offense" added insult to injury as far as Adeena was concerned. The urge to vent her frustration by pummeling Sal was so raw she took a step back. If some lunatic hadn't marked her for termination she probably would have dealt better with the snide remark, the fucking royal use of "we." But not today. "Listen, Thomasina, you may not know, but I do!" She used her finger to punctuate her point. "Somebody came after me with a fucking gun today. What that means, if you need to understand, is that *I* do know Heather is my twin and that there is no doubt in *my* mind that this shit goes all the way back to *our* birth. That would be mine and Heather's. *Our* mother died during childbirth and someone still went to the trouble of burning down her house. A house that still had her family in it. I challenge you to look at a photo of Lucy Mae Brown and tell me I don't look exactly like her. I challenge you to look me in the eye and tell me how my birth mother, who happens on paper to have the same name as Heather's birth mother, signed a document three days after her death." She folded her arms over her chest and silently dared Sal to tell her again Heather wasn't her sister.

Sal adjusted her glasses once again and cleared her throat. "Uh, yeah. Cynthia forwarded the material you sent her, and I found Lucy Mae Brown. That is, I found her photo, a copy of the obit, and yeah, no way did she sign anything on the twenty-eighth." She gave a wan smile. "Well, the, uh…the thing is, what Cyn, what Cyn and I can't understand is why you believe Heather was your twin. Not that I think you're a liar," she said quickly. "But I have to say again you look nothing alike. You're black and she wasn't."

"What, you with the red hair and the freckles don't know black people can come in all varieties?"

"That's not the point. What I mean is that the only thing linking you is the names on a birth certificate. Fictitious names at that."

"I don't care about that!" She flung out her arms, torn between anger and frustration. As far as weeks went, this one sucked and she didn't need some smartass woman to make it worse. "I'm willing to take a DNA test, compare it to Nathan. Even if we don't look anything alike and our skins are a different color, genes will show a close familial relationship between me and him and therefore Heather. Will that satisfy you and Ms. Kennedy?"

"I can't speak for Cyn," Sal said stiffly. "I can say Cyn is serious about tracking down the lawyer who did the adoption and getting answers to any other questions surrounding Heather's birth."

Ian put a hand on Adeena's shoulder as if sensing her mood. "What about this private detective? Who hired him and why is he checking out a dead woman? Is the cheating husband involved?"

"Not unless he found a way to pay him without taking money out of any of his accounts. Believe me, I checked." Sal glanced down at the dog sniffing at her high-top sneakers. "What do you know about the background of your parents? That is, the people who adopted you."

It was galling to have to admit to a stranger how little she knew. "Some. They were from Georgia. I grew up believing they moved to Nevada before they had me."

"I did a deep search, and the Joy and James Minor Jr. who were your parents didn't seem to exist until after your birth."

"You work fast." She didn't consider it a compliment. Obviously Sal and her pal had decided she was after something. She wouldn't be surprised if they had a detective looking into her. Not that it mattered. She had nothing to hide. "I guess I can tell you I found other birth certificates for both of them. Walter Morrow and Jessica Simmons. I'll tell you right here and right now that I don't believe they had knowledge of or were involved in the kidnapping or the fire. They were good people."

"We should go inside," Ian urged. "It's been a tough morning."

Adeena fumbled as she tried to get the keys into the lock. Despite the heat from the sun, she felt frozen inside. Tough didn't begin to describe the situation she found herself in.

"Let me do that." Ian took the keys, unlocked the door and walked her to the open living area. "You sit. I'm going to make some of that tea you like so much."

"I'll help." Andi followed Ian to the kitchen, which was separated from the living room by a half wall.

"I'm sorry if I said anything to upset you." Sal fingered her glasses. She was standing in the front foyer, looking like she wanted to be anywhere else.

It was almost funny, Adeena thought. She too wanted Sal to be anywhere else. Manners had her saying, "Can't be helped. You might as well have a seat." When Adeena sank into the sofa, Diablo immediately jumped into her lap. Obviously he'd picked up on the tension. "I'm sorry you got dragged away from the casinos. I'm guessing from your accent that you're from the northeast. Wouldn't Atlantic City be a lot closer?"

A smile flashed across Sal's face. "Cyn asked me the same thing. And like I told her, I prefer Vegas for a lot of reasons. Plus it's far enough from New York City to feel like a real vacation."

"Give me New York City any day. Now that's a city. Of course I was only eight the one time I was there. The buildings probably won't seem as tall to me now."

They fell into an awkward silence. Sal studied the room while Adeena studied Sal. The other woman looked so geeky, Adeena wondered if it was a disguise. A true geek would surely have brought a laptop or other gadgets.

"Tea," Ian announced unnecessarily as he was carrying a tray with four cups.

Adeena took one of the cups. The liquid slid nicely down her throat, warming her insides. "You can tell Ms. Kennedy I'm going to Georgia," she said and once again watched Sal closely for reaction. There was none. "I was going to Seneca, but that's changed. I need to go to Savannah, talk to the lawyer, see what he knows, see if my adoption was legal."

Sal opened her mouth, then closed it without speaking.

The pained expression on Sal's face said it all. Adeena exhaled, leaned back and stared at the ceiling. "And you already know it's not legal."

"Never filed. Neither was Heather's."

"Was that lawyer licensed to practice?" Ian demanded, reaching for Adeena's hand.

"Was and is. He's filed a lot of legal adoptions. Before and after you, which makes motivation hard to pin. Doesn't look like it was for money. No big house, no snazzy cars, no big deposits, no second property."

"The money must be in an overseas account," Andi said. "Swiss bank or in one of those island countries that keep money away from prying eyes."

"I'm in the computer information business. I can assure you he doesn't have one. I've checked forward and backward and there is nothing in his lifestyle or his records to suggest he took money to keep the two adoptions off the record."

"Then I definitely want to talk to him."

"Cyn already hired someone to do a follow-up with the good lawyer."

*And to check up on me,* she thought. "I'm still going to Savannah. I know my birth mother and her family are dead, but she had friends, other relatives. I'll look for them. She was almost full-term when she supposedly died in the fire. Someone in her circle knew who the father of her babies was. Either he was in on her death or he knows something. Maybe seeing me in person will make people talk or make him feel guilty."

"And maybe he'll fall on his knees because you put yourself right in his murdering-ass hands!" Ian slapped his hand against the coffee table. "This is much worse than going to your parents' house alone."

"You yourself said they wouldn't look for me there," Adeena pointed out. "How many times do I have to say that I need to do something? Face it, doing nothing's almost gotten me killed. Three times."

"Then find her friends, her family's friends and take the information you get to the police. They're the ones who get paid to deal with murderers."

"Fine. We'll try it your way. But if it doesn't work…" She didn't feel the need to state the obvious. And there was nothing that said she couldn't go to the police with her information and then go see Daddy Dearest immediately afterward. She wanted to see his expression when he realized she'd bested him.

Sal cleared her throat. "If I may be of help? I think I have a solution you both can live with."

# CHAPTER TEN

Conlin received no satisfaction when his burner phone hit the wall with a loud thud and fell apart. He'd been in tight spaces before, considered it the price of doing business. But he didn't think they'd ever felt this tight. And they'd never been caused by his own misjudgment of the situation and of the man he'd put in charge.

So maybe he could be forgiven if his hand shook a little as he poured a generous serving of scotch. Expensive scotch he'd received as a gift from Eugenia Tanner. A reward for a nasty job well done. As he downed the liquor in one gulp, he wondered if there wasn't some irony that he was drinking it now for a job that had gone anything but well. A job that was supposed to be his last, his swan song. The way things were going, it would still be his last, only not with the ending he anticipated.

He poured another generous shot and considered the worst. It wouldn't be his death. No, he was too cautious a man for anyone to get the jump on him. But it would mean slinking off with his tail between his legs. He'd known Eugenia Tanner too long not to realize that today's attempt, failed or not, would bring her wrath. A direct order had been disobeyed. It wouldn't matter that he had instructed his man to only watch the girl, not kill her. No, Eugenia Tanner only saw his assignments in black and white, success and failure. He'd made the decision not to go to Nevada and deal with the situation himself after two failed attempts, which meant he bore sole responsibility and would be dealt the sole punishment.

Thankfully he had ears at the Vegas PD and knew about the failed attempt before his man called him. Now he had enough time to put his retirement plans into action.

Conlin downed the shot and his initial panic subsided. Later tonight he'd be on his way to a place where no one knew his real name. It was a damn shame he'd have to do it without the big payoff this job should have brought. If he didn't have to worry about the likes of Eugenia Tanner, he'd make a stop in Nevada and show that idiot Osbourne the true folly of trying to think for himself. As it was, he didn't have that luxury.

But there were other ways to make up for the lost score. Once he was settled, he could see about bleeding some money out of the old girl. Keeping her secrets, and there were many, had to be worth a good deal. He poured himself another shot, contemplated the amber liquid and decided he'd be better off waiting on the blackmail until that womanizing son of hers was closer to getting that office in Washington. Dear Eugenia would be more easily persuaded to pay up then.

\* \* \*

"Here we are." Sal unlocked the door, then gestured for Adeena to enter. It had taken a lot of talking on her part to convince Adeena she'd be safer at the Bellagio than at her apartment. Sal believed Ian throwing his support her way had closed the deal.

Adeena clutched her overnight bag and looked around the room. "Nice."

Sal wondered if the other woman would talk in one-word sentences from now on. Adeena had hardly said a word as they first took a cab to the airport, walked around the terminal for thirty minutes, then grabbed another cab to the hotel. "You get the room to the left. I need to make some calls, then we can, uh, plan some more." She pushed up her glasses. Something about Adeena Minor made her nervous. She was far from the blond and beautiful types she usually chased, but the intensity of those eyes, the obvious intelligence and the show of courage made her skin itch. Sal hated itching. "I thought we should eat in. You know, just in case. I mean, if that's okay with you."

"Fine. Bath. I'll take a bath."

"Bath?" Sal's voice went up an octave. Bath meant naked and she did not want her mind to go there. "Bath. Yeah. You go do that while I, umm, yeah…" Sal could feel her head nodding like one of those bobblehead dolls, but she couldn't stop. She needed to get herself under control if she was going to make it through the next few days with her sanity intact, she thought as Adeena left the room. There was too much to do before they could get to Savannah for her to be standing around mentally drooling like some pubescent boy.

"Focus." Sal blew out a breath and forced her thoughts away from a naked Adeena frolicking in the tub to what had to be done if they were to succeed. She'd already changed the destination of her flight from Atlanta to New York City. It would be easier for her to create the documents for Adeena's new identity in her office. From there they would fly to a private airport outside of Savannah under assumed names, rent a car, register at a hotel and then search for relatives or friends of Walter Morrow or Lucy Brown. She knew what high school Walter had graduated from, knew that he'd lettered in track while at Savannah State College, married Jessica Simmons in his junior year and graduated with a degree in history. A week after Adeena was born he'd gone off the radar. Three months later, James Minor Jr. had moved with his wife and child to Nevada, where he had led a quiet life as a history teacher.

Sal figured that finding out what he'd been doing before and after Adeena's birth was crucial to solving one of the puzzles. They also had to find someone credible who could give them the name of the father of Lucy's babies. Adeena seemed convinced he was behind the murders of the Brown family and the current murder attempts, and Sal had to admit it fit. It was too damn bad the person who'd sent Adeena the letter hadn't seen fit to mention a name. But then the hunt wouldn't be as challenging, she reasoned, and she did love a challenge.

Checking her buzzing phone, she winced. She'd foolishly believed there'd be a little more time before she had to talk to Cyn and admit what she'd gotten herself into. "What's up?"

"Did you find her?"

"I did. Yes." She went to her bedroom and shut the door. She was going to have do some fast talking to keep Cyn from killing her and it was best Adeena didn't overhear.

"And?"

"She's legit, Cyn. At first I didn't think so, but once she laid it all out I could see it. And then you add in those files from the lawyer. Did you read what I sent you about the twins?"

"For hell's sakes, Sal, that doesn't mean Heather was her twin. It only means she was adopted through the same shady lawyer."

"Think about it, there were only two kids with the same birthdate, the same parents. That is *not* a coincidence."

"You like her."

"What? No. I...uh, sure she seems uh, nice. More important she's in trouble and she could well be Heather's sister, so of course that's why I want to help."

"One hit-and-run does not trouble make. What if she set it up? A way to garner our sympathy."

"Then I suppose she set up getting shot at as well." As soon as the words were out of her mouth she wanted them back. She hadn't meant to mention that particular detail. Knowing Cyn as she did, she held the phone away from her ear. Even then she had no trouble hearing the response.

"Shots? Somebody's shooting at her now? What have you gotten yourself into this time, Thomasina Salamander?"

Sal rolled her eyes. Cyn was conveniently forgetting that she was the one who'd gotten Sal involved in this situation. "Hey, it wasn't at me. Some guy took a few shots at her and missed. It happened before I got there, so no danger to me. Yes, I checked and the incident was reported. One of the witnesses was a cop. All aboveboard."

"Says you."

"Says the facts. It did happen, Cyn. Tell me you can see why she needs my help."

"No. Your problem? Why is this your problem, Sal? Doesn't she have family she can go to, hide out with?"

"She doesn't. As far as she knows, her parents didn't have relatives. She's on her own, Cyn, and she plans to go to Savannah."

"Good. Then you need to get your ass back to New York and forget you ever heard of Adeena Minor."

"And do what? Go on like always and let them get to her? What if she's Heather's sister? Would you really want me to walk away, leave her swinging in the wind? You should know I can no more do that than I could walk away if you were in trouble."

"You should know what happens when you hang with women targeted for termination. Bullets don't know names, Sal. Don't care about names. I can't lose another sister."

The anguish in Cyn's voice got to her. It wasn't a matter of Cyn not caring. This was a matter of her caring too much.

"Listen for a minute, Cyn. We're not going into this dumb and blind. You know me. I'm taking extra precautions. For one, we'll be traveling to Georgia under assumed names. For two, we're only looking for information to get the cops interested enough to take another look at how Lucy Brown supposedly died." Sal didn't cross her fingers, reasoning there was enough truth in what she'd said for it not to be a lie. She didn't want to walk away from this. It had been a long time since she'd been directly involved in such an interesting situation. "If that doesn't reassure you, I know people who know people in Savannah. We'll be covered."

"You know people who know people everywhere."

"Damn right. So you know my backup is solid. Don't ask me to step away and I won't disappoint you." A loud sigh and silence met her request. "Come on, Cyn. You're the one always spouting off about truth and justice. Even if it turns out she's not Heather's sister, she needs answers before it's too late."

"Sal, Sal, Sal. Most people would run screaming in the other direction, but not you. Never you. Damn. And I'd be the one at fault for asking you to turn away from who you are, now wouldn't I? Fine. You have my understanding if not my blessing. I do expect you to check in regularly. You also have to promise you'll call Dani if you get into real trouble. She used to be a cop. But I guess I already told you that. What I didn't tell you because I didn't know before is that she looks like she can handle trouble."

"Cyn, you forget that while I may not look like I can handle trouble, I can. We'll be okay. I promise."

"Don't make promises about things you have no control of. If you get yourself killed, I'm going to be seriously pissed for infinity and beyond."

"I love you too. Don't worry. I fully expect to be out of Savannah before they figure out we're there. If not, I'll make sure the whole world knows the reason we're there. It's harder for people like this to do what they do under a spotlight."

Sal's next call was easier. When she ended the call, she had the name of a couple of contacts in Savannah who knew about local guns for hire. That was only useful if the hiring had been done in Savannah, but she was willing to bet it had. Most likely the person doing the hiring was a prominent figure from a family with old money. She'd found those who hid behind a façade of being upstanding citizens were the most dangerous.

She could work with that, Sal thought, as she relocated to the common area and her laptops. She would need to put together a list of the white influential families who'd been in Savannah at least thirty-five years ago. She could eliminate any who didn't have males between seventeen and forty back then. Once she'd narrowed down the list, she could run financials, see if anyone had large unaccounted-for withdrawals. After cracking her knuckles, she set up one of her laptops to begin the hunt.

Sal had knocked off a lot of her "to-do" list by the time Adeena joined her. Adeena had changed into a San Francisco T-shirt and jeans, which hugged her in all the right places. Sal resisted scratching the itch between her shoulder blades, silently damning those expressive eyes. Instead she returned her attention to her laptop. "Bad news. Our lawyer seems to be AWOL. Went on vacation and never made it back."

"You think he's behind this?"

"Doubtful. No big withdrawals to pay for a hit. In fact, no movement in his financials since a couple of days after your face got splashed all over the place. I'd say that means dead."

"I'd say that means someone's cleaning house." Adeena hugged her stomach and dropped into the chair directly across from Sal. "Nicholson was a long shot anyway. The way I see it, he wouldn't know who's trying to kill me. The person the mastermind hired to get rid of my mother is probably the one who dealt with Kenneth Nicholson. As far as mastermind knew, there were no babies for Nicholson to arrange adoptions for."

"You are so right." Sal squeezed her head, realizing she needed to move the puzzle pieces around. She gave up pretending to look at the screen and set her laptop aside. "So mastermind sees you, realizes he was double-crossed thirty-four years ago, goes back to original hired gun and finds out what really went down."

"Maybe he even forces hired gun to kill me to make up for what he didn't do before."

Sal shook her head. "Better if—we'll call him MM for short—hires a new hired gun to kill old hired gun, all those the old hired gun dealt with and, unfortunately, you. Why trust someone who's already proven untrustworthy? You wouldn't."

"Which means the people who killed Lucy and her family are dead or will be soon."

"Technically they didn't kill Lucy. Childbirth did."

"Bullshit!" Adeena exploded out of the chair. "Think about it. Heather and I weren't born in Savannah. No. We were born in some barely there town miles away and not in a burning house. How do you think she got there? Not on her own. Can you imagine? The stress of that could've triggered the labor, probably did. Or maybe it was bad timing all around. Either way, in a hospital with doctors on standby she could have survived the births. She would have had someone who cared about her well-being looking out for her instead of someone who only cared about harvesting what she was carrying. The fact that they denied her that alone makes them responsible."

She closed her eyes and took a deep breath. "That doesn't take into account the fact that they would have killed her if she'd survived our births. There can be no doubt about that. No doubt about what MM is responsible for."

"Right again." Feeling like a total jerk, Sal went to stand beside her. "I'm sorry. I...well, I've been looking at this as a puzzle to be solved when to you it's much more. She would have been your mother and they stole the possibility of that and of being a family from you, from Heather and from Lucy." She rubbed Adeena's arm. Her heartbeats sped up when Adeena rested her head on her shoulder, if only for a fleeting moment. "We'll get him," she found herself promising. "MM. We'll get him and we'll make him pay. If not in criminal court, then civil court and the media, which must matter to him. I'm the queen of stealthily leaking information."

"Agreed. Exposing his actions for all to see is probably the worst punishment for someone like him." Adeena wiped her eyes and looked into Sal's. "Queen, huh? Should I ask what it is you do?"

"Only if it matters to the outcome."

"Then no, I won't ask. Exposing him and what he did before, is doing now, has to lead to a police investigation. Even if they can't gather enough evidence to convict, I'll be happy to have him live the rest of his life with the stench of accusation as his constant companion."

Sal stroked Adeena's cheek lightly and found the brown skin as soft as it looked. "'Stench of accusation' sounds good. You, uh, you need anything? Drink?"

"I'm good." Adeena dropped back into the chair. "And ready for what's next. Whatever that is."

Sal grabbed her laptop and positioned herself next to Adeena. "We'll go to New York this evening, get you a new look and an ID to go with it, then fly to Savannah first thing tomorrow. Another charter flight to keep us off MM's radar as long as possible."

Adeena's face lit up. "New York? I went there once. But I already told you that."

"Was it a family vacation?"

"I wish. It was supposed to be a reward for winning a big competition. Best elementary school math whiz in Carson City. My mom was almost bursting with pride. Dad too. But he was proud of everything I did. Even the little things." She waved her hands. "Okay. Anyway, I remember looking out the window as we were flying in and thinking the city looked like a whole new world. Unfortunately, I spent most of the time going to museums and getting quizzed afterward on what I'd learned. At nine that felt more like punishment than reward. I always swore I'd go back. Funny the things you forget."

"Wish there was more time to show you the fun stuff this time, but we'll be there seven hours tops. But do you know what that means?"

"We'll be in the city seven hours tops?"

Sal laughed. "No. It means you have to come back another time. My place is better than your average crash pad. I know the city like the back of my hand, so you'd get to know the non-tourist parts as well."

"So impulsive. After this is over you may regret you ever met me, let alone invited me to your apartment."

"Not a chance." Sal rubbed her hands in anticipation of what they were going to pull off. "This trip is going to be awesome."

"Except for the part where someone may try to kill us."

"You got me," Sal said. She shrugged. "Won't happen on my watch. Too smart for that. For backup I was thinking we should contact a reporter at one of the Savannah news stations. Not the ones who do the evening news, but the ones who do the live shots in the middle of the storm or the middle of the night. They're still looking for that story that will make them famous. Your story has 'attention getter' written all over it. They'll dig and hard. Might save us the trouble and find out the identity of the father of, umm…the father." It was easier for her not to think of the man who'd gotten Lucy pregnant and was most likely responsible for her death as Adeena's father. "I know someone who could get me a name fairly quickly."

"I can work on writing something up on the way to New York. We should include photos. The famous flying video. Then have it hand delivered to the station. How long before they would go live with something like that?"

"We can give them forty-eight hours to air at least a tidbit before we say we'll move on, give the story to another reporter. I don't believe it will come to that. With you being a celebrity and the spitting image of a woman who supposedly died *before* giving birth, they'll be salivating to break this story."

"And Heather?" Adeena crossed her arms over her chest and thrust her jaw forward. "I noticed you didn't mention her. Don't you think they'll be salivating more over me having a white-looking twin?"

"Well…yeah, about that." Sal gave a pained smile. "The problem is we don't yet have concrete proof of that part. I'm afraid mentioning it could have them discounting the other stuff. My thinking is someone knows Lucy was expecting twins. No. Wait. We should say you were told you have a twin. A fraternal twin, who was adopted by a different family. One that you're looking for. Yeah. That's an even better story."

"Yes, yes. The news media love those types of stories."

"Once they air it, people will come forward. Maybe we'll get the identity of the baby-daddy that way. Lucy told someone."

"That's fine except people have faulty memories or they lie outright. For all we know an old boyfriend could step forward wanting the hype."

"That's why we'll be doing our own digging. There's no law that we can't reach out to anyone who comes forward, pump them for specifics, offer money if they need that sort of motivation. I'm also doing a search on murders in Savannah that have occurred since your rise to stardom. The lawyer won't be the only one. He won't even be the first."

"No. The first hired gun will be the first. Had to get to him to know who else needed to be gotten rid of. You're really good at this, Sal. I would never have thought of doing that."

"Here's where I confess to knowing something about the way the scum of the earth do things. I've never sunk that low, but I have dipped a toe into waters that weren't, say, strictly legal." She looked to Adeena and waited for any fallout.

"Did that water have in it the blood of innocents?"

"Not even close."

"Then it's not a problem. I want to go to her neighborhood. Lucy's. Get a feel of where she lived and who she might have been. I still want to find someone who was around back then who knew her or her family. Before doing the reporter thing."

"Then we'll do that first. One other thing." Sal adjusted her glasses. "For the, uh, the flight to Savannah we'll need to change your appearance. I'm thinking drastically."

# CHAPTER ELEVEN

Adeena knew she was acting like a starstruck tourist, but she didn't care. New York City was eye-opening. Like Vegas on steroids times a thousand. Everywhere she looked, the buildings were tall like in her memory. Vegas and the danger to her life seemed far away in the wash of lights.

"You like?"

She turned to Sal, who had encouraged her to view the scenery through the open sunroof of the limo. "Love. I love it! This, this is a city."

"Coming up on one of my favorite areas. Times Square."

"Now this is like Vegas at night. Only more. Hey, I recognize that billboard. They always show it on TV. Now I wish I had a video camera. One that's better than the one on my phone. And I'd better sit before I get dizzy." She sank into the leather of the roomy back seat. "It was dangerous showing me that. Might be forced to take you up on that offer of a future visit."

"I don't view that as a threat. My place is always open to those who show the proper respect for my city. This is only one facet. You'd need days to see it all. Manhattan, the Bronx, Staten Island, Harlem… I could go on."

"So long as I don't have to take a test afterward."

"No test."

"Where do you live."

"Upper West Side. It's a straight shot to Times Square on the subway. It's nerdy, but I get a kick out of saying I live on Broadway."

"Because if you make it there, you can make it anywhere?"

Sal grinned, flashing her dimple and gave Adeena a shoulder bump. "You get it. You definitely have to come back now. I mean, you know the song."

Adeena laughed. "After a few shots, I can sing the newer one by Jay Z and Alicia Keys." She returned to gawking and sooner than she would have liked, the limo came to a smooth stop in front of a tall white building that looked more like an office building than an apartment complex.

"Home sweet home," Sal announced. "And here comes Damon. Best doorman in the city. How's it going? The kids?"

"Great, all great. Both looking forward to that gaming camp you got them in." He held the limo door open for Sal and Adeena to alight. "Haven't had to say a word about homework, chores or cleaning rooms. We owe you."

"It was nothing, but I wouldn't turn down another invite to Sunday dinner."

Damon grinned. "Say the word and it's done."

"I'll let you know." Sal handed the limo driver a tip when he delivered their bags. "Listen, Damon, I'm only going to be here for a few hours. If anyone comes sniffing around, I'm here alone and don't want to be disturbed."

Damon nodded. "You want the boys to continue seeing to your plants?"

"Yeah. Not sure for how long, but I'll let you know. And tell them not to be besting any of my top scores."

Damon laughed. "You on your own with that." He went ahead of them and opened the door.

Adeena grabbed the handle of her carry-on bag from Sal after they entered the building. Inside, it looked nothing like an office building. The lobby was spacious and bright with cathedral lighting and stained glass windows. "Nice. Somehow I think I'm going to be saying that a lot around you. But don't for a minute think I'm talking about you."

"You're okay, Adeena." Sal put out a hand to hold the elevator open and motioned for Adeena to enter first. "I think you'll like the view." She pushed the button for the top floor.

*She lives in the penthouse*, Adeena thought. Her brain couldn't wrap around the amount of money it would take to rent a penthouse in New York City. Certainly more zeros than she'd ever see on a paycheck.

She stepped inside Sal's apartment and stopped, stunned by the wall of floor-to-ceiling windows that let in New York City at night. Adeena was sure she could stay in this spot and enjoy the view forever. It probably looked even better at sunrise or maybe sunset. "Okay, 'nice' is not going to do it."

"You like?"

"There's that tepid word again. 'Love.' No. 'Adore.' No. 'Lust for.' Let's say it's 'absofab,' and I'm so jealous you get to see this view all the time." Curiosity propelled her forward. She took in the lofty ceiling, the hardwood floor, the colorful rugs and the mixture of modern furniture and antiques. "You definitely should not have shown me this. I may never leave."

"But there's more. You must see the terrace before you decide whether to stay forever." Sal walked toward what looked like a closet but turned out to be an elevator. "I usually use the stairs, but..." She pointed to their luggage.

"You have more than one floor?"

"Three."

"Three floors?" Now Adeena knew her mind couldn't conceive of the number of zeros on the rental agreement. She entered the elevator and thought she was in a different reality. A great different reality.

Sal pressed the middle button and the elevator ascended smoothly. "You're surprised. Probably think I'm a big-time criminal now."

"No. I…this is New York. I was expecting something, I don't know. Something a little bigger than a breadbasket. Not this. Not the elevator, but everything else. I'm dazzled."

"I admit it's over the top. I spent a number of years in a breadbasket. Swore I was going to have better one day. I've had a little luck here and there, my job pays very well, so now it's one day."

"Can you buy me a lottery ticket before we leave?" Adeena asked as she stepped out of the elevator. "Or maybe I'll rub your arm, hope some luck rubs off."

The dimple flashed. "Rub away. This adventure keeps getting better and better."

Being reminded of why they were here was sobering. "I'd almost managed to forget about the rest. View envy will do that."

"That doesn't mean you shouldn't enjoy the view. In fact, it means you have to enjoy it more."

"Because I might not make it back?"

Sal's expression turned serious. "Having faced down death means you're obligated to enjoy life more. Push yourself harder, embrace new experiences with open arms. Well, that's my belief. As borne out by the kick-ass media room you'll get to see later. But for now, we'll park your luggage in this guest room."

The room had a slightly different view as the one downstairs but one just as striking. It seemed Sal believed in color for everything, from the red walls to the yellow window treatments and the rainbow-colored bedspread.

"Bathroom and closet through the door on the right. If you want, you can catch a few hours now and do your ID later."

"Now. I want to stay focused. But maybe I can see that media room first?"

"You got it. Back in, say, five."

Once Sal was gone, Adeena walked to the window and looked out. She took a mental snapshot and promised herself that no matter what she found in Savannah, she'd remember the awe she felt for this city. And for Sal and her wisdom. But now she needed to check out the bathroom.

Sal was waiting when she returned. "You hungry? You didn't eat before, so I thought you might be hungry."

"I could eat. You cook?"

"Actually, I do. But I was thinking of calling down and ordering calzones or pizza if you prefer. It's been more than a week since I had one."

"You like calzones?"

"There's that tepid word 'like' again. Love. I love calzones."

"Smartass."

"The biggest."

\* \* \*

Beau tried to lock the front door quietly. It was late to be out on a Sunday night and in his defense, he'd spent the evening studying with Sinead and a couple of other friends and not partying. Still, he winced, spotting the light spilling from his father's study. He'd been sure he timed his arrival so that the soon-to-be senate candidate would be off discussing strategy in his assistant's bedroom. He considered taking the back way but quickly dismissed that as cowardly.

"Beau? Need to talk to you, son," his father called out before Beau passed his office.

He entered his father's domain with the oversized desk, the many photos of his father with dignitaries and the lingering smell of cigar smoke. Beau had never liked this room. This was where he got lectured, got told bogus bullshit that was always supposed to be for his own good and never was. "Yes?" He refused to be like Phillip and add the sir.

"You're out late. Date?" Jackson gestured toward the chair next to his desk. A tall, handsome man, he worked hard at keeping his body in shape. It was one of the few things Beau felt they had in common.

"Studying. Finals."

"How's that going for you?"

"Fine."

"Listen son, your grandmother asked me to speak with you."

He didn't bother to cover up a groan. "If this is about Sinead, don't bother. We're just good friends. No benefits." Friendship was something his grandmother knew nothing about. As far as he could tell, she tended to value people based on how useful they could be. More recently it had been how useful they could be to his father's campaign.

"You and she spend a lot of time together. Your grandmother has concerns. It's natural."

"Like you or she would know what's natural," he muttered and pushed blond hair off his forehead. "You want to know why I spend a lot of time over there? Maria isn't there. Nobody bugs me about how I look, how I act. Nobody worries about what I might say next or tries to brainwash me. And Sinead gets the whole running for office thing. What's the big deal? I thought the Tisdales were rich enough, *Republican* enough, to be acceptable."

"It's okay for you and Sinead to be friends. What I want you to know is that I understand if your feelings for Sinead have changed over the years." Jackson smiled.

"What are you trying to say?"

"I'm letting you know it's okay if you and Sinead are having sex and—"

"But we're not!" Beau threw up his arms. Would they ever listen? "How many times do I have to say it!"

"Settle down, son. I'm not here to judge. Despite what your grandmother may say, there's no shame in bedding black women. The problem is you're almost eighteen and at that age it's easy to get caught up, as you kids say. Happened to me at your age." Jackson leaned back in his big, black chair and propped his feet on his desk.

He couldn't say he was surprised, considering the number of women his father had gone through. "Bet that went over well."

"Your grandmother was concerned." Jackson loosened his tie. "It's a fact of life that you see things differently when you're young. Think differently. I was no exception. For a while I thought it was okay to think there was a future for us. Eventually I came to see I hadn't been thinking things through, that it couldn't work out. Your grandmother helped me understand, put me on the right path."

Beau wondered what would happen if he told his father his black girl was a black boy. He'd probably stroke out, he decided, and that fallout was not something he was willing to deal with now. "What happened to that girl? The one you thought you loved till Grandmother told you you didn't."

"I went my way, she went hers. Heard a few years later she died. I was really sorry to hear that. So much potential wiped out too soon."

"Sounds to me like you still think about her. I don't care what Grandmother says. You weren't wrong if it was love."

"You're missing the point, Beau. Love isn't always enough. We're Tanners and as such we have obligations. More is expected of us. I know that's tough for you to hear at your age, but it needs to be said. Bottom line is that sex with Sinead is okay, but it can never be more than that. You're young. Trust me, when you get older you'll realize love does not make the world go around. Not when it's between you and someone with a different social standing."

"Get real. You mean race! Don't try to pretend you don't." Beau slumped back against the chair. Just once he'd like his dad to surprise him, say something that didn't make him want to cringe. It obviously wasn't going to happen today or any other day. But that didn't mean he had to stay, had to hear any more.

Resolve propelled him out of the chair as if he were a rocket. "I can't take this bullshit anymore! If you really believe what you're saying, then I'm glad I'll be old enough to vote next year. If you really believe a black girl isn't good enough for your son, then you don't deserve to be a representative of the people!" Too angry to stay, he ran from the room and almost took down his mother in the hallway.

"Beau, what's wrong?"

*You don't really want to know*, he thought as bitterness ate at his insides. She never wanted to know. "Ask your husband."

He brushed past her without giving her time to respond, tore up the stairs and, once in his room, locked the door and threw himself on the bed.

He should have taken Sinead up on her offer to spend the night. Tomorrow was the official announcement day and his dad would be too busy to lecture him about black women and sex. What a joke. Sex and women were the farthest thing on his mind. Even if it wasn't, his dad was the last person to lecture *him* about sex. He wasn't the one fucking every woman that moved.

He ignored the knock on his door. He didn't want to talk to anyone. But he especially didn't want to talk to anyone in this house.

"Beau, please open the door."

The gentle pleading in his mother's voice got to him. Feeling like the weight of the world was on his shoulders, he unlocked the door.

"May I come in?"

He stepped back, stood even when she lowered herself onto his bed.

"It seems we never talk anymore."

"Did we ever?" he shot back.

"Yes. When you were younger." She patted his hand. "You seemed upset downstairs and I thought talking might help. I know your father's run for senate seems like it's taking over your life."

"Only because it is," he retorted. "He hasn't even officially announced he's running and we're already on display like show dogs. Do this, don't do that. And the worst is Maria. When did she become the boss of all of us? I used to think this was my home, but now…"

"All of us are going to have to make sacrifices, Beau. Maria is only doing what's best for your father, his campaign."

"So we don't matter? Only the great Jackson Tanner matters? Not to me. And I won't vote for him or any of his ridiculous Republican cronies. They need to realize we're in the twenty-first century. The world is not the same as it was even ten years ago. And hello, it won't be the same five years from now. It can't."

Hope Tanner reached for his hand and held it to her chest. "You're still young, full of youthful idealism. And that's as it should be. But your father feels like he can do some good if he's elected to office. Frankly, politics isn't all that it seems from the outside. To get elected, your father has to be willing to compromise on some of the issues. I don't expect you to agree, but that's the way the system works."

Beau snorted. "The system is broken. Everyone knows that."

"Not everyone." She turned his head so he was looking at her. "You have a few more weeks of school left and then you'll be off doing good deeds. All I ask is for you to work with us for those weeks. I promise to speak with Maria, tell her to give you some space, if you'll promise to have a little more understanding of the process your father has to work through. If you'll agree to quietly disagree."

He took his time considering the deal. With Maria off his back he could ignore the rest. Nothing he said to his parents was going to make them change their mind. And in a few weeks he'd be gone, out of their sphere of influence anyway. "My friendship with Sinead has nothing to do with our deal. No matter what they think, we are *not* having sex. We've never had sex."

"I know that. That's your grandmother's concern, fueled by events from the past. You're a good son, Beau, and I appreciate your willingness to listen."

"What do you get out of it? I mean, won't your life be messed up the most?"

"Why, I get a chance to be a senator's wife. And once your father's in office, there's nothing to say his policies can't be tweaked." She kissed his cheek. "Get some rest and let me worry about your father and Maria."

Later, as Beau drifted off to sleep a thought jolted him awake. His mother most likely knew about the other women, about Maria. He wasn't sure what that made her for staying all these years. Maybe it made her smart and ambitious. And considering the deal they'd struck, it made her a better politician than his dad. He couldn't say if that same quality would make her the better senator.

# CHAPTER TWELVE

Adeena landed at the small airport outside of Savannah as Lisa Mitchell. Sal, going by the name of Tim Thomas, had done a great job of exaggerating her eyes, slimming her nose and accentuating her chin. Her breasts were considerably larger and the long, curly wig she sported was a garish reddish-blond. She didn't know what the hair, the breasts and the suggestive clothes did for anyone else, but they made her feel like she should be on a street corner hawking her wares.

She'd argued the name was too obvious, but Sal overruled her by pointing out that MM most likely didn't know the name on her birth certificate. And since Sal had been the one to create the necessary fake documents and pay for two flights on what she would term luxury airplanes, she finally conceded, somewhat graciously. Initially she'd been worried about what she'd owe in return, but Sal quickly made it clear that being able to participate in the great adventure was payment enough. Adeena figured she owed Cynthia Kennedy a huge thanks for sending Sal, her money and her dubious connections.

"I still think you overdid it with the tits," she argued, clutching her small backpack to her breasts. "Did we really have to go there? And I won't talk about the hair." She growled when Sal's gaze dropped to her breasts. "Quit drooling. You of all people know they're fake."

"Still." Sal wiggled her bushy black eyebrows, which matched her darkened hair and a ridiculous-looking mustache. "Would your friend Ian recognize you?"

"I guess that's a damn good point in your favor. If I break my neck in these ridiculous heels, I'm suing." It didn't help that Sal was dressed as a man and got to wear comfortable shoes.

"So noted." Sal pulled their bags toward a waiting limo.

"Being with you is constantly being forced to say 'wow.'" Adeena looked down at her heels, then accepted Sal's help with maneuvering into the limo. It amazed her what a big difference shoes could make. "Wouldn't a rental car be more practical? Not that I'm complaining."

"It'll be waiting for us at the hotel. You'll be happy to know I followed your suggestion and went with a boring sedan instead of a flashy sports car."

"It only makes sense for us to try and blend in. Flashy does not blend." Adeena resisted the urge to stroke the soft-as-butter leather seats. Maybe she did need a newer car. "Hold up. Do you know how to drive? Being from New York City, I mean."

"I spent most of my adolescence in a suburb of Boston. I can drive. I'll show you the toys I have to prove it when you come for that visit."

The limo ride was smooth enough to lull Adeena to sleep. Excitement about being in New York and nervousness over what was to come meant she'd gotten little sleep the night before. The next thing she knew, they were pulling into the half-circle driveway in front of a hotel that looked more like a large house. She pulled her head up from where it was lolling against Sal's shoulder, rubbed her eyes and surreptitiously swiped the sides of her mouth, thankful to discover no drool had been involved. "Nice."

"Welcome to the Portman. I believe you'll like the accommodations."

Adeena stepped out of the car with help from the driver. Inside, the lobby spoke of tasteful luxury. It looked more like a home library, with bookcase-lined walls and comfortable seating. There was, however, nothing that looked like a check-in desk. Before she could ask, a nattily dressed staff person was there, tablet in hand. They were checked in with quiet efficiency, and before she could do more than yawn, the bellboy was ushering them into a suite on the top floor.

"Be sure to check out the rooftop lounge." The bellboy pocketed the tip from Sal. "Everyone loves the view and the specialty drinks. There's a nice park right across the street if you feel like a walk or a run. Be sure to call if you need anything. We pride ourselves on our service."

"We'll do that." Sal closed the door behind him. "You run?"

"Only if someone's after me. I walk my dog every day. Does that count?"

"Don't tell me I was supposed to rent one of those?"

Adeena laughed. "If anyone could…"

"I'll make a note for next time."

"For my visit to New York, right?"

"Exactly. You want to finish your nap or go check out the neighborhood?"

She was running on reserves and was afraid if she fell asleep again she wouldn't wake up for a week. "Neighborhood. I hope we can find someone home this time of morning. It'll be close to nine thirty by the time we get there."

"This is the perfect time to find the nosy neighbor. You know, the type who doesn't work and has time to keep up with everyone's business. With a little finesse it shouldn't be hard to get them to share information."

"If she or he was the nosy neighbor thirty years ago, they might be dead," she pointed out.

"It's a statistical fact that nosy neighbors live ten point four years longer than the average person. Something about being too busy to worry about their own situation."

"You totally made that up."

"Yeah, but I was quick with it. Should get points for that."

"No need to worry about points with me. I'm here without a killer riding my butt because you stepped up. I won't forget it."

"I don't work for gratitude."

Because Sal looked uncomfortable, Adeena poked her arm and said, "You can't get away from mine. Do you think I should change? Looking like this won't make anyone think of Lucy."

"Good idea, but grab a hat and sunglasses until we find that nosy neighbor. I'll get the car while you change and meet me downstairs."

Adeena grabbed her bag and raced for a bedroom. A quick shower made her face her own again. She threw on the first outfit she came across, eager to find someone linked to Lucy's past.

Sal was waiting downstairs as promised. "That was quick. I'm used to waiting longer."

"Won't have to with me." Adeena hopped in the car and fastened her seat belt. "I don't like to be kept waiting."

"Good to know," Sal said as she eased into traffic. "Tell me something about Adeena Minor. Who is she when she isn't running from murdering bastards?"

"Dull, boring, ordinary. Pick your adjective. I work a lot and I walk my dog. Pathetic huh? Maybe I should be thanking MM for getting me out of my rut." She turned to look out the window, wanting to think that Lucy had seen some of the same sights.

"Not even close. What is it you work at so hard?"

"My team and I manage the models that forecast traffic volumes for the Las Vegas region." Her job was more complex than that, but she'd found it was easier for all concerned to give the short answer.

"For the government?"

"Quasi. The work I do is federally required, and while we are supported by public funds, my agency isn't technically part of the federal, state or local government."

"And is that fun for you?"

"It's complicated. I enjoy what I do, but I'm ready for a change in scenery. And I have a new boss who is...challenging. We'll leave it at that."

"Why not quit?"

"Pesky things like bills that need to be paid. I have been looking. Eventually something will come through. Of course, my boss might decide to fire me for being out of the office so long."

"You don't sound cut up about it."

"Actually, it could be the kick I need. Being without steady income would force me to look harder."

"You have somewhere in mind?"

Adeena talked about her top choices, which led to a discussion of the cities Sal had visited and the sights she'd enjoyed the most.

"Sounds like helicopter tours are your favorite touristy thing to do." Adeena was feeling envious of all Sal had experienced.

"I guess they are. It's the best way for me to get a sense of the city. I like cities."

"I'd like to experience more." Adeena consulted the map in her lap. "The street's coming up," she said a step ahead of the instructions from the GPS unit. "I guess you could say I use paper maps to get a sense of a city. I collect them, like to pull them out and look at them."

"Nothing wrong with that." Sal slowed down and turned on her blinker. "I don't know about you, but I haven't noticed a lot of buildings that look like they've been around longer than ten to fifteen years for the past ten blocks. Could be they spruced up this street." She turned, drove down to the stop sign. "According to the address the house was down on the right."

Adeena took in the newer, larger-sized houses, the perfectly manicured lawns. She wasn't going to find a sense of Lucy or her family here. "No nosy neighbor from thirty years ago. Looks like Plan A got kicked to the curb."

"I would say it was a result of the fire, but judging by the style, none of these houses date to back then. Almost as if the whole neighborhood received a makeover."

"Yeah, I doubt anybody here remembers Lucy or the fire except anecdotally. Sorry I dragged you out here for nothing."

"It's not nothing. I now can cross flying into Savannah disguised as a man off my bucket list." Sal fingered her fake mustache.

Adeena smiled. Seemed Sal was a bucket half-full kind of woman. "You're a nice person, Sal."

"Don't let that get around to my associates." She pulled into a driveway and turned the car around. "I think we should hit the hotel, catch some Zs, then figure out what next is."

"That works. One of the steps should be checking into the history of the neighborhood. It obviously went through extensive gentrification. There have to be articles of before and after. Most likely there were some protests of the new development by those getting displaced. With any luck, we could find where some of them got shuttled off to."

"See. Not such a waste after all." Sal programmed the hotel address into the GPS unit.

She heard the teasing and smiled. "Don't make me have a chat with your associates about your niceness."

* * *

Eugenia glanced at the clock and frowned. She thought she'd been clear that Conlin was to call with an update at three o'clock. It was fifteen after now and she was beyond being upset. Lateness might seem like a minor thing to some, but to her it was a sign. In this case it was a sign that Conlin had perhaps outlived his usefulness. Jackson was announcing his candidacy in forty-five minutes and she needed assurances the Minor girl wouldn't be a problem.

Why she expected this part of the operation to go any smoother than the rest, she couldn't say. She'd found out from Burlett that the Minors weren't who they claimed to be. Before he could pinpoint where they'd been around the time Lucy had given birth, he'd have to first unearth their true identities, which would take longer. For Eugenia his report had only solidified her belief the parents had played some part in what happened thirty-four years ago. They might even have been present at the birth and snatched up the girl right then.

"Is everything okay here?"

Eugenia stowed her phone in her purse and gave Maria a cool smile. While she truly believed Maria was an excellent choice for Jackson's campaign, she had yet to decide if she could trust her with the Minor matter. Women like Maria collected dirt better than dust rags. The good ones knew when to use the dirt to their advantage. For now she thought it best to hold this particular problem close to the vest. "Everything's fine. I would hope all is in place for the announcement?"

Maria's perfectly arched brows rose up her forehead as if in annoyance. "Of course. I wanted to speak with you privately about Beau."

"Beau will fall in line. I'll see to that." She took exception to Maria's tone. It was one thing for her to express concerns about Beau. She was family after all. Maria wasn't.

"Actually Hope requested that I, shall we say, give him some space. Apparently he and Jackson had a major difference of opinion over his relationship with Sinead Tisdale. Why Jackson felt the need to discuss it with him is a mystery to me. He should have realized it only serves to give the relationship more importance to someone's of Beau's age. We'll be lucky if he doesn't run off and get married. Men," she added with a shake of her head that seem to classify all men as clueless.

Eugenia gave a disapproving sniff. "I myself asked Jackson to speak with the boy. Beau is young and headstrong. It is my strong belief that he needs guidance from his father, and his father alone, at this stage in his life."

"I see." Maria smoothed down her knee-length black shirt, looking every inch the successful political consultant she was. "In the future it would be better to run these issues through me. The next month will set the tone for Jackson's campaign."

Eugenia gave her a hint of a smile. "I have been around the block a few times, *dear*. I understand very well what's at stake. I also understand about family relationships and Beau's feelings toward you and your current role in his life. If Hope asked you to back off *her* son, I'm certain she had a good reason."

Maria gave an elegant shrug. "I would hope we *all* understand Jackson is my primary concern. That is to say, getting Jackson elected. If you'll excuse me, I have a few last-minute details to attend to."

Eugenia seethed as she watched Maria strut off. Closing her eyes against the anger fighting to erupt, she knew she must be getting old not to have picked up sooner on the addition of sex to Jackson and Maria's relationship. She must have been thrown off by the fact Maria was older than Jackson's usual women. And while Maria made the best of what she had to work with, she wasn't the drop-dead gorgeous type he favored.

Apparently neither of those details mattered in this case and that was worrisome. She couldn't help but think Jackson was surely mad to tangle with someone he needed to keep on his side far longer than his dalliances usually lasted. With all else that was going on, she didn't need to be worried about what would happen when his interest turned to a younger, prettier woman. And turn it would, as Jackson was involved.

As far as she knew, there had only been one instance when he'd been completely enthralled with a woman and that had created the disaster she was dealing with now. Much like now, she'd been caught flat-footed by what was going on right under her very nose. Back then it had taken a few words from the housekeeper to let her know how far Jackson had dug in, how deep the relationship had grown. She'd felt she had no choice but to shove Jackson back on the right track. That was a mistake she'd realized too late.

In hindsight Eugenia had come to see the relationship would have eventually fizzled to nothing on its own. There had been no need for her to send the little upstart packing. When Jackson found out, he'd been furious on the girl's behalf and outraged he'd been used to deprive her of a job. In his anger he'd defied her edict about having any contact with the girl. He'd gone to give her money and ended up leaving something behind.

Eugenia hadn't found out the girl was pregnant until it was too late to get rid of it. Again it was her housekeeper who brought her the news the girl had returned to town eight months pregnant. According to the housekeeper, Lucy was keeping the name of the father of the baby a secret.

But like the housekeeper, Eugenia had done the math and come to the logical conclusion. She'd given the girl an out and was rebuffed, leaving Eugenia no choice but to take drastic measures. Any mother would have done the same. Her son was much too important to have his life spoiled by a girl of no consequence. End of story.

To Eugenia's regret her relationship with Jackson had changed. It was as if she was the one who caused the problem. He became distant, not making the effort to hold up his part of the conversation at mealtimes. Most of his time was spent alone in his room with the door shut and the music on high. She'd told herself their relationship would improve eventually. And when she shipped him back north, she had consoled herself with the knowledge the right thing had been done.

He'd gone back to dating the right type of girls, proving her right. It hadn't mattered to her that they came one after another after another. He'd been too young to settle down. Then came senior year. He met Hope and Eugenia had allowed herself to hope as the relationship grew and held. And eventually there had been grandsons for her. Handsome grandsons who would carry on the Tanner name and with luck, have fine sons of their own when the time was right.

"It's showtime, Grandmother."

She came out of her musings with a start and gave Beau a quick once-over. He looked quite dashing in the black suit, the crisp white shirt. She made a note to speak with him about the length of his hair. The blond locks were brushing his shoulders and falling into his eyes, obscuring his good looks. "Don't you look handsome." She took his arm and let him escort her out of the cramped back office to the main room at Jackson's campaign headquarters. "I hope you realize how much your father appreciates your presence today."

"Mom and I struck a deal."

"Oh." She made the connection between the deal and the request for Maria to back off. It seemed Hope was smarter than the rest of them. "I hope you're looking forward to working in Haiti this summer."

"Totally. The people there need a lot of help. Sinead and I started a donation thing. A senior give-back thing." He shrugged and brushed the hair off his forehead. "It's something more."

"Wonderful, dear." She patted his arm, thinking they would find a way to use that. Maybe in one of Jackson's speeches. "I realize how much you feel smothered by the recently imposed restrictions and I sympathize. This trip will be good for you, something to polish your résumé."

Eugenia gave out the last round of air kisses and accepted her grandson Phillip's offer to escort her to her car. The first official fundraising dinner had gone very well. "You did well tonight, Phillip. Perhaps one day it will be you running for office."

He would make a great candidate, she thought. He was handsome, with his mother's good looks, his father's dark hair and blue eyes. A star athlete in both basketball and football, he was also very well spoken. And unlike his older brother, he was eager to please. They would have no worries about Phillip spouting off at the mouth at a fundraising dinner or at any of a number of events Jackson and his family were going to have to be seen at over the next ten months.

"I don't know about that, Grandmother. Right now my number one goal's to be starting quarterback this fall." He waved off her driver, opened the door and helped her get in.

"I'm sure you can do whatever you put your mind to." She held up her face for his kiss, gave a wave and settled against the backseat of the roomy sedan.

"Where to, Ms. Tanner?"

She allowed Charles the easy familiarity because they'd been through a lot together over the years. She trusted his discretion implicitly. As a former marine, he could be counted on to follow orders and understood the game of life couldn't always be played by society's rules. "I haven't heard from Conlin. I believe it's time he and I had a chat. Face to face."

"Yes, ma'am. I have the address."

"I don't know what I would do without you, Charles." On the way across town, she replayed the day and thought about the suggestions she would share with Maria over the next month. She considered it the most crucial time to establish their message and get the money people firmly committed.

When the vehicle pulled into a cracked driveway barely bigger than the car thirty minutes later, she took in her surroundings in disdain. Eugenia had never understood why Conlin chose to live in this tiny one-story, two-bedroom house located in a questionable neighborhood. This was the first and last time they would meet here, she decided. If Conlin couldn't be bothered to come to her, she would find someone who would.

As Charles came around to open her door, he triggered an extra bright security light. The light amplified the house's flaws, from the sagging gutter and the missing shingles to the desperate need for a new paint job. "I hope he doesn't have anything armed to blow," she said. She took Charles' hand so he could help her get out of the vehicle.

"Probably not to blow." His smile showed the gleam of white teeth against his dark skin. "Conlin never deals with bombs."

"I guess there's something to be thankful in that."

"Would you like me to go in and bring him out here, Ms. Tanner? Save you a trip."

"I'm already out, but thank you for offering to sacrifice yourself, Charles. I only hope this trip isn't a waste of time. He should have spotted us on one of those surveillance cameras I'm sure he has set up. And come to think of it, there's not a light on inside. In a neighborhood like this, you think he would set them on a timer to discourage burglaries."

Charles rushed ahead and rang the doorbell, then returned to help Eugenia up the three steep cinderblock steps.

"I do so hate to waste my time." Eugenia walked to a window and peered inside. There was no movement. "I don't like this at all. Ring that bell again."

The result from the second ring was much like the first—no response. She cocked her head, listened closely and still could not discern any noise from inside. "We might as well go," she said and huffed. "If he is here, he obviously does *not* want to see me. And either way, I absolutely refuse to stand out here on this porch waiting for entry like I'm some common solicitor."

"Understood, Ms. Tanner." Again he helped her down what served as stairs and to the car. He closed her door and walked around the car. Opening the front door, he asked for permission to check with the neighbor across the street who'd just walked out of his house.

He was back moments later. "Bad news," he said as he slipped into the car. "Conlin was packing up that truck of his about this time last night. When the neighbor across the street returned a couple of hours later, it was gone. He says he heard that Conlin sold his house to the company that's been coming in tearing down old houses and putting up bigger new ones on the next block. I slipped him a little cash, asked him to call me if Conlin should return."

"Damn!" Eugenia didn't normally give in to vulgarity, but too many things had gone wrong lately. "That girl. It has to be that girl. Something obviously went wrong and he's too much of a coward to tell me. And after all the work I've sent his way over the years."

"I got a buddy out there who can look into it. Owns his own business and does good work."

"Tonight? Get in touch with him tonight. Now that Jackson has announced his candidacy, every second counts."

"I'm sure that won't be a problem for him."

"I'm willing to pay a bonus if he works fast."

# CHAPTER THIRTEEN

"I think I found the Holy Code." Adeena did a happy seat wiggle. It was Tuesday morning, but she felt like she'd been searching for information on Lucy's old neighborhood for weeks.

Sal laughed. "Holy Code. Good one."

"This guy, Dr. Anthony Rucker now, wrote about the transformation of the neighborhood for his master's thesis. He's from here, got his degree from Georgia Tech. What's good for us is that the Georgia Tech library gives anybody online access to some of their documents and his thesis is one of them. Couple of hours and I should have more names for you."

"If there's a goddess, some of the former residents will be the ordinary type and have known the Browns as opposed to the activists you uncovered yesterday. Not that there's anything wrong with activists."

"I know what you meant." Adeena opened the file and began reading it. Like Sal she hoped for names of residents who had known Lucy well enough to be able to name the father.

"Remember to scan, not scour."

Adeena didn't roll her eyes. The caution was needed. But it wasn't her fault the information on the neighborhood sparked her interest. After reading the first few pages of the thesis, she promised herself she'd come back and read for depth later.

"Here it is! First chapter. The Stingray. Owned and operated by the Fishers for fifty years. That's Harrison Fisher and his wife, Lana Marie Fisher. Apparently it was the place everyone in the neighborhood visited regularly." Adeena scanned a couple more pages. "They opened a restaurant after the store closed. The Soul Garden in—"

"Got them. Retired ten years ago and turned the management over to their daughter, Essie Newsome. She's only a couple of years older than Lucy. They probably went to school together. The restaurant opens at eleven."

"We should go there now. Someone has to be there to open, start cooking."

"Better if I went at eleven, bought lunch, chatted up the waitress, then asked to speak to the manager."

"Why you? With my face there's no need to chat up a waitress."

"Me, because I'm the lookout. This is only the initial meet. A chance to feel her out, see what she knows, see if anyone else has been asking questions about Lucy and her pregnancy. Safer that way."

Adeena put a hand to her stomach. "You found something, didn't you?"

"Someone. A guy named Bonnie Franks. His badly beaten body was found in a park not twenty-four hours after your world debut. Definite signs of torture. And Franks lived in Lucy's neighborhood, had been in trouble since his teen years."

"You think he was the first hired gun. The one MM hired years ago?"

Sal nodded. "There'll be others. Maybe waiting to be discovered."

She tried to tell herself they deserved it, but the knowing still made her feel sick. "Why wasn't I first?"

"That I don't know. I could speculate, say it's a distance thing." Sal pushed at her glasses, frowning. "Sounds terrible, but maybe MM thought Franks was more, uh, of a threat."

"You were going to say important. It's okay. The person who knows where the bodies are hidden is more important if you're a murdering bastard. Get to him and he leads you to the others. Me, I'm just one person."

"And way more important than Franks from my viewpoint. You're alive and we need to keep you that way."

She took in Sal's earnest expression and some of the sickness faded. "Which brings us back to you going to the restaurant, doing the reconnaissance and bringing important-me Southern food. That means—"

"Collard greens, mac and cheese, fried chicken, yams, cornbread and real sweet ice tea. My grandmother never let go of her Southern. In thought or in the kitchen."

"I was going to ask for fried pork chops, but chicken works too. And cobbler. Peach if they have it. Oh, and I think you should go as Tim. You need to be safe too. Can't lose my free place to stay in New York."

One of Sal's devices sounded a strident alarm. "I need to take this." She grabbed her phone and went into her room.

*Probably her girlfriend*, Adeena thought and chewed on her bottom lip. Who, if she had any sense, wouldn't want another woman staying at her girlfriend's apartment. Maybe they had an open relationship. The kind where Sal took trips to Vegas on her own and picked up strange women in trouble.

She pretended to be reading when she heard Sal's return.

"I may have a way to find our new hired gun. I'm told I can only get information on him in person."

Her relief that the caller hadn't been a girlfriend was overridden by her concern for Sal's safety. "Is that wise? We know what he can do."

"That's precisely why this has to be done in person. Don't worry. It's all on the up. If not, I have contingency plans for my contingency plans." Sal grinned. "That's how I roll."

"Fine. Don't forget my cobbler."

*She's used to this kind of thing*, Adeena told herself after the door closed behind Sal. Anyone who bent the law had to know how to protect themselves. Which meant she was worrying over nothing. "So stop."

Easy to say, hard to do, but eventually she was able to bank the worry and get back into reading about Lucy's old neighborhood. It felt strange to read about the fire, find out ten people had been killed and three houses destroyed. In the back of her mind, she thought it might have ultimately been the catalyst for the neighborhood transition years later. Strange in a sad way, she decided, because a community had also died. Its death had changed many more lives.

Her cell phone ring broke through her melancholy. She snatched up her phone when she saw Sal's name. "You okay?"

"I'm fine. Mrs. Newsome is at the hospital waiting for her third grandchild to be born. Which is okay because there's photos of the old store all over the place, and a teenage Lucy is in one of them."

"Yeah?" Adeena laughed in relief. "Surely that means they know her."

"Drumroll, please. No? Okay, it means they know her *and* the girl in the photo with her."

"No way!"

"Way! Cleta Robinson, nee Jones, was Lucy's BFF."

"Cut the bull. There is no way some waitress was able to give you all that."

"While I'm hurt by your assessment of my charms, I'm forced to agree. They annotated the photos. The name is right there for all to see. Smart, huh?"

"Fricking brilliant is what it is."

"I left Mrs. Robinson a message saying I was looking into my family tree and wanted information on the Browns. She's a manager at Macy's, so she might not be able to call back until this evening. And if she doesn't, me and your face will go see her tomorrow."

"I can't believe we're so close to an answer." Adeena exhaled and put a hand to her stomach to quiet the butterflies. "Part of me wants to march right into the store. But part of me thinks it's better to wait, temper my expectations."

"Why temper? She's alive, meaning chances are slim she's on MM's radar."

"Or she knows nothing. Hired gun charges too much to kill for no reason. Sorry, snarkiness isn't called for. Nerves. I'm nervous."

"But it's true and that's in our favor. And since you brought it up, I should tell you I found our hired gun. Problem is he's like a ghost unless he knows you. Goes by Conlin. Word is he might have slipped town in the dead of night and to stay away from him. Far away."

"Sounds like a great idea. We don't need him, do we? Better he's in Vegas trying to kill me."

"Except he wasn't in Vegas when we were. He has some men he hires out regularly. Contractors."

"Our hired gun's a businessman? Great. Any idea where he is?"

"None. Which is a shame. It would be sweet to hand his ass to the police. This definitely calls for more digging. Hey, food's here. See you in twenty."

"Take care," Adeena told the dial tone.

She hugged the phone to her chest. They had two names. Conlin they could ignore for now, but Cleta Robinson was a person of interest. And wouldn't it be great to sit down with her and learn more about Lucy? She got almost giddy thinking about it.

Once again her phone interrupted her thoughts. She checked for the caller. Ian was early today, she thought. "No, we haven't discovered his identity yet, but we're closer. And yes, I still have not been attacked."

"How close?"

"Hopefully this evening close. My research paid off." She paused for effect. "We found her best friend, Ian. That is, we, Sal, left her a message. I'm scared, I'm excited, I'm everything."

"Keep the scared. Some guy's been asking about you. Claims he's working on a suit with a couple of the parents from your mother's school and wants to talk to you about joining. He seemed legit, but given your situation, I told him you'd taken yourself off to parts unknown to get your head together. Told him to leave a message on your office phone because you were checking them. He seemed to buy it."

"That's good thinking. If he is legit, he'll leave a message." She thought of Conlin, the ghost. "What did he look like?"

"White, dark brown hair, brown eyes, serious build for a lawyer and a couple of inches shorter than me. Late thirties, early forties. Italian suit and a Rolex, so maybe he is a lawyer."

"If he's making that much, why is he looking for clients? Assassins make a lot of money too. He give you a name?"

"And a card. Vincent Fabbrini. Downtown office. I could drive by, see—"

"No! If he's who I think he is, this guy is major trouble, Ian. I'll get Sal to check him out. She's good at that. Very good."

"How's it working out? Being with her?"

"Great. What's not to like about flying on chartered airplanes, the breathtaking view from the terrace of her penthouse apartment and the luxury suite I'm currently staying in? It's been first class all the way."

"Besides that."

"She's helping. A lot. She's kind and funny, despite the serious expression she has most of the time. I trust her, Ian. Considering the mess I'm in, that is the highest compliment I can give."

"Same beds or no?"

She laughed and it felt good. "Noneya. As in mind your own. How's my baby boy?"

"I'm good, despite the slap-down you just delivered. Oh, you probably meant Diablo. Fine, as he was yesterday."

"Meaning Mrs. H is still letting him keep her company during the day." Mrs. Henson was Ian's neighbor, who considered him a surrogate grandchild. Diablo reaped the benefits. "He's going to be spoiled rotten by the time I get back."

"Your point would be? I need to go. Work calls. Be careful, and call me if you need me to check out the lawyer."

"I won't. Seriously, Ian, this guy is bad news. Let it go." She didn't end the call until she got his reluctant promise.

"Deveraux. Talk to me."

"There was a failed attempt to kidnap her Sunday morning."

"Shit! What happened?"

"An off-duty cop happened. Adam Osbourne was charged with attempted murder among other charges. He screwed up in every way possible."

"Son of a bitch. Orders were to observe only." *No wonder that bastard Conlin packed up*, Charles thought. "Where's Osbourne now?"

"Jail. Bail denied. There's talk he tried to run her over before. He working with you?"

"Very loosely. Freelances for Conlin."

"Conlin's in this?"

"Was. He's been AWOL since Sunday night."

"Conlin? Never known him to run."

"Never known him to fuck something up. Boss lady's gonna be pissed. She told him to go out there and take care of this himself."

"'Nough said. Next steps?"

"Deal with Osbourne like by yesterday. He's a lightweight, probably offer to make a deal. After that, set up surveillance on Minor. We need to know what she knows about what's going on. Get me your account info and we'll get you the money."

Adeena jerked out of a disturbing dream to find herself in the dark. Her breath caught in her throat as she tried to remember what she'd been doing before she fell asleep and couldn't. Testing, she moved her arms and legs. Good, they hadn't tied her up, she thought. And they hadn't killed her either. She had a chance.

Trying to be quiet, she eased off the bed and when her bare feet sank into plush carpet she remembered.

"Hotel. Savannah." She hadn't been abducted by MM's minions. She was in an upscale hotel with curtains that did a great job of blocking out light, unlike the cheap blinds in her apartment. She sank back on the bed.

A knock on the door had her remembering more. She was with Sal, sharing a suite, and despite the dream, she was safe. "Come. I'm awake."

Sal stuck her head around the door. "Thought I'd remind you Dani's due in forty-five."

"Danny?" Him she didn't remember. He must be one of Sal's numerous sources.

"Dani Knight. The PI Cyn hired."

Memories of yesterday's conversation surfaced. They'd decided Dani should be the one to approach Mrs. Robinson. Or rather, she'd convinced Sal it was the right thing do. The lawyer who'd talked to Ian hadn't left a message on Adeena's office phone, leaving her to conclude MM knew she wasn't in Vegas. "Right, right." She rubbed her gritty eyes and peered at the alarm clock. It was almost one o'clock, which meant she'd managed six hours horizontal. Time to get her brain in gear. "Forty-five minutes."

"You up for pizza? There's this place nearby with good reviews and they deliver."

"Wouldn't mind." And neither it seemed did her stomach as it grumbled approval. "I'm not picky. Get what you like."

"What if I want anchovies?"

She heard the teasing in Sal's voice. Yeah, she was safe for now. "Then order them, smartass. And add brussels sprouts." She laughed at the expression of horror on Sal's face. "Fine. No brussels sprouts."

After Sal left muttering about desecration of the pie, Adeena stood and stretched. It felt good to have something to laugh about. Today was their third day in Savannah. If there was a goddess, Dani was going to tell them they had a meet with Mrs. Robinson, and her work email would stay quiet long enough for her to recover from the all-nighter Bobby-boy had just forced her to pull.

Yawning, she shed her pajamas and made her way to the bathroom. She'd gotten a call from her boss at ten last night.

One of the scripts they'd run a thousand times before had failed, and of course Bobby-boy needed the output the script generated for a report he'd been sitting on no later than this morning. For Adeena, that had meant painstakingly reviewing each line in a twenty-page script. When she'd gotten to the brink of losing her mind, she found the misplaced decimal point. Someone, and she had her suspicions his name began with Bobby, had committed the offense of altering the script without inserting a comment. With her brain cells leaking from her ear, she'd made the fix, rerun the program and sent an email to her boss to let him know it was done. She'd included a snarky comment about messing with code and asked him to remind the team the purpose of adding comments.

Adeena frowned as she turned on the shower. Perhaps she should have skipped the snarky. Someone was going to get blamed. In her absence she feared it might be her. Sure, most of her coworkers would know that was crap, would know she would never change a script without leaving a detailed comment. Still, principle.

Stepping into the shower, she let the hot water beat against her shoulders and reminded herself she had much more important problems to worry about. According to Sal, no one had come looking for her in New York. Sal had paid for the flight, so it wouldn't show up on her credit card, but there was no time to cobble up a fake ID so she'd had to fly under her real name. It was only a matter of time before someone discovered that and possibly who she was traveling with. The sooner she and Sal talked to Mrs. Robinson, got a name or a better source for the name, the sooner they could move on. Which meant she needed to start thinking about next steps. Returning to Vegas wouldn't be safe until MM was arrested. "Or exposed in the media." Before that could happen, they had to settle on a reporter.

She grabbed the perfumed soap bar and lathered her body while channeling optimism. Maybe not being able to return was a sign for her to shake things up, make the move she'd been talking about for almost a year. She could send a resignation email today, then work the two-week notice from anywhere. Hell, she could do three weeks as long as some of her time was spent actively looking for a job.

"I can do this. No! I will do this."

Bristling with energy, she joined Sal as the pizza was being delivered. The scent of tomato sauce and garlic hit her taste buds hard. She could've wept in gratitude. "God, that smells great. Starving."

"Soda and water in the fridge." Sal placed the pizza on the glass table in front of the sofa, tore off a couple of paper towels and opened the box. "Man. If this is half as good as it looks and smells, I'll be in heaven." She took a huge bite and groaned.

*And we have heaven*, Adeena thought as she made her way to the kitchen area. Though she pledged allegiance to Diet Dr. Pepper, she had to make do with the Cokes she found in the fridge. She figured Sal, being one of those skinny people, couldn't even see diet drinks, let alone buy them.

She was enjoying her own groan-inducing bite of pizza when someone knocked on the door. She and Sal had a stare-down before she reluctantly parted with her slice, saying, "Why don't I get it?" Sal's response was a grin. A really cute grin.

Adeena was about to the open the door and thought about the reason they were there. "Wait. What does she look like?"

"Tall, athletic, blonde." Sal stuffed the rest of the pizza in her mouth and rose to join Adeena. "But it never hurts to ask for an ID."

"Not like they can be forged or anything." She rolled her eyes and opened the door, leaving the chain on. "You have ID?"

The woman holding up an ID said confidence and family in a GLBTQI way to Adeena. After carefully studying the ID, she shut the door, took off the chain and opened in again. "Just making sure. Adeena Minor." She shook Dani's outstretched hand, looked into her blue eyes and decided this was someone who got the job done. "Pleased to meet you, Ms. Knight."

"Dani will do."

"Then I'm Adeena."

"Sal. We talked yesterday." She pointed to the pizza. "You hungry? We have plenty."

"I'll pass, but I wouldn't say no to one of those Cokes."

"I'll get it," Sal said. "You guys sit."

"Were you able to see her? Speak to her?" Adeena asked.

"Sorry. Maybe you should tell us about the lawyer first." She picked up her slice, but didn't take a bite. She fully expected to hear about the discovery of the lawyer's body and suddenly the pizza wasn't so appetizing.

"I was able to speak with Mr. Nicholson's paralegal late yesterday afternoon. According to her he's in Montana. Goes to Glacier National Park about this time every year."

"I doubt he got that far." Sal handed Dani a Coke and perched on the arm of Adeena's chair. "They took him out here, figuring it would be a while before anyone would look for him."

Dani nodded. "Back to the paralegal. She wasn't at liberty to speak about his cases. Didn't end up being important as she's only worked for him for five years. However, thanks to her, I was able to track down his old assistant, Ms. Estelle Lancaster. After I explained my interest, she graciously agreed to meet with me this morning. I showed the baby photo of you and Heather, told her a little about your situation and she admitted there had been two adoptions done hush-hush. She remembers it so clearly because she first thought the girls were twins due to their time of birth. Then she found out one was white and one was black and that disabused her of that notion." Dani smiled. "Her words. Nicholson took care of all the arrangements for those two adoptions, which wasn't their usual process. It also means only he knew who the babies went to. Mrs. Lancaster did know the parents' names in the official files were made up. Nicholson told her it was to protect the babies from coming to harm and she believed him. She was quite firm that Nicholson's a kind, generous man who would go out of his way to help anyone in trouble."

"How old is she?" Sal asked.

"I'd say late sixties, early seventies. Not young and naïve at the time of the adoptions. Makes me inclined to buy her take on Nicholson. Apparently they did a lot of adoptions in her day and a number of them were done at no or little cost to the prospective parents."

"So our bad guy isn't a bad guy," Sal said. "That jibes with his financials."

"Not only is he not a bad guy, he's also most likely another victim." Adeena sighed. "Dead because he tried to help me, maybe my parents. It's not right. And I know life isn't always about right, but this is turning into a horror movie. How many have to die so one man can rewrite his history?"

Sal stroked Adeena's arm. "I know one who won't. One, who along with her trusty sidekick, will bring him down. That's what we focus on."

"You're absolutely right." Adeena smiled a thanks up at Sal before turning her attention back to Dani. "Mrs. Robinson?"

"After some fast talking on my part, she's agreed to meet me this evening after she gets off work."

Adeena's heartbeat sped up. The desire to have the opportunity to speak with someone who knew the woman who'd carried her for nearly nine months was suddenly overwhelming. "That's fantastic. I'd like to come."

"I was counting on that. I kept with Sal's story that you're a relative looking for more personal information on the Brown family. That you'd hired me to do preliminary research."

"What's she like?"

"Polite, reserved. What you'd expect with me being a stranger. She's interested in genealogy herself. I believe that helped convince her to meet with me."

"Whatever the reason, I'm grateful for the opportunity to talk to someone who knew Lucy. Thanks."

"Yeah, good job, Dani."

"The two of you did most of the work." Dani set the soda can on the table between them. "I have a couple of threads to pull, but I'd be happy to swing by here at six, give you a lift."

"We'll meet you there," Sal said. "I know I'm not invited to the meet, but I can be nearby, keep an eye out. Seems to me we're close to uncovering a secret someone has killed to keep buried. Backup's a no brainer."

"That's true. They've had a day to track me to here," Adeena said. "Even with the fake name and the disguise."

Dani shook her head. "I believe they would've shown themselves by now if they had. But Sal's right. Extra precautions never hurt. My plan was to meet with Mrs. Robinson first, check out the coffee shop, then bring you in. You sticking with Sal while I scope out the place works even better. We're meeting at the Coffee Bean in downtown around six thirty. She said it was small with not a lot of weeknight traffic."

"Small is good. Helps with surveillance." Sal keyed the name of the coffee shop into her phone. "Got it."

"If something comes up, text me. I have Sal's number, but I'd like one for you as well, Adeena."

Adeena rattled off her number.

"Barring any last-minute glitches, I'll see the both of you at six thirty or so."

"We'll be there." Adeena walked Dani to the door. "I hope you're taking extra precautions as well."

"I'm always on my guard. However, I don't see any harm in you or me having a conversation with Mrs. Robinson. If I did, I wouldn't have suggested it."

Adeena closed the door behind Dani as hope and nerves warred. She was hours away from meeting with Lucy's best friend. Hours away from discovering who her enemy was. What happened after that, she didn't know. With a name, they might not need the reporter. She could call the cops in Vegas, tell them what she'd learned. If they bought her story and forgave her for holding back information, they might call Savannah PD, get them to take a look. Maybe she could let that be enough.

"What are you thinking?"

"Not thinking so much as trying to work out next steps. That's after I meet with Mrs. Robinson and get the final answer to the puzzle." She plopped down on the sofa and curled her legs under her body. "Which you don't have to attend if you don't want to. You're the one who said no one's followed us the times we've gone out. Plus Dani doesn't think there's any danger, and if there is, well, she'll be right there. She looks like she can handle herself in any situation."

"You can never have too much backup." Sal picked up her pizza. "I'm as interested in hearing what she has to say as you."

"No one can be as interested as me. I hope she remembers."

"Of course she remembers. It had to be traumatic to lose her friend to a fire. That kind of thing has to stay with a person. If not, one look at your face will bring it all back."

"You're right. I'm being silly. It's just I'm going to get the chance to talk to someone who actually knew Lucy. Someone who can tell me what she was thinking, what she was feeling." She rubbed her arms. "It gives me goosebumps thinking about it."

"And while you're finding that out, I'll be the dashing counterspy on the lookout for bad guys." Sal flexed her scrawny arms. "I'll wear all black, bring high-tech equipment."

"My shero."

"You'd better believe it. Now about that reporter…"

"I thought we could, you know, just go the police. Let them take care of it."

Sal shook her head. "The media is more powerful than the police. They certainly'll act faster. I'm not saying don't go to the police. I'm saying we should do both."

"Because you can never have too much backup?"

# CHAPTER FOURTEEN

"She's clean."

Adeena gave up all pretense of sightseeing. "What? Who?"

"Mrs. Robinson. I checked her financials and there's no unexpected lump sum in any of her accounts. And technically she's not a Mrs. anymore. She and her husband of twenty years split two years ago. Coincidentally, she filed for divorce shortly after their only child went off to Spelman College in Atlanta."

"I'm not even going to ask how you got your information."

"Most of it's public record or on social media. Makes my job easier."

Adeena rubbed her temples. She couldn't stop worrying just because Mrs. Robinson was clean. MM could be using the poor woman without her knowledge.

"Problems?"

"What if this is a trap? Not for me because they don't know I'm here, but for Dani or anyone asking questions about Lucy. They'll torture her until she tells them about me, about us, then—"

"I believe it was you who not that long ago pointed out that Dani could take care of herself. She won't go into this blind. Not that I think there's anything to worry about. MM's too busy trying to eliminate you and the people involved thirty-four years ago. He doesn't have time to worry about Lucy's best friend or a PI working for Cynthia Kennedy."

"And you checked her financials because…?"

"Maybe there was a very slight chance they're watching Mrs. Robinson. Not now. Not anymore."

"Good to know. You've been on the money so far. This shouldn't be any different."

"By George, I think she's got it."

"Don't call me George." She smiled and patted Sal's thigh. There was no one like her. "Is it okay to admit how glad I am she's not with them? Mrs. Robinson. It's kind of nice to think she could still be Lucy's best friend in her mind."

"I'm glad too. Makes things a lot cleaner in theory. Hey, we're about a block away. I think we should park here and walk. If anyone is watching her, they won't know what vehicle we're in."

"Making us harder to track. See I'm learning. On top of that, it's probably easier to get lost on foot downtown. In case we have to run." There were other places for them to duck in, hide out. And taxis, she noted. They could leave the car and grab a taxi if need be. She donned the hat, the big sunglasses and said a quick prayer they wouldn't need the hiding places or the taxis. Prayed this friend of her mother would tell them what they needed to know.

She looked at her buzzing phone, saw the text from Dani telling her it was okay to come in.

"Go ahead," Sal urged when told the news. "I'll be there in a few." She kept on walking, only stopping to peer at a display in a gift store window three shops down from the coffee shop.

The walk to the coffee shop seemed too long and at the same time too short to Adeena. She would soon know the name of the man who had a part in creating her *and* trying to erase her. That had to be why she felt so off-kilter, so unsure of which emotion she was supposed to be experiencing.

Adeena entered Coffee Bean and was bombarded by the heavenly scents of coffee coupled with the smell of something baking. She breathed in deeply, then took a moment to check out the place. It was small as advertised and crammed with tiny tables. Other than Dani and Mrs. Robinson there was only one other person, who seemed more interested in her phone than her surroundings. She also looked like she was in high school, so Adeena dismissed her as a spy.

Hoping her nervousness didn't show, she stepped up to the counter and ordered a Frappuccino. While her drink was being prepared, she pretended not to study the woman sitting across from Dani. Mrs. Robinson was thin, beautiful and stylishly dressed. She looked nothing like the image Adeena had in her mind.

Adeena knew it was dumb, but somehow she'd been expecting someone who looked more like Lucy—more down to earth and less glamorous. She wondered if as a teen, Lucy, with her medium build and above average height, had ever envied her petite best friend. Adeena had some experience with that particular emotion. She'd gone through puberty early and filled out in different ways than her mother. Consequently she'd been put on a diet until she went to college. Eventually she'd realized she was never going to be slim like her mother and that it was okay she had thick thighs and a big behind. Eventually she'd realized it didn't make her any less of a woman.

It occurred to her that she might have reached that conclusion earlier had she known she was adopted, that her shape was hereditary. Just as it was obvious Heather had taken after the other side, from him. It seemed neither of them had gotten his mean streak. Sure, she had her bitchy moments like anyone else. And from all accounts Heather had been a kind and loving person. It wasn't a stretch to believe Heather would've been a kind and loving sister.

She blinked her eyes rapidly as the sudden longing for that loving and kind relationship took her by surprise. Somehow seeing Mrs. Robinson had turned her into a mushball. She had to do better.

"Here you are."

The server's voice cut through her grief. Adeena accepted her drink, then was careful not to look at Sal, who was behind her studying the menu. She stopped to remove the hat and the sunglasses before she made her way back to Dani and Mrs. Robinson. Taking a deep breath, she said, "I hope I'm not late." She wasn't disappointed at Mrs. Robinson's reaction. The other woman's eyes got impossibly wide as she clutched at the white pearls around her neck.

"This is the client I mentioned would be joining us," Dani said into the silence.

"My name is Adeena Minor." Adeena's hand was ignored as Mrs. Robinson continued to stare. Uneasy, she looked to Dani, wondering if they needed to do something and what that something might be. Thankfully Mrs. Robinson blinked her eyes and Adeena took that as a signal to sit.

"Excuse me." Mrs. Robinson reached for her bottle of green tea and took a healthy sip. "You look like…like someone I knew a long, long time ago." She cleared her throat and took another sip. "Oh Jesus, I remember you now. Saw you on the television. You were crying and I thought to myself how like her you looked. How if she'd had a daughter, she'd look like you, be the same age. But here…in person, the resemblance is unbelievable."

There was a longing in Mrs. Robinson's eyes that brought back the mushy feelings. Adeena steeled herself, made herself remember she was on a mission. "Like Lucy Mae Brown you mean? She was my birth mother."

"Can't be." Mrs. Robinson shook her head vigorously. "That can't be. Lucy died in a house fire before she gave birth. It was early Christmas morning." She gave a shudder. "I remember it so clearly. A time that should have been happy, joyful, only it wasn't that day. I lived a few blocks away. We heard the sirens, could see the clouds of smoke, smell the burning wood. Of course I didn't know it was Lucy's house then, only wondered who was going to have a bad Christmas." When she reached for her tea her hands shook. "Oh God, she was my best friend. They never found any bodies. It was horrible. A horrible time for me, the neighborhood and on Christmas Day. And to see you here, looking so...It's a shock."

"Do you know who fathered Lucy's babies?" Adeena leaned forward and gripped her cup.

"I sure do. It was supposed to be a big secret. She wouldn't tell anyone, not even her own mother. But I knew. She graduated early, you see. Got a full-time job at the Tanner Estate to save for college." Mrs. Robinson smiled. "I think I first noticed the change in her in March. Never could get her to tell me what was going on. Then when school was out, I got a job there as well. He was already home then. At first I teased her because I could see how he went out of his way to get in her way. How he only came around the kitchen when it was her lunchtime. How he stayed in his room later and later in the mornings as if waiting for her to come up and clean his room. I stopped teasing her because I could see he meant something to her. And you know, it seemed like she meant something to him. So, no. They didn't fool me none."

Adeena couldn't stop herself from reaching for the other woman's hand as her heartbeat sped up. "Who? What's his name?"

"Jackson Beauregard Tanner the second. He was a year older and handsome for a white boy. Big blue eyes with dark hair and charming when he wanted to be. Lucy never had a chance once he set his sights on her. Must've been when he was home for spring break. I'm sure they kept in touch when he went back to college. Ivy League, you know. Then about three weeks after he came back for the summer, she gets fired by the head witch herself. That would be his mother, Eugenia Tanner. It was strange. Up until then that woman didn't have a thing to do with us. Everything came through the main housekeeper. Another evil witch if you ask me. Except Miss Betty was black and should've been looking out for us, for Lucy."

"Did Mr. Tanner know she was pregnant? Know she was carrying his child?" Adeena unconsciously squeezed Mrs. Robinson's hand.

Mrs. Robinson frowned, seeming to come back from the past. "Lucy told me early on that her baby didn't have a father. That the person who got her pregnant didn't deserve to be the father of her baby."

"Could he have found out? Mr. Tanner," Adeena clarified. "Seen her on the street when she was showing?"

"I don't see how. He wasn't around much after that if I remember correctly. And once Lucy Mae Brown made up her mind, it was darn near impossible to get her to change it. There's no way she would've had anything to do with him."

"Her family probably didn't have a lot of money," Dani said. "Is there any chance she went to Mr. Tanner? Asked him for help? By rights he bore some responsibility for the pregnancy."

"Absolutely not. Her family might not've had a lot of money, but they would've made do. That's what we did back then. And Lucy was resourceful. She had money she'd saved for college and she could make more sewing fancy-looking clothes. She sewed a lot of dresses for the prom. As good as those you could get in the store, but at a reasonable price."

"I meant no offense, ma'am."

"We just need to know how he knew," Adeena said, deliberately drawing attention away from Dani.

"That I don't know, child." She smiled at Adeena, patted her hand. "I do know you're here, and looking at you I can believe she's here. Of course she was dark like me. Other than that, I know she would've looked exactly like you if she hadn't passed too soon."

"What was she like, your Lucy?"

"Smart. Won some money to go to college. Dreams. She had lots of dreams. And she was kind of shy, especially around boys. Thought she wasn't pretty enough. And her good grades intimidated some, so they made fun of her. But she was the sweetest person, always willing to do for others. Lucy was the best friend I could ever wish for." Mrs. Robinson tapped her forehead. "I almost forgot. Lucy was away for most of the time when she was showing. Near Greensboro, Georgia. She had some relatives there. Her daddy's people."

"Are you positive she was in Savannah in December?" Dani asked.

"Came back as big as a house. She was having twins and wanted to have her babies in a big city hospital. I sure was happy to have her back. I was going to the technical college and had myself a boyfriend I wanted to show off. We talked a lot in those last few weeks. I was real glad we had that time after she was gone."

"Has anyone else asked you recently about Lucy, the father of her babies?" Dani asked.

"Why, yes." Mrs. Robinson rubbed her arms. "Said to call him Conlin, claimed he was asking on behalf of the family of the man who owned the house back then. The one that burned down. Said someone was talking about suing after all these years. That the son of the owner thought it might be the father of Lucy's unborn babies and did I know him. I didn't believe him." She clutched at her pearls again. "This Conlin. There was something about him. Something about his aura that made me uneasy the whole time we were talking."

Dani took a photo of Roman Burlett from the folder in front of her. "Is this the man?"

Mrs. Robinson shook her head. "The man I'm talking about was tougher looking, mean. Even when he smiled. I thought he might be ex-military because his hair was so short and the way he carried himself, kind of stiff like. I admit I lied. Told him I thought it was an old boyfriend of hers. That everyone thought that. And the last part was the truth, so I told myself it wasn't all a lie."

"What's the old boyfriend's name?" Dani turned a page in her little notebook.

"Gregory Charles Selman. He was a year older. Broke up with her right before the prom our junior year. It was so he could take this girl who had a reputation of putting out." Mrs. Robinson sniffed. "Lucy was saving herself and he was putting pressure on her to have sex with him. They'd been going out for a whole year and he still did something like that to her. She was crushed. Course he tried to get her back after the prom. Bought her this nice necklace. She told him to get lost and take the necklace with him. He kept trailing after her for months like some lost puppy. When she started showing and there was no boyfriend in sight, people assumed he'd worn her down."

"He deny it?" Adeena asked.

"Not that one. He'd just grin. Lucy denied it though. Denied ever being with him. I was one of the few who believed her, one of the few who knew about Jackson."

"So if this Conlin found anyone else to ask, they'd tell him the same thing as you." Dani tapped her pen against her chin. "Which means someone thinks getting rid of Adeena solves the problem."

Mrs. Robinson looked at Dani, her expression puzzled. "I can't think why any of this matters. I'm telling you, Lucy died in that fire and I really do doubt Jackson ever knew she was pregnant."

"You said this Gregory Charles tried to get her back, so why not Tanner?" Adeena asked. "He could've gone to see her after she came back, found out that way."

"He didn't come back that Christmas. After Lucy came back…well, I asked one of the women who worked there to keep an eye on him. For Lucy's sake. I didn't want him catching her in a weak moment, what with her condition."

"Jackson Tanner. Sounds vaguely familiar." Dani flipped through her notebook. "You mentioned an estate. Does the family have money?"

"Old money. They're the closest thing to royalty for some people around here. The family owns lots of land and has businesses in and around Savannah, maybe the state. Jackson's a partner in a big-time law firm now. I've been hearing talk he's going to run for the US Senate, but I don't pay much attention to politics. Seems like they're all crooks."

Adeena felt as if she'd been knocked upside the head. Motive with a capitol M. An illegitimate child could be explained, forgiven as a teenage mistake. But she was more. Alive, she was proof Lucy had given birth, casting doubt on her death by fire. Doubt that could lead to questions Tanner wouldn't want answered. "If Lucy went into labor early, was there anyone not connected with the hospital she would've reached out to?"

"What are you trying to say?"

"I think you know, Mrs. Robinson," Adeena replied gently. "Lucy was my birth mother. She had me and my sister after she was kidnapped from her home. Something went wrong and she died during childbirth. Most likely the fire was staged to make it look like she never gave birth."

"How can I believe that?" Mrs. Robinson shook her head slowly, then more vigorously. "I can't. There was a fire. I was there, I saw that there was nothing left of her house or the ones on either side of hers. I saw and I knew then she, her family, they were all gone. It was terrible. Like something you'd see on TV or at the movies. Only it was real."

"The fire was real, Mrs. Robinson. Lucy wasn't in the house then," Adeena explained. "You saw me on TV and noticed the resemblance. Tanner probably did the same. And maybe someone else as well. I received a letter last week that said Lucy was kidnapped and died after giving birth. The letter writer claimed my life was in danger. I thought it was crazy until I saw a photo of Lucy and realized my life had been built on a lie. Now thanks to you, I know the source of the danger."

"None of this makes sense. It's true Lucy wasn't at church that night. That she was home with her uncle. I can't believe her parents wouldn't have noticed she was missing. Wouldn't have called the police to report just that when they returned from church service. I want to believe you. I do." Mrs. Robinson took another sip of tea. "It doesn't make sense."

"Maybe they forced her to leave a note or put pillows to make it look like she was in the bed," Adeena replied. "Unfortunately the letter writer didn't tell me everything that happened that night."

"Maybe they didn't know," Dani said. "What we do know is Adeena looks like Lucy, that she's survived two auto accidents and an attempted kidnapping *after* her face appeared in the news."

"What? No!"

"It's true. That's why I needed to know about Tanner. He's the only one who would benefit from my death. That's especially true if he's running for office. Surely you can see what a liability I would be."

"That's crazy." Mrs. Robinson put a hand on Adeena's arm. "Your story is something like out of a movie. Like the fire, only worse. I don't want to believe this and yet you're here with Lucy's face and Lucy's eyes."

"I realize this is quite a shock, Mrs. Robinson, but do you have any idea who could've sent the letter?" Dani asked. "Or who might've helped Lucy give birth?"

"I wish I did. She was interested in medicine, wanted to be a doctor. Lucy trusted the hospital, the nurses, her doctor. If she'd gone into labor early, she would have had someone to take her to the hospital. I'm sure of that." Mrs. Robinson closed her eyes briefly. When she opened them, they were moist. "If she did give birth outside of a hospital, it wasn't her choice. Do you have the letter?"

Adeena pulled it from her bag, smoothed it out and placed it on the table. "Any chance you recognize the writing?"

Mrs. Robinson squinted as she read. "Sorry, but no. You don't see handwriting so much anymore. I do know this town the writer mentions. It's west and east of here. Back then it was little more than an intersection. Most of the people lived out, in what we considered the country. She wouldn't go there by choice."

"Did she know anyone who lived there? Did you?" Adeena asked.

"I wish I could say yes. I wish I had some of the answers you need, child." Mrs. Robinson reached for Adeena's hand and cradled it between hers. "What happens next? What will you do next?"

"It's best you don't know until we get to the bottom of this, Mrs. Robinson," Dani said. "It's also best if you didn't mention this meeting. Adeena's life is still in danger."

"I won't say a word. Do you think this Conlin person will come back to me?"

"No," Adeena said. "He obviously believed you about Gregory Charles. He thinks you don't know anything. You're safe."

"I can hope you're able to say the same soon. You've had a rough time of late. I hope when all this is done you come back to see me. I'd love to tell you more about Lucy, get to know more about you."

"I'd like that very much, Mrs. Robinson. She sounds like she was a very special person."

"That she was. Life is peculiar." Mrs. Robinson pulled a handkerchief out of her purse and dabbed at her eyes. "I'm happy and sad. I so wish Lucy could be here with us. You should take some comfort from knowing that she loved you so much, was determined to give her best for her girls. If you don't learn anything else about her, know that."

"I will." Adeena fought off tears. If she started crying now, she wasn't sure when she'd stop. "Thank you for that." She grabbed her bag and dug out one of her business cards and a pen. "I'm adding my cell number and personal email address to this. I want you to have it, to know I will get back in touch with you when I'm able."

Mrs. Robinson looked at the card, then smiled even as she once again patted at tears. "A PhD. Lucy would've been so proud of you. So proud of the person you are and what you've accomplished."

She nodded, unable to speak, unable to do anything but welcome the hard hug. With Mrs. Robinson's arms around her, Adeena rested her head on her shoulder, breathed in the sweet smell of her perfume and was comforted. It was one of those perfect moments, one that she knew she would always remember.

She watched until Mrs. Robinson was out of sight, then covered her face and took a deep breath. She'd gotten so much more than she thought she would. Her mother had loved her, had loved Heather, had wanted them.

"You okay?" Dani asked.

She swiped her eyes with the back of her hand. "I'm a little overwhelmed. It's just...a lot to take in. In a good way."

Sal walked over, patted Adeena's shoulder and grabbed a chair. "You'll be interested to know Jackson Beauregard Tanner officially declared his candidacy for the US Senate late Monday afternoon." When they looked at her, she shrugged. "Okay, so I was doing some electronic eavesdropping."

"Of course you were." Adeena poked Sal's shoulder. "You're a dangerous woman, Thomasina Salamander."

"I'll take that as a compliment." She puffed out her scrawny chest. "He was on my list of possible fathers."

"What list?" Adeena asked.

"Men with money whose families have been in the area for fifty years or more and who were between seventeen and forty-five when Lucy got pregnant. I started it back in Vegas, then kind of forgot about it. And now that we know Tanner's our guy, I say our next step should be adding his name to our packet and sending it to our reporter."

"What packet?" Dani looked from Sal to Adeena.

"Plan B." Adeena blotted her eyes with a napkin. "Sal and I thought it would be a good idea to share parts of my story with a reporter, have her do some checking. You know, in case we couldn't figure out who the father was."

"And protection," Sal added. "If something were to happen to Adeena—not that I plan on it—but if something were to happen, there'd be someone other than us to get the word out."

"That works," Dani said, nodding. "Insurance is always a smart idea."

"Exactly." Sal tapped on the table. "Our plan's to give the info to a reporter looking to move up. Cold cases are big these days, so we thought she'd dive in. But now that we have Tanner's name, know he's running for office, I bet we could get a big name to dig into the story and make a huge splash."

"I think we should stick with our plan. I like the idea of giving someone a leg up. Something good to come out of this mess."

"Good point. We'll stick with Kristy Moore. I'm told she's the next big thing. Plus, she's African-American and should be sympathetic to Adeena and Lucy."

"What's the step after that?" Dani asked.

"Go to the police, see what they have to say?" Adeena guessed. "I don't know. What else can we do? We don't have any solid proof."

"Follow the money," Sal said. "Now that I know Tanner's behind this, I can access his accounts, see who he paid and share it with the police. Anonymously of course. But given what we've just learned, I suggest such digging be done anywhere but Savannah. Politics is not for the weak."

"What about Tifton? My mom—Joy Minor, that is—once mentioned coming from there. We could look for her relatives. They might know where she was thirty-four years ago. May help us figure out how she and Dad got involved in all this."

Dani's cell buzzed and she excused herself.

"We don't have to be in Tifton to locate your relatives," Sal said. "I'm going for bold and suggesting we head up to Seneca. Proving a genetic connection between you and Nate would beef up your connection to Heather. We go there, meet with Cyn. She sees you, talks to you and I bet between the two of us we can convince her to have Nate's DNA tested, compared to yours. And not only can you get to know your nephew, you can learn about Heather from her other sister and her parents."

"I don't know, Sal." She rolled the cup between her hands. "I'm not the pushy type. Outside of work, that is. But there I absolutely know what I'm doing. This is iffy to me. I want her to like me, not resent me for pushing myself on her. What if she thinks I'm trying to take over her nephew? And I don't want to think about what her parents will think."

"They're really nice people."

"Yeah, but they're really nice people who are dealing with a motherless grandson, a slimeball of a son-in-law and the media fallout. Me being in their face, claiming a relationship, is not a good idea for anyone. I mean, didn't you tell me that the man had a heart attack not that long ago?"

"You may have a point." Sal adjusted her glasses. "Okay, consider this. We go, talk to Cyn and let her decide if her parents can handle this now. She'll know what they can stand."

"Only if you call her first, tell her our plans, *and* she willingly agrees to meet me. And I do only mean willingly."

"Deal. 'On the road again,'" Sal sang and rubbed her hands together. "Next stop Seneca."

"A veritable metropolis. And yes, that was sarcasm. I understand how coming to Savannah could be considered an adventure, but Seneca, Georgia? It's more suburbs than town from what I've read. Why are you still excited? Why are you still doing this for me now that we know the who?"

Sal leaned forward and puffed out her cheeks. "Because we're still on the hunt. I'm invested now and I'm mostly convinced Heather was your twin. Cyn is my sister. Heather was her sister and you're Heather's sister, so that sort of makes us sisters." She frowned. "We'll say sort of family. Family always helps family. Number one rule, hard and fast."

"According to whom?"

"My parents. First thing they taught me. And we have to add Heather's side into the mix. She would've been fascinated by your story. I'm willing to bet money she would be the first in line to do the DNA test. The first to want to know if you're her sister. Since she's not here, I'm doing it for her. If that's not enough, then what was done to Lucy Mae Brown, to her family, to you, to Heather needs to be exposed and the person responsible needs to be punished."

This close to Sal, Adeena could see that although Sal's eyes were dark, there was a difference between the iris and the pupil. She wondered how the dark could seem so warm, so caring, and concluded it was because the eyes belonged to Sal. "I don't care what you say, you *are* nice. No, don't say it. Lips are sealed.

Your associates will never hear it from me." She gave Sal's hand a quick squeeze and got one in return. *Connection made*, she thought.

"Need to go," Dani said upon her return. "I've got a lead on where Mr. Burlett's staying. I think it's time he and I have the chance to chat face to face now that Nicholson seems to no longer be in the picture."

"Is that wise?" Adeena asked. "He could be armed and dangerous, no matter what Sal says."

Dani's smile was fierce. "So am I. What did you decide to do?"

"We're going to see Cyn," Sal replied.

"Smart. That should be the last place they'd look for Adeena."

"Then it's a good thing we're leaving off the Heather angle. Sal thought the idea of Heather and me being twins might strain credibility to a point the reporter would take a pass on the story."

"That probably doesn't matter now that we have Tanner," Dani pointed out. "Anything involving him will be huge. I would think your reporter will want to first establish a relationship between him and Lucy. Then link him to you and, if she's good, insinuate his candidacy's a good reason for your recent spate of incidents."

"Too bad we can't get his DNA, compare it to mine. It's fine to have the media speculating, but to nail him we need to show he fathered me."

"Never underestimate the power of media speculation," Sal said. "And we shouldn't leave social media out of the mix once the story's out. We hit online conversations about Tanner's run, talk up the story. Hit pages of potential and known opponents as well. This is going to be a public hanging of biblical proportions. Stick with me, kid. We're going places."

Adeena laughed. "That's what I'm afraid of."

# CHAPTER FIFTEEN

As Dani was rushing to the Holiday Inn Express on Gateway Boulevard East, Roman Burlett was ringing the doorbell at the Brooks residence in a northwest suburb of Savannah. According to his research the woman who answered the door was in her late sixties. She looked younger. Shirley Brooks was one of the many sisters of James Louis Early, a man he was having little luck tracking down.

She eyed him suspiciously. "Can I help you?"

"My name is Roman." He handed her one of his cards. "I'm looking for Mr. James Louis Early. I'm told he's your brother."

"Don't know why you'd be looking for him over here. After our mother died, I told that drunk fool not to bother coming over here for looking money. I'm not like my mother. I'm not about to give him any of my hard-earned money so he can buy liquor and drugs. Couldn't tell Mama nothing, but I knew that's what he always did with the money. Go and get drunk as Cooter Brown, then like a fool try to pick a fight. I'm sorry if he owes you anything, but I ain't got it," she looked at his card, "Mr. Burlett."

"It's not a financial matter, ma'am."

She peered at his card again, then gave him a once-over. "Inspector. You the police? Should've known. He's been in trouble just about my whole life. What's he done now? Ain't no bail money if that's what you're wanting," she was quick to add.

"I'm a private investigator, ma'am. Let me assure you this is *not* a police matter. I'm trying to locate an old friend for a client. He was a friend of your brother and I was hoping he might have a way to contact a Walter Morrow."

When she laughed, her portly body shook. "Contact? That drunk fool doesn't have any contacts. And even if he did, he's got no way to contact anybody. I say if you're looking for any of Junior's friends look in prison. All of them were as much trouble as him. Some more."

"This would have been over thirty years ago, ma'am." He managed to hang on to his smile as he pulled a photograph from his coat pocket. During his investigation of the seamy side of Lowrents, he'd been lucky to find someone willing to answer questions in exchange for money. He'd not only identified as Walter Morrow a photo of Minor taken when he first began teaching in Nevada, but he'd given him Early's name as well. He'd remembered Morrow because he was one of the few boys who'd gone to college, let alone graduated. "Is there any chance you recognize him?"

"Thirty years? Who remembers from thirty years?" Despite her words, she took the photo and studied it intently. "Sure is handsome, but he don't look familiar. What would a professional-looking man like this have wanted with Junior anyway? Looks like he's got some sense. Those hoodlum friends of Junior never had any."

"He would've been younger, ma'am. Same age as your brother."

She looked again, then shook her head. "Sorry."

"Do you have the names of any of your brother's friends? Maybe they'd be able to help me."

"Number one loser would be Bonnie Franks. I always thought he was so mean because his people gave him a girl's name. I'd look for him in prison too. Or a graveyard. Had a temper on him like nobody's business. Add on dreams of making it big and all you got is trouble. That one never let the law get in his way. Tried to tell my brother that, but he didn't want to listen."

"You've been a big help, Mrs. Brooks. I'd like to thank you for your time, ma'am. If your brother does drop by, could you please give him my number?"

She sniffed. "I can. But like I said, he knows better than to come around here with his hand out. Depending on my mood, I just might cut it off."

"One more thing. Did you know if your brother knew a Lucy Mae Brown per chance?" He could tell she did by the way her face softened. His source had mentioned Mr. Early's name in connection to a fire that had wiped out Ms. Brown's family thirty-four years ago. Because Lucy was only a few years younger than Walter Morrow, Roman was also looking at her for a connection to Morrow and at the fire as a connection to Morrow's activities. It wasn't a stretch to think Morrow could have been involved, gotten nervous and changed his name to get away from his past.

"Lucy Mae. I haven't thought about that girl in forever. Lived round the corner from my sister in the old neighborhood. She was so sweet and so smart. Never could figure out what she saw in that nephew of mine."

"Lucy Brown was involved with your nephew?"

"Until he got stupid. He's my oldest sister's only son. Pansy spoiled him rotten. Got so you couldn't tell that boy nothing. Some no-account shook her behind in his face and he dropped poor Lucy just like that. Of course that fool eventually realized his mistake and tried to get her back. She was smart, though, wouldn't give him the time of day. There were plenty who thought Gregory Charles was the father of her baby, but me, well, I never believed that. Kept that to myself I did on account he was my nephew. If he wanted to pretend he put that baby in her, wasn't up to me to correct that lie."

Wheels began to turn in ways he didn't like. There had been no mention that Lucy was pregnant. "Did you know who the father of her baby was?"

She shook her head. "She was the quiet type. I figured some boy was able to have his way with her because Gregory Charles broke her heart. But we'll never know on account of how she died in the fire."

"A fire?"

"Christmas morning." She put a hand to her heart. "It was terrible, I tell you. The whole family perished. Nothing left but ashes according to my sister. She lived near there, you know."

"Yes. So you said. That's tragic. Thank you again for your assistance, Mrs. Brooks."

"Good luck finding that man you're looking for. Like I said, I doubt my brother could tell you where anyone is. That is, if you can find him."

"Is there any chance your nephew could have known Walter Morrow?"

"He did hang around James more than he should've. They were closer in age, you see." She gave him a phone number. "If you can't reach him there, try Zane's Automotive tomorrow. He works there."

He decided in person was better. Easier to tell if this Gregory Charles was telling the truth that way. "Would his last name be Early?"

"Selman. Gregory Charles Selman."

He thanked her again and, feeling as if he finally had a solid lead, returned to the rented sedan. If Selman had been a good friend of Morrow, he might have a general idea of what Morrow had been doing thirty-four years ago. The general would lead him to the specific.

Roman now had a way to solve the mystery. As he drove away from the curb, though, he had to question Mrs. Tanner's interest in Walter Morrow. Thirty-four years ago, Morrow and his wife had added a daughter to their family, become the

Minors and moved to Nevada. The cynic in him wondered about the connection between that child and the Tanners. Jackson Tanner was a few years younger than Morrow. And while he hadn't found any connection between them, it wasn't a stretch to imagine Morrow and his wife had agreed to take Tanner's love child and move across the country. Selman would know if Morrow's wife had been pregnant when they disappeared. But knowing that wouldn't tell him how any of this was linked to a house fire and the death of another pregnant woman. Dead women didn't usually give birth.

At the hotel, he backed into a spot by the back entrance. He'd considered it a good sign that he hadn't yet checked out of this hotel when Mrs. Tanner gave him the additional assignment. Now he wasn't so sure. There were too many seemingly unrelated pieces to make the assignment straightforward. Not the least of which was finding the article about Minor's daughter's close brush with death within a week of burying her heroic mother. It could be that Mrs. Tanner had seen that article and remembered something or seen something in the daughter. Pure supposition on his part, unfortunately. But something to be considered.

On the positive side he did have a possible connection between a man named James Minor and a Vicki Adams, the goddaughter of the lawyer who handled the adoption of the woman Mrs. Tanner had hired him to research. This particular James Minor, who had also been married to a Joy Minor, died the year before the James Minor he was researching had surfaced, along with his Joy Minor. He'd left a message for Ms. Adams, who'd worked at the hospital where the Minors had died, to contact him, and if he didn't hear back by tomorrow morning, he planned to visit her at the children's hospital where she currently volunteered on a regular basis. She could be a very important piece in the puzzle he was assembling. It would be a kick to piece together how these cases were related.

He did a quick scan of the lobby, as was his habit, and only then did he proceed to the elevators.

"Mr. Burlett? Roman Burlett?"

He turned, saw the cool blue eyes assessing him and thought cop. He'd covered a lot of ground the past few days, but none of it had veered from the legal. "Yes. Can I help you?"

"Dani Knight." She held out a card. "I thought we might have a chat about overlapping cases. I've been hired to look into a matter concerning Heather Garson-Kennedy."

Intrigued, Roman scanned the card. Talking done right could result in answers. "I haven't had dinner. I hear the Metro Diner up the road's not bad." When she gave a nod, he added, "Forty-five minutes?"

"I'll be waiting."

*I'm sure you will*, he thought as he watched her walk away. Only then did he push the button to summon the elevator. In his room, he searched the Internet and found enough information to know a meeting with Dani Knight would be on the up and up. Anyone who consulted with the police, as he himself had done, had to adhere to certain standards.

Grabbing a bottle of water from the tiny refrigerator, he wondered about Knight's angle, wondered if Mrs. Tanner had hired someone to check his work. If she had, that said desperation, and given that her son had recently announced his candidacy, it made the water harder to swallow.

Roman told himself that intrigue was part of the job and checked the results of the search he'd left running. He frowned at seeing another potential source eliminated. Bonnie Franks had died two weeks ago. Bruising and cut marks on the body suggested he'd been tortured before being left hanging from a tree in a popular city park. Because Franks had a long history of marketing narcotics, the police had essentially ruled his death the price of doing business.

"Damn." Time for him to change tactics. Diversify. He might be able to get information from Selman and Adams tomorrow, but he should also look more closely at the Minors' daughter. To him there was nothing in her face that suggested Jackson Tanner had a part in her DNA makeup. Looks could be deceiving, though, which he knew very well.

Roman smoothed down his goatee, then glanced at his watch. His allotted time was almost up. Perhaps talking with Knight would give him another perspective.

As he stepped into the elevator with his duly licensed gun covered by his jacket, the badly beaten body of Vicki Adams was discovered by a group of teenagers in a heavily wooded area.

* * *

When Ian's cell shrilled as Wednesday turned into Thursday, it caught him in postcoital glow. His first reaction was irritation, his second, worry. Worry that somehow Tanner had found Adeena. Ian reached over Andi's naked body and grabbed his phone. "Yeah."

"Is this Ian Zucker?"

He blinked when Andi turned on the bedside lamp. "Who's calling?"

"This is ADT. Your alarm was tripped. Is this Ian Zucker?"

"Yes."

"Is everything okay?"

"What? No. I don't know. I'm not home right now." He rattled off his passcode when asked and threw back the covers. "I'll meet them there."

He sprang from the bed and reached for his clothes. "I need to go meet the police. My alarm went off."

"I'll come with you."

"No. Stay, sleep. It's probably a false alarm." After fastening his pants, he leaned down and gave her a kiss. "This is not how I wanted our first sleepover to end."

Andi smiled sleepily. "Then we'll have to try again."

"Friday? We can stay at my place. I make killer French toast." He kissed her again, aware that he was being sappy and not giving a damn.

"Friday," she agreed.

Ian cut five minutes off the drive to his place. There wasn't a police car in sight. "Great. Just great." He'd left Andi's warm bed for nothing.

Yawning, he walked to the side of the building where his place was and looked up. The door to the balcony was closed and the lights were off. Definitely a false alarm. As he turned to go to the front, he caught a movement out of the side of his eye. Before he could process what he was seeing, pain exploded in the back of his skull. His vision wavered as he grabbed his head. The face in front of him looked a little different, but the eyes were the same. "You!"

His assailant grinned and grabbed his arm. "Yeah, me. This time you might want to stick with the truth, Zucker."

Ian pulled, but couldn't loosen the other guy's grip. "Let me go. I don't know what you're talking about." A hard fist to the stomach took his breath and brought him to his knees. For a moment he was afraid he was going to die as no air filled his lungs, then in a rush of pain, his breath returned and he wished it gone.

"My client doesn't like liars. More important, I don't like liars. You and I are going to take a little ride, have another chat."

"No!" Ian tried to yell it, but it came out small, weak. Fighting through pain and fear, he attempted to crawl away only to have his foot grabbed and twisted. Pain radiated up his leg, stopping any movement.

"We can do this the hard way, which I would love, or the easy way. Either way you're going to tell me where Adeena Minor is."

*Liar*, he thought. This guy was all about the hard way. But it seemed the only way to survive long enough to escape was to pretend to go along. "Easy." The quiet laugh sent chills down his spine.

"Good choice. We're going to return to your car, take a drive and if I like what you say, I'll let you live. If not..." He pulled a gun from behind him and pointed it at Ian's head.

"Okay, okay. I'll tell you everything."

"Your kind always does." He pulled Ian to his feet. "One word and the first bullet goes in your spine. Then things get fun."

Ian walked to his car feeling the constant pressure of the gun against his back and the throb in his twisted ankle. His only hope to get away would come when they were getting into his car. That plan died when he spotted the big man sitting on the hood of his car.

*Now or never*, he thought and faked a stumble. When the maniac bent down toward him, Ian reared back with his head. When he screamed, it was for help and from the excruciating pain in his head. His vision blurred, then dimmed to nothingness. He didn't hear the obscenities or feel the fury of the kick that damaged his ribs—at least not then.

# CHAPTER SIXTEEN

When Adeena's alarm blared out music at three forty-five a.m., Ian was already dead. She immediately rolled out of bed ready to take on the day. In spite of the excitement of meeting Mrs. Robinson and her worry about meeting the Kennedys, she'd managed a solid seven hours of sleep and was ready for the eight-hour road trip that would eventually end up in Seneca. Sal had arranged for their current rental car to be picked up at the hotel in case anyone had gotten wind of their presence. They were going to take a taxi to the airport and rent another car under her Lisa persona. Once again, she wasn't certain the subterfuge was strictly necessary, but Sal was convinced driving to Seneca was the best way to continue to keep them off MM and his hired gun's radar. And as Sal was once again picking up the tab, it was hard to object.

A quick shower taken care of, she put on her slutty-girl getup for all the fifty minutes plus it would take to go to the airport and pick up the car. It seemed like a waste of time—hers. But according to Thomasina Bond, it was necessary. Adeena's argument that the hotel staff could identify the real her had been shot down as well. According to Sal, the hotel staff was paid well to not recognize anyone.

Adeena carried the heels as she wheeled her bag into the shared area. Sal was lounging on the sofa, squinting at one of the two laptops she always seemed to have open and looking like she'd spent the night with them. "You do remember? Taxi, fifteen, right?"

"Yeah, yeah, bags packed." Sal waved a hand toward her luggage and yawned. "I think I'm on to something big, but it takes a while to take the pieces of the puzzle apart and put them together so the image's correct."

"Should we stay?"

"Nah. I can do this in the car while you drive. We can have Dani do any follow-ups if needed." Sal finished off a Coke, then began packing her equipment.

"Fine. I want coffee." She moved to the kitchen area and prepared a cup of much-wanted coffee. She didn't really need the caffeine yet. Not with her adrenaline amped up. She just loved the taste of the expensive brand she couldn't bring herself to buy at home. She was definitely going to miss living in the luxurious setting once she was back in her apartment. But she sure wouldn't miss not seeing her baby. Their one video call had only upset her and confused Diablo. She'd decided their next interaction would be in person.

Downstairs it was too early for her costume to draw many looks, but the taxi driver gave her a once-over that suggested he'd like to ask how much she charged. Sal, busy with her phone, seemed oblivious to the byplay.

The look she got from the guy at the car rental counter was full of suspicion and disdain. He made a show of checking her driver's license and handling the cash with only two fingers. Adeena imagined he would run to the bathroom and scrub his hands as soon as they were gone. The thought amused her while she spent time in the bathroom of a nearby gas station turning back into herself. Or she would have been herself if she wasn't once again wearing oversized-sunglasses and a New York Yankees baseball cap.

"Cigarette?" Sal gave up slouching against the wall and held out a pack.

"I didn't know you smoked." She pulled down her cap as they walked past the store clerk at the island of registers and out the door. She wondered what he made of her quick makeover.

"I don't. And that's why no one will think it was me buying cigarettes. I'm a genius."

"You are something. Okay, next step registering at a Savannah hotel we will *not* be staying at."

"Once you see it, you'll thank me for not making you stay there." Sal opened the driver's side door of the spiffy, red Mustang and motioned for Adeena to get in. "It's not in the best of neighborhoods."

She waited for Sal to skirt around the hood and slide in the passenger seat before asking, "Then why bother? Who's going to believe you'd stay at anything but the top of the line?"

"Someone who thinks I'm trying to fool them by staying off the radar. How many more times do you want me to explain?"

Adeena swallowed a snarky response. "What about the car? Won't it get stolen before we finish registering? I told you we should have gotten something nondescript."

"Don't worry. I got this covered. And yes, I know people who know people."

"You and your people. Put the address into the GPS," Adeena ordered and pulled off the sunglasses so she could see. "This is one time I do not want to get lost."

"As you command."

Adeena gave her the look before backing out.

The Inn was located on the south side of Savannah. Adeena thought calling it an inn was a stretch. It was two ugly rows of rooms and much past its prime, which had probably been in the fifties. "I'll wait in the car."

"Can't. The clerk has to be able to describe you should anyone come looking."

"Take a picture with your cell."

"We're registering under your real name, remember? Ten or so minutes, in and out. Think of it as an adventure."

"I bet the roaches have roaches in this place." Adeena tried for a pitiful-me look which garnered no response. "Okay, fine. But if I catch something, I will sulk for days." She got out of the car, clutching her bag to her chest. "Don't see why we can't register in your name."

Sal sighed. "Who are they looking for?"

Adeena shut up.

The inside was surprisingly decent, absent an army of roaches ready to take them hostage. Adeena was further surprised when the burly guy behind the scarred counter actually asked for, then scrutinized their IDs.

He handed Adeena the keycards, then gave them the spiel about checkout time and the ice machine location.

"Now that wasn't so bad, right?" Sal asked as they walked back to the car.

She shrugged.

"Good. Now for the hard."

"Hard? What hard? There was no mention of hard."

"You need to go in the room." Sal said it quickly as if that would make it more palatable.

"No."

"Yes. To make this work. Twenty minutes and the clerk will have stopped watching. I'll drive around the back, then you come join me."

"Why can't I drive around the back? And who wants to be alone in this neighborhood in the dark? There's no telling what's out there."

Sal slung an arm around Adeena's shoulder and pulled her close. "Odds are good they'll figure out today we're in Savannah," she said quietly. "I want them to think you're at this hotel for as long as possible."

"And you think twenty minutes will do it?"

"Twenty minutes and a sleight of hand. Later today, someone with your build will be seen going to the ice machine and the car will be parked out front."

"You should have told me all this sooner. I'm not so good with last minute."

"It only came to me this morning. But that's no excuse. We're partners and I should have laid it all out. I'm sorry."

As one who had trouble admitting when she was wrong, Adeena was easily swayed by the quick and sincere apology. "Forgiven. Twenty minutes and not a second longer. And I'll be the one driving while you figure out if they're on to us."

"Deal. I'll be back later," Sal said loudly. "As promised."

"Whatever," she replied for the benefit of the unsteady couple passing them.

It took a lot for her to enter the room, only to find that yet again, things weren't as bad as she'd imagined. The bed was made and from where she was standing she could see a coin slot. "It vibrates." She took out her phone and snapped some photos to share with Ian. He would get a kick out of that and the mirror on the ceiling. She'd send them with appropriate captions while he was at work, hopefully in a meeting.

With ten seconds left, Adeena eased open the door, shut it carefully and hurried in the direction Sal had taken. She found Sal leaning against the car, talking to a skinny black guy. Money was exchanged and the guy walked away on foot.

"I won't even ask," she said and took the keys Sal was dangling. "One of your people?"

"I thought you weren't going to ask." Sal sauntered around the car. "In my business it pays to pay contacts. Money makes them more inclined to be loyal."

"Oh kay." She slipped into the driver's seat and fastened her seat belt. "Is this the same car? It sort of looks the same, but it feels different somehow."

"Because it is different. How else can our car be parked in front of the room later?"

"I bow in awe of your preparedness, Mistress Sal. Next step on our tour is Atlanta. Where we will register at another hotel we won't be staying in. It's a good thing you're rich."

Sal gave a queenly bow of her head and booted up her smaller laptop. "And since I am so rich, I could use more caffeine. Coke please."

"And you didn't get one at the last place why?"

"Didn't go with the cigarettes. We passed a gas station a block over."

"This car will not be stopping until we leave this neighborhood behind. Far behind." She shuddered as they passed a ramshackle house with grass a mile high. There was no telling what kind of predators were lurking within it.

"Why do I get the impression you've led a sheltered existence?"

"Because I have. Not ashamed of it."

"No reason to be. I can wait until we hit Highway 16 for that caffeine. It's not that far."

Adeena shot Sal a quick glance before she made the next right as ordered by the mechanical voice. "I hope I didn't offend you with comments about the neighborhood. I suppose you didn't always live the way you do now."

"No worries. My skin's tougher than it looks."

"But you did live in a neighborhood like this, right?"

"It was worse and it was only for a little while. I don't have any baggage left over from that time if that's what you're getting at. According to my grandmother, I'm an optimist."

"What do you think you are?"

"An adventurer. Every day can be an adventure, a chance to experience something new. It's what helps me bounce out of bed."

"Adventurer. I like the sound of that." Adeena saw the sign for I-16 a split second before she was told to take the next left. "Looks like you have your choice between Quick Trip and Chevron."

"Quick Trip. Like the name."

"You got it. Next time I come back to Savannah, I'm def—"

"Son of a bitch!"

Adeena almost put her foot on the accelerator despite the red light. All she could see was a set of headlights in the rearview mirror. There was no way to tell make, model or if there was a homicidal maniac pointing a gun. "If you think we're being followed, you need to tell me now." Her voice sounded calmer than she felt. Maybe they should have rented a Hummer with bullet proofing.

"What? No. The asshat who tried to shoot you is dead. They discovered his body yesterday. Stabbed to death."

"How can that be? He's in jail."

"You need to get out more, *Lisa*. Criminals frequently inhabit jails. Not a stretch to think one took money to off him. Wonder if he was going to spill his guts for a deal. That on top of the failure to complete the mission would be more than enough reason to dispose of him."

"Maybe the reason is because we're dealing with a psychopath who's decided we all must die in order for him to rule the word. He did have an occupied house burned to the ground to get rid of his baby-mamma. And most likely we'll find he's gotten rid of anyone else involved in the kidnapping, birth and adoption. What stellar genes I come from. Makes me so proud." She punched the steering wheel.

"Remember the letter writer," Sal said, sounding hesitant. "Hard to mail something if you're dead. Someone out there knows his secrets and is still alive to tell."

"Was Tanner's name mentioned in that letter? No! They don't know his secrets. They know *my* secrets. And they could be dead by now." *Probably are dead*, she thought and tried to swallow the lump in her throat. All because she hadn't died when he wanted her to. That was the kind of monster she came from.

"I, uh, I disagree. I think the letter writer is still alive. They might not know Tanner's secrets, but they have to know enough to know they're in danger."

"I hope so. I don't want to think of what the death count is up to."

"Then don't."

"Easier said than done. A hell of a lot easier." Adeena sighed as she made the left. "Life. What can you do?"

"Scream. Wouldn't you know it? Now that asshat's dead, I'm that much closer to figuring out who paid him. The Orion Group. Probably a shell company with a name like that."

"Any luck hacking Burlett or linking him to Tanner?"

"That's a negative. Guy knows his stuff or hired someone like me. Wonder if Dani got anywhere with him yesterday?"

"If he even agreed to talk to her. Frankly, I don't see why he would."

"To see what she might know. Since he's here, odds are he's trying to find info on Heather, and finding out who sold her would be a great place to start. Which begs the question why anyone would care. There's nothing to gain."

"Because he wants to kill them." Adeena tightened her grip on the steering wheel and wished it was Tanner's neck. "Remember the part about taking out everyone involved with everything?"

"Then Tanner picked the wrong dude. Burlett doesn't give that kind of service. Told you I checked him out and he's one of the good guys."

"And people are good until they aren't." She put on her blinker, then turned into the Quick Trip's empty parking lot. "He has to be not so good to work for Tanner, who we've already established is a psychopath."

"Speak for yourself. Could be Tanner's just an egomaniac. And Burlett might not know he's working for Tanner. Easy to have someone he knows hire Burlett. But I'd bet you money Burlett's job is to locate people, not kill them."

Adeena rolled her eyes and thought, *Smug bitch. Easy to bet money when you have so much.* "Me, I don't bet. But if you find someone and they then get killed, you're just as guilty of killing them in my humble opinion."

Sal chuckled. "I doubt there's a humble bone in your body."

"Whatever." Feeling disgruntled about Sal's attitude, Tanner's murdering ways and the state of the world, she yanked the key from the ignition. "You want anything to go with that drink?"

"Cheese danish. Make that two. Two Cokes as well. Make that one Coke, one Cherry Coke."

When Sal reached for her wallet, Adeena waved her off. "This I can handle, rich girl."

Inside the too-bright store, she lost her mad before she made it to the cooler. It was stupid to get upset with Sal for disagreeing with her. She'd seen Sal's thoroughness for herself, so if she said the investigator was okay, then he was. It wasn't his or Sal's fault she had crazy for a sperm contributor. The sooner she reconciled herself to that bitter disappointment, the better for her mental well-being.

She paid for her purchases and left the sleepy-looking clerk with a cheery wish that he have a great morning. When she returned to the car, the look on Sal's face destroyed her new found cheer. "What now?" she demanded. "Have they traced us to Savannah?" Adeena fastened her seat belt, put the key in the ignition and mentally prepared herself to run.

"You have a habit of thinking the worst. My grandmother would not call you an optimist."

"You think?"

"I really do." Sal, seemingly oblivious to the heavy sarcasm, calmly pulled a danish out of the bag, tore open the package, took a big bite and chewed slowly. "Tanner and company continue to stay one step ahead of me and it's starting to seriously piss me off. Vicki Adams. Who is that you might ask? Let me tell you. Ms. Adams was working at St. Joseph/Candler Hospital as a nurse when James Minor Jr. died at the ripe old age of ninety-three. His wife, Joy Minor, had died at the very same hospital two months earlier. And Ms. Adams, through her father, is connected to our lawyer friend Nicholson."

Hope bloomed. "You think she sent me the letter? That she was there when I was born?"

"We'll never know. Her body was discovered yesterday. According to early reports, it looked like someone worked her over before they strangled her. No sign of rape, so not your average run-of-the-mill killer. Not that I'm an expert on killers."

Adeena put the car back in park, turned off the ignition and rested her head against the steering wheel. Fear and panic, thicker than molasses, squeezed her heart. They had to go to the police now, tell what they knew. The situation was way beyond their control. But first there were others to be seen to. "We should call Dani. Make sure she's okay. Make sure he didn't kill her. I can't…can't believe it. Oh God, and I have his DNA inside of me."

"Wait a minute." Sal put a hand on her arm. "I've always been on the nurture over nature side of the argument. Sure, my parents were grifters, but who knows what I might be if they hadn't taught me the game and the rules not long after I could talk. And sure they taught me to bend the law a little bit, but you won't find me breaking it in half. That, my dear, is nurture."

"Or is it your nature to be a good person at the core?"

"If it's mine, then it's obviously yours too or you wouldn't be so worried about it. And if that's not enough, it's obvious the people who raised you nurtured you right. See, no worries."

"No worries? I can't do that. Not when I'm also stuck in disbelief. Come on, this should not be happening to me. It's like I'm on a soap opera only I don't know my lines. Hell, I don't even know what role I'm playing." Adeena put a hand to her chest, felt the rapid beat of her heart. "We need to go back, talk to the police. Tell them about the other dead guy you found."

"And tell them what exactly? It's our word against a guy who's a member of an established Savannah family. I say we wait until I find the money trail. What we can do is have Dani go talk to the police. She'll know how to feel them out, see if they're receptive to any information we have. She was a cop, remember? They'll believe her before they believe us."

"You're right as usual." She exhaled and felt some of the panic smooth out. "She knows how to speak their language. Smart enough to sense any danger. I did say she looks like she can take care of herself. That could work."

"Will work. Now don't you feel better?"

"I do. I do." Adeena fumbled with the top of the Diet Dr. Pepper bottle she'd bought for herself and finally managed to twist it off. "I can't tell you why that poor woman's death rattles me so much. It just does."

"Because it proves how deep this mess is, deep and wide. Use the rattled nerves as motivation. I do it all the time."

She nodded and then guzzled half of the bottle. When she opened her mouth to speak, a thunderous burp erupted that seemed to reverberate around the inside of the car. "Excuse me." Covering her mouth in embarrassment, she checked Sal's reaction.

"Impressive." Sal held up nine fingers. "You ever do competitions?"

The emphatic "no" she had planned came out as another loud burp. It was quickly followed by a giggle she hadn't realize was coming. Another glance at a grinning Sal and she began to laugh. Soon they were both howling with laughter.

Adeena used the back of her hands to wipe her eyes once the laughter was under control. "I think I needed that."

"I've always found burping to be cathartic. Not quite as good as farting, of course." Sal flashed a dimpled grin.

"You're a sophisticated woman, Ms. Salamander. Who knew?"

"When you come for that visit I'll show you the depths of my sophistication, Ms. Minor. There will be shock and awe."

"I'm sure there will be." Adeena smiled as she started the car and backed out. "You're a woman of many talents. So along with hacking and creating impressive Lego buildings, what else do you do?"

"You know Vegas and gambling, so let's see…Hanging out in Times Square, movies. I'm a serious movie buff. Action, adventure, sci-fi and some comedy. How 'bout you? What do you like to do when you're not tracking down killers?"

"We've already talked about my boring life. Even conservatives would have problems accusing me of having a 'big gay agenda.'"

"Gay? We didn't talk about that. My gaydar must be busted. Didn't even give me a little ping."

"You pinged big-time on mine." She checked for traffic before shooting across the road and making the right onto the ramp and then merging onto Interstate 16. "I do like to read. Mysteries and thriller have always been a favorite. I've discovered, though, it's a hell of lot more fun to read about mystery and murder than to be caught in the middle of either. In retrospect, being unexciting is not such a bad thing."

Sal washed the last bits of her first danish down with soda and opened the second package. "Don't forget about the thriller part. We've had that too."

"One of these days I might look back on running for my life and facing a guy with a gun as thrilling. Maybe. Or maybe not. Most likely not."

"You misunderstood. I was talking about your Lisa outfit. There's been more than one guy and yes, probably some women, who got a thrill. Mr. Taxi Driver looked ready to empty his wallet for some of your time."

"Oh?" Brows arched she glanced at Sal only to find her once again hunched over her laptop. "I thought you didn't notice."

"Oh, I noticed," Sal said, never looking away from the screen. "And appreciated."

"Yeah? Well, don't get too used to it. Strictly temporary."

"Understood. I can appreciate more than one look. Despite what you may hear."

*Interesting*, Adeena thought. Anyone other than Sal and she would have seen that as a show of interest. With Sal she wasn't sure and that wasn't necessarily a bad thing. Between work and inertia she hadn't given her social calendar much consideration. There had been a couple of forgettable dates and not much else in the past eight months or so.

And now there was Sal. Super geek mixed with sweetness, topped by soft eyes. *And an uptown residence on the opposite side of the country*, she reminded herself. But there was also the adorable dimple that flashed when Sal grinned, the unassailable loyalty to family and family of family, the bravery to stick by a woman with serious problems. All good qualities. Since she was adding the plusses, she'd needed to throw in brains. The woman was obviously smart, and, yeah, she needed to acknowledge the loaded part. That couldn't be understated.

"Damn," she said without any heat. The points were skyrocketing too fast for her liking.

"Problem?"

"Something I need to work out. Later." Time to shelve the little pull of attraction. Later, when she was sure she had a future to worry about, she could take it back out, dissect it and decide if it was something worth pursuing.

# CHAPTER SEVENTEEN

Charles set aside the paper with a grumble. It was getting so he couldn't enjoy his morning coffee in peace. He frowned at the caller ID. "Farrago? Orders are you are to go directly to her now."

"It's bad. Real bad, Deveraux."

"Shit. Tell me."

"The girl's in Savannah and—"

"What? When? When did she get here?"

"Monday. Came on a chartered flight from New York City with a Thomasina Salamander."

"Damn! Must have left right after the botched kidnapping attempt. How sure are you about this?"

"Very. I got it out of a reliable source. Had a friend do a little sniffing around in New York to verify. But what's important is they're staying at the Portman Hotel under assumed names. And it gets worse."

"How the hell can it?"

"She found out yesterday that Tanner's her biological father."

"Fuck!" Charles banged his fist on the table, knocking over the coffee cup. "Goddamn son of a bitch! No way she should know that. How? Conlin got to everyone."

"Apparently he didn't. Something about a mysterious letter and a thesis from Georgia Tech. My source was crapping out on me by then. He did tell me that the girl contacted Cynthia Kennedy. Something about her being Kennedy's sister's twin. It was Kennedy who sent Salamander to check things out. Now I can't get there for hours, but I do have a couple of associates who can handle things until I get there. Will the old lady go for that?"

"Not much choice. This shit's got to be dealt with and fast. Send your men. Have them snatch 'em up for now. More instructions to follow. Is Vegas contained?"

"It is now."

"Then get here as fast as you can." Charles dropped the phone on the table and grabbed his head. It was a fact that Mrs. T was going to fucking stroke out when she heard. They'd been together long enough for him to know she wouldn't shoot the messenger. But boy would she be like a bear with a splinter in its paw to deal with. Too bad she hadn't let the boy sort out his own mess all those years ago and all the years since. If she had a blind spot it was for her boy, Jackson. No matter how many beds he slipped out of, she was always there to support him.

*Like I'm always there to support her*, Charles thought. Mrs. T had been good to him over the years and he owed her a lot. Maybe when this mess was cleared up, he'd go find Conlin, bring him back and let Mrs. T have a go. Yeah, he could do that for her, he decided, as he put on his professional mantle in preparation for ruining his boss' day.

"I expect you to call me from now on, Mr. Farrago. Whatever the news." Eugenia ended the call in midsentence, slipped the phone into the pocket of her robe and put a hand to her rapidly beating heart. She wasn't worried about a heart attack, but a stroke wasn't out of the question. What an affront it was for that girl to be here in Savannah, near Jackson, near his campaign. If

Jackson caught as much as a glimpse of the girl with Lucy's face, it would undo everything she'd ever wanted him to have. One glimpse and he would start to question, start to dig until he had all the answers. No matter what he might say, he wouldn't be able to turn Lucy's child away.

"That damn Conlin!" That girl shouldn't have survived three attempts on her life, let alone found her way to the city where she should've been born. There was no possible way the girl had figured out her roots by herself. The parents must have known about Lucy and Jackson. They must have left a letter for their daughter to read after their death. A letter that explained her origins. She should have thought of that earlier, should have instructed Conlin to interrogate the girl first and then dispose of the body so that no one would find her. These matters were always clearer in hindsight.

Eugenia crossed to the window overlooking the well-cared-for backyard and only saw broken dreams. If the wrong people saw that girl, had the chance to speak to her, they might begin to remember Lucy. In remembering Lucy, they would remember the pregnancy and how Lucy's offspring would be the same age. These days it only took one set of loose lips to start an avalanche that would wipe out Jackson's good name, along with their family's good standing in Savannah and in Georgia.

"No!" That was *not* going to happen to her son. Farrago had to get rid of the girl. That was the only solution. But this time she would be the one calling the shots. Done right, the death of Adeena Minor would never be connected to Jackson. She would tell Farrago how to set the scene that would lead the police to the conclusion she wanted them to reach. Conlin may have disappeared, but she would still gladly throw him under the bus in absentia. As an added bonus, the police would be wasting their time trying to find both Conlin and his connection to the Minor girl.

Sal looked up from her laptop and rotated her neck. As much as it pained her to admit it, she'd hit a dead end. Whoever had set up the account for the Orion Corporation was a fucking genius and as much as it pissed her off, she also felt admiration for a job well done. Her stomach rumbled and she tuned back into her current surroundings to discover they'd been on the road for almost four hours. Breakfast time. "I'm getting hungry."

"Back to this world then." Adeena paused the book she'd been listening to on her phone. "I could eat and I certainly wouldn't mind a chance to stretch. I wonder what people did before audible books."

"Fell asleep at the wheel or sang along with the radio." Sal checked her phone. "There's a Cracker Barrel about an hour from here. They do a decent breakfast."

"Cracker Barrel? Really? Do you think they know what else 'cracker' can mean?"

"It's the South, so yeah, I assume they know. Maybe it was founded by the Cracker family. Or maybe they like crackers. I do know we're getting closer to Atlanta and the traffic there sucks during the morning and evening commute and sometimes in between."

"They have some of the longest commutes in the nation, courtesy of sprawl. I almost applied for a job at the Atlanta equivalent of my agency. Read up on the area first."

"Why didn't you?"

"My girlfriend at the time lived in Oakland. And I was younger and believed my relationship with my mother would eventually turn around. Turns out my girlfriend and I split up and my mother never got around to approving of me."

Sal didn't know how to respond. She only had good memories of her mother. "That's, uh, too bad."

"That's life. At least now I can tell myself I understand why she never loved me. And, hey, I really was adopted."

"Don't forget while you're talking to yourself to tell yourself how much your birth mother loved you. It has to balance the scales some."

"It does. So did my dad. Love me. There was never any doubt he loved me, would've been proud of me even though I didn't become a medical doctor. That's what my mother wanted for me. Smart little girls become doctors. I guess I should be grateful her plan wasn't for me to marry one."

Sal thought about Lucy, about how she planned to be a doctor. "Is there a chance your mother knew Lucy? Wanted you to become a doctor because she knew Lucy wasn't able to?"

"Doubtful. For my mother, my being smart was a status symbol. Something she could brag about when she was with her cronies. Medical doctors rate a lot higher than someone with a PhD."

"I think a PhD is impressive. What would also be impressive is if you could stop at the next gas station for a bathroom break. My bladder woke up with a vengeance."

Adeena sped up. "According to the last sign, the next exit's in a couple of miles."

"Good. Maybe getting out and stretching will jump-start my brain."

"What exactly are you looking for?"

"I'm trying to follow the money back to the source and hitting a roadblock. Make that a cliff. There's no going around, only over to nothingness."

"Meaning?"

"Meaning I can't prove Tanner paid for a damn thing and it's seriously pissing me off! Most people leave crumbs, damn it. Crumbs you can follow." She covered a yawn.

"Maybe he borrowed it from someone else's account like your brother-in-law did." Adeena cleared her throat. "That should be allegedly. Guilty until—"

"No allegedly about it in Stephen's case. He's guilty as hell."

"So then why can't MM be stealing from his wife, no, his mother's—"

"His mother!" Sal smacked the dashboard. "His mother. Say you're eighteen and find out you've knocked up the girl your mother warned you about. What do you do?"

"Hire someone to kill her?"

"No. You're young, you're stupid at eighteen. Most people that is. You twist, you turn, then you go to the person who thinks it's her job to look out for you."

"His mother!"

"Bingo. She's already proven she cares about you by pulling you from the clutches of a no-good woman. So she pats him on the head, tells him she'll deal with it. She's the one who did the hiring, the paying. Why didn't I think of this sooner?" Sal rubbed her hands together. "I can work with this. Eugenia Tanner, open wide. I'm about to do a deep cavity search."

"Okay. I'm forced to ask what it is you do. And no, it doesn't really matter, but curiosity's raised its ugly head. It's a flaw, I know."

"Me?" *Crunch time, as they say in* Star Trek *world,* Sal thought. In her world it meant shit or get off the pot. The itch was getting stronger with each mile. If she was going to get anywhere with Adeena, she needed to give more. Better to find out now if what she did was a deal breaker. "A little of this and a little of that. Some people want things found, others want things hidden. I can do both for a hefty fee if the client checks out by my standards. Disclaimer. It's not all strictly legal."

"That's almost funny. We're running from people who had no compunction about killing a pregnant woman and her family. Not strictly legal is barely a blip on my radar anymore."

"Good point. But I thought you should, uh, you should know that about me."

"Now I know. Disclaimer. Your 'not strictly legal' is what's kept me alive. Would be damn hypocritical of me to slap at you for it." Adeena threw a quick look at Sal. "I imagine that skill came in handy when you found yourself living in less than ideal circumstances."

"Sounds so sanitized. 'Less than ideal.'" It wasn't often Sal spent any time thinking about those two years. When played against the rest of her life, it was a small slice. Of course, while she was living it, surviving it, time had seemed to slow.

"Sorry. I shouldn't have brought it up again."

"That's okay. It was what it was. I lost a lot, but I gained too." Sal preferred to remember gaining a grandmother and regaining her belief in family rather than the death of her parents and the terrifying path that her family of choice had chosen. It was better to remember surviving, growing stronger and wiser. "Gained the skills to keep me in fancy digs."

"I can attest to that. I would say 'drink to that' if was after noon. Although, it's always after noon somewhere."

She smiled, relieved Adeena had picked up on her cue to lighten the subject matter. "Mimosas. That's what you can drink before noon. It's a Southern thing and we are in the South, so it's all good." The thought of drinking reminded her that she had to go to the bathroom. "Anyway we can go a little faster?"

Adeena sped up without asking for a reason. "They sell them at this Cracker Barrel you speak of?"

"Not in the middle of the week. We are in the Bible Belt. I'll fix you some when you come to New York."

"And will you cook?"

"Chicken and waffles."

"Stop. You'll make me hungry. And this exit doesn't have a decent place to eat." Adeena switched lanes. "So how did you end up in New York City instead of Boston?"

"New York's my heart." Sal thumped her chest. "I did as my grandmother wanted, graduated high school, then college. She knew I always intended to go back there. I can't imagine living anywhere else in the world."

"That means you've traveled?" Adeena pulled off the highway, made a right at the intersection, then another right into the gas station.

"I'll love you forever if you let me out at the door. May the Goddess bless you," Sal said as they came to a stop.

She was exiting the stall by the time Adeena entered the bathroom. After washing her hands, Sal checked her email messages. She quickly saw that all of them could be dealt with once they were settled into the hotel in Seneca. Cyn was going to join them for a late lunch, then the three of them would decide what the next step should be. She hoped that step would be DNA testing for Nate.

Adeena joined her at the sinks. "Everything's so clean. It pays to hit public restrooms early."

"We have to get our jollies where we can, I guess."

"I certainly hope I can do better than a public bathroom. Hey, I've been thinking. What do you think about the chance of getting like a strand of hair or a toothbrush from Tanner? I figure some of the people you know might know people who could do that kind of thing. We sort of talked about it earlier, but nothing was decided. I think having defendable proof would take away the necessity of killing me and anyone else."

Sal heard the underlying worry in Adeena's voice. "I know someone who can tell me how easy or hard that would be to do. Hell, for enough money, I bet she'd do the job herself." She checked the time, then flipped through her contact list. It would give them some breathing space while allowing her to get the financial evidence needed to tie Eugenia Tanner to a "murder for hire" scheme. "I should have thought of this when you mentioned it yesterday."

"We can't all be geniuses like *moi*."

Sal laughed. "Remember what I said about you and humble. Rae…Yeah, yeah. I know it's early, but it'll be worth your while… You know me, I'm good for it." She explained what she wanted done. "Get me confirmation it's at the lab and the money'll be in your account."

"You're handy to have around." Adeena opened the bathroom door. "Buy you a drink?"

"For now, but I'm counting on you paying for breakfast too."

"I'll even pay for lunch. That means it'll be your turn at dinnertime."

"Yeah? That means you're down for breakfast tomorrow."

"You're on." Adeena stopped in front of the cooler. "Breakfast is usually the cheapest meal."

"Why is it I always get the women who want me for my money?"

"Maybe you've been associating with the wrong kind of women, Salamander. Could it be you're not giving them what they need in other areas?"

"Hey. I'm a very good driver," she whispered, affronted by the insinuation.

Adeena's mouth dropped open before she threw back her head and laughed. "Priceless." She threw an arm around Sal's shoulder and gave her a quick squeeze. "Thank you for being you."

Sal caught the subtle hint of perfume, enjoyed the feel of Adeena's body pressed to hers and hung on. And the itch morphed to something more. What a bad time to give up the forgettable blondes, because now she didn't have them for distraction, didn't have them to keep her out of trouble. Trouble that wouldn't be solved with a new Lego set. If there was one thing Sal knew deep inside, it was that Adeena wasn't the type of woman she could easily get over by buying a million toys. "Thanks, but you're still paying for breakfast."

"And a Coke." Adeena waved the bottle at her and then grabbed a Diet Dr. Pepper.

"I meant to say something about you being a Pepper earlier."

"I hope you noticed it's diet in case you feel the need to stock up on supplies at a later date."

"Yeah, but I don't get that. The no sugar thing. Ruins the taste."

"What a surprise."

"You're full of sarcasm this morning. I think I like it."

"You know what I don't get? Glasses. They have surgery to correct vision. Surgery that's been perfected over a number of years. Ever thought about throwing some of your dead presidents that way?"

Sal pushed her glasses up her nose. "Would you tell Clark Kent to have laser surgery?"

"No. His glasses are clear. He only wears them to hide his secret identity. Something that wouldn't work in today's world."

Sal crossed her arms over her chest as Adeena counted out change for the cashier. "So you're claiming you know my secret identity?" She wanted to howl at the look she was getting from the female cashier. "No? Enough said. I'll be outside with the car."

She didn't have long to wait.

"We'd better hurry," Adeena said as she unlocked the car. "I think the cashier's calling for a padded wagon."

Sal looked up toward the sky and sighed dramatically. "See what we superhero types have to live with? It gets to be demoralizing. If I hadn't taken the oath to do no harm I'd have leveled this world years ago."

Adeena firmed her lips as if trying to suppress a smile. "And you, my dear, are full of shit. Get in."

"Okay, but know you're crushing my ego." She settled in her seat and fastened her seat belt.

Adeena got in, put the key in the ignition, then turned to Sal. "Okay. I get it. You don't want to say about the glasses. Fine." She started the car. "We have ways of making you talk."

"Get me in bed and I can't keep my mouth shut."

"I will take that under advisement," Adeena replied primly.

# CHAPTER EIGHTEEN

Normally Eugenia wouldn't be as rude as to answer her cell phone during one of her ladies' luncheons. Today was an exception. Noting the number, she excused herself saying, "Sorry. Jackson's campaign."

"What's the status?" she demanded as soon as she was outside the restaurant.

"She left the hotel this morning with Salamander and moved to a dump on the south side."

"How can you be sure?"

"She registered under her own name. My man went in and once the guy at the desk was satisfied he wasn't a cop, he identified Minor from a photo. We also got a lock on the car she rented and it's sitting right outside the room. Do you want my man to take them out now?"

"No. I want them taken out quietly after it gets dark. Take extreme care. No one should be able to trace this back to your man or you."

"My men and I are professionals, Mrs. Tanner. I believe that's why you hired me, ma'am."

Eugenia heard the affront in his voice and wondered what the world was coming to. She hadn't realized hardened criminals had thin skin. "And you're doing a fine job, Mr. Farrago. But I can't stress enough how important it is that this be done right. A lot is riding on it."

"Understood, ma'am. You want us to dispose of the bodies?"

"I want Minor's body buried in a particular backyard. Not so deep a cadaver dog can't sniff it out."

"You want the body found, ma'am?"

"That is what I said, Mr. Farrago. Please remember that I am not some feebleminded old lady."

"No offense meant, Mrs. Tanner."

*Too late*, she thought and gave him Conlin's address. "It's the type of neighborhood where you shouldn't have to answer any questions. Send me a text once you've left the property. I'll take care of the rest. Is that clear?"

"Crystal, ma'am."

"Don't disappoint me, Mr. Farrago." She ended the call and made another. "I don't have a lot of time, so listen carefully. I need you to go to Zane's Automotive. Find a Gregory Charles Selman and see how much it'll take for him to swear he was the father of Lucy Brown's babies. No more than ten thousand, but given his current financial situation, he should be willing to take less. And Charles, be sure to stress this is a one-time payment. I trust you'll let him know what happens if he gets too greedy?" She laughed at his response. "I'll find my own way home…Well, if you're sure…Thank you, old friend. I know I can always count on you."

* * *

As Eugenia returned to the restaurant, Dani and Detective Alexa Benson were taking the elevator up to Burlett's hotel room. After a call from Sal, Dani had done a little research into the Savannah PD. She'd singled out Detective Benson because she was the detective with the least number of years with the department and because she was African-American. Dani had hoped both of those qualities would make Benson more likely to take her seriously.

Dani had to admit she was surprised to get the call from Benson, asking her to join her for a talk with Burlett.

"I'd like you to take the lead initially," Benson said as they approached Burlett's room. She was tall and lean, with a no-nonsense manner Dani respected. "He knows you, has probably looked you up."

"'Knows' is too strong. We spent over an hour jockeying for position. Like I said, he's too smart to give up much."

"Let's say he knows more about you than about me then."

Dani nodded and knocked.

Burlett opened the door and looked at Dani, then the woman standing beside her. "Ms. Knight."

"Mr. Burlett, this is Detective Benson, Savannah PD. We were wondering if you were up for another informal chat."

He studied the badge thrust at him, then took a step back. "Come in."

Dani glanced around the room after choosing the sofa and found it neat and tidy. Detective Benson settled next to her, and Burlett positioned himself in the chair opposite them.

"What's this about?"

"We'll start with Ms. Vicki Adams," Dani replied. "Detective Benson's the detective in charge of investigating her murder."

"What about her? I know of the case. But so is the rest of the newswatching public."

"Did you know her?" Detective Benson's voice seemed deceptively mild.

"I knew of her. Planned to ask her some questions. I'm sure by now you've checked her answering machine, found my messages."

"What was the nature of your relationship?"

"We didn't have one. I'm attempting to locate someone on behalf of a client and believed she could provide me with information. Nothing more, nothing less."

"The name of the someone you're looking for?"

"It's not a secret. James Minor Jr."

"He's dead," Dani said, watching him closely for his reaction. As she'd expected, there wasn't one. "The real Minor died over thirty years ago. The fake Minor nineteen years ago."

"I see." His lips curved in the faintest of smiles. "It seems you've done my job for me."

"What was Ms. Adams' connection with the Minor you're looking for?" Detective Benson removed a small pad and pen from her suit jacket.

"I can't be certain there was one, Detective. As I explained, I believed she might have information on Mr. Minor. That was one of the reasons I needed to speak with her."

"I see." Detective Benson cocked her head and smiled. "Saying one of the reasons means there are more, Mr. Burlett. Would one of those reasons have anything to do with Kenneth Nicholson, the lawyer who handled the adoption of Heather Garson-Kennedy perchance? The same Kenneth Nicholson whose badly beaten dead body was discovered in a parking lot in Alabama?"

*Got you*, Dani thought, catching the fleeting widening of his eyes. "Any chance your client is Jackson Tanner?" She asked the question for Detective Benson's benefit. Thanks to Sal, she knew which Tanner Burlett probably answered to.

"None whatsoever."

"Who is your client, Mr. Burlett?" Detective Benson lost her mild tone.

He gave another stingy smile. "I'm sure Ms. Knight would agree that discretion is the name of the game in our business, Detective. For the protection of my reputation I'm going to have to insist you get a warrant for my records if you want that information."

Dani could tell they'd taken the wrong tack with him, had gotten his back up. And he seemed like the type who could keep his back up a long time.

"Mr. Burlett, are you familiar with Adeena Minor? She's the daughter of the Minor you're searching for. Adopted daughter, as she found out not that long ago. Kenneth Nicholson was involved in her adoption as well."

"Her name came up during my investigation," he admitted. "I have, however, not met or spoken with her. Nor was she part of my assignment."

"Are you aware that there have been three attempts on her life over the past few weeks?"

"Attempts on her life? My information says there was one incident involving a drunk driver."

"That's changed. The Las Vegas PD arrested someone for attempting to kidnap her at gunpoint a few days later." To Dani's satisfaction, his reaction was much more pronounced this time. Maybe she'd made the right decision. "Are you aware Ms. Minor has information that Lucy Mae Brown was her birth mother?"

Roman cleared his throat. "I certainly am not. But I fail to see what that has to do with me. As I previously explained, Ms. Minor is not my assignment."

"I'll tell you what it has to do with you and your assignment, Mr. Burlett," Benson said. "Lucy Brown supposedly died in a house fire when she was eight months pregnant. It would have been impossible for her to give her children up for adoption. Maybe now you can understand why we're asking questions about your client and why the SPD is somewhat suspicious of his or her interest in the fake Minor at this particular time."

"There is also credible evidence to suggest Jackson Tanner had a sexual relationship with Ms. Brown and is the biological father of Adeena Minor." Dani couldn't detect a response this time. Obviously he'd come to that conclusion on his own.

"Now me, I'm a cop and we cops don't generally believe in coincidence. I have to think that the timing of certain events— Adeena Minor's face being splashed in the news, the sudden murder attempts, Tanner announcing his candidacy—are, shall we say...suspicious." Detective Benson leaned forward. "I add in the timing of the death of Ms. Adams, of Mr. Nicholson, of Bonnie Franks, your client's interest in the Minors, and I can't help thinking something smells rotten. We came to you hoping you might have put some of these pieces together to make a bigger picture. I'm here to ask if you're willing to work with me. Make no mistake, I will get to the bottom of this matter. Your help will get me there sooner. I firmly believe the dead deserve justice, Mr. Burlett."

Any hint of a smile left his face. "I hope you realize what you might be going up against, Detective Benson."

"A murderer is a murderer. They need to face the consequences no matter *who* they are."

He nodded slowly. "I should start at the beginning. My original assignment was to look into Heather Garson-Kennedy's background, see if she'd ever made an attempt to find her birth parents. I was to do this without alerting the Kennedys. My conclusion was she'd never made the attempt or had the interest. I reported such to my client and was subsequently directed to find information on James Minor. Specifically, details about what was happening in his life thirty-four years ago. I, as you did, quickly discovered he hadn't existed by that name until about thirty-four years ago. Once I set about finding who he might have been before, I came upon the name of Ms. Adams."

"Whom you did not have a chance to speak with."

"That's correct, Detective Benson. I have a couple of other people who I also haven't been able to speak with. My client directed me to Minor's old neighborhood where I was given the name James Louis Early as a possible source of information about Minor. In trying to locate him, I spoke with his sister, Mrs. Shirley Brooks."

Benson made a notation in her notebook. "This Early was a friend of Minor?"

"Acquaintance perhaps. Once again, I can't be certain as to the nature of their relationship. I have yet to locate him, let alone have a conversation. You might be interested to know his name came up in conjunction with a Christmas Day fire that happened around thirty-four years ago. Nothing concrete, mind you, but I'm told there were plenty of rumors floating around back then. Apparently the police had that information. What they did with it, I couldn't say."

"The police require more than rumors, Mr. Burlett."

He shrugged. "Given that the fire fell into my time frame and the possible connection between Early and Minor, I did a little more digging. I discovered that a very pregnant Ms. Brown and her family perished in the fire. I did not hear of any connection between Minor or his wife and the fire. I did find out that Early's nephew was believed to be the father of Ms. Brown's babies. His aunt disagreed."

"Did she give you a name?"

"She did not, Detective Benson. According to her, Ms. Brown was a private person. Nonetheless, I began to draw conclusions. I may not be a cop, but I am skeptical of coincidences. The fire, the birth of the Minors' daughter, the interest in his life around the same time." He cleared his throat. "I'm feeling the need for something to drink. Can I interest you in a drink? I have water and soft drinks."

After filling their requests, he settled back into the chair and took a sip from his bottle of water. "Where was I? Ah yes. Uneasy suspicions. I was giving consideration to contacting your department," he admitted. "Like you, the more I dug, the worse things smelled. I read about the death of Bonnie Franks, who was a friend of Early's, and feared Early might have met the same fate."

"Are there any other names on your list, Mr. Burlett? Seems like almost everyone you mentioned turns up dead."

"Gregory Charles Selman. He's James Louis Early's nephew and dated Lucy Brown at one time. He was also friends with Minor when he went by the name Walter Morrow. Mr. Selman was under the impression that Walter and his wife had joined the Peace Corps and moved to Africa. He couldn't say whether she was pregnant or not as he hadn't had as much contact with Morrow once he got married. When I asked him about being the father of Lucy Brown's baby, he smiled while telling me he didn't kiss and tell.

"The name Jerome Henderson also popped up. He was supposed to have been an associate of Bonnie Franks back in the day. He's been dead twenty years, however, I heard he had a girlfriend and a child in his hometown of Pimberton. They were on my 'to do' list if Adams didn't pan out."

"Name of the girlfriend?" Benson asked.

"Minnie Johnson or Jones. I wasn't able to locate her during my initial search."

"I have someone who can find her," Dani said.

"She's no longer of importance to me." Burlett took a sip. "At this point I want nothing more to do with this assignment. This is not the kind of work I do, Detective Benson. Nor is it the kind of work I want to be associated with. A check of my history should have shown you that."

"No one is accusing you of anything, Mr. Burlett. I'm curious. Who would you have gone to in our department?"

"I never got that far. As you mentioned earlier, the police require facts. I don't have a single piece of evidence that my client was in any way involved in anything illegal. Coincidence and my gut do not constitute admissible evidence."

"They can lead an experienced detective such as myself to the admissible."

"You should be aware that the man who attempted to shoot Ms. Minor was found dead in his cell," Dani said. "Stabbed."

"I assure you that I can and will take care of myself should the need arise." He seemed to hesitate. "I was hired by Eugenia Tanner. I realize she has some juice in this town."

"That doesn't matter to me, Mr. Burlett. I'm charged to protect and serve. Our department is run differently these days. The SPD appreciates your support." Detective Benson's cell phone buzzed. She looked at it, quickly excused herself and left the room.

"You've done the right thing, Mr. Burlett."

"I hope she has some concrete evidence. Mrs. Tanner has a reputation of being untouchable."

"She went after the wrong person this time. They'll get her for this."

"What's your stake in this?"

"Keeping Adeena Minor alive while trying to find that concrete evidence. I was originally hired because the Kennedys were concerned about you and your questions."

"Are Adeena Minor and Heather Garson-Kennedy related through Jackson Tanner?"

"That's a working theory."

"Interesting. I wish you luck, Ms. Knight."

She took his hand. "Thank you. It was interesting sort of working with you."

She found Detective Benson in the hallway. "What do you think? About Burlett, about Mrs. Tanner?"

"I think he told it straight. The term 'steel magnolia' is apt in Eugenia Tanner's case. I've heard talk of some of the deals she's orchestrated behind the scenes, and while I can't say with a hundred percent certainty that she gave any orders to kill, I believe she has it in her. She has the mindset of old. Lucy Brown, a black girl, having a grandchild of hers would have been an affront to the family name and not what she had planned for her son."

"What about Jackson Tanner? Is he the kind of man to look the other way, let his mother do his dirty work?"

Benson frowned. "That I don't know. Talk is he's an upright guy. I checked and his boys have never been in any kind of trouble with the department. I would hope that means something about the kind of person he is."

# CHAPTER NINETEEN

Adeena stepped onto the tiny hotel balcony. Seneca, Georgia, was definitely no New York. It was, however, close to Nate and the Kennedys.

"You still worried?" Sal joined her on the balcony. "I told you it would be okay."

"Your worry scale and mine don't match." She leaned against the rail and let the midday sun warm her face. "We're asking a lot and at a difficult time."

"It's not a lot. A simple mouth swab to be compared against yours, and Tanner's if we can find a way to get it. I personally think it's best for all concerned to know the truth."

There was something in Sal's voice that made her turn. "You found something?"

Sal nodded. "The name on the account she uses is Phillip Marcus Tanner."

"Her grandson? She's using her own grandson?"

"Social doesn't match. I checked, his middle name is Dawson. The Phillip on the account is her husband's dead brother. Not sure how she got on the account, which was opened before the older Phillip died. Of interest is that she recently wired a big chunk to a Vincent Farrago."

"Farrago? That fits. Remember Ian said a Vincent Fabbrini was looking for me? Same guy. I'd bet on it, but I—"

"Don't bet. As Farrago he has a little office in Vegas. PI, supposedly. You go down a couple of layers and you see he's been in the business of mayhem for ten years. Amazingly enough, one couldn't tell how lucrative his business has been looking at his tax returns. The IRS won't like that."

"Was the money to take care of me or the guy who tried to take care of me?"

"Best guess? The guy who tried to take care of you. Poor Mrs. Tanner doesn't seem to be getting the best from her hired guns."

"My heart bleeds. Wonder how long before he figures out where I am."

"Not as long as I'd like. He or someone using his name landed in Savannah an hour ago. What I don't know is how he figured out you were there. My guy in New York swears no one has asked about our flight."

"My name is on record at The Inn. And has been since early this morning."

"I don't like it. They shouldn't have found that place this soon. There are plenty of other hotels in Savannah."

"Are you worried they'll find us here? Maybe we should leave. I wouldn't want to see anyone else hurt because of me."

"It's not because of you, Adeena. It was never because of you. You're the innocent victim."

Adeena exhaled. "You're right. Sometimes I forget it's not all about me."

"It's about you. What you have to remember is 'about' and 'because' are two different words. It's because of Ma Tanner and maybe son Tanner. The responsibility for any murder and mayhem lies with them."

"Hearing it from someone else helped a little. Hope Cynthia Kennedy agrees."

"She's smart."

"That may be. I only hope she's open-minded enough to give me the benefit of a doubt."

"Let's go see."

They went down to find the lobby teeming with technology convention attendees. Cynthia Kennedy was scheduled to attend some sessions tomorrow, which made it the perfect hotel for them to hide in plain sight. This time they were registered under one of Sal's female aliases.

"Everyone's trying to get a room before the opening session starts," Sal remarked. "Perfect cover for us."

"Except it makes it harder for us to spot her."

"Not really. Ken, over here." Sal waved a hand to get the attention of a tall woman wearing sunglasses and a wide-brimmed hat.

Adeena was relieved that Cynthia Kennedy was dressed casually in jeans and a polo shirt as Sal had promised. She stayed silent as Sal and Cynthia exchanged a long hug. Their affection for one another was there for all to see.

"Didn't we just do this?" Sal stepped back and looked Cynthia up and down. "You're looking good. What I can see of you, that is."

Cynthia grinned and removed the hat and glasses. "It's only been a few days. How did you expect me to look?"

"Doesn't matter." Sal held out a hand to Adeena. "Come meet Cyn. My BFF."

Adeena felt a prick of alarm at the sudden coolness in Cynthia's blue eyes. Here was someone who seemed to be judging her as wanting. She lifted her chin and held out a hand. "Adeena Minor. Glad to meet any friend of Sal's." *And Heather's sister*, she thought but didn't dare say. "Thanks for agreeing to the meet."

"It seems to be necessary for all of us."

Adeena found the words as cool as the eyes.

"We can talk down here, then go to lunch or go up to the suite, then come down and go to lunch. I'm told they have an excellent buffet." Sal pointed to one of the semiprivate seating areas that was out of the way of lobby traffic.

"Down here is fine." Cyn finger-combed her hair as they crossed the lobby. "The paparazzi should still be chasing Nick to nowhere."

"They're still hanging around?" Sal asked and dropped into an oversized chair. "Figured they'd moved on."

"Then you missed yet another interview with Stephen's sidepiece. I'm told she hired an image consultant to make her come across as more sympathetic."

"As if. Sorry I missed that one."

Cyn glanced toward Adeena, seated to the left of Sal. "You've had other things on your mind."

"Not an excuse. I'll pay better attention. Did she have anything new to say?"

"More bull about being sorry for duping Heather." Cyn sniffed and put on a sad face. "This is what she looked like the whole time. That is when she wasn't crying prettily for the cameras. Totally fake."

Adeena pressed a hand to her stomach and wondered if that "fake" had also been meant for her. It was obvious she didn't have a fan in Cynthia Kennedy. "I'm sorry your family has to go through this."

"The timing could be better. We'll get through it, Ms. Minor. We're strong."

"Call her Adeena," Sal said. "I, for one, am glad the sidepiece changed her tune. For a second it seemed like she was trying to insinuate Heather's death might not have been an accident."

"She was. I bet a word from Stephen's lawyer closed that tap. There was no truth in that anyway. But we're not here to talk about that."

When Cyn turned her attention to her, Adeena felt it to the bone. She cleared her throat. "I feel I need to make it very clear to you that this isn't an attempt on my part to steal your nephew or get money."

"Then what is it?"

"Connection. The woman who adopted me was never very...we'll say 'motherly.' So when I found out I'd lost my birth mother and my twin sister, I thought maybe there was some kind of family connection left to find through Nathan. I've seen his photo and he has the look of her. I thought he might have her inside as well." Adeena looked away from those cool eyes and ran her palms along her thighs. This woman was probably a titan in the boardroom. "It probably sounds crazy to you, but it's true."

"Of course it's true." Sal put an arm around Adeena's shoulder. "This has been a big shock for her, Cyn. Finding out your own grandmother wants you dead isn't any more fun than finding out your brother-in-law is a sack of shit."

"I know that," Cyn said heatedly. "But we can't all think with something other than the head on our shoulder."

"How can you say that to her? No." Adeena held up a hand when Sal opened her mouth. "Sal's been your friend for a long time, so I don't understand how you can think for one minute she's not thinking with her brain. She's not naïve and she's damn well not stupid. I think you can agree to that. So why the hell are you sitting there looking for a scam that isn't? Please don't bother telling me you don't trust her to suss out a scam. You have to know her history better than I do." She sat back, folded her arms across her chest and dared Cyn to dispute a damn thing she'd said.

"I know Sal, but I don't know you. It's damn suspicious you discover Heather is *supposedly* your twin when my family's dragged into the spotlight."

"You and your family are not that important, Ms. Kennedy. If I was after money, why the hell would I bother with your family? If Sal's so under my spell she can't think straight, then why would I be here? I could be sitting on my ass in that swanky apartment of hers in New York City. Bird. In. The. Hand."

"Okay, okay." Sal motioned with her hands as if patting the air. "Let's take a minute or two or five. We're on the same team."

Adeena rolled her eyes. The only team they were on didn't count in this instance. Cynthia Kennedy was a cold bitch with delusions of grandeur as far as she was concerned. "It would obviously be better if the two of you talked. I'll be in the room." She got up before they could object or agree and stalked to the elevator. Once there, she decided a walk outside would do more good than stewing in the room.

"So she has a temper," Cyn said once Adeena was out of sight. "You didn't tell me that."

"Come on, Cyn. She had some good points. Cut her some slack."

"The two of you certainly looked cozy. What's going on with that?"

"She's smart, she's courageous, she's cute. What's not to admire? It's not like you to be so judgmental. What's really going on?"

Cyn sighed, hung her head. She knew she'd been in the wrong. "It's stupid. I expected to see something of Heather in her and there's nothing. How can they be twins and look nothing alike? They supposedly had the same parents. They should look more alike."

"Fraternal twins don't necessarily look alike. Doesn't mean they're not twins."

"I know that. I read what you sent, saw the pictures of the black and white twins. I guess it's like her looking to Nate for family connections. I thought maybe I'd get to spend a little more time with Heather." Cyn blinked her eyes rapidly. It didn't stop the tears from springing in her eyes. "Which is stupid."

Sal moved to perch on the corner of Cyn's seat, rooted around in her pockets and came up with a worn, but unused napkin. "It's okay. I understand now. I should have thought this through more before springing her on you."

"Not your fault." Cyn mopped at her damp eyes. "I owe her an apology. And you."

"Don't worry about me. I know this on top of the other is hard."

She exhaled. "Doesn't excuse my behavior. You should call her. Tell her I'm ready to listen with my mind open and my mouth shut."

"Let her walk off her mad. She needs it. It's been a tough couple of weeks for her too. And damn it, it's not over."

"You really like her. You know, she looks nothing like Rachel and—"

"And nothing!" Sal interjected heatedly. "She's *nothing* like Rachel. Nothing. And I do like her a lot. I also admire her. She's had some serious shit thrown at her and she deals. If that makes you question my judgment, so be it."

"That's not what I meant."

"Then what, Cyn? Rachel was a long time ago."

"And yet she continues to control your actions. Every woman you've panted after since then has been some fluff piece, who seem to have a fleeting love for your money. While you seem to have a fleeting desire for their looks and not much else. Admit it, you've been afraid of dealing with any woman capable of touching your feelings. That is until now. I can look at you with her and tell Adeena's different. That you feel something for her. She certainly was quick to put me in my place for daring to question you." Cyn smiled. "If I hadn't been insulted because she was right, I would have liked it. Damn. I do owe her an apology."

"You said it, not me. You should know I'm responsible for her being here. She didn't ask me to bring her here. In fact, she was against it."

"Then why bring her?"

"It's the right thing to do. For all of you. And because she's Heather's sister and she needs that connection. Has probably missed it her whole life and never realized what it was. At least that's how it supposedly is with twins." Sal fiddled with her glasses. "Following Adeena's brilliant suggestion, I hired someone to get something of Tanner's we can use for a paternity test. We found a lab in Atlanta affiliated with one in Savannah. Adeena did the cheek scrape and they sent it by courier to Savannah. More weight to sink him and his mother. If not in legal, then in civil court. They and their army of thugs are *not* going to get away with what they did. You can bet on that."

Cyn heard the steely determination in Sal's voice. Considering what Sal had managed to do to Stephen, she had no doubt the Tanners were sunk. "Sounds like you have things under control. And now you want me to allow Adeena to meet Nate," she said even though she knew there was more.

"That and I'd like you to say you're onboard with having Nate tested. We know for a fact Lucy was pregnant with twins, that Tanner was the father. We know Adeena is one of those twins. We know Nicholson only fixed Adeena's and Heather's adoptions and they have the same information on their fake birth certificates. I say that adds up to Heather and Adeena being twins."

She'd been expecting it and still it threw her off guard. The testing made sense and it would add weight to Adeena's claim. But it would also make Adeena...Cyn didn't know why her knee-jerk response was to say no when the answer needed to be yes. Adeena deserved to know if Nate was related. Hell, Nate deserved it too. And Tanner, his family, needed to know what he'd thrown away. "I need to run it by my parents, make sure they're okay with it."

"Goes without saying. I'm not sure when that reporter will do her thing, but the sooner it gets done the better."

"So you contacted someone?"

"I thought I told you that." Sal rubbed her forehead. "Too much going on. Kristy Moore. Her name is Kristy Moore. And she's supposed to be ambitious. Switching gears, I checked and there's a place in Peachtree City that can do the DNA test. I figure it's only twenty minutes, so it wouldn't mess with his day too much. Or yours."

"This means I have to tell my parents everything. But that's okay. They already know the adoption wasn't legal. At least now I can give them some assurances Heather's birth family isn't going to try for custody. That is...Adeena's not looking for custody, right? Sal? Talking to you."

Sal looked up from her phone. "No. Absolutely not."

"What's going on?"

"Some guy appears to have our room at the dump staked out. He's checked out the car, but he hasn't tried to enter the room."

"Maybe he's waiting for the cover of darkness."

"Then they don't know that place very well. It gets busy at night. Lots of room turnover. What bothers me is how they found us so fast. I was sure they wouldn't figure out where we supposedly are until tomorrow." Sal frowned.

"Could the information have come from the guy you went to see? You know, the one who told you about that Conlin guy?"

"He didn't know where we were, and he sure as hell didn't know our plans."

"Maybe he followed you."

"I can make a tail, Cyn."

"Then how?"

"I have no idea. That's the problem."

"You should send Dani the financial info you uncovered."

"Already on its way to Detective Benson."

"Then send her after the guy at the hotel."

"For what? He hasn't done anything yet. But perhaps she's smart enough to wait until he does."

* * *

Adeena was soaked with sweat when she let herself into the suite. She'd decided to spend some quality time in the hotel gym to give Sal and Cyn more alone time. Gyms were usually not her thing, and she and her body were regretting that decision.

"You look warmish."

She only had the energy to give Sal a lukewarm glare. "You have a habit of stating the obvious."

"It's a gift."

"From the demons of hell. So, what did she think? Did I pass?"

"No test was involved. She did think you were courageous and kind of nice once you calmed down."

"She did *not* say that."

"I made that part up. Not the courageous part though. She does think her parents will go for the testing. Mainly because they'll want the answers. I would bet—not you because you don't bet—but anyone else I'd bet big money we get an invite to dinner. Mary Francis likes to feed people."

"I like to eat. Anything else I need to know?"

"Well…" Sal looked up at Adeena, then quickly away. "I, uh, I wonder who you told about coming to Savannah. It was only Ian and Andi, correct?"

She frowned, wondering where this was going. "You were there when we talked about it, Sal. Then we didn't stay in Vegas much longer. There was no time to tell anyone else. What's this about?"

"Them finding the dump and so soon. I spoke with the pilot who flew us to Savannah. No one asked him about us. But he mentioned one of the newer guys was seen talking to a lowlife named Rico. The new guy, when prodded, admitted Rico asked him to confirm we flew to Savannah."

"Meaning someone already knew."

"Exactly. So if only the four of us knew, who talked? What do you know about Andi?"

"Nothing really. You can't think she's working with MM's hired hand." Adeena shook her head. "If they were going to plant a woman, it would have been a blonde with big tits. That's what Ian usually goes for." She could tell Sal was still skeptical. "Check her out. Last name Wilson. I'm willing to bet ten dollars she has nothing to do with either Tanner or Farrago."

"Ten whole dollars? Wow. For the record, when you have a sure thing bet high."

"Fine. A hundred."

"Better. It wouldn't hurt for you to talk to Ian while I'm checking her out. See if she's been asking questions about where you might be."

"I suppose I could." Her stomach churned as she sent a text for Ian to call. This felt wrong. "You don't think Ian could be in danger, do you?"

"I don't see why," Sal replied, her attention back on her laptop. "But if he doesn't call right away, maybe you should call him at the office, let him know about Farrago."

"I'll give him an hour to call me, then I'll call. But you should call Dani, tell her…No. Call Cyn, have her call Dani. There's nothing more for her to find in Savannah but grief."

"She already pulled out on Detective Benson's recommendation."

Adeena snorted. "Detective Benson? Let me guess. First name Olivia? Works with Special Victims?"

Sal grinned. "Wrong. Alex works in homicide. I checked her out and she's solid."

"Then why hasn't she arrested Eugenia?"

"I assume she has to convince her higher-ups to go to the DA for a warrant. I'm sure it doesn't happen as fast in the real world as it does on TV. But…Might be an easier sell when Kristy Moore pushes harder with the story."

"Justice should be faster. Yeah, yeah. I know that's not the way of our world." She sniffed her shirt. "Shower for me. I stink."

"I wasn't going to say it," Sal mumbled.

"I heard that."

Adeena took her phone into the bathroom to make sure she didn't miss Ian's call. *Kind of ridiculous*, she thought as she removed her sweaty clothes. He could easily be too busy at work right now. Or he could be exchanging sexy texts with Andi, who surprisingly had not yet been jettisoned. Adeena hoped he'd keep Andi around. She'd proven herself to be good in a crisis and she was a vast improvement on his usual type.

After her shower, Adeena checked her phone for a call from Ian. "Damn." What the hell could he be working on that he couldn't take a minute to call or text her? Then she remembered about his date with Andi the night before. Maybe his phone was in another room with his clothes. It was a scenario she found much more likely. She'd give him another hour to recover from a vigorous night. But first she sent him a photo of the room at the Inn and captioned it "I know what you've been doing."

A knock on the bedroom door had her reaching for one of the hotel-provided robes, then opening the door. "You rang?" Sal's expression said she had bad news. "No. Not Andi."

"Worse." Sal rubbed a palm across her forehead. "Andi's dead and Ian's a person of interest. The police can't find him."

"What?" She clutched the doorjamb. "Dead? Ian's a suspect? That's ridiculous. Of course he didn't do it! How could they think for a second he did?"

"He's missing and several people were too happy to tell reporters they saw him with her last night."

"Oh shit! Shit!"

"I, uh, I think you'd better sit down." Sal took her arm and led her to the bed.

Adeena, grateful for the assist, dropped onto the bed, her chest so tight it was hard to breathe. "You're sure it was Andi? Ian's Andi?" Her heart shattered when Sal nodded. "No!" If Andi was dead, then... "Ian's dead too." All her fault. Her fault. The tears rained down her face as she rocked back and forth.

"I'm so sorry." Sal sat beside her, pulled her close, held her until the storm passed.

"How can this be?" Adeena wiped her face on the sleeve of the robe, then steeled herself against a new flood of tears. She didn't have time to mourn. Not yet. Not while those murdering bastards were free. "Tell me everything you know."

"She told a friend they had a date last night."

"Dinner and a movie. He was hoping for more."

"Looks like he got more. With her consent. There's no sign of forced sexual activity."

"Of course not. Ian is no rapist. Is that what they're trying to say about him? That he raped and killed her?"

"Not at all. It's standard procedure when they find...it's standard."

"How did she die?"

"Strangled. Some things were overturned like they had a fight."

"So he suddenly snapped? He has no history of abuse. The police should be able to figure that out." She stood to pace around the room. "They killed him too, then took his body to make him seem guilty. That's how they knew where we were. What time did she die? What time did Andi die?"

"Most likely around the time we left the first hotel this morning. It was pure chance they discovered her so soon. Big rig carrying hazardous materials overturned and they were evacuating her complex. A neighbor spotted her car, noticed she hadn't come out and got concerned."

"It was Farrago. Had to be. And that's how he knew I was in Savannah. They've had all day to find that damn hotel. Bastard! That bastard!"

"There's more. Ian's car was found at his condo. Neighbors put it there since before six."

"They didn't know him. Didn't know he wouldn't have gone home that early."

"He did have to go to work the next day."

"Doesn't matter. Ian wouldn't have left. If he left, he couldn't get in another round the next morning. Wasn't for Diablo either. He was having a sleepover with Ian's neighbor." She looked for her phone and was surprised to find it in her hand. "I need to call the police, tell them he wouldn't have left Andi's place. Not unless he didn't have a choice. They need to be looking at Farrago, the Tanners. I need to tell them everything this time."

"You do that and Farrago knows you know, has to wonder how you know. We need him to think we're at The Inn, Adeena. We'll go to the police later if it's still necessary."

"Once again you're right." Adeena pressed fingers against her eyes and exhaled. Maybe she should've told the Vegas police everything. Or told Ian nothing. It hurt to think that while they thought they were laying a false trail, Ian was being forced to talk. It wasn't right. Something had to be done.

*Think*, she told herself. And not about Ian. She could think about him later when she had time to fall apart. But that couldn't happen until she and Sal were out of danger. There was one way to speed things up. Risky, and yet worth it. "You're not going to like what I say next, but please wait for me to finish. I need to get back to Savannah and do an interview with Kristy Moore. I can't have anyone else dying because of me. It's almost three thirty. We can be back there in five hours. Maybe do something for the late night news. I know it's risky as hell going there where Farrago and company are. I know that. And still, I need to go. Need to do something."

"Not so risky when they think you're holed up at The Inn. It could work. We'll make it work. How soon can you be ready?"

She felt the relief in every cell of her body. Sal couldn't know how much her continued support meant, but she did. Somehow she'd find a way to show her when this was over. And it would be over. Even if that meant knocking down doors at wherever Jackson and Eugenia Tanner called home.

First she had to get there. "Twenty minutes tops." Adeena hurried to the dresser and yanked open the top drawer.

"Good." Sal rubbed her hands together. "However, it'll take me longer than that to get everything in place. I'm thinking we can do better than a five-hour road trip. I'm also thinking we should wait to contact Moore until we're on our way to Savannah. Cuts down on leaks."

"This Detective Benson. What about inviting her to the interview? And Mrs. Robinson? She might be willing to talk about the relationship between Tanner and Lucy."

"Why don't we wait on that. Let Moore do the contacting. We need to get you in front of a camera. As for Benson, I've got something else in mind for her. A sting operation."

"Whatever you think is best. I know you don't like to hear it, but thank you. I'm not going to insult you by saying I'll pay you back. Just know if there's ever anything I can do, I'm there."

Sal squeezed her shoulder. "That I do like to hear. Give me forty-five. Don't worry about packing. We'll be back."

Adeena held her breath, then exhaled slowly as the door closed behind Sal. She wasn't alone. Even better, she was with Sal and that meant anything was possible. And that was a great feeling.

# CHAPTER TWENTY

This time Adeena landed at that same small airport as herself. The limo that picked them up and whisked them north to a hotel near the Savannah International Airport was bigger than the last one. In addition to the driver, there were two bulky guys, who sat across from them. Sal had introduced them simply as Mason and Ratchet.

Adeena spent the ride practicing what she wanted to say. The very worst thing would be to come across as a nut. She figured if she told the truth and sounded sane, the viewing audience would come to some conclusion. If she was lucky, they'd get the connection between her face and the problems that had plagued her.

She had debated the need to mention Ian and Andi during the interview, then decided against it. It wasn't right to sensationalize their misfortune at this time. Ian was her best friend and deserved better.

As she squeezed her eyes to hold back tears, Sal reached for her hand.

"I should call work," she said when she could talk. "Tell them something. My boss thinks I'm coming back to town tomorrow."

Sal pulled out her phone, typed a message and held it out for Adeena to see.

A laugh bubbled up, catching her by surprise. "I…You can't send that. I would not…," she trailed off remembering they had company. "Erase it," she demanded, trying—and failing—to look stern. A giggle escaped as she imagined Bobby-boy's reaction to being told to do something anatomically impossible.

Sal shrugged. "Only trying to help you out."

"You cheered me up, so thanks."

"Figured out what you want to say?"

"The truth so it sounds believable. Should be one and the same and yet…How much longer?"

"Airport's coming up, according to the last sign."

"I saw some clips of her reports. She seems okay."

"She's good considering the conditions she has to report in. I especially like the one where she almost got nailed when that car hydroplaned. Never missed a beat."

"We're here." Adeena took a deep breath as the limo pulled up in front of a hotel. "Promise you'll signal if I start to sound crazy."

"What kind of signal? Discreet like scratching my chin? Or more obvious, like waving my arms and wiggling my butt?"

There was no one like Sal. "Discreet is probably better. But maybe later you can demonstrate the butt wiggle."

The dimple flashed. "You're on."

With Mason in front and Ratchet bringing up the rear, Adeena and Sal entered the hotel. No one seemed to pay them any attention as they crossed to the elevators.

Sal pressed the elevator button. "So far, so good."

"Fingers crossed it stays that way." Adeena entered the elevator after Sal and rubbed her stomach as they winged up to the sixth floor.

"You'll be fine. I bet you've given presentations at work. Think of it like that."

"This should be easier than explaining to bored board members how activity-based travel models work."

Kristy Moore opened the door soon after they knocked. She was fully made up and smiled like she was already in front of a camera. "Adeena Minor. I would have recognized you anywhere. I can't thank you enough for choosing me. I've made good headway beyond what you sent me, but this interview will push us over the top."

Adeena had her hand pumped. "Thank you for agreeing to do this on such short notice, Ms. Moore. This is my friend, Thomasina Salamander. She deserves the credit for picking you."

"Come in, come in. The only other person here is my camerawoman, Jules Barnes. We go way back, so no worries about being scooped." Kristy gave them another beaming smile.

"That never crossed my mind." Adeena's worry was more about life and death than story credit. She acknowledged the tall, well-built camerawoman with a nod.

"The first thing is to make sure you're comfortable." Kristy patted a chair. "This would be a good place for you to sit, Adeena. I'll sit across from you. Makes things homier. Just us girls, right?"

"Right. Format?"

"I'll start by introducing you to our viewers, tell a little about you. You know, the school shooting, your mother's death." Kristy put a hand on Adeena's arm. "Will you be okay talking about your mom?"

She nodded. "It was the catalyst."

"We won't stay on that long. I'll say a few more words to set up your story and then you can take it from there. I'll interject information here and there, help you out if needed. I think you'll be fine."

"Can you get this on tonight?" Sal asked.

"I can guarantee it. The Tanner name is big around here."

To Adeena's relief, Kristy lost the over-the-top mannerisms once they started. She was somber without being tragic as she did her opening, then led Adeena through her part of the story. Kristy finished by talking about Lucy Mae Brown. She mentioned the type of person she'd been, the type of student and her dreams of being the first person in her family to complete college. She closed by asking viewers to be on the lookout for updates on her story.

"That was perfect," Sal said once the camera had stopped rolling.

Kristy flashed her megawatt smile. "Thanks." She turned to Adeena. "You made it easy. Ever thought of getting in front of the camera?"

"I'll leave that to you." Adeena removed the mic pinned to her shirt. "I won't be surprised to see you go national not too long from now."

"Aren't you sweet. I do my best. Now, Adeena, I purposefully did not bring one tiny piece up now." Kristy smiled. "I know Lucy was expecting twins. Something you didn't happen to mention. Is it because the baby died with her mother?"

Adeena glanced at Sal. "It's complicated, Kristy. I can tell you my twin is dead."

Kristy's eyes narrowed. "That means you know who she was."

"I do. However, I won't share that at this time. You know what's happened to me. Her family deserves the anonymity for now."

"Do the Tanners know about her?"

"I believe they know her family's no threat to them. We were fraternal twins, not identical ones."

Kristy pursed her lips. "Would you be inclined to share the name if Jackson Tanner drops out of the race?"

"I'd have to speak with her family first. Get their permission." Something Adeena had no intention of doing. Cyn and her parents knew about the interview, had approved. Adeena thought they deserved the chance to make their own decision about whether to join the media frenzy her interview and Kristy's story would cause.

"That's fair. How can I get in touch with you? There may be some follow-up questions."

Sal rattled off a number. "We're not sure where we'll be. Any follow-up can be done by phone."

"Hope it's far from here," Jules said. "Especially after this airs. Tanner will have some hard questions to answer, whether he wants to or not. That would piss anyone off."

"We're prepared for whatever," Adeena said. "A recent experience has brought home how desperate these people are."

Kristy Moore looked intrigued rather than frightened. "Do tell."

"That's for another day," Sal said firmly. "We need to go. Our transportation's waiting."

Adeena gave silent thanks when only Ratchet and Mason were waiting for them. Their presence hadn't yet been discovered.

"I'm hungry," Sal announced once they were in the limo. "You hungry?"

"I want to see Tanner." Adeena hadn't planned to say that, hadn't planned for the anger to overflow. "I want to talk to him face-to-face, have him give me a justification for killing Ian and Andi. I need to know why the hell he's so damn special." She clenched her teeth as tears threatened to return.

"Okay. I can get his address, we could drive by, see if he's home." Sal pulled out her phone.

"Not at his house. His wife and kids will be there."

"It's guaranteed they're going to find out anyway. You realize that, right?"

"But not by me going off on Tanner. His campaign headquarters would be better. Tomorrow. He must go there regularly."

Sal's smile was sly. "I can certainly get him there if you want."

"I do," she said, nodding. "I really do. He or his people will have seen the interview by then. He'll know I know what's been done when I confront him."

"You do remember it's his mother who's paying the bills?"

"I don't care. He may have been a teenager back then, but he's a grown man now. A grown man who's still letting his mother do his dirty work. It's him I want to talk to." Adeena exhaled. "Ignore me. I'm acting like a diva. Let's stick with the plan, fly back to Seneca. I'll drive back here tomorrow. He probably doesn't go in until later in the morning anyway. Sorry. I wasn't thinking about anyone but myself."

"I'm here for the ride. What you want is what we'll do. Our pilot's loose. He won't mind flying back tomorrow. She sent Ryan a text about the schedule change. As for accommodations, we're checked in at the Portman. Might as well use it." Sal pushed the intercom and notified the driver of their new destination. We can have dinner on the rooftop again. Wonder if they'll have lobster."

"Just like that, huh?"

"What good's having money if you can't use it to be spontaneous? And I like the idea of you confronting him. I wouldn't mind exchanging a few words with him as well."

* * *

Eugenia watched as Maria made her way to their table. It wasn't hard to tell by the way Maria carried herself that she was walking fury. Schooling her face to show mild interest, she wondered who had gotten in Maria's way this time. They were in one of Savannah's more prestigious restaurants, one owned by a good friend, having an early family dinner. In reality it was a good opportunity for Jackson to glad hand. They had already had a number of potential supporters stop by for a word, for the chance to shake Jackson's hand. Even Beau had managed to dress up and bring a civil manner. All in all a good evening. She took a sip of wine in a silent toast.

"Sorry to intrude on your night off, Jackson." Maria's smile was as tight as her short skirt. "Eugenia, could I beg a moment of your time?"

"Of course, dear." She excused herself and followed Maria. In the kitchen, she had a quick word with the manager and secured the use of one of two tiny private offices behind the kitchen.

"How long have you known?" Maria had thrown off even a hint of the anger suppression cloak. Her eyes glittered with fury as they bore into Eugenia hard enough to scrape skin.

"Perhaps you could be more specific, dear. It pays to know many things these days."

"Don't be cute. I'm talking about a woman named Adeena Minor. Talking about her being the result of Jackson's relationship with an African-American girl. I received a courtesy call from a trusted source, warning of a forthcoming story about her, about her pregnant mother who was supposed to have died in a house fire thirty-four years ago and about their link to Jackson. What the hell are we supposed to do about this? How the hell are we supposed to respond?"

"Could you please keep your voice down?" Eugenia wasn't sure how thick the walls were and Maria's voice carried when it reached that annoying high pitch. "First off, there's no need for you to concern yourself with empty speculation. There have been rumors circulating off and on for years that Lucy was pregnant with Jackson's child when she died so tragically. I happen to know it wasn't Jackson's child. Speak with a Gregory Charles Selman and ask him who the father of Lucy's child was. Ask him what she planned to do with the baby once it was born." The last part she threw in for distraction.

"Lucy? You have a name? I wasn't told a name." Maria seemed to falter for a moment. "You knew about this!"

Eugenia took exception to Maria's accusatory tone. "There really is nothing to know. Her name was Lucy Mae Brown. She worked at the house for a short time. Jackson was momentarily infatuated with her. Then he wasn't. When he came to me, asked for me to fire her, I did. She slunk back to her old boyfriend once she realized I wasn't going to allow her to pressure Jackson into a relationship. Unfortunately she died in a fire some time later."

"But she was pregnant. How do you know it wasn't with Jackson's child? You yourself admitted he was infatuated with her."

"Do you think she wouldn't have come to me begging for money if she was carrying Jackson's child? Even if she thought she could convince me it was his she would have been on my doorstep with her hand out. That's the kind of person she was." The words came out exactly as she'd practiced them, and she could tell they were having the desired impact. "Lucy Brown is long dead. Yes, Jackson bedded her. But I hardly think allegations of teenage Jackson being involved with a black girl will sink this ship. What you should be doing is checking to see what the station has collected in terms of background information on this Adeena Minor. Once you've done that, then you can choose to come to me in a panic."

"What do you know about her?"

"Why nothing," she lied with aplomb. "Obviously she's a liar. But that none withstanding, I'm certain background checks are standard procedure in this kind of situation. You should consider ordering one yourself if they didn't. It always pays to know potential stumbling blocks. Now is this girl actually *claiming* to be Jackson's child?"

Maria frowned. "I don't know and it hardly matters! The information had to come from somewhere, so it's only a matter of time before she does."

She sniffed. "Where's the proof? It's a fact that Lucy died in a house fire before giving birth. For anyone to say otherwise, to say Jackson has a daughter, is ludicrous. You might want to warn them to check their facts before they think about airing this story, Maria. Lawsuit is such an ugly word, but if needs must…" She gave an elegant shrug.

"That's neither here nor there. Jackson needs to be told as soon as possible. He needs to have a response prepared if questioned."

"I'll talk to him. Only later, after dinner. Even you would agree that he is entitled to this last quiet family dinner out."

Maria looked as if she wanted to object. "Fine. But be sure he hears it soon, Eugenia. I'm going to sit down with him tomorrow and work up a statement. I will not have him caught unaware!"

"Of course not, dear."

"You should also know Adeena Minor has survived a couple of murder attempts. They're trying to insinuate those attempts are tied to Jackson's run for the senate. This is serious, Eugenia."

"Utter nonsense. Again I say don't be pulled in by empty talk. Their lawyers won't let them air such trash. Really, Maria." She gave a long-suffering sigh. "I expected better from you."

"Empty? Do you have any idea the damage that would be done if something like that got out? Doesn't matter if it's true or not. Once made, false claims can never be erased from the public's mind. This could tank us before we've even started."

"I suggest you keep your voice down and find your dignity, my dear," Eugenia said with an undertone of steel. "It's preposterous for you to think that anyone with sense would believe Jackson would be involved with such sordid matters. He was a boy when this happened. Do you honestly believe I didn't know everything my son was involved in? Instead of interrogating me, you should be finding a way to get that erroneous story blocked. You should have something you can use in that blackmail file you keep."

Eugenia feigned unconcern even as she seethed with rage on the inside. Maria had overstepped her bounds this time and she would let her know. Not here where there was only the illusion of privacy, but in her home where they would be alone. No one talked to her this way and got away with it. "Is there anything else or may I return before my food is served?"

"I think we should meet. Not here. Perhaps at your place. Put all the cards on the table so I'm not working in the dark."

"If you insist. Though it's entirely unnecessary. Call me tomorrow and I'll see when I can pencil you in. Now I would like to go and spend some quality time with my family. Something I don't believe you know anything about." She sailed out. As she did, she thought she caught a glimpse of movement out of the corner of her eye, but when she turned, the hall was empty and she put it down to an overactive imagination.

Wondering if she was more rattled than she thought, Eugenia stopped by the restroom. She took some deep, cleansing breaths before returning to the table as if she hadn't a care in the world.

"What was that about?" Jackson asked.

"Nothing that couldn't have waited until tomorrow. You know how Maria can be sometimes."

"Over the top," Beau said. "She really needs a life of her own. Maybe then she'll stop trying to live ours."

"Now, Beau, Maria is working very hard for me, for my campaign. Show her some respect."

Beau glared at his father. "Maybe if she showed me some I would."

"Not here," Hope said firmly. "This is a family dinner. We won't talk about Maria, we won't talk about campaigns."

"Then what else is there?" Beau demanded. "We haven't talked about anything else in days."

# CHAPTER TWENTY-ONE

Beau wasn't sure how he got through the long drawn-out dinner and dessert. But he managed, this despite the knots churning in his stomach from listening in on his grandmother's conversation with Maria. He had vague memories of some stupid saying of nothing good coming from listening. He could now say that was true.

As soon as he was safely locked in his room, he opened his laptop. Finding information on Adeena Minor was easy. He skipped the videos of her dodging some drunk and focused on her professional bio. She was thirty-four. Doing the math, he noted his dad had been nineteen when she was born and eighteen nine months before that.

It fit. As much as he didn't want it to, it fit with what his dad had told him. That meant his grandmother had lied to Maria, just like his father had lied to him. The only reason to lie was to hide the truth. Beau wasn't sure he wanted to know the truth.

But eventually curiosity had him searching for Lucy Mae Brown. He found a story about a fire, saw the grainy newspaper photo of her and her family that went with the story and knew there had to be more. More that he wasn't going to get from the Internet, he thought, and he closed his laptop. His "more" source was downstairs in the form of his father.

He sat on his bed for ten minutes, almost sick with apprehension and fear his father had done something bad. He could ignore this, wait for the story to hit the news, but that struck him as cowardly. He was almost eighteen, almost a man. A man wouldn't hide in his room afraid of what could be. A man would go downstairs and demand answers.

Beau flew down the stairs, not giving himself a chance to chicken out, to act like less of a man. He channeled the rush of anger he'd felt in the restaurant when listening to his grandmother and Maria. As usual their concern had been for his father's campaign and not on how the news could destroy the lives of the other people in the family. It was like he, his brother, his mother didn't matter, weren't worth any consideration. Well, he did matter and now was the time to show it.

He knocked on the closed door, then entered when bidden. His father was sitting at his desk, papers spread everywhere. Beau tried not to think that some of those papers could be about Adeena Minor and her death.

"What is it?"

The impatient tone had Beau licking his lips with what little spit he had. This was way harder than he thought it would be. "Did you steal your child from Lucy Mae Brown and give her away?"

His dad looked at him as if he'd grown another head. "I don't have time for your foolishness tonight, son. I'm busy."

"It's not foolishness! Maria was talking about it with Grandmother at the restaurant. There's going to be a story. About the baby. Your baby with Lucy Mae Brown. But she died in a fire, like you said. But the baby didn't. Why didn't the baby die?"

"That's ridiculous. You obviously misunderstood, son. Do you really believe Maria wouldn't have come to me with something like this if it was true?" Jackson leaned forward, a sorrowful look on his face. "It's true Lucy died in a fire. I told you that. She wasn't pregnant. Your grandmother would've told me if Lucy was pregnant. Would've taken great pleasure in my knowing Lucy was pregnant with another man's child."

"Why couldn't it have been your child? You had sex with her."

"She didn't contact me. Lucy would've gotten in touch, told me she was pregnant. She knew I would do right by her. Knew I would've seen she had what she needed. Seen that the child had what it needed if she chose to keep it."

"But would you have married her?" Beau pressed. "Isn't that what doing right by her means?"

"She knew that was out of the question, Beau. She understood how things work. I loved her in my way, but she knew it couldn't be more than it was."

Beau shook his head. "That's sick! I don't believe that. I can't think that way. I refuse to think that way."

"That's neither here nor there. Lucy was not pregnant, Beau. I don't know what you think you overheard, but it wasn't that."

"Then why didn't Grandmother tell you about it? She told Maria she would." Beau could see he was getting nowhere. He pulled out his phone, did a search for Adeena Minor. "This is Adeena Minor. The one they say is your child." He thrust the phone in his father's face and watched all the color leach from it. "Dad? You okay?"

"Who is this?" His father's voice was barely above a whisper as he clutched the phone.

"Adeena Minor. The woman Maria was talking about. At the restaurant."

"Has your grandmother seen this?"

"I don't know." He grabbed his head and brought the conversation back to mind. "I don't...no, Maria didn't mention any photos or anything. She just said someone who owed her a favor told her about a story that was coming. She said someone had tried to kill this Adeena Minor and it was linked with your campaign."

"You're sure that's all? This is important, Beau. Tell me you're sure."

"I'm positive. Call Maria if you don't believe me. She was acting really pissy about it. Like it was a big deal. Ask her if you don't believe me."

Jackson leaned back in his chair and closed his eyes. "I will."

"Do you know who she is? Is she Lucy's child?"

"I don't know, son. I don't know."

"You have to know. What if there's a story? What happens to me, to Phillip, to Mom? We matter too!" He slammed his fist on the desk, convinced his dad knew something, was hiding something. "It's not fair to keep the truth from us. You think I want to hear it from my friends? Other kids at school?"

"Am I interrupting father-son time?"

Beau's mood took a downward turn upon hearing Maria's voice. "Yes!" he said without looking at her. "This is a family matter."

"I need to speak with your father alone, Beau. It's important."

Beau turned to face her, his fists clenched. "So you can tell him more about Adeena Minor? I overheard you and Grandmother." He sneered when he saw the surprise. "Yeah. I know."

"I'd still like to talk to your father in private." Maria placed a file in front of Jackson. "I had to call in a couple of markers to get this. You should read it. Every word. Then call me."

Jackson shook his head as if coming out of a trance. "Beau, please excuse us?"

*Should've known*, Beau thought in disgust. Maria always wins. "Whatever." He stormed upstairs and slammed the door to his room hard enough to rattle the windows. They were trying to keep him in the dark. He wouldn't stay there.

Downstairs Jackson closed the file and pressed his fingers against his throbbing head. The gesture didn't do much to erase what he'd read, couldn't erase the image of Adeena Minor. She didn't have Lucy's youthful look, and yet it wasn't hard to believe he was looking at a photo of Lucy at thirty-four.

"Did Eugenia mention this to you?"

"We got sidetracked talking about her luncheon, the donations she wrangled and the need for tasteful gifts. Seems shallow in retrospect. Of course, Lucy has always been a sore subject. For both of us." He tried to smile. "Before this evening I would've sworn it was impossible for Lucy to be pregnant without me knowing."

"And now?"

"She looks like Lucy. Like Lucy should've looked. I can't look at her and not see Lucy. How she would have looked if she'd had the chance." He dropped his hands and looked up at Maria. "I don't know what to think. How can this be? How could I not know she had a baby? It had to be mine. She should've contacted me. She knew how to get word to me."

"Here's a crazy idea. Why not drive over, talk to her face-to-face? You weren't that far away."

"I was. I disobeyed the rules, went to see her after Mother fired her, to make sure she was okay, see if she needed any money. Things got out of hand." Jackson rubbed his mouth. He could still see Lucy, see how disappointed she'd been that he couldn't stand up to his mother for her, the sake of their future. "She thought it meant more than it did and she kicked me out. Told me not to come back. My mother knew as soon as she saw me. She got me a summer job and shipped me off to Martha's Vineyard. But Lucy knew how to contact me. No matter how mad she was, she should've let me know when she found out. She had to know I would've helped out." Jackson looked away, full of regret and shame. Lucy might still be alive if only he'd treated her differently.

"I want to believe, Jackson. But what about later? There was surely news about the fire, about the death of a pregnant woman, her family. It was Christmas Day. A traditionally slow news day."

He tried not to be offended by her accusatory tone. Given the facts, he couldn't blame her though. "You have to understand how it was between me and my mother. She didn't react well to my relationship with Lucy and I didn't react well to her reaction. I stayed away to punish her. Went to Tahoe with buddies from college that Christmas and learned to ski and pick up women in hot tubs. I admit I was a jerk back then, treating Lucy the way I did. No denying that. But I'll tell you like I told Beau, I did not know she was pregnant, let alone with my child. This insinuation that I had something to do with the fire? It's categorically not true. I don't know what happened then or what's happening to Ms. Minor now. Believe me when I say that I intend to find out."

"Good, because that's only part of the story. A larger part is how a baby managed to survive the fire. Once this story hits, reporters are going to be all over you. Which will lead to the general public demanding answers. I think you need to prepare yourself that the police will have questions as well."

"Let them. I'm innocent. There's nothing linking me to any of this. Nothing, Maria."

"You're a lawyer. Don't be so naïve. You know it isn't always about innocence. You would be the first one to advise a client to say nothing without legal representation present."

"I'll call my lawyer tomorrow on the slim chance it comes to that."

"That's a start. You and I need to sit down, talk strategy. This situation has clusterfuck written all over it." Maria slung her purse strap over her shoulder. "We need to get in front of public reaction with a preemptive statement. Write down where you were, what you were doing. Add the names of those friends. Any chance you're in touch with any of them?"

"Maria, tell me you believe I had nothing to do with this."

She looked him in the eye. "I believe you have nothing to do with this, Jackson. However, you should think about the one person who desperately wanted Lucy out of your life permanently."

Jackson jackknifed out of the chair. "What are you trying to insinuate?"

"You know."

His first reaction was denial, then outrage. Not his mother. "My mother can be a demanding woman, but what you're suggesting is obscene. You know her, Maria. How can you think she had anything to do with this...this fiasco?"

She put a hand on his arm. "That's a knee-jerk reaction. Take some time and think it through. If it's not you, then who else would it be?"

"Someone from her neighborhood. It was miles away from what it is now. She told me once about this guy who dealt drugs, how she wished she had the nerve to turn him in because he was rotten to the core. And he wasn't the only dealer. Maybe she went to the police and one of them found out. Burned down the house to send a message to anyone else thinking of doing the same."

Maria shook her head. "Wouldn't that be neat and tidy? I hope that's what this is. I hope that a drug dealer kidnapped Lucy, sold her baby and lit the fire. But if that's the case, why kill Adeena Minor? There's no evidence linking anyone to the fire. Trying to kill her now only brings attention to the old crime. Think about it. And call your lawyer in the morning, then call me to set up a time to meet. We should do this at headquarters, show everyone you're still in the game. I'll see myself out."

Jackson wished her arguments weren't so believable. His mother's hatred of Lucy had been beyond irrational. His behavior hadn't done anything to diminish that. Somehow his mother had figured out how deep his feelings were, how conflicted he was over being with Lucy and doing what was right. And God help him, if Lucy had come to him, told him of the pregnancy, he might not have been able to turn her away for a third time. That would have been the ultimate betrayal in his mother's eyes. She wouldn't have stood for that.

Feelings of being disloyal swamped him. His mother had nothing to do with this. Lucy would never have gone to his mother with any problem. There was no way his mother could've known she was pregnant. He was following Maria down the wrong road.

He took another look at the folder of evidence. If someone had killed Lucy's family to cover the birth of her baby, that had to mean his mother wasn't involved. She would have no reason for wanting the baby kept alive, wouldn't want her to come back to haunt her son as she was doing now. On the other hand, she *would* have reason to want Adeena Minor dead. It was all so confusing.

"What's going on with you and Beau?"

Jackson closed the folder, cursing himself for not shutting the door. He needed time alone to deal with this situation, time to figure out how to proceed. "You know Beau," he said to his wife. "He seems very unhappy these days."

"Mostly with Maria. I saw her leave. What's really going on, Jackson? I think I deserve the truth."

A line from some movie about not being able to handle the truth flashed through his mind. But in reality, he was unsure of how she would react. Their lives had always been separate but equal to the satisfaction of both of them. "My past, or rather a twisted version of my past, has raised its ugly head."

Hope sighed. "Who is she? Or rather, how old is she?"

"She's thirty-four and she's my daughter. Surprise!" He almost laughed at the comical expression on her face.

"Daughter?" Hope sank into the chair Beau had vacated. "I'm not sure how to take this."

"That makes two of us. I've always been very careful about this type of…situation."

"I know. Thirty-four? That would've made you—"

"Nineteen. Eighteen at the time of conception."

"I was going to say that would have made you a kid yourself. Is the mother asking for anything? The daughter?"

"The mother's dead, Hope. Lucy's been dead a long time."

"Lucy? The Lucy Eugenia—"

"Loves to throw in my face from time to time," he finished for her and rubbed his temples as the headache intensified. He didn't want to think about his mother and the things she'd said about Lucy over the years. "And yes, she was African-American."

"That shouldn't matter. It's not the fifties, Jackson."

"You've lived in the South a long time and yet you can say that with sincerity. Amazing."

"It didn't hurt Strom Thurmond."

"He was already well established when it came out. On the waning end of his career really. I'm trying to get my foot in the door. You should know there are worse things than her race that need to be addressed and soon."

Hope smiled. "Is that what had Maria in a tizzy earlier?"

"Deservedly so. There could be a criminal element. Not a problem for me," he added when her smile disappeared. "But it must be dealt with nonetheless. I'll be speaking with the lawyers tomorrow."

"You need to tell me everything. The boys need to be protected."

With a nod, he laid it out for her as he understood the problem.

"That's a hell of a complication, Jackson. What will you do?"

"Tell the truth. I didn't know she was preg—"

"Not that. What are you going to do about your mother?"

"My mother. What is it with you and Maria? My mother isn't involved."

She frowned. "Don't play dumb now. We both know how much your mother still hates Lucy. I can only imagine how it was back then."

"She hated her with reason. I was enthralled. Think about how you would feel if Beau came to you with notions of marrying Sinead."

"As I don't have poor Lucy to warp my senses in the present, I know I don't have to worry about that. Sinead is gay, Jackson. She's got a big letter L on her forehead."

"You would know," he taunted and immediately regretted it.

"That was an ineffective jab. Even for you, Jackson."

"I'm sorry. You're right. That was cheap." He'd known her preference from the start. It was the main reason their marriage was a success.

"And I'm right about the influence of the incident with Lucy as well. On you, as well as on Eugenia. What does she have to say about this uncovering of the grave as it were?"

"Nothing so far. I'm sure she expects this will blow over."

Hope mirrored Maria's doubtful expression. "She never has in the past. Why would she start now? Be reasonable, Jackson, and admit she wouldn't say nothing. At the least, she would throw the incident in your face once again. You're going to want to talk to her about this. And even more important, you need to be prepared to take a big step back if you want to have a chance in this race."

"You know her, Hope. How can you think she had anything to do with this?"

"I do know her," Hope said solemnly. "I know that Jackson Beauregard Tanner the Third and his well-being come first with her. I see her for who she is. You never have. Go talk to her and listen with your ears wide open this time."

"I will. You'll see she had nothing to do with this." He quelled the doubts that wanted to surface. Drug dealers had killed Lucy out of revenge. That was the only reasonable explanation.

# CHAPTER TWENTY-TWO

Sal hesitated, then joined Adeena on the balcony of the Portman Hotel. She was worried. Adeena had been so solemn since they finished dinner. "What are you thinking about?"

"My life in Surrealville. This is the third balcony in the third city that I've stood on in less than a week. This view's nowhere as good as yours, but it is a step up from Seneca. It's hard to wrap my mind around it, to know how I'm supposed to feel from one moment to the next." Adeena took a sip of coffee. "I've decided not to watch the report. I already know how it ends. And I hear the camera adds ten pounds." She closed her eyes. "Maybe I should watch it. Worrying about ten extra pounds would be preferable to thinking about Ian, to thinking about what he would say about me bitching about ten pounds."

"What would he have said?"

"That my weight was fine the way it was. Of course I would be compelled to ignore that as always. This was coming from a guy who consistently dated women the size of a stick. They had to have big boobs."

Sal grimaced. Add in blond hair and Adeena could be talking about her preferences. How embarrassing was that? "Andi wasn't a stick."

"Andi was the exception. I think she would've stuck. That she would've made him think beyond the superficial. And now…" She blinked rapidly. "Now they won't have the chance to find out and I won't have the chance to rag him about it. I won't have the chance to rag him about anything ever again. Or have him rag on me. He was like my brother. Family in a way my mother never was. I don't know how—" Her voice broke as the tears flowed.

"I am so sorry." Sal took Adeena into her arms, held her close while she cried. She stroked Adeena's back and tried to come up with a better, more descriptive word than "sorry." There had to be one, but for the life of her she couldn't think of it.

When the tears slowed and died, she continued to hold on. And maybe there was a little bit of guilt that she enjoyed the feel of Adeena in her arms. That she enjoyed the closeness that felt like intimacy. She'd felt that only once before, but this was more, better.

"You got any tissues?" Adeena's voice was husky. "My nose is running like a faucet. Forget I said that." She sniffed. "Maybe that's why I don't have a girlfriend."

"I doubt it." Sal reluctantly took a step back and searched her pockets. She came up with a napkin. "Take this. I'll get more."

Adeena was holding onto the railing when she returned. "I won't ask what you're thinking this time."

"I'll tell you anyway." Adeena took a deep breath and accepted the pile of tissues. "I was thinking how glad I am that it's you here with me. I don't care what you say. You're a *mensch*, Salamander."

She thrust her hands in her pocket, rocked back on her heels as heat flooded her cheeks. "So you're saying I'm a person as opposed to…"

"I've embarrassed you, haven't I?" Adeena gave her a watery smile. "I'll have to remember that compliments weaken you. That's sweet."

"Like kryptonite," she said solemnly. "Only worse."

"Poor baby." Adeena stroked her cheek. "Wouldn't want to interfere with your ability to fly."

"Ha." She trapped Adeena's hand between her shoulder and her cheek. "You should have more respect for the blue cape."

"No cape, dah-ling."

"Huh?"

"All those kids' toys and you don't know Edna from *The Incredibles*? A superhero like you would want to keep up with other superheroes. Your education is sadly lacking."

Sal hung her head and tried for pitiful. "I was never invited to attend that university for the gifted."

"You are a poor baby." Adeena lifted Sal's chin and gave her a quick kiss. "We need to rectify that." Another kiss followed, this one longer.

Sal's itch was replaced by heat as she pulled Adeena closer and feasted on impossibly soft lips. Her head was swimming when she pulled back and sucked in air. "Seems you have hidden powers as well."

The alarm on Sal's phone blared out noise, startling them both. Sal turned it off. "Uh, I forgot to turn it off. The news."

Adeena's expression turned serious as she once again gripped the railing. "I almost forgot. Thanks for the reprieve."

"I should be thanking you. Sure you want to go see Tanner tomorrow? You really don't have to."

"I feel like I need to face him, have my say before I can set it aside. He should be at his headquarters by ten thirty, right?"

"We'll get him there one way or the other. I figure one look at your face should do it. Even if he had forgotten what Lucy looked like, he'll remember now."

"Who knew my looks would ever come in handy?"

"Remember what Mrs. Robinson said about Lucy? How she thought she wasn't pretty? Well, she was wrong and so are you if you don't think your looks would come in handy. Now my face? That's a different story. A different book."

"Now I get to tell you you're wrong. To me, you're adorable. I like the red hair, your freckles."

Though she was grinning, Sal covered her face. "Kryptonite! I'm melting."

Adeena gave her a hip shot. "Crazy woman. But maybe I shouldn't say that seeing as I have another favor to ask."

"Yes."

"At least hear me out first. I need to get back to Vegas. The sooner the better. I need to go back to work. With Ian gone they're going to need me to help out. I don't care about my boss, but I do care about the other people on my team. I also need to let my boss know he's got six weeks to hire a replacement for me. And I need to see my baby. I know Diablo's getting the best of care. I…" She slowly exhaled. "I need to be with him. He loved Ian too and this has to be confusing for him."

"Whatever you need." Sal ran a hand down Adeena's arm, then grabbed her hand. "I did miss out on my last night of gambling. I bet I can get a room at the Bellagio. Maybe stay longer than one night."

"I can't ask you to do that. You must have work to catch up on, and you've done so much already."

"You're not asking, Adeena, I'm volunteering. I know it's been less than a week, and you have a lot of extra stuff to deal with—"

"Which you've been a huge help with. I'd love if it you could come back to Vegas with me for a little while. I'll have to work, but there's lunch, after work and this weekend."

"I know it's backward, but what about a date? Dinner on Saturday and a helicopter tour of Vegas at night? Maybe a show."

"I would love to take a helicopter ride with you. Instead of a show maybe you could show me how to gamble."

"I'm your woman."

Adeena's phone sang out. "I have to get this. I told Mrs. Henson to call me if she heard anything."

As Sal stepped away to give Adeena some privacy, her phone rang. She frowned seeing Dani's name. "Everything okay?…I suppose…She's on the phone…You sure it's okay?…I trust you." She ended the call, her mind racing furiously. Going to a police station was never easy under any circumstance. She could only hope going to the Savannah station wouldn't be dangerous to their health.

"They found him. They found Ian's body." Fresh tears filled Adeena's eyes. "He was tortured. Like the others you found. My fault. I don't know how I can live with this, Sal."

Sal crossed and pulled her close. "I'm so damn sorry, but it's not your fault. That blame lies squarely on Eugenia Tanner's shoulders. I thought we already decided this." Her response only provoked sobs. Sal's nerves were stretched thin as she considered what the correct time was to inform Adeena they had a date with a detective.

* * *

By the time Jackson arrived at his mother's house, he was mentally and physically tired. Beau had tried to corner him again, then Maria had called about rumors that a live interview had been shot earlier in the day. All that on top of Hope and her suspicions. She did know his mother, giving him no choice but to have suspicions of his own. At this point he barely had the energy to worry about the damn campaign, much less what the pundits would have to say about his chances once the interview aired.

He imagined turning around, finding a bar and knocking back a few. He could pick up a woman, have meaningless sex and maybe get the image of an older Lucy in the form of Adeena Minor out of his head. Maybe stop thinking about how much Lucy would be disappointed if he didn't attempt to reach out to the child they created together.

Martha opened the door, dashing any hopes of finding anonymity in a bar.

"You okay, Mr. Tanner? You've been standing out here for at least five minutes."

He worked up a smile. "I'm fine, Martha. I have a lot on my mind these days. Is Mother home?"

"She sure is. Went upstairs about ten minutes ago. You come on in, have a seat. I'll go get her."

"Thank you."

It took his mother twenty long minutes to make it downstairs. He stood automatically.

"Jackson? What are you doing here this time of night? It's after ten. I had already retired for the evening."

A look at her face said that was a lie. Her face was as perfectly made up as it had been at dinner. "I apologize for coming so late, but it is important." It occurred to him that apologizing to her was something he'd been doing as long as he could remember. She never apologized to him.

"Well, what is it? I'm tired." She sighed as she sat. "Please don't tell me you're having trouble with another clingy woman. Really, Jackson, we've talked about this repeatedly. It's of the utmost importance that you are on your best behavior."

"It's much worse." He pushed his hands into his pockets, feeling as if he was that wayward teen who needed a good talking to. "Oh wait. I hear you already know about Lucy and the child. My child."

"Not that. I can't believe Maria came to you with that hackneyed story. And after I told her how to deal with it."

"If only it were hackneyed, Mother. I've seen her picture. She was born in December. She has to be mine."

"Ridiculous." She waved a hand in dismissal. "I looked up that young woman claiming to be your daughter. She looks nothing like you or anyone else in our family. Listen to me, son, and leave this alone. That young woman need not concern you."

"It's not like you to be so naïve, Mother. That young woman may have a lot to do with me. My relationship with Lucy is a fact, she's the right age and she looks exactly like Lucy. Or how Lucy would have looked if someone hadn't decided she didn't deserve the chance to live longer."

"They say we all have a doppelganger out there. I can't believe you would accept this woman's word with no proof except her face. She could have had facial surgery for all you know. And you need to remember Lucy died while she was pregnant. This is a hoax. One I can't believe you're falling over yourself to believe. Really, Jackson, I thought better of you."

*There it is*, he thought. The "I thought better of you" card she'd played all of his life. It was always accompanied by the same pained expression she was sporting now. He remembered as a boy thinking she must practice it every day. "Be that as it may, a simple cheek swab will dispel any doubt."

"Surely you wouldn't agree to this? We're Tanners and that means a lot in this town. A Tanner does not kowtow to scam artists. It's up to this woman, this nobody, to prove you have anything to do with her. I realize this has come as a big shock, son. I suspect you have some unresolved feelings about what happened with Lucy and that you're letting them cloud your thinking."

"Did you know Lucy was pregnant?"

"Of course I knew. It was in the paper."

"Before the fire. Did you know before she died? Surely you kept an eye on her, made sure she stayed away from your precious son."

"Nonsense. I cut the knot binding you to her when I sent you away. Why would I need to concern myself about her anymore? She was a no one, a nothing. A fact you seem to have forgotten."

*Another lie*, he thought. Even with him away, she would have kept an eye on Lucy. Dread filled him as Maria's words came back to him. "Why didn't you mention the pregnancy when you told me she was dead. Given the timing of the pregnancy, you had to know I'd be interested, that I had a right to know."

She sighed and pulled at the lapel of her fancy robe. "Frankly, I assumed you wouldn't want to hear she was pregnant with another boy's child."

"Except she wasn't. The child would've been partly my responsibility."

"Do you truly believe you were her only bed partner? If she slept with you without the benefit of marriage, she slept with others. Really, Jackson, you disappoint me."

*The other card*, he thought. Disappointment. He always seemed to disappoint her. Lucy had been the biggest disappointment, which explained the hostility, the unreasonable hatred. "Trying to slander Lucy is weak. She was a virgin, Mother. A virgin. I do know she made love to me and only me." He closed his eyes and tried to will away the deepest shame. "She made love to me because she believed in the person I wanted to be. A person with ideals. You've always tried to belittle her. You were wrong then and you're wrong now. She was a better person than I can ever expect to be. I would've been a better person if I'd found the courage to stay with her."

"You fool! Do you honestly think I was going to let you throw your life away? And for her? She was a little upstart who didn't know her place. She would have ruined you, Jackson. I was not going to let that happen!" She put a trembling hand against her chest. "You have your own children now. Two boys. Surely you can see how I had no choice. I had to protect you."

He couldn't be hearing right. She couldn't mean what he thought she meant. If it did—No! That couldn't be right. He wouldn't let it be right. He shot jerkily to his feet, feeling as if he'd stopped at the bar. Feeling as if alcohol had already slowed his thinking. That had to be the reason he didn't know what he was supposed to do at a time like this, didn't know what he was supposed to say. He, a lawyer used to thinking on his feet, used to charming juries to his way of thinking, was without a single word. He'd dealt with corporations who'd committed egregious crimes in the name of profit, had gotten some off, had gotten some reduced fines. But this was his mother and the enormity of what she might have done stunned him.

"What is wrong with you, Jackson? That girl would—"

"Stop! I...don't say any more. What have you done?" His name, he thought. It had been done in his name. The weight of the guilt had him dropping down, had him covering his face. Nightmare. He was stuck in a nightmare. But when he opened his eyes she was still there, still looking at him as if he was the crazy one.

"Typical. You're just like your father. Love the benefit, but don't want to be bothered with the nasty details." She pounded the arm of her chair. "You should be thanking me for having the guts to protect your future. You should be on your knees in gratitude for all I saved you from."

He shook his head. "There was no need. There was no need."

"There was every need! I could hardly let you be saddled with her, with her…her offspring for the rest of your life. She tried to pretend she was so high and mighty, that she didn't need my money. But I knew. Knew she would eventually be back. First for your money, then to steal your life and make it hers. I alone saw in her what you never could."

"And what do you think will happen when this comes out? Where will I be? Where will the Tanner name you're so damn proud of be? Did you ever think about that?" He wanted to scream it but didn't. The horror was too great.

Again she waved her hand in dismissal. "I'm not without resources. None of this will come out. Even as you curse me, I'm protecting you, your name, your campaign."

"It was never my campaign. It was always yours."

"Do you hear what you're saying? Grow up, Jackson. I suppose I've always known you didn't have what it takes to be a good leader. Your uncle always said true leaders are born, not made. I should have listened."

For the first time Jackson let himself see her hard core, see the ugliness of it. See that he too bore the blame for going with the flow, for never standing up to her tyranny. "I hope your righteous indignation keeps you warm at night, Mother. Because of our relationship, I sincerely hope you manage to keep your friends in high places once this blows up in your face. You're going to need them." He hesitated in the doorway until he realized there was nothing more to say. She was as obdurate as she'd always been, so sure in her right to do what she wanted and damn anyone else.

After letting himself out, he stood on the porch and took a deep breath. The evening was warm and humid, hinting of the summer to come. A summer that would be like no other. He had little doubt this story was going to blow sky-high and take his mother with it. And him. Then by association, the innocent—his wife, his boys.

*So much to do*, he thought as he got in his car and pulled out of the driveway for the last time. His family deserved to know first he was dropping out of the race. Then Maria, his diligent volunteers. They should all know before he made the official announcement tomorrow.

And then there was Adeena Minor. It was hard and easy to look at her photo. She had Lucy stamped on her face and he wondered if she had Lucy stamped on her personality. She was certainly smart like Lucy had been. Lucy would've been so proud of Adeena's accomplishments.

He stopped at a stop sign and stared blindly ahead. God how he missed her, his Lucy. She'd been so sweet, always willing to listen to his grandiose ideas of saving the world, always willing to share hers. She'd been set to start technical college in the fall, get good grades, then transfer to Georgia Southern. After she graduated with honors, she was going to join the Peace Corps and see some of the world. When her two years were up, she planned to attend med school, then work in areas where doctors were needed the most.

How impressive she'd seemed to him, with her life mapped out, with the certainty of what she wanted her future to be. All he'd had were barely verbalized dreams and pressure from his mother to live up to the Tanner name. Tanner men studied law, joined the right law firm, married the right type of women and produced offspring. Girls were okay, but boys were better, his mother always said. Boys would carry on the Tanner name. It's how things were done.

But for a brief time, he'd been able to dream, to imagine forgoing Yale and enrolling in Georgia Southern to be within an easy drive of Lucy. He'd dared to dream of joining the Peace Corps with her, of working side by side, of doing good. When they came back, he would go to law school while she was in med school. He would work at a big firm, save money while she earned her degree. In their plans, they would find someplace far from Georgia to settle down, get married, work and later have beautiful children. Girls or boys, it didn't matter because their children would be free to do whatever they wanted, be whomever they wanted to be. Most of all, he would be free of the Tanner name and all the obligation it entailed.

Jackson sighed and thought back of their last carefree weekend. He'd snuck into town and whisked her off to Hilton Head. What fun they'd had. But with Lucy everything was fun, was new, was bright. It must have been then she'd gotten pregnant. If only… He sighed again and rubbed his face.

If only. But they'd been so young, so naïve, with immaturity added in on his part. He'd been a rich kid with the world for him to take. That is until his mother sat him down, straightened him out. With barely a token protest, he'd let the best thing in his life be ripped away. He would always bear the shame of how spineless he'd been, how much he'd crushed Lucy's heart by doing nothing. Now he'd have to add more guilt to that. Because of him she'd suffered far worse than a crushed heart.

"Oh, Lucy. I did love you."

# CHAPTER TWENTY-THREE

Eugenia sat for a while after Jackson left. *He'll be back*, she thought. He always came back. She would take longer to forgive him this time. He deserved it for throwing Lucy and that girl in her face as if they mattered.

Shaking her head, she couldn't help wishing it had been Phillip who had gotten her pregnant. Phillip had been strong, had known what it took to be in command, to stay in command. Phillip's son wouldn't have gotten caught up with the likes of Lucy. That she knew. But it had happened, and though she tried her best to nip it in the bud, disaster had struck.

She had no trouble recalling the day she'd confronted Lucy, demanded she do the right thing. Eugenia had dressed carefully for the meeting, purposefully set at a place outside the city where she wouldn't easily be recognized. And even knowing the girl was pregnant, she'd been shocked when Lucy arrived, looking as if she could deliver any minute.

Eugenia had started with polite, had asked the girl about her health, the health of the child.

"Children," Lucy corrected her. "I'm having twins. Girls." She patted her stomach, looking as proud as she could be.

"Girls? Are you sure?"

"Reasonably, as the technician didn't see any boy parts during the ultrasound. They're not identical twins. Fraternal. They can tell that now. Science is a wonder."

"And what do you plan to do with two babies? Surely you and your family barely have enough money to raise one."

Lucy's lips tightened. "My girls and I will be fine, Mrs. Tanner. I'm not afraid to work hard to provide them with everything they need."

*Aren't we putting on airs?* Eugenia thought. "I think we can agree your definition of what they need and mine are vastly different."

"They'll have what *I* think they need. Love, attention, understanding. But I'm sure that's not what you came here to hear." Lucy shifted on the hard bench and stretched her back. "I admit I was surprised to hear from you."

"Is that why you slunk out of town? Trying to stay off my radar?"

Lucy smiled. "You think too highly of yourself. I went away for Jackson's sake."

"Jackson? Do tell."

"I don't expect you to understand how I…how I felt about your son. He can be sweet, kind. But he'll never be able to stand up to you, to your vision of his future. No matter how much he hates it."

"I am his mother! I know what's right for him, and you and your wild ideas are not it. Did you really think I would let someone like you get your hooks into any child of mine? I know your type, always looking for a handout, an easy way to make money."

"You don't know me at all. Please don't insult me by pretending you do. If you need to hear that Jackson and I are over, then consider it said. If you need to hear that I don't want anything from him or you, consider that said as well. You Tanners think that money is everything. You're wrong. And I don't want any child of mine to be brought up thinking they're above everyone because of how much money they have or the last name they carry. It's true my girls won't be brought up in the lap of luxury, but it's also true they won't grow up without a soul."

"Easy enough to say when you're not having to worry about diapers or formula. Easy enough to say when you're not worried about where their next meal will come from. I've seen how you and your people live. If you agree to give those kids up for adoption, I can make sure they go to better homes, will have greater opportunities than you ever had. I'm even willing to throw in money for college. I'm told that's what you were aiming for."

"Keep your money." Lucy levered herself off the bench. "I don't want it, I don't want your son and I don't want the Tanner name for myself or my girls. Me and 'my people' do fine, don't you worry your pretty little head about us. We'll survive. And I may have to delay college for a few years, but I'll get there, my girls will get there. Goodbye, Mrs. Tanner. It hasn't been a pleasure and I don't want to see you or your son again. These are my children."

"You go too far, Lucy Brown. You'd do good to watch that smart mouth of yours, to show me some respect."

"I'll show you respect when you earn it."

"We'll see about that." Eugenia exhaled as she watched Lucy walk away without looking back. That girl had made a serious mistake, one she wouldn't get the chance to correct. No one talked to her like that and got away unscathed. No one.

Eugenia unclenched her hands, surprised to find the anger was as hot as it had been all those years ago. The utter nerve of that little nothing. She should have been there to see Lucy's demise. If she had, she wouldn't be in the situation she was now. She could be spending her full energies on Jackson's campaign, instead of cleaning up past screw-ups.

She noted the time, then pulled her phone out of her pocket. There was still time for her to see Lucy's daughter get what she deserved. And she would enjoy it.

"Can I get you anything else this evening, Mrs. Tanner?"

Eugenia jerked in surprise. "I'm fine, Martha. Go to bed. If I need anything later, I'll get it myself."

"It's no trouble for me to stay up, ma'am."

"No. Go. I'll be fine." She waited to call Charles until she couldn't hear Martha's footsteps. "I find myself in need of a ride. Give me ten minutes, then pick me up around back...No, the truck, for this one. No need to advertise our presence." She'd give Farrago the new instructions once they were at The Inn.

"Damn!" Vincent Farrago was coming to regret not doing more research before taking this job. Because of that, he'd badly underestimated his opponents.

"Problem, boss?" Blue Rivers asked. They were parked outside The Inn, waiting for the right time to grab their prey.

"Found another registration in a hotel in Atlanta. How sure was that clerk's ID of Minor?"

"Solid. She wasn't wearing a disguise and he checked her driver's license. He made Salamander as well."

"Atlanta must be a ruse. It'll be a pleasure to take care of both of them. Fucking amateurs," he added, even as a tinge of doubt tickled his consciousness.

"What'll we do with the bodies? Could weigh 'em down, take 'em out on my cousin's boat and toss 'em overboard."

"The broad who's paying wants Minor buried in a shallow grave. Wants her to be found to fuck with someone else is my take."

"Who?"

"Don't know and don't care. It ain't me."

"Takes all kinds, I guess."

"She is all kinds. This is one cold broad. We need to mess up Salamander and leave the body."

The clock on the dashboard showed eleven. "Let's do this before the next round of sexcapades starts." Farrago pulled down his cap to shield a good portion of his face, while Rivers donned a big cowboy hat to go with his fake mustache and took a healthy sip from a flask. "Spill some of that on your shirt. We want you to be remembered as being sloppy drunk."

Rivers splashed some cheap rum on his shirt and the seat of the stolen truck. He opened the door and pretended to almost fall out. Laughing, he held onto the door and swayed. "Let's party!" Stumbling, he made his way to the sidewalk where Farrago took his arm.

Farrago shook his head and grabbed Rivers' arm. "After we get inside, you take right. We'll do this quick and without a lot of noise." Using a stolen card, he eased the door open, motioned for Rivers to enter, then entered and eased the door shut. He donned night vision goggles and could make out the two shapes sharing the bed. Thinking they had to be light sleepers, he removed the gun with the silencer from the small of his back.

After Rivers did the same, he approached the person on the left, ripped the pillow from beneath her head and fired two shots. Again, Rivers mimicked his moves. "I love it when they make it easy. Now for the torture."

As he reached for the bedside lamp, the room was flooded with light, blinding him.

"Drop your weapons! Hands up!"

Farrago whipped off the goggles and after a quick assessment lowered his weapon and held up his hands. The room filled with cops in full riot gear, making him feel like the fucking amateur. Obviously they should have sent someone to check on the occupants earlier. It would have been hard for the two life-sized dolls lying butt to butt to pass as either Minor or Salamander.

"Vincent Farrago, you are under arrest."

Farrago tuned the cop out. He knew the drill, knew every word, but especially his right to have an attorney. "I want a lawyer."

"I want a lawyer," Rivers echoed, sounding as scared as he looked.

The flashing blue lights were visible before Charles and Eugenia pulled into the parking lot at The Inn.

"Slow down, but don't stop," Eugenia demanded. She peered out the window as Charles followed her instructions.

The activity seemed to be centered on one room. She didn't doubt whose room it was. "Damn! What could've happened?"

"Don't know, Ms. Tanner. Farrago should've been better than to get caught."

"Could the girl have spotted Farrago's man and called the cops?"

"I'm thinking it was a setup. No way she'd be able to pick out Farrago or his men. Seems like she's been one step ahead since the third failure." He checked the rearview mirror and sped up as they left the area around the hotel behind. "What's next? It's obvious she's already talked to the police."

"Yes. The question is will your man talk?"

"No worries about that, Ms. Tanner. At most they could get him on trespassing or carrying an unregistered weapon. A good lawyer could plead that down to much of nothing given he's got no record."

"That's good, but it still leaves the girl untouched once again. We have Mr. Selman to add to the confusion. He had an uncle who was supposed to be in on the Lucy job. There might be a way to throw suspicion his way. I'll have to think about this. For now, take me home. There will be no satisfactory resolution tonight."

Eugenia exhaled as she stared out the window and saw nothing. It seemed the story would come out, and perhaps it wasn't the end of the world. There was nothing to tie her or Jackson to any crime. Jackson might face some heat initially, and that could eventually have a positive outlook on his campaign. At first the public would rush to find him guilty, then as the facts emerged, that same public would rush to exonerate him. He would rise in the standings and walk away with the vote.

There would be an initial interest in the girl and her relationship with Jackson. Especially if Jackson went along with a DNA test. Luckily the public's interest didn't stay in one place very long and soon that interest would wane. Of course an opponent might try to keep the flames burning bright. Their side would simply have to push the "he was only eighteen" card.

And it was hardly Jackson's fault the girl failed to tell him she was pregnant.

The fire would be the trickiest part to deal with. Someone out there knew what had happened. Someone that Conlin couldn't get to or hadn't known about. Eugenia couldn't help wondering if that someone had any more bombs in their arsenal. If that someone was going to be sending the girl another letter. If only she knew who it was.

She caught the flicker of lights seconds before Charles brought the truck to a stop.

"Police. What now?"

For a moment she was dumbfounded. Police and her neighborhood, her house, didn't match. The utter gall. "Go around the back to the garage. It's not a crime to go out at night. I have nothing to hide."

An officer flagged them down when Charles pulled into the driveway.

Eugenia lit into him as soon as Charles rolled down his window. "What is the meaning of this?"

"Eugenia Tanner, we have a warrant for your arrest. Please get out of the vehicle slowly."

"There must be some mistake. I demand to speak to your superior. Do you know who I am?"

"Yes, ma'am, you're Eugenia Tanner."

The last person Adeena expected to see after spending a grueling hour being questioned by the police was Eugenia Tanner. But as fate would have it, the stone-cold bitch was being escorted into another room at the same time she was escaping a small, dingy interview room. Adeena could tell the second she was recognized. Eugenia's eyes narrowed and her face twisted in hate. "Hello, Grandmother. Fancy seeing you here. I do hope you caught my interview with Kristy Moore."

"You! How dare you speak to me. How dare you presume to call *me* grandmother. You're nothing to me. Nothing to my family."

"How dare you try to have me killed, *Grandmother*." Adeena pasted on a smile even as her insides reached boiling point. "Too bad your hired guns failed not once, but four times." She waved four fingers. "As you can see, I'm alive and well. And doing a hell of a lot better than you. Tell me, how is my father the Senate candidate faring? I hope I haven't ruined his chances with my revelations."

Eugenia lifted her chin. "As if the likes of you could touch Jackson. You're nothing. Just like your mother was nothing. We'll see what happens once my lawyers get these ridiculous charges dismissed."

"Are you threatening me?" She took a step closer and looked down her nose at Eugenia. "I could remind you how well your previous attempts worked, but people like you never learn from past mistakes. You might also remember you don't have the advantage of surprise now. Of course, this is if your lawyers can perform miracles and get you off. I'm willing to bet they can't, Eugenia, and I don't usually bet. I'm also willing to bet your murdering ass is going to be popular in prison. There'll be a bunch of women fighting over who gets to make your arrogant ass their bitch. I'm almost sorry I won't be there to see it."

"Not as sorry as you're going to be," Eugenia said with a cold smile. "You don't scare me."

"Right back at you, Granny. You don't scare me."

"Adeena, you didn't tell me there was a party going on," Sal said as she joined the group. "And with the top dog herself. Former top dog, I should say, once the judicial system gets through with her."

"She seems to think she has nothing to worry about." Adeena took Sal's outstretched hand and threaded their fingers together. "Must mean she's looking forward to some caged heat action."

Sal laughed. "Maybe she can get a cameo appearance on *Orange Is the New Black*."

"Laugh all you want now," Eugenia said. "I'll be the one with the last laugh."

"Good luck with that," Sal told her. "You might want to check your account balances if you somehow manage to get out on bail. Errors can occur at the strangest times. Now we've taken up enough of your time. Wouldn't want to keep you from chatting with the police."

"What was that about?" Adeena asked after they were out of hearing range. "The accounts bit?"

"A little thing called 'Fuck you, Granny.' She moved a big chunk of money into the dead Phillip's account this evening. I took the liberty of moving most of the money to a new account in case she was planning to run. Not that I see her as the running type, but it pays to be safe rather than sorry."

"She's more the strike-back type. And she must have chunks of money in other accounts to strike back with."

"Which is why I put alerts on those accounts as well. She doesn't get to retaliate or skirt answering for murder on my watch. I can't go back and fix what happened in the past, but I can damn sure keep it from happening again if the justice system won't do its job." Sal exhaled. "I wanted to punch her. Standing there so damn smug, so damn sure she was going to get away with murder yet again. Surely those cops saw that."

"I don't think smug looks are admissible as evidence."

"They damn well should be. She's going down if it's the last thing I do."

Hearing Sal's words and seeing the disgruntled expression on her face made Adeena's heart swell. Sal was on her side, and that was one weapon Eugenia couldn't countermand. "Thank you for being you." She squeezed Sal's hand. "It's crazy, but in addition to wanting to punch her, I wanted to thank her for bringing you into my life."

"Could say the same, but I want to punch that smug expression off her face more."

Adeena put a hand to her heart. "My shero."

Sal stuffed her hands in her pockets. "Yeah, well, uh, you'll be interested to know the other Tanner's scheduled a press conference for tomorrow."

"Perfect. I'll talk to him there." She covered a yawn. "Now I'd like to sleep. We're getting close to being up for twenty-four hours."

# CHAPTER TWENTY-FOUR

"You're positive he'll be there?" Adeena pulled down the visor so she could check her appearance. Saying she was nervous was a gross understatement. She was terrified.

"He called the press conference. I think it's safe to say he'll be there. What did you decide to do about your boss?"

"I sent him a link to the interview. Along with my six-weeks' notice." She looked away from the road when Sal threaded between a bus and a semi. "We're not in that much of a hurry."

"What? This is how we drive in New York. Did I ever tell you I was a taxi driver? Great way to see the stars."

"You must mean the kind of stars you get when you bang your head against the windshield," she replied, then held her breath when Sal zipped across two lanes to make a sudden left. "Please tell me we're almost there."

"We're almost there."

"Really?"

"Define 'almost,'" Sal said as she sailed through on the last second of a yellow light. "GPS woman says it's one point one miles. It's taking longer because of rush hour traffic. He could have waited until nine, nine thirty, when everybody and their dog wasn't going to work."

"It isn't every day your mother's arrested. He probably wants to get the questions out of the way, make sure we know he's innocent of any wrongdoing."

"Appalled. He'll also be appalled at any accusations of wrongdoing on the part of his mother. He is a lawyer. I think they have to say that as part of their creed."

"Doesn't matter what he says, he's between a rock and another rock. I wouldn't be surprised if he dropped out of the race."

"No way. Doing that makes his mother look guilty. Better to stay in, have her attorney file motion after motion to delay the trial until after the election. If she's convicted after he's in office, then he can throw her under the bus."

"That'll never work."

"Do you know how many criminals get elected to office? And as far as he's concerned, we don't have anything linking him to any crimes. His people will preach that loud and clear. I'm willing to—"

"I know. Bet money. This time you're wrong. Like you were with Andi." *Shouldn't have mentioned that*, she thought and bit her lip to keep the tears at bay. She wanted Tanner to see her as cool and dignified, not as the "angry black woman." But she was black and she was angry, damn it. And she had a right to be both.

"What are you thinking?"

"That I'm angry, and because I'm black and a woman, I can't be here today and get taken serious. It's unfair. I deserve to be angry at what's been done to me. What was done to me thirty-four years ago. But because I'm showing emotion while black, then I'm obviously a hostile person."

"Unfair and a no-win situation. I say be who you want to be. What do you care what Tanner thinks? At best he treated Lucy so badly she wouldn't even tell him she was pregnant. At worst, he conspired to kill her and you. He doesn't deserve a second of your consideration, Adeena."

She patted Sal's thigh. "Don't you get tired of being right?"

"It is a gift and a burden. And we're here." Sal pulled into a parking lot down the street from Tanner's campaign headquarters. They could see the news vans up ahead, the sidewalk teeming with reporters and camera operators. "I think the hat and glasses are in order. Now that you're a two-time celebrity."

"What fun for me." Adeena donned the straw hat, the oversized glasses. "Let's go before I change my mind." When she got out of the car, the noise from the reporters carried. She wondered if Kristy Moore was in the crowd. What would she do if Kristy saw through her disguise? Her stomach clenched and she considered getting back in the car and having Sal drive them to the airport. Too cowardly. She wanted this chance to face Jackson Tanner. *Needed this opportunity*, she reminded herself. "Wait."

"You okay?"

"I will be. You need a disguise too. I just thought. Kristy's bound to be here and she knows what you look like. If she spots you, it won't matter if I'm disguised."

"You're right." Sal popped the trunk, rummaged through her carry-on bag, removed a cap and pulled it low over her forehead. "This should do if we stay in the back."

Adeena took a deep breath. "Okay." The closer they came to Tanner's office, the faster her heart beat. "What if he won't see me?"

"Then you tell his staff you'll be happy to give the media another interview. He'll talk to you."

"That simple, huh?"

"I've found channeling your inner bitch can be helpful."

"I believe my dear grandmother would agree with you."

Sal winced. "Of course, some take it too far."

Before they made it to the door, the media people surged into the building. "Something's going on." Adeena picked up her pace. "Why would they go inside now?"

"To hear what Tanner has to say."

"Then why were they camped out front if he was inside? There has to be a back entrance."

"Politicians don't use back entrances unless they're doing something wrong."

"I think this one did." She reached the door and pulled it open before Sal could. There was a short hallway that opened into a big room. Jackson Tanner was near the podium in the front of the room. Adeena recognized one of the women he was talking to as his wife. She checked and was relieved at not seeing his sons.

"I wouldn't want to be him right now," Sal said. "You have to give him points for doing this."

"I don't have to give him anything," Adeena said curtly.

"Well, maybe points for not parading his kids around."

Jackson Tanner stepped up to the mike and thanked everyone for coming, then talked about Lucy Mae Brown and what she could've meant to the world. He finished by announcing his withdrawal from the race and asked for privacy for his family. He did not mention his mother.

"I did not see that coming," Sal said as the questions from the press and one Kristy Moore, came fast and furious. "No way he was involved."

"You're right again."

When the questions began to wind down, Adeena made her way to the front of the room. She wasn't exactly sure how'd she'd get his attention, but she knew it would be easier to do it from the front of the room.

"What are we doing?" Sal asked as she followed along.

"Trying to figure out how to catch him before he goes out the back way." She raised her hand.

"No need for that. I have his cell phone number. His campaign manager's too. But now I'm thinking we can do one better. Take off the glasses, the hat." Sal put her fingers in her mouth and gave two shrill whistles, then ducked down. All talk stopped momentarily.

Adeena saw him track the noise with his gaze, saw his eyes widen when he spotted her, heard him falter in the middle of an answer. She put the hat and glasses back on, then looked around as if she too was trying to figure out what the noise was about.

Jackson Tanner cleared his throat. "That's all the questions for now. Again I'd like to ask for privacy for my wife and my children." He stepped back from the podium, keeping his gaze trained on Adeena until he was surrounded by his volunteers.

She closed out the movement, the noise of the media hurrying out to get their story on the air and really looked at him. Even in his early fifties he was fit and movie-star handsome, with that touch of gray at his temples that supposedly made him look distinguished. Imagining how he looked thirty years ago, she could see why Lucy hadn't stood a chance of holding out against him. According to the gossip Sal had dug up, there weren't many women who could resist him.

Lucy must have felt special when he singled her out, when he showered her with attention, Adeena thought. Mrs. Robinson had mentioned Lucy was shy around boys and Adeena wondered how hard Tanner had had to work to break through that shyness. She hoped he'd meant some of the words he'd spouted to a shy girl.

"It seems I owe you money," Sal said. "How much did we bet?"

"A couple of million. I'll put it on your account. You seem to be good for it." Adeena watched as Tanner shook hands and said a few words to each worker. "Do you think he had that perfect smile thirty-four years ago? My knees might quiver a little if he turned that and the charm on me. Imagine what it would do to an eighteen-year-old girl."

"Don't have to imagine. Some of those volunteers are barely past that. And even the older women are hanging on to every word he says."

"You're right. I wasn't paying attention to that." She made herself look away from Jackson Tanner, made herself look away from an image of him and Lucy as a couple, of them as her parents. This meeting was about something else and now that it was almost here, she wasn't sure what that was. "I don't know what to say to him. I mean, I dragged you here and now I don't know what to say."

"You could tell him his mother sucks cocks in hell."

"What?" She turned to Sal as what was said sunk in. "Where did *that* come from?"

"An old horror movie. *The Exorcist*. Saw it when I was a kid and couldn't sleep without a light on for weeks."

"I should tell him his mother's possessed?"

"No, but I made you smile. You looked like you could use one."

"You are certifiable. I really like that about you."

"Excuse me. I'm Maria Cousins. Jackson asked me to bring you to his office."

Adeena eyed the brunette she'd seen talking to Tanner earlier. "Uh, sure."

"I hope this won't take long. We have a lot to do, what with closing down the office."

Adeena didn't reply. If Tanner wanted this woman to know what was going on, he could tell her.

Jackson Tanner was standing in his office, looking out the window when they entered.

"Here you go," Maria said. "Don't forget we have to get the financials to the accountant today."

"I won't. That'll be all for now, Maria." He gave her a nod of dismissal. "Please close the door. Thanks."

Maria seemed surprised, but she did as she was told.

Jackson cleared his throat. "Have a seat." He sat on his desk after Adeena and Sal were seated. "I assume you have questions."

Adeena nodded, then removed the glasses and the hat. Once again she felt the intensity of his gaze.

"Let me start by saying this is a big shock to me."

"Which part?"

"All of it. I had no idea Lucy was pregnant. I knew she died, found out three months later. But believe me, I had no idea she was pregnant when…that she was pregnant or what was done to her." He cleared his throat again. "I assume by now you know my mother has been charged with conspiracy to commit murder. Of course you do, you heard the questions at the press conference."

"I did." She had no intention of mentioning her meeting with his mother. It was his job to give her information.

"Then you know simply saying I'm sorry isn't enough. Would never be enough for what's been done to you. Then or now."

She grudgingly gave him points for sincerity. "I do wonder how much you knew."

"Nothing! I knew nothing until yesterday. Lucy obviously didn't think enough of me to tell me. Not that I blame her. I don't." He wandered back to the window, stuck his hands in his pockets. "I was young, immature. And weak where she was strong. I honestly thought for a while that I could be the person she and I wanted me to be. In the end my mother put down her foot and I folded." Jackson turned so he was facing her. "I'm not proud of it, but it is the truth. It's also true that I had nothing to do with her death. That I would never have had anything to do with her death."

"Did you ever love her?"

"She was my first love. Part of me will always love her. I'd be the first to admit I failed Lucy, that I'll regret that failure for the rest of my life. Like I said earlier, she was a very special person. Much better than the likes of me. My mother didn't see it that way, needless to say. She had a powerful hate for Lucy. But I stayed away, so I thought it was forgotten."

"It probably would've been if she hadn't been pregnant." Adeena found herself feeling a little bit sorry for Jackson Tanner. The guilt he'd felt before must have paled in the face of what his mother had done. "I don't know if you knew that I, uh, I was… had a twin. She's dead now."

"Twins? Lucy had twins?"

"Twin girls."

"This keeps getting worse. One more death on my head. It's ironic. All my mother did was supposedly for my future, for the future of the Tanner name." He laughed without humor. "That's shot to hell now. And there's some justice in the fact she has to live with the knowledge that she's responsible for the taint on the Tanner name. That will cause her more pain than any action from the court of law. It's not enough to pay for all she's done."

"But it's something," Adeena said, and because he looked so miserable, she added, "I can't give you a name right now. Don't ask me that. I can tell you that my twin's death is not on you. She died in a car accident five months ago. The family that adopted her has been made aware of the events of the past. They'll ultimately make the decision whether they want to reach out to you or not."

"Thank you for that. Is there...is there anything I can do for you?" He grimaced. "I can reimburse any unexpected expenses you've incurred—"

Adeena held up a hand to stop him. "No need, but thanks."

"What about a place to stay? Are you all set there? I...I feel like I should do something for you. That Lucy would want me to do something for you."

"Perhaps one day when things have settled down you can tell me about her."

"I'd like that," he said, nodding. "My oldest son, Beau, he'd like the opportunity to meet you. Not now, but in the future if you could see your way to that. Phillip as well. He's very confused right now."

"Yes. I would like that, Mr. T—"

"Jackson. Call me Jackson."

"Adeena. I'm Adeena. And this is my savior, Sal. Thomasina Salamander. She's the reason I'm still alive."

"You did a lot of it yourself," Sal told her. "She can think on her feet," she told Jackson.

Jackson crossed the room and held out a hand. "I owe you a debt of gratitude, Sal."

Sal shook his hand. "That debt's been paid. I would do it again. No questions asked."

"Then please accept my sincere thanks."

There was a knock on the door before Maria stuck her head in. "We really need to get going on this, Jackson."

"We need to get going as well," Adeena said. She took a card out of her bag. "This has my contact information on it."

He put the card in his wallet and took out another one. "Call when you feel ready."

"I will."

"If you need anything, anything at all, get in touch. I do mean that." As if he couldn't help himself he stroked Adeena's face. "I would've recognized you anywhere. I can't tell you how sorry I am you didn't have the chance to know her."

Adeena donned the hat and glasses and battled tears as they made their way outside. The street was all but deserted now that the media representatives had closed up shop.

Sal exhaled. "I never thought I'd say this, not in a million years, but I actually feel sorry for the guy."

Adeena wiped away tears. "He loved her in his way. You could hear it in his voice, see the grief on his face."

"I could see it in the way he looked at you. The way he touched your face at the end."

"I almost lost it at that point. He was looking at me, but you knew he was looking at her."

"Wishing for her. That's kind of sweet."

Adeena reached for Sal's hand. "It's funny. That's the way I'd describe you. Kind of sweet."

Sal frowned. "Only kind of?"

"Just enough. Perfectly balanced with the not-so-sweet to make things interesting."

"Great save." Sal brought Adeena's hands to her lips. "What do you say we blow this joint, get you to Vegas so you can fulfill your obligations and then see what's next?"

"I say yes to all. Especially to seeing what's next if you're in it."

"I am. You can bet on that."

# EPILOGUE

*Six months later*

Adeena was mentally dragging her feet as she returned home from yet another job interview. Like the other interviews she'd gone on, her answers to all the questions thrown at her had been well received, there was rapport between her and the two people interviewing her and when it was done, she felt like she had a great interview. Unfortunately, she exceeded the qualifications and most likely wouldn't get the job.

*It is what you expected when you applied for the job*, she told herself as she summoned the elevator. Knowing that didn't help her mood one bit. On other occasions, she'd been able to take some solace from being selected for an interview. Today was not one of those days. She was definitely in a funk.

Maybe she could blame it on the time of year. Thanksgiving was coming up, to be followed by Christmas, which meant it was almost the official start of the holiday season. And her thirty-fifth birthday, which she was absolutely not going to think about. She was down enough without thinking about being unemployed and a year older. According to Sal, she was in the best city to celebrate the holidays. And she certainly had the best girlfriend to celebrate with, but something was missing and it was inside her.

The elevator came and instead of getting on, she turned around and walked out of the building. She wasn't ready to see Sal, wasn't ready for the unending supply of cheerfulness that Sal seemed to have. Not today. Not when she was coming back from another job interview knowing she wouldn't get the job despite having given her best. Not when she felt like she was at the bottom of the bottom.

Without thought, she went east toward Central Park. Maybe a walk through the park would help her find the balance she desperately needed to have before facing Sal. Without that balance she might be tempted to spew her frustrations all over Sal and that wasn't fair. Sal had been nothing but supportive and helpful since she and Diablo had made the move north. And any other day, Adeena wouldn't need the walk, wouldn't need to find her balance because her life with Sal was all about balance. Her life with Sal was all she could ask for.

A cold breeze whipped at her face and she pulled her scarf tighter, though the temperature fit her mood. The cloudy sky did too. It was a good day for feeling down, for feeling like a failure. She was angry at the world and at herself for being angry at the world. In her situation, being unemployed was not the end of the world. She had a great place to live and no money worries. It wasn't like she was sitting on her ass binge watching TV shows and eating junk food. She was actively looking for a job, as evidenced by the many job interviews she'd been on.

She certainly wasn't feeling any pressure from her great girlfriend about not having a job. She had money to pay for her meager needs combined with few expenses since Sal refused to accept any money toward their living expenses. And she was doing consulting work for her old boss. All in all, she had no reason to be feeling down. There were plenty of other people who had it worse, and she was being a Grinch for feeling as she did. She should be back in the apartment giving the two most important beings in her life some of her attention.

Unmindful of the pedestrian traffic around her, Adeena stopped, took a deep breath and tried to find her center as she'd learned to do in her yoga class. In addition to Sal, she had gained two brothers and a nephew whom she was convinced would eventually get used to her, would eventually come to love her. Plus she had Cyn and her parents. Adeena was forging a steady relationship with them. She didn't have Ian, and that still hurt, but compared to last year this time, she had more people in her life who cared about her.

Despite the muttered curses being directed at her as other walkers made their way around her on the sidewalk, she felt better. Maybe she had needed this time alone to grieve.

Another deep breath and she turned around and retraced her steps. This time she stopped to chat with Bruce, the retired ex-cop who guarded the door during the day, before she went upstairs.

Diablo's bark began the second she put the key in the lock. "It's me." She bent and accepted his exuberant welcome.

"How did it go?" Sal asked as she came down the stairs.

"I got the pained 'we love you but you're overqualified' look. Never mind that I would be doing a lot of the same things I did in Vegas. It's discouraging. I'm not used to failing."

"I'm sorry." Sal gave her a quick kiss, then pulled her into her arms. "Maybe you read the look wrong. Maybe it was a 'I can't believe we hit the jackpot' look. You are a first-class prize."

Adeena couldn't help but smile. "And you're a first-class optimist. Yin to my yang."

"That's good, right?"

"That's perfect." She tightened her grip and realized she should always come to Sal's arms first. It was better than the walk, the solitude.

"Good. I wouldn't want you to regret, you know, moving here."

She pushed back so she could see Sal's face. "What are you talking about? Of course I don't regret it. I could never regret being with you. I was existing before and now I'm living. Even if it takes me another four months, a year, to get a job, I can't regret making the best decision I ever made. I may be feeling a little down, but know I'll come out of it. I love you, Sal. Period."

"I love you too. And if there's anything I can do, you have to let me know. Say the word and I'll help you set up your own company."

"I'm not ready for that kind of responsibility. Don't know that I ever will be. But thanks."

"Then I think you should take a break from the search until next year. Nan and Beau'll be here Thanksgiving week, then we're going down to Seneca for the week after Christmas. It's actually good that you don't have a job yet. Now you don't have to worry about getting the time off. Which you probably wouldn't, being the new hire."

"Enough. I'm convinced. I won't apply unless it's the perfect job. And only accept if they give me those two weeks off."

"Deal. We okay?"

"We're okay." She showed Sal with a kiss.

"Hate to say good again, but good. Now for potentially bad. Eugenia killed herself. Pills. The housekeeper found her this morning. Jackson thought I should be the one to break it to you."

Adeena didn't know what to think. Eugenia's death meant there wouldn't be a trial. No trial meant Eugenia didn't get to rot in prison. No trial meant they might never know the whole story. But Eugenia's death might mean that whoever wrote the letter, unless it was Vicki Adams, might come forward, might contact her again. "I…I can't be unhappy, but what a surprise."

"I know. I wouldn't have bet on her being the type to commit suicide."

"How did Jackson sound? Guess I should call him." They had sort of established the beginning of a relationship. She had a much closer relationship with Beau, who had immediately claimed her as his big sister.

"He sounded shaky. Said you should expect to be contacted by the press and to call if you needed anything."

She sighed. This would happen when she was enjoying her return to anonymity. "Will it have any effect on Farrago's trial? Whenever it happens."

"Shouldn't. Hard for her to testify against him when she was still denying everything. May help. The innocent don't usually knock themselves off. Not that it matters. He's toast, thanks to the anonymous source who sent his digital ledger to the police." Sal's expression was one of innocence.

"That was provident." She took a step back and wandered to the living room windows. "I'm conflicted. On one hand, it's good that she's not wasting taxpayer money. On the other hand, she's not going to spend a single day in prison. I was looking forward to thinking of her being there."

"Well, yeah, it totally sucks that she gets to go out her way." Sal slid her arms around Adeena's waist and pulled her close. "In control."

"That's exactly it. I didn't want her to be in control. I wanted her to see how it felt to have other people pulling on her strings. It's not fair."

"Look at it this way. When you die, you go up or down. She went down and hell has to be worse than prison, right? In her hell, she's getting bossed around by all the people she's screwed over. Probably poor and in rags too."

"Her hair's gray and thinning, and she's wearing clothes fit for rags. And has bad teeth. She looks like a hag." Adeena smiled. "She'd hate that with a passion."

"Because she can't turn around without seeing herself in the house of mirrors. I bet she's already screaming and tearing at her hair. Making it even thinner. We should celebrate her arrival in hell. I'm thinking calzones for lunch. And rum and Coke without—"

"The rum. Make mine—"

"Diet Dr. Pepper. And I'll have them add spinach to your calzone to make it healthier."

She grinned. "You know me well. How could I ever regret following you anywhere?"

* * *

"Lord Jesus!" Letha Douglas put hand to her chest as she closed her eyes and bowed her head. She gave a silent prayer of thanks that her prayers had been answered. She hadn't wanted Eugenia Tanner dead, because she was a god-fearing woman after all. What she had wanted, had prayed for, was an end to the danger of secrets unknown.

"Granny!" Nicki said as she ran into the room. "You okay? I heard a noise!"

"Come here, baby." Letha held out fingers, swollen with rheumatoid arthritis, to her thirteen-year-old granddaughter. "Your granny is doing fine. Just fine."

Bella Books, Inc.

*Women. Books. Even Better Together.*

P.O. Box 10543
Tallahassee, FL 32302

Phone: 800-729-4992
**www.bellabooks.com**